Henry VIII:
WOLFMAN

Praise for *Queen Victoria: Demon Hunter*

'It deliberately steers as close to history as is possible in a story that at its heart makes a scion of the royal family into Buffy the Vampire Slayer, using details revealed in Victoria's journals for verisimilitude.

That's not to say there isn't some deliciously black humour in the story, as well as a neatly ironic use of contemporary circumlocutory style (it's catching!) . . . Mixing history with anachronism, the novel manages to both explain the supposedly scandalous relationship between Victoria and John Brown, and culminate in a showdown in a lunatic asylum and a zombie-infested House of Commons!'

www.totalsci-fionline.com

'The effect is that of a lost Gilbert and Sullivan operetta written under the influence of opium, absinthe and black pudding.'

Washington Post

Also by A. E. Moorat

Queen Victoria: Demon Hunter

Henry VIII: WOLFMAN

A. E. Moorat

HODDER

First published in Great Britain in 2010 by
Hodder & Stoughton
An Hachette UK company

First published in paperback in 2010

1

A CIP catalogue record for this title is available from the British Library.

B format PB ISBN 978 1444 70520 1
A format PB 978 1444 70643 7

Typeset in Berkeley Book by Palimpsest Book Production Limited,
Falkirk, Stirlingshire

Printed and bound by Clays Ltd, St Ives plc

Hodder & Stoughton Ltd
338 Euston Road
London NW1 3BH

www.hodder.co.uk

For Granny, with apologies for
all the rude and horrid bits.

Acknowledgements

Firstly, many thanks to you if you're reading this. Thanks and love also to my wife, Claire, and all family and friends for their interest and enthusiasm; to my agent, Antony Topping and all at Greene and Heaton; to my editor, Kate Howard, and everybody at Hodder.

Henry VIII : Wolfman

PROLOGUE

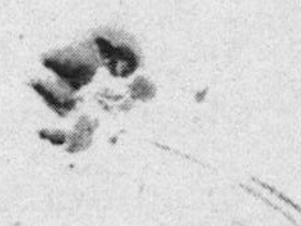

It was his time of the month and Henry was getting hungry.

If only he could find a body in a gibbet, he thought, he could eat that.

Yes. His stomach rumbled at the thought of a freshly gibbeted corpse. One the crows had yet to find, open wounds still oozing blood. Or a livestock thief burnt at the stake then left in a hanging cage. Smoked peasant.

But what a shame that peasants were never fat, he mused. Not like noblemen or clergy. Perhaps he should burn a stout priest at the time of the next full moon and see to it that the remains were displayed close to the palace. He could drag bits of it through the bars of the cage to feast upon.

Henry groaned in pleasure to think of it. Of the charred skin crackling and the tender, bloody flesh beneath, done to perfection: raw, but with that distinctive wood-smoked flavour – a real taste sensation. Positively drooling at the thought.

No, he really *was* drooling at the thought, he realised. Great, huge threads of it hung from his mouth to the oak floor of his chamber.

Which meant that it was happening. The Change was coming.

He was in his closet in the secret lodgings of his Privy Chamber, a room reserved for reading, contemplation, acts of devotion, and, now, for his transformation. Here was where he'd learnt to come at the time of the full moon. And wait. And hope that the cure had worked: that this time would be different and the beast inside would not emerge, because it would want to hunt.

The walls were lined with timber panelling so the closet was dark apart from light at the window. The light of the full moon. He looked out over the grounds of the Palace of Greenwich and towards the Thames, over which hung the moon like a sacramental wafer. He drank its rays, feeling the pull of it, the all-too-familiar longing. He was breathing heavily now. A scraping sound came from within his own head and all of a sudden he could hear with more clarity – heard the rustling of trees in the grounds, the movement of animals. He had a sense of movement, of running with the pack. He felt something within that was nameless and ancient.

He groaned, knowing what it meant: the metamorphosis had begun in earnest. All of his senses were suddenly heightened. In his nostrils was the scent of earth, of loam, and something else in the room. Fear, he realised. His own.

But it was a feeling that belonged to the old him and he laughed at his own weakness. At the same time his chest expanded and his jerkin burst, while from below came a ripping sound as his hose tore. He shouted in pain at the pricking of a thousand needles as his fur pushed through his skin. He felt movement in his skull, of grating bone as his snout pushed aside his human features. Then there was a cracking sound from within his torso and he grunted, still pushing – pushing his wolfen form through his human skin.

He felt his entire body filling out and his height increasing. He felt his skull pulse and change, his ears growing, forehead lengthening and pulling back; heard the scraping sound of the hair pushing through. There was a rasping sound from the stone floor as his feet bulged and grew and the muscles in his hind legs became firm. He opened his mouth, working the jaw to prepare it for the arrival of his fangs, throwing back his head and grinning to feel his long, sharp incisors push through the gums with a tearing noise that sounded more painful than it felt. He looked down at his chest to see thick, brown hair in place of pink, fragile and easily irritated skin.

And then Henry stood, fully transformed and lupine fresh. He made a tentative sound and yes, it was a growl, deep and low in his throat. His full senses came to him now, too, so that the smell of the burning wood in the hearth was almost overpowering.

And he laughed to think of himself sitting there as he had been, a man, fretting about changing, resisting the inevitable. After all, why deny it? Why fight this, when it was so *good*? He jumped to the window ledge and then to the Privy Gardens below.

Back went his thoughts to food as he ran across the lawns, feeling the rush of the night, feeling more free than he ever felt as a man, as King, when even here in his Privy Gardens, though shielded from the world by tall hedgerow, he was constantly accompanied by advisers, grooms, pages and yeomen of the guard. But not now. Now he dropped to all fours, speeding up, relishing the sensation of the soft ground beneath his paws, the scent of the wild. Human things, the preoccupations of men, fell away, so that he was aware only of the earth and that which lived upon it. Things he wanted to eat.

He stopped, resting back on his haunches, placing his long forearms to the ground, and feeling the vibrations of the earth beneath him. Around him, hedges cut into the figures of animals silently regarded this new creature in their midst. A low mist bubbled at the grass. Raising his snout he breathed in freezing night air and sniffed, gathering the scent of his prey.

Then: *fox*.

A wily fox. A cunning fox. His head snapped in the direction of the treeline and he rose to his feet, running until he met the trees. He could smell it more strongly now and there it was, some feet away. Her eyes shone from the undergrowth but she stood her ground, watching him, not moving.

You're standing there for a reason, aren't you, clever Mistress Fox? thought Henry.

For a moment or two he and the fox regarded one another, the two beasts sizing each other up. Henry's stomach rumbled once more. But why wasn't she moving?

Then another sound and Henry smiled. Of course. What he heard was the sound of cubs mewling for their mother and he twisted to see a pile of knotted tree roots. From within, the sound of the cubs. He turned back to look at the mother, who had tensed, knowing her ploy had been unsuccessful; she had failed to draw the wolfman away from her young.

Bad luck, Mistress Fox. Henry reached to within the roots and scooped out a cub from the burrow, biting into the juicy stomach. Not-so-clever-now Mistress Fox dashed back with a scream to protect her cubs but Henry chortled and grabbed her and tore off her head then finished eating her young.

But the sounds of the killing had cleared the area and Henry stalked the woodland looking for fresh quarry without success. He went to the waterline and found nothing but mud and empty boats on the shore. From further upriver came the sounds of life, of singing and shouting and fighting and sex, but there also were lights and fires, so he avoided those. As he retreated into the trees he chanced upon an unlucky rabbit but it still wasn't enough. And as he squatted, cleaning the blood and intestines from his coat with his tongue, he found his thoughts going back – back to the palace.

Between his bedchamber and that of the Queen was a gallery so that they might visit one another at night. He pictured her now, lying in her bed and he found his mouth watering as he thought of her pretty dukkies and imagined sinking his fangs into them, the soft flesh opening, blood squirting like the juice of ripe fruit. He thought of the meat on her thighs and her behind, pictured himself tearing it from the bone with his teeth. He had enjoyed fox and rabbit for a main course, why not a Queen for pudding? He would regret it, he knew, when he changed back, he would regret eating the Queen; but tonight he did not care. Tonight he simply wanted to feast.

Able to stand it no longer, the thought of burying his snout into the warm innards of the Queen finally too much to bear, Henry sat back, howled triumphantly into the night sky, then turned and set off back to the palace . . .

When dawn arrived, Henry was still feasting upon the Queen. As the new day's light filtered into her chamber, he transformed back into his human self, and, raising his head from his wife's ravaged stomach saw himself in the mirror, black gore caking his mouth. He looked at the blood on his hands and was consumed with horror and self-disgust at the thing he had become. Once upon a time, long ago, Sir Thomas More had tutored him in the ways of a monarch and he had pledged to be a good king, just and fair. And he had tried, but failed, becoming instead an animal, cruel and savage, drunk on bloodlust.

And nothing would change, he knew. He had lived with the curse for too long. His humanity was gone, he mourned it, and what made it worse somehow was that he knew – he remembered clearly the day that he lost his humanity and he thought back to it now. He'd woken up hungry that day . . .

Part One

THE WOLFEN

I

The court of King Henry VIII, that vast travelling household of over one thousand nobles and servants, was accustomed to moving between residences. The most frequently inhabited were the palaces at Greenwich, Richmond and Westminster, but lately His Majesty seemed to have settled; indeed, the checking of calendars would confirm that they had now been at the Palace of Greenwich for four months. Here, Henry had spent his days hunting and feasting as usual, but even so, it was an unusually long period of time for him to spend in one place. The sharper-minded might have wondered why.

So it was that the household was operating with the complacency bred by uninterrupted routine and this day began as did any other, with Henry yawning, blinking and focusing on the murals of St John that decorated his chamber, rubbing his head, sore from banqueting, and dropping back to his bed to gather his thoughts for the day to come.

It would start with breakfast – his stomach registered its approval at the very thought – then after that some time spent dealing with affairs of state. As little time as possible, he hoped, in order to leave room for plenty of jousting practice in the tiltyard, followed by a hunt and then later a banquet for which he had made great provision. Such special provision, in fact, that he was amused to learn of many who had come to the conclusion that today was their last at Greenwich for the time being; indeed, some were so sure of the fact that they had already begun a little surreptitious packing, convinced they were soon to be on the move. They couldn't have been more wrong, of course . . .

He smiled to think of it, and closed his eyes. And he was just about to ease back into sleep when there came a knock at the door.

Though Henry's predecessors had all enjoyed the benefits of private quarters, it was he who had truly developed the idea, so that the Privy Chamber now constituted a household-within-a-household and boasted a staff of its own, many of whom remained within the quarters at all times, playing dice or cards until needed by the monarch.

Mornings commenced when he awoke, which that day was at eight o'clock. For the grooms tasked with warming the chambers, this meant that they had enjoyed an extra hour in the lap of sleep before pulling themselves from their pallets to light fires and wake the more senior staff. They in turn gathered, stifling yawns and scratching their beards, quietly trading gossip of the previous evening, much of it involving the twelve Gentlemen of the Privy Chamber, six of whom were on duty at any given time, and who, at the urging of the page, would have begun assembling. Henry's Gentlemen were handpicked, and they were the best men in the land; their noble looks were finer, the cloth of their garments more colourful and exotic, the light that danced in their eyes brighter than other men. Between them was a great camaraderie.

They came into his chamber now, and Henry greeted them, then his barber, also in attendance. The barber carried water steaming in a bowl, a cloth over his arm, knives, combs, scissors, all for trimming and dressing the King's head and beard. Henry liked his hair close cut, his beard neatly trimmed, and he submitted to the man's scissors as the Gentlemen bustled around them, Henry at the centre, calm and smiling, still very sleepy and a little thick-headed if he was to be honest with himself.

Once the poor put-upon barber had withdrawn, Henry stood and allowed himself to be dressed. Grooms and ushers had prepared garments the previous night, ensuring all his apparel was sufficiently warmed, and were on hand to assist the six Gentlemen as they went about the business of clothing him. Only these six were allowed to lay hands upon the Royal person; no other would ever presume to do so unless given special dispensation, and they worked with great delicacy and sensitivity, dressing him first in a loose silk shirt embroidered with gold, then silk netherhose fastened with a garter, and then trunk hose, also of silk. At his waist the King usually wore a bejewelled dagger and sword, while around his neck hung either a medallion or diamond. His colours were purple, gold, silver and crimson – colours the lower classes were forbidden to wear, even if they could afford such finery – and today he wore purple, the corresponding jerkin brought forth. Next, Sir Edmund Small indicated for an usher, who stepped forward, the light of the bimbling fire behind him, and proffered the doublet that Small slipped over the King's shoulders then knelt to fasten.

Henry, as he often did, detached himself. All of his life

he had been dressed and undressed by others but that didn't mean he particularly cared for the experience – quite the contrary – and he had learnt to deal with it by taking himself away, mentally, if not physically. Now, he found himself staring from the window, past the gardens, orchards and dormant fountains, luxuriating in the magnificent view of the Thames, with its stone jetties, swans, sailing ships and rowing boats. Sometimes the occupants of the boats would wave at the windows of the palace, little knowing that the King was watching them. He loved to see that; was pleased that he could. After all, it was not so long ago that there was no glass in the windows, and they were covered with thick drapes in order to try to block the icy chill. Now he could stand and admire the river that ran like a vein through his realm . . .

Just then he became aware that his body was being tugged. And pulled. And constricted. And the very breath was being forced out of him until he could stand it no more.

'Hell's teeth, Edmund, what's going on?' He laughed. 'Is this some kind of assassination attempt? Should I summon the guard?'

Sir Edmund Small held out a hand for an usher to step forward and help him up. He touched the brim of his hat and bowed, grinning sheepishly at Henry. 'Your Majesty,' he said, 'I can only apologise for the discomfort. It seems we have a problem with the jerkin. As the French might say, a "*défaut de fonctionnement de garde-robe*".'

'A what?' said the King, relishing the view of Sir Edmund at a loss almost as much as he had been admiring the view of the early-morning river. 'Say it again, but in English.'

'That the jerkin . . .' Sir Edmund could be seen struggling for diplomacy, 'has, um . . .' he looked to the Gentlemen of the Privy Chamber who either smirked or found something of interest to see in the fire, '. . . shrunk? Yes, shrunk. That the jerkin has shrunk and we shall be having a terse word with housekeeping, Your Majesty, whose wages shall be docked in accordance with this outrage.'

'Nonsense,' laughed the King, and he patted his stomach. 'It is not housekeeping we should penalise but instead the kitchen we should congratulate. Indeed, shall we send them a case of ale from me? I think we should. In fact, let's send them two. Your King is getting fat, gentlemen. Sir Edmund?'

'Yes, Your Majesty?'

'My compliments on a situation delicately handled.'

'Thank you, Your Majesty.'

'Though I'm not sure those in housekeeping would agree.'

The Gentlemen burst into laughter so unusually loud that those outside wondered what commotion was being caused within.

Moments later, the door was opened and out filed the grooms, ushers, and five of the Gentlemen of the Privy Chamber, Sir Edmund Small still shaking his head with mirth as he closed the door behind him.

II

The one Gentleman to remain inside the Chamber was Sir William Compton, the Groom of the Stool and thus the Senior Gentleman of the Privy Chamber. He had a sandy-coloured beard and close-cropped hair the same colour, and though he had amused eyes was more serious than the other gentlemen; had a certain bearing the others lacked. In his presence Henry could finally relax; so he did, letting himself fall into the seat of a large, wooden armchair.

'Do you think it will be today, William?' he asked.

'Well, not being a physician myself, it could be difficult to say, Your Majesty,' replied Compton. Friend or not, like all subjects, the groom was wary of giving opinions – even when asked for them.

'They said it could be any day now,' sighed Henry, 'as ever they resisted giving me a conclusive answer.'

'Then perhaps today might be the day, Your Majesty.'

'Perhaps.'

There was a long pause. Logs in the fire crackled. From outside came the sound of swans on the river.

'And what of the day, William?' asked Henry. 'What does it have in store?'

'First breakfast . . .'

Henry's stomach rumbled. 'And then?'

'I'm told Sir Anthony Knyvett is keen you should see some sport in the tiltyard.' At this, Henry brightened. 'But before that some matters concerning the realm.'

Henry pushed out his bottom lip. 'Really? Must I?'

Compton chuckled. 'Sir Thomas More requests an audience.'

'Oh.' His old friend and tutor. But even so. 'I suppose he wants to talk about ghosts and ghoulies.'

'Today is wolves, I believe.'

Henry groaned. 'Wolves? Really?'

'Yes, Your Majesty.'

Henry sighed theatrically. 'Then there is but one question of great moment.'

'Majesty?'

'What is for breakfast?'

Compton laughed. 'Whatever pleases Your Majesty, though I took the liberty of asking that kitchen prepare a roasted peacock.'

'And marzipan?'

'I can of course see to it that marzipan is an accompaniment.'

'Perfect.'

Henry chuckled then fell into silence. His eyes were half-closed, a smile upon his face.

'I dreamt of my lady last night,' he said.

Compton smiled. 'Of Queen Katherine?'

'Of who else would I dream?' retorted Henry, a little too crossly, as one does in defence of a lie. Because the fact was he had not dreamt of his Spanish love last night.

He was sure he loved her, of course, just . . . he did not dream of her.

As though reading his thoughts, Compton said, 'Is it not possible to have nocturnal thoughts of another, Your Majesty? A certain maid of honour whom I believe I saw Your Majesty admire a short while ago. Miss Seymour. Most fair, she is, too; I'm sure you wouldn't mind—'

'Stop,' snapped the King, 'I trust that you are not about to make a lewd joke that involves wanting to "see more" of her?'

'Um, no, Your Majesty.'

'Good. And let me tell you that while Miss Seymour is *obviously* attractive – what was her first name, again?'

'Jane, Your Majesty.'

'Quite. Well, I have absolutely no designs on "seeing more" of her. What do you take me for?'

Compton chuckled. 'A man, Majesty. Who showed grace and kindness to Her Majesty Queen Katherine when your brother, her husband, died and she found herself without consort in a foreign land. Who made her his bride. Whose actions were driven by compassion and admiration, certainly. But love . . .?'

'*William*.' Henry gave his groom a sharp, reproving look, which, were he to have given a name, he would have called 'The Tower of London'.

In response, Compton gave a short bow.

There was silence for a moment. Henry brooded. He watched the flames and thought of love.

'You're wrong, William,' he said at last. 'I am not a man and I can't think like one. I am a king and I must behave accordingly. Which is why last night, when I dreamt of my lady, it was Katherine of whom I dreamt. Do you understand?'

'Yes, Your Majesty.'

III

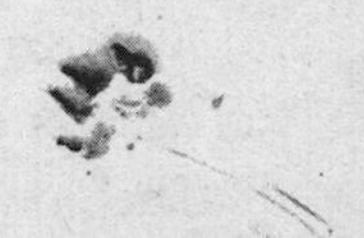

Much later that day, four cardinals crept up the hillside towards Darenth Wood and the lair of the wolfen, murmuring prayers in the half-light of the full moon, their breath freezing in the cold.

Below them was the valley; above them the pasture rose, a mist starting to gather; after that the dark treeline of the wood.

Three of the clerics were armed with an arquebus and a forked staff on which to rest it. Each man had readied his rifle with powder and ball; then, mindful of the environment and the weapon's tendency to clog, had wrapped it in a blanket, stuffing the muzzle with cloth before lashing it to the staff. On their backs they wore custom leather packs, each made up of a sword in a scabbard, the handle jutting over the shoulder, as well as a quiver in which was stored extra ammunition, an unlit torch and several tapers. Close to their body, dry, warm and folded into their robes, was a tinderbox; in a sheath tight to the calf a spare blade, a knife or dagger. And thus laden they trudged in single file towards their fate. On point was Simonetti; behind him, the commander, Morante, and after him, the big man, Pignatelli – the muscle.

Bringing up the rear was the fourth holy man, Barbato, who also had a blade strapped to his calf, carried a tinderbox and wore a sword. But in place of an arquebus he was armed with a longbow, while the quiver at his back held no torch but arrows in its stead.

And Barbato, like his comrades, was as prepared to die as he was to mete out death.

The four were members of the Protektorate, the elite tactical unit trained to engage unearthly forces and entities. Demon hunters. Appointed by the Pope himself, they had all served at the Vatican before their tour of duty and were now stationed at the Observant Friary adjacent to the Palace of Greenwich, where, in these days of accord between man and inhuman, they existed primarily as a peace-keeping force, a deterrent. As such they rarely ventured forth – except for operations such as this one.

On point, Cardinal Simonetti stopped suddenly, and clenched a fist, signalling the team to halt. His hand went to his waist, making a motion like he was patting the head of an obedient dog and behind him the clerics dropped to one knee, watching their point man as he knelt to the ground as though to anoint it with a kiss. But in fact was listening.

Darkness pressing in. The sound of a breeze in the trees. From somewhere an owl.

Then the point man was straightening, twirling his finger above his head to indicate the squad should turn about. In a harsh whisper saying one word: '*Horse.*'

At the rear, Barbato the bowman shifted around, squinting in the moonlight to look across the valley. His eyes followed the lie of the land and then he saw it – a shape on the other side of the valley. No more than a dark blur but it was making its way downhill, and moving fast, too.

'I see something,' he said. It had reached the bottom of the valley and was negotiating the stream. Either it had two riders or one large one . . .

'Target?' the commander's voice came from behind him.

'Acquired,' he replied, perhaps a little too loudly. He snatched an arrow and fitted it to the bow, finding his mark. Too dangerous to go for the rider if it turned out there were two. Go for the horse. He adjusted his aim for the front flank of the steed. Behind him the squad had turned and he heard them draw their swords.

Blade in hand, Morante scrambled back to crouch beside Barbato, drawing his robes around him with his free hand.

'Easy,' whispered the squad leader in Italian. 'Easy now. It could be a farmer. A friendly.'

The rider stopped on the hill. Barbato tensed. Yes: there were two men on the horse. Both wore black, hooded capes buttoned up against the cold. One of them, his head bent, was reaching for something that he pulled out and held up. A standard. The Royal standard.

Morante placed a hand to his forearm so Barbato lowered the bow, then the commander stood and waved. The riders turned in their direction and seconds later the horse was upon them, one of the men jumping down and sweeping back his hood to address Morante.

'Good evening, Your Eminence,' he said.

'Sir Thomas,' replied Morante.'You gave us quite a fright.'

Sir Thomas More, the King's secretary and adviser, passed the reins of his mount to the second man, who wore the robes of a minor cleric, and beckoned Morante away from the other cardinals.

'My deepest apologies if I startled your men, Your Eminence,' he said to Morante, his voice low. 'Did you think me a wolfen?'

'We take no chances,' whispered Morante in English. Not a language he felt a great affinity for. 'But what is the meaning of this, Thomas?'

'I offer most humble apologies, Your Eminence,' said More, who could speak Italian perfectly, but had chosen not to reveal this fact to the Protektorate, gaining a private and somewhat guilty amusement from their attempts to negotiate his mother tongue. 'But my mode of transport was chosen for its speed, not its silence, for I bring you a command it is most important to heed. You are to stand down.'

The Cardinals erupted. A moment ago they had been due to attack, hearts and heads prepared for the assault. Now they were denied: boldness replaced by doubt, courage by fear.

As Morante quietened his men, More continued with his instructions. He was to remain with them, he said. It was his responsibility to see to it that they did not commence the operation until a signal had been given.

But the waiting was dangerous, they protested (knowing that to do so was futile), the beast would almost certainly send out patrols; each moment spent in the open increased their risk of discovery. Of death.

More spread his hands. Sorry, but the order was that they should stay on the hillside and out of sight. Light no fire for warmth or food. They should wait.

Not long later they had seen a fire glow on the horizon, known that the cleric was there. They had moved to the shelter of an old oak tree, the perimeter of the wood perhaps two hundred yards away, and they settled down at the base of the tree as though to absorb its fortitude and wisdom, and they took solace from prayer as they awaited their order.

Which would come from some thirty miles away, at the Palace of Greenwich, from the quill of Cardinal Wolsey.

IV

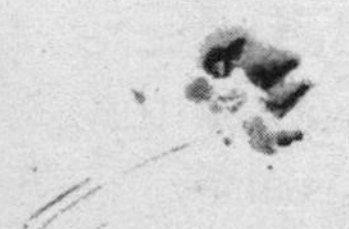

The King's Lord Chancellor, Thomas Cardinal Wolsey, was apt to chew upon the handle of his cane when he was beset by nerves, and he was beset by them now, so it was all he could do not to gnaw at it as he strode quickly through the Palace of Greenwich, his chains of office bouncing at his chest, robes billowing about him.

Oh, fuck, he thought. He had a meeting with the Belgian ambassador. A meeting for which he was already late. *Oh bloody, bloody hell.*

Despite his bulk he moved quickly, his cane clacking on the flagstones, servants stepping out of his way and bowing their heads as he passed. Hurrying with him was one of his many young clerks, Dudley, who was among his most trusted and wore his household's crimson velvet livery embroidered with a cardinal's hat. Dudley carried a large wood-carved writing board, worn on his back – so heavy he was almost bent double beneath it – and fastened to his body with large straps that criss-crossed across his chest. In his hands a silver tray on which was a quill and inkpot, and a rolled-up sheet of parchment.

They reached the Long Gallery heading towards the Great Hall. Wolsey was used to seeing it in the daytime when members of court used it for exercise, couples walked together, and servants exercised dogs. Tonight, however, there were celebrations in the palace and several of those unable to take the rambunctious pace had found their way out into the gallery and collapsed there, snoring on the wooden floors so that Wolsey and Dudley were forced to step over them, the noise of the party growing louder as they approached the hall.

Wolsey would rather have avoided it, of course, being keen not to see the King, who would no doubt insist he join the festivities. But through the hall was the most direct avenue to the chambers in which he had arranged to meet the ambassador. Other corridors might be unlit and they would definitely be wet and cold and Wolsey did not like the idea of feeling his way along damp, lichen-covered walls while the ambassador waited.

No, the only way to be sure was to go through the centre of the palace. He would have to bank on His Majesty being so caught up in the moment that his passage went unnoticed.

Then they were inside and moving between the great hanging tapestries and the long banqueting tables that lined either side of the hall.

Servants attempted to clear the remains of what had obviously been a magnificent feast. Some guests had remained in their seats, where they conducted loud conversations or gossiped scurrilously, in which case they leant to whisper in each other's ears, feathers from hats tickling their noses; some had adjourned upstairs, where they lingered on balconies or in the galleries overlooking the Great Hall, figures cloaked in darkness, gathered among the yellow ochre beams; most, though, had congregated in the middle of the hall, laughing, flirting and dancing. Among them moved minstrels creating an infernal racket that caused Wolsey such vexation. The noise of it was almost deafening.

Now he was adopting his well-practised smile as he picked his way through revellers, some masked, some not. All, it seemed, in a state of great intoxication. It was his court smile, the one he always wore in the face of such celebrations. As though he did not find the festivities tiresome, self-indulgent, trivial and repetitive, and think the sound of the lute redolent of lax morals and the relentless high-pitched recorder pestilential beyond description. But thought they were joyous. Why, the very fabric from which life was woven.

The cardinal wore his smile well. For there were those – naming no names Thomas Boleyn and Thomas Howard, the Duke of Norfolk – who would be watching assiduously, who would be more than happy to report any sign of displeasure to His Majesty; say anything to weaken his standing with the King. Norfolk's beard was black, Boleyn's ginger. Otherwise there was little to differentiate them; they were both as conniving and ambitious as each other. Thomas Cromwell, his erstwhile assistant, would be around somewhere, too. Cromwell was more discreet about his ambition than the other two, which probably made him even more dangerous. Wolsey did not stop to seek them out as he moved through the hall. But they would be there, he knew, in a gallery or dark recess, in the flickering shadows; they would watch him with drunken, resentful, heavy-lidded eyes; and they would talk behind their hands so that his clerks were unable to read their lips.

So his smile stayed fixed. Even when he was brought

up short by a leering young man in a colourful slashed doublet who staggered into his path, swigging from a leather bottle of wine. Oblivious to the cardinal, the partygoer lurched away, grabbing a young woman by the waist and pushing his face into her cleavage, which she greeted not with a gasp of horror but with a scream of laughter, her head thrown back in delight. The young man pulled away, raising his leather bottle and calling, 'Hypocras. More Hypocras.'

Good God, thought Wolsey, *the revelry is even more Bacchanalian than usual!* And had he paused to consider why this might be, he might have come to the conclusion that the King was toasting a particularly successful day's hunting, or perhaps celebrating in honour of Queen Katherine, who must have been the most regularly and lavishly honoured woman in the entire kingdom, for these were the usual reasons given to excuse the palace's descent into debauchery. But Wolsey did not wonder. Instead he concentrated on moving onwards, on avoiding the King and on the suppression of his nerves. To chew upon his cane in public, like a famished dog at a sun-bleached femur, would be most unbecoming for the man they called *alter rex*, the 'other king', upon whom rested all of the great responsibility of power.

The Lord Chancellor was not of noble birth. The son of an Ipswich grazier he had risen through the ranks of the church and then court, having gained favour with the father, Henry VII, then the son, whose confidence he enjoyed and who relied upon the cardinal in almost all matters, ceding complete authority to him.

Oh, the King pretended, of course, being wily enough to

know that he should be *seen* as being at the seat of power. 'If my cap knew my counsel I would throw it in the fire,' he once declared during Privy Council, much to the private amusement of Wolsey who had been watching His Majesty slowly lose a battle against sleep.

No, despite his disingenuous proclamations, the King was a sybarite. It was Wolsey who would sit at his writing desk for days at a time, his concentration on the King's matters so complete that he stopped not even to piss; Wolsey who, after the King, was the most powerful human being at court, and thus in the land. Wolsey who was the power behind the throne.

Wolsey who was now tasked with the problem of the wolfen.

No wonder he ached to chew upon the cane.

Earlier an envoy had come to Wolsey's chambers bearing the Vatican seal, a response to Wolsey's petition to Rome, in which Wolsey had explained the situation to His Holiness: that in Kent local people had been disappearing, presumed murdered; that a local had reported seeing a woman borne off by a wolfman.

Usually such sightings tended to excite the local populace but merely titillate those further afield. However, Protektorate intelligence believed the locals were correct; that a wolfen cell led by the renegade Malchek was responsible for the disappearances – Malchek, who had vowed never to abide by the treaty, a sworn enemy of humans and a diplomatic embarrassment for demonkind.

Using the locations of the disappearances as a guide, they had narrowed down the area in which Malchek might be found. They conducted extensive reconnaissance and surveillance, eventually reaching the conclusion that he and his accomplices were holed up in a disused church inside Darenth Wood.

Wolsey's proposition was that they launch an assault on the hideout. Wipe the insurgents off the face of the earth.

He knew, of course, that the Pope's blessing for this endeavour was not a foregone conclusion. Wolsey did not like the idea of rogue wolves at large on what he considered to be his territory. The Pope, on the other hand, was of the opinion that occasional demonic activity was to be tolerated. Tales of beasts, possessions, witches and werewolves frightened the people. And frightened people attended church.

Mindful of the Holy Father's views, Wolsey had ended his petition by reminding His Holiness that the last thing they wanted was for locals to take matters into their own hands. The message was sent, and Wolsey awaited his reply.

And waited.

Until he could wait no more so had dispatched the force that morning, Thomas having gained the King's permission.

Shortly afterwards, of course, a messenger had come to Wolsey's chambers. A boy who was the bearer of bad news. For it came back that the blessing was to be given on one condition. That Wolsey met with the Belgian ambassador and gained his approval for the attack.

More had been despatched to stop the cadre before the assault. They were dug in outside Darenth Wood, so he'd been told, where they awaited his command to attack. Meantime, he had set up a meeting with the ambassador and cursed the delay, hoping against hope that villagers weren't, even now, taking up cudgels, pitchforks and stout staffs against the wolf.

V

Master Gregory Hoblet and his wife Agatha were on the trail to Darenth that evening when three men stepped into their path: a collection of labourers bearing pitchforks and stout staffs.

Agatha rode on a horse, but she insisted that Hob, as Witchfinder General, ride on an ass. This, she said, was how Jesus used to travel. And like Jesus it was their job to roam the countryside doing God's will – though by torturing and burning young women rather than distributing fish or healing the sick.

Moreover, just as Jesus Christ had a humble ass, Hob's was similarly lowly. Literally so; it sat much lower than Agatha's horse, and he would often find himself being flicked in the face by its tail, plus he had a greater familiarity with the stallion's lower anatomy than he would have preferred, being in closer proximity. But worst of all his ass was bony and hard and not at all pleasant to sit upon, especially over long distances.

'Perhaps we should exchange mounts for a few miles,' he'd suggested earlier, the very thought a triumph of hope over experience.

She cackled, hawked and spat. 'Oh, but what if someone

were to see, Hoblet,' she rasped derisively. 'It wouldn't do for the Witchfinder General's wife to be getting ideas above her station now, would it?'

He sighed. 'Look, Agatha, why don't you just be the Witchfinder General from now on? It's really more your sort of thing than mine anyway.' He imagined himself back at the farmhouse, tending to the garden and looking after his bees . . .

'Nobody would be happier about that than me,' she said haughtily, 'only we seem to be stuck in the dark ages when it comes to us women round here. I would be more than happy to take on the title of Witchfinder General; it would only be fitting and right seeing as it's me what does most of the work. Oh, but our enlightened society dictates that witchfinding be left to the men. And seeing as you're the only man around here, and you do have the beard for the task, and a certain bearing, I'll give you that much, then that makes you the Witchfinder General. So stop moaning about your ass. And remember to talk right an' all.'

'Yes, dear,' Hob had said, gazing over the fields and to the huge mass of Darenth Wood.

Then: 'Look sharp,' Agatha muttered. 'There's folk up ahead. From Darenth village if I'm not very much mistaken.'

Sure enough, and now the village people were clustered around them, one of whom stepped forward, spat and wiped his mouth. 'Would you be the Witchfinder and his wife?' he asked, voice like a rusty saw.

Agatha removed her pipe. 'Aye, that we be, countryman.'

'And you have come to question the wolfman?'

By his wife's side, Hob had been trying to look sinister and impassive, which was not at all easy given that Agatha's horse was flicking its tail enthusiastically, awarding him the occasional faceful of dung-scented horsehair. He hid his true thoughts, his happy thoughts of his garden and his hives. And for that reason it took a second or so for the word to register. What Hob had been expecting to hear did indeed begin with 'W', but it ended in '-itch', just as he had been led to think it would by his wife. They were, after all, witchfinders. So, for that second, his brain, still in the garden at the farmhouse, struggled to comprehend this new, unfamiliar word: *wolfman*.

Hoblet craned his neck to stare at his wife in astonishment as she continued. 'We hear tell of an animal stalking the region. That he has been taking folk from the land and visiting upon them the foulest of atrocities, such as could not be spoken of, for to even hear of such deeds would be to darken the soul beyond repair. And that in your village a man stands accused of these crimes and of the crime of . . .' she paused, removing the pipe from her mouth and leaning forward in the saddle so that the wart on her chin was only inches from the face of the nearest villager '. . . *lycanthropy*.'

Obligingly, a bird chose that moment to make a sudden commotion in the branches of a nearby tree, and as one the countryfolk jumped in fear, the witchfinder's wife sitting back in her saddle and chuckling to herself, puffing on her pipe.

When the villagers had settled she said, 'Now perhaps you would be so kind as to show us to our accommodation. We have ridden many miles and Master Hoblet needs his rest in order to conserve his strength for tomorrow's questioning.' She widened her eyes, looking from one man to the next. 'Which is sure to be both harrowing and horrifying. Isn't that right, Master Hoblet?' She looked at him enquiringly.

'Yes, that's right,' said Hob.

She narrowed her eyes at him. Inwardly he sighed. He hated having to talk like a yokel.

'Aye, that it be, Mistress Hoblet,' he growled obediently. 'Most harrowing. Most harrowing it be.'

Later, they were installed in rooms above a tavern, much to Agatha's disgust, she being more accustomed, so she said, to manor house accommodation, when Hob questioned her about the nature of their assignation, choosing his words carefully so as not to enrage her.

'Agatha,' he said, 'my love, my light at the end of the tunnel—'

'Don't be calling me that,' she growled. 'Just spit it out you – what you want?'

'It's just that . . . *wolfmen*?'

Exasperated, she threw up her hands. 'There's no bloody pleasing you, is there, Hoblet? It was you who said you was tired of burning witches. What about all those *nightmares* you were having. I thought burning a wolf might make a nice change. Help you with that tender *conscience* of yours.'

'It's not a tender conscience, Agatha. It's just *a conscience*.'

'Whatever.'

'But, look, that's not the point. The point is . . . what do we know about wolfmen, for God's sake?'

She sighed and closed her eyes as though gathering the strength to speak to a particularly stupid clergyman. 'Listen here, Hoblet, ours is the business of fear, and the fear business is changing. People ain't afraid of witches no more, that's the sad fact of it; they're afraid of wolfmen now. And if we want to keep a roof over our heads we can't go on clinging to the old ways. Witches are last year, they're over. If the public want to see lycanthropes put to death, then that's what we've got to give them. Cos if we don't someone else will. And afore you know it, it'll be Fred Bloggs the Wolffinder General, and do you want that?'

'No, dear,' he said, but if Hob knew his wife she was thinking of her chimney. Their farmhouse was little more than a yeoman's abode, but Agatha had grand plans for the chimney. It had a spiral, twisted design and chequered brick-work, so that their builder, Master Brookes, would stand and scratch his beard and say, 'Chequered brickwork? Now you're asking, Mistress Hoblet . . .' and quote them ever-increasing figures for its construction – money that had to be found from witchfinding. And when one night, Hob had drily remarked on the irony of burning witches in order to pay for a chimney, Agatha had been moved to fury and threatened him with a hand axe. Because new accusations were infrequent, the chimney remained unfinished. And every day Agatha would stand in the yard, one hand on her hip and the other shielding her eyes, scanning the horizon for sight of a messenger who would have travelled from one of the villages in the area and who would tell of a woman accused of witchcraft – an unmarried woman more often than not – witnessed talking with her familiar, usually a cat, sometimes a stoat, even a grasshopper once. She would have been imprisoned, this accused witch, she and others who had fallen under suspicion because they were un-married women and were known to have associated with the accused, or had been witnessed speaking in tongues. And fearing the spread of these satanic crimes the magistrate had sent for the Witchfinder General: he who was licensed by parliament and the King (which was what Agatha told folk, though it was not strictly speaking accurate or, in fact, true at all) to rid the region of the abomination of witchcraft.

And Agatha would get all excited. With bright eyes and a spring in her step, she would see to it that Hob donned his robes and hat and that his white beard was trimmed, and she'd brush his eyebrows into menacing points. She herself would dress in her very best apron and cap, and from the wall she would take her collection of pricking irons wrapped in a leather case. She would fetch their mounts and, giving Hob's ass a hearty slap, they would set off for the village. Arriving, they would find the villagers hard at work building a fire in the village square, a sense of anticipation in the air.

Agatha did not disappoint. You had to hand it to her, for as night replaced day, when Agatha Hoblet questioned a witch, a confession would surely follow. Along with home improvement, torture was something for which she had a genuine creative flair. Her favourite form of persuasion was the *strappado*, which involved taking a length of rope, using one end of it to tie the victim's hands behind her back, and feeding the other through a pulley until the accused was suspended in excruciating pain that increased as weights were added to the legs. Hob had seen more limbs wrenched and dislocated than any man should. Luckily, Agatha was expert at returning them to their sockets with a brisk pop. So that the screaming could begin again.

She enjoyed force-feeding the accused large amounts of

water until their stomachs were so bloated and distended as to be almost transparent, and they would be shrieking in agony.

She liked pulling out their fingernails with hot pincers, or filling their noses with lime and water, so that it burnt holes in the nostrils. She had chopped off ears, fingers, noses, toes, even labia.

She relished gouging out eyes and holding them up for the appreciation of the crowd, burning brandy or sulphur over their prone bodies, strapping them to tables lined with hawthorn, forcing spiked rollers on their spines . . .

In short, there was no end to her invention when it came to exposing witches, and she had the success rate to match. Because if the accused died during questioning, then it was a sure sign of witchcraft; if she displayed taciturnity, then it was a sure sign of witchcraft; if she passed out, then it was the devil putting her out of her misery, and a sure sign of witchcraft; if she would not admit her abominations, then the tortures would be increased until such a time as she did. And if the accused confessed to witchcraft, then that was a sure sign of witchcraft, too.

Confession extracted, Agatha would turn her attention to execution, by hanging, burning or drowning, and leaving any remains to act as a warning to others tempted to consort with the devil. Then they would collect the money – for the Good Lord paid in silver for every witch delivered unto him, as Agatha was fond of saying – before returning home, where Agatha would brood and moan and make life a misery for Hob and Brookes the builder . . .

Now, Hob watched his wife place her leather wrap of pricking irons on the bed and he wondered what other methods of persuasion she had in store for the wolfman. He stared through the wooden slats of the window and into the village square below. It was calm now, quiet, but he knew how that would change when news of a burning was in the air.

VI

'Thomas!'

The King's voice, as magisterial as his bearing, seemed to cut through the merrymaking and Wolsey came to a halt so suddenly that Dudley almost collided with him. The cardinal restrained himself from chewing upon his cane.

'Thomas,' repeated the King. Then he was clasping the cardinal in a bear hug, bringing with him a magnificent cloud of sovereignty, and the fumes of fine wines.

From the looks of the King he had been imbibing it in even greater quantities than usual. Not only was his affection conveyed with extra vigour but his cheeks were ruddy and his eyes gleamed happily. His gown had been cast aside, so that he wore just his doublet over a shirt with a drawstring at the neck, black velvet hose and an ornate codpiece. His short hair was in disarray and his beard glistened. Next he appeared to do what was a little jig, whirling to finish and flinging out his arms in the manner of a showman making an introduction of the great capering at his back.

'Welcome,' he said. And though Wolsey was larger than the King he still marvelled at the size of the man. Famously athletic and well built, which he had no excuse not to be considering his daytime pursuits of hunting, hawking and jousting, the King would habitually negotiate the night with a great feast, each a minimum of three courses, each course made up of at least twenty dishes: meats roasted on a spit, pies with decorative tops, exotic fruits, songbirds, sea otters, dolphin. All of it caked in spice. Oh, and marzipan. He loved marzipan. Those who said he ate and drank more than was healthy had no feel for the energy of the man, no idea of the sheer size of the palaces in which he lived, and how cold they always were. All that food he consumed – he needed it. For his mind, body and spirit. For life.

Wolsey smiled in reply to the King's dance. 'Very good, Majesty,' he said, raising his voice to make himself heard. The fire roasted his back.

'It's good to see you at court, Thomas,' grinned Henry, 'we don't see enough of you.'

Wolsey bowed his head in a gesture that he hoped conveyed his deep regret at not visiting court more often. 'I trust my dispatches keep Your Majesty informed,' he said. These would be taken from his home to court – where, Wolsey was sure, the King ignored them altogether.

'Oh yes,' replied the King. 'I mean, I'm a little behind, of course, you know how it is. Now, won't you tarry a while? Come take a drink.' He indicated to the huge top table piled high with uneaten food. Of Her Majesty, Queen Katherine of Aragon, there was no sign and Wolsey briefly wondered when he had last clapped eyes on her.

'Come, please, come,' urged the King, and with reluctance, Wolsey followed him to the top table where a line of servants stood, Sir William Compton in charge of them.

Their eyes met. Compton waited a moment, no more than the strike of a drum but enough for Wolsey to register the slight. Then Compton indicated to two of the servants, who seated Wolsey and placed a goblet before him.

In front of them, the party continued. Perhaps this was all the King required, hoped Wolsey: simply for him to show enthusiasm for the festivities. And as the King threw up a hand to whip the players into greater volume, Wolsey increased the intensity of his smile, nodding his head in time to the music as though the musicians delighted him, not that he'd like to see the fuckers thrown on the fire.

'How about a rendition of "Pastime with Good Company", Thomas?' yelled the King into the face of Wolsey who recoiled a little, the King adding, 'Oh God, sorry, did I just breathe fumes all over you?'

'Oh, no, Your Majesty.'

'No to the fumes or no to the song?'

He really was quite merry, thought Wolsey. 'Er, no to the fumes, yes to the song. The song would please me very much.'

Wolsey was fibbing, of course. He loathed the song. It had been composed by the King himself in yet another tribute to the Queen, and was by far the worst song Wolsey had ever heard.

Before he knew it the King was rising from his seat. 'Godfrey,' he called to one of the players, beckoning him over, and Wolsey had to restrain himself from pulling away as Godfrey and his accursed lute came closer. As if the sound were not bad enough, the man had an ingratiating posture and a particularly despicable beard. First bowing his head obsequiously, he then smiled at the King and his eyes flicked momentarily over the King's shoulder as he inclined his head to hear his instructions.

As Henry spoke, Godfrey's eyes wandered once more and Wolsey turned slightly in his chair to see Compton, a smile on his face.

Then Godfrey was straightening and indicating to the other players and in moments they had struck up 'Pastime with Good Company', the entire room joining in the song.

'I love, and shall until I die.
Grudge who will, but none deny,
So God be pleased, thus live will I.'

Christ, but it was shit, thought the cardinal as he shared a helpless look with Dudley, who stood bent over, still holding his tray. Then, when the singing had at last finished, Wolsey made a great show of applauding, bowing his head to the King, then making to stand, offering a silent prayer that he might be allowed to depart.

A regal hand came to his forearm. The King leaned towards him. 'A moment, Thomas, please. I have something to tell you.'

Wolsey settled. 'Yes, Your Majesty?'

'It cannot have escaped your notice that tonight's festivities are more joyful than ever, yes?'

'Certainly,' said Wolsey, 'Your Majesty's great beneficence has been noted.'

'Then I wager you would like to know the reason why?'

Wolsey nodded his head vigorously.

The King leant towards him. 'It is the Queen, Thomas. She is with child. We are to have a son.'

For a moment the sound of the festivities fell away as Wolsey absorbed the news.

The Queen. Pregnant. Again.

This was – it had to be said – a surprise.

'Your Majesty,' said Wolsey, picking his words very, very carefully. His smile never wavered. 'What wonderful news. If only she were here in order that I could offer my congratulations in person.'

'She is resting,' beamed the King.

'Then in her absence, may I submit my warmest congratulations and assurances that I shall be offering prayers for Her Majesty.'

'As well as a toast, Thomas.' The King nudged him, raising his own goblet to his lips.

'Indeed, Your Majesty.' Wolsey took up his own drink. 'May I ask, how far advanced is the Queen?'

She wouldn't make it full term, he thought, taking a gulp. These celebrations were ludicrously premature. The Queen was last with child some years ago, with the sixth of her pregnancies, and a more torrid catalogue of tragedy it was difficult to imagine, a series of stillborns and miscarriages with just one living child, Mary, to show for it. Most at court now felt that the Queen's childbearing days were over; she was, after all, almost forty years of age. No, she would miscarry within a month. He had no doubt of it.

'She is nine months pregnant, Thomas,' confided the King. 'My beloved is due to give birth any day now.'

Cardinal Wolsey coughed. He felt his lungs flood. He banged his goblet to the table, chest tight, trying to get some words out.

'Went down. Wrong hole,' he managed, feeling himself go red, still unable to breathe.

'Thomas . . .' laughed the King. He stood and thumped

the Lord Chancellor on the back so hard that Wolsey thought he might have cracked a rib. Although it did at least have the desired effect.

'*She's almost due?*' he gasped incredulously, trying to recover his composure. 'Your Majesty, why was I not told? This is the kind of information I need to know. I must notify Rome.'

'Nonsense, Thomas. Nobody needs informing until my son is born.' The King leant even closer, bringing those fumes with him again. 'My lady is advanced in years, you know this. Why, I saw it in your eyes.'

Wolsey made what he hoped was the correct face.

'For me,' continued the King, 'it is a distressing matter having the world think my wife is incapable of carrying a child – a son – and that I am incapable of providing her with the care and support she needs in order to do this successfully. Do you understand? It is my wish that no announcement is made until the baby is born and pronounced healthy. That is why nobody but a very, very select few know the truth.'

Wolsey thought back to the last time he had seen the Queen, many months ago. They had passed in a hallway and he had acknowledged her with a short bow. In return she inclined her head, a rather virtuous and self-satisfied smile about her lips. A smile of triumph that seemed to say that despite their many conflicts she would prevail, she had the devotion of the King. Now Wolsey knew there was something else in that smile. That she had the devotion of the King and soon, she would have his son.

But Wolsey had seen the fatigue in her eyes then, and he didn't doubt that if he were to visit her now he would see that same weariness and maybe something else, too. Doubt, perhaps, and fear.

'May I ask, Your Majesty, who knows the secret?'

'Just those who need to know. And if you don't mind, I'd prefer we leave it at that.'

Wolsey nodded, but his mind was now racing in order to assess the implications of the news, all the possibilities and outcomes. Looking up, he saw Boleyn and Norfolk together in one of the galleries, faces in shadow, gazing down upon him, watching him. Norfolk, stocky, his beard black; Boleyn, slighter than his co-conspirator and weasel-like with his abominable ginger beard. Would they know? He felt Compton's eyes boring into his back. Surely he would know?

'Your Majesty,' Wolsey said, 'despite this most joyous news, I must beg my leave, for I have urgent business to attend to; indeed, that business My Lord Sir Thomas More spoke of this very morning, if you recall . . .'

The King looked perplexed. 'Yes, there was something. Something to do with . . .'

'It's of *utmost* import to the Crown,' pressed Wolsey.

'Greater than celebrating the imminent arrival of my son, Thomas?' chided the King. 'His name is to be George – a saint to serve England. Don't you want to toast the future King George?'

But Henry was joking and he clapped the cardinal heartily on the back, giving him leave to stand and depart the table, which Wolsey did, bowing to the King before crossing the room, collecting Dudley and swiftly exiting the Great Hall. With a huge sigh of relief, he left the heat and noise behind him.

'Is the Queen's physician still that Vittoria fellow?' he barked to Dudley as they hurried, the gallery to themselves.

'Yes, Your Eminence. Dr Fernando Vittoria.'

'Good. Arrange an appointment. I need to see him. A medical matter, tell him. Say it's for my gout. That my own physician is indisposed. I need to see him as soon as possible.'

'Yes, Your Eminence.'

'And, Dudley, listen . . .'

'Yes, Your Eminence.'

The cardinal lowered his voice. 'There's a minstrel called Godfrey. Put someone on him. I *especially* want to know if he fraternises with Compton.'

'Yes, Your Eminence.'

'And, Dudley?'

'Yes, Your Eminence.'

'Who at court currently has the King's eye?'

'Your Eminence?'

Wolsey stopped. Dudley stopped, too. Bent half over, the board strapped to his back, he looked a little like a tortoise, craning his neck to stare up at his master, who bent to address him.

'Dudley,' said Wolsey, 'tell nobody of this, but the Queen is with child.'

His clerk's eyebrows shot up in surprise.

'Quite. And she has been pregnant for some time; indeed is expected to give birth *any day now*.'

Dudley's jaw dropped.

'Where do you think the King has been taking his pleasure these last nine months?'

'Your Eminence,' stuttered Dudley, 'I'm . . . I'm quite sure I don't know.'

Wolsey frowned and regarded Dudley, who looked anxious. He was Wolsey's eyes and ears, yet the King's trysts – and there would have been trysts, Wolsey knew – seemed to have escaped him.

'Then he has obviously been discreet,' said Wolsey.

Dudley relaxed.

Wolsey thought. 'Who was his last fancy?'

'Your Eminence,' said Dudley nervously, for he was almost as aware of the politics of the court as the cardinal himself, 'I'm afraid to say it was the Boleyn girl. Mary.'

The colour drained from Wolsey's face.

'Good God, how could I forget?' he exclaimed. 'Mary Boleyn, of course. Oh bloody hell.'

Wolsey hurried on, Dudley falling into step behind him. Wolsey's mind raced. Now he understood the demeanour of Boleyn and Norfolk. Those pimps. Perhaps they were unaware of the Queen's condition but they would indeed know that the King had been paying visits to Mary's bed. What was it they'd called the girl in France? *A great prostitute*. For the King, a willing bedmate. For Boleyn and Norfolk an opportunity to further inveigle themselves at court and supplant Wolsey. They even had another, it was said. A sister to Mary. Another whore to pimp out.

Worse than all of this, of course, was that when he and his assistant reached the meeting chamber, as was almost inevitable, the ambassador and his party had gone back to his own quarters, no doubt.

Wolsey turned to look at Dudley, who regarded him with trepidation, and he sighed. 'Fuck,' he said.

VII

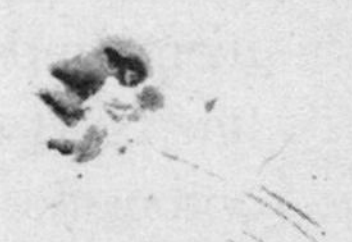

Sir Thomas More always wore a hair shirt next to his skin. For penance and atonement. To chafe and scratch at his flesh, to scour his soul and keep him from attaining comfort in a life ripe with enticements.

He was glad of it tonight, though, for the warmth. That, his robes and the thickest of his thick cloaks was helping to keep the English winter at bay. He glanced over at his companions. Secretly he did not especially approve of the cardinals' usual mode of dress. All those shining, flowing robes and chains. He found them a little ostentatious. Neither were they particularly practical, he mused now, wrapping his cloak around him and looking over at them: Morante, Barbato, Simonetti and Pignatelli lying between the roots, their arms wrapped about themselves, sleeping.

More closed his eyes and let his head rest against the bark, thinking of his children, as he often did. All it took was thoughts of them, or of God, to soothe his soul . . .

Then, awaking from his ruminations with a start, he heard distant conversation, which came from the treeline. He pressed himself to the tree trunk and squinted out into the darkness, hoping to pick out the source. The voices were coming closer. Two people if he heard correctly: a man and a woman, nothing clandestine about them judging by the tone and volume of their voices. The female laughed, even. Could it be two people out for an early-morning stroll? Perhaps so, because now he saw them. They walked in the pasture, close to the boundary of the wood. They were young, by the look and sound of them, and they wore the clothes of labourers: she a white linen coif tied under the chin and a smock, though not an apron; he a woollen hat he had adorned with a feather, a rather rakish touch, and typical of a gentleman suitor. They walked with a carefree, close gait. Again, a laugh. She took his hand and rested her head on his upper arm as they walked.

More chewed his lip, wondering whether he should take action. If he was right then they would at some point be entering the wood. There to find shelter for whatever activity it was they had in mind – he had a good idea what that might be.

They might find themselves caught up in the operation; moreover, there was the danger that a member of the wolfen might be on the prowl, perhaps looking for their next victim. The girl – surely aware of the disappearances – thought she would be safe with her suitor. No doubt he had calmed her nerves by telling her so, thinking more of the beast in his breeches than the one at large in Darenth Wood.

More shifted, watching them walk across his line of sight, then find a break in the trees – a well-worn spot – and go through. He wasn't so sure they'd be safe. Not so sure at all.

And what was this now? As they vanished into the undergrowth another movement caught his eye. A third person was moving quickly across the plain, crouched low and closing the distance between himself and the courting couple. As they disappeared from sight he broke into a stealthy run. A black leather jerkin glimmered and he wore no hat, his long, greasy hair bouncing as he hurried across the grass.

Jesu. With the third man gone, More scuttled around the base of the tree and shook Cardinal Morante awake.

Morante shot into a sitting position with a gasp, eyes finding the horizon where the fire still burnt, instinctively reaching for his sword.

'Your Eminence. So sorry to disturb you,' began More, who was not at all sorry; indeed, if the situation were not so serious, he might rather have enjoyed the sight of the cardinal in disarray. He told Morante what he had seen.

'I shall send a man,' whispered Morante, in English.

More laid a hand on his arm. 'My orders were explicit. You are to remain here. I'll go.'

'Have you the arms?'

'A short sword,' replied More, suppressing a grin despite himself. 'It will have to do. It's of paramount importance that Malchek is stopped. If I can prevent collateral damage, then all the better.'

Morante gave him a searching look. 'So be it.'

More nodded and stood, pulling up his hood. He took a deep breath then made off in the direction of the treeline.

VIII

Wolsey took a deep breath and knocked hard on the oak door of the Belgian ambassador's chamber. Moments later it was opened by an aide in embroidered silk, who raised his eyebrows, saying, 'Your Eminence.'

Wolsey dipped his head to acknowledge the unusual circumstances that brought him, the Lord Chancellor, to the door of the ambassador.

Then again, he thought, as he was ushered into the chamber, Dudley trooping in behind him, this was no ordinary ambassador. He was not a man as others were – though he took the form of one for his dealings with humans. And while it was true that he was the representative of a foreign power, his was even more powerful than France and the Holy Roman Empire combined.

To most at court he was Laurent Cassell, the Belgian ambassador. To Wolsey and the Protektorate he was Lefsetz, a high-born demon and a representative of the Baal clan that held sway over all demonkind, and who had, since the treaty of 1520 – signed in secret at the Field of the Cloth and Gold – remained at court as the demon ambassador to England.

Lefsetz was moving into the middle of the room now, a

gold earring glinting orange in the candlelight of his private chamber. He wore a voluminous white linen shirt and slashed hose and he grinned, his arms outstretched in order to embrace Wolsey who found himself, as always, wanting to shrink away from the man.

'Your Eminence,' said Lefsetz. His voice was like honey dripped over that pronounced European accent that the ladies at court found so very seductive.

'My old friend,' purred Wolsey in return.

As they clasped one another, Wolsey found himself aware not of the man, but of the creature beneath. Did he imagine it, or when they embraced could he feel the body flex and change beneath his arms with a rustling sound, like that made by aged parchment or the wings of an insect?

Perhaps it was just his mind playing tricks on him. All that marked Lefsetz as different from humans was his teeth, which Wolsey swore would become markedly more pointed when he smiled, especially when he was discussing those subjects that interested and excited him: war, rape, punishment and torture. Other than that Wolsey had not seen the ambassador take his true self and hoped he never would; indeed, Lefsetz had once said that his natural form was capable of inducing insanity or even death in humans. He'd smiled when he said it. And his teeth had seemed to grow and sharpen.

'I owe you an apology, Your Excellency,' said the cardinal, pulling away from the embrace.

'For keeping me waiting? Think nothing of it, Your Eminence. As soon as I heard that you had been taken to the King's table, there to drink with him . . .'

'Ah,' Wolsey smiled, 'you had word.'

'But of course, Your Eminence.' He indicated a high-backed chair. 'Won't you please take a seat, so that we may talk.'

They did so. Wolsey opened proceedings. 'It appears we share a problem, My Lord.'

Lefsetz's shoulders slumped theatrically. 'Ah, Malchek. Tiresome, and an Arcadian. Could there be a worse combination?' He wrinkled his nose.

'You don't hold Arcadians in high esteem, do you?'

The aide arrived with goblets on a tray.

'Not really.' Lefsetz took a sip of his wine. 'As you know, they are of subordinate rank among demonkind. They are as dogs or horses are to humans. Suitable for menial tasks only. They –' he stopped, frowning, '*most* of them anyway – have no guile or cunning, no lust for evil. No *hunger*.' He grinned. 'They are curs. Wolves without fangs.'

'Though it suits you to have humans believe otherwise,' said Wolsey. 'These tales of werewolves that spread throughout the regions must please you greatly.'

'Don't they please you?' smiled Lefsetz. 'We both prosper when fear is at large.'

Wolsey shook his head. 'Not us, My Lord.'

Lefsetz smiled, revealing his teeth. 'Doesn't it please your masters in Rome?'

'We take no gratification from carnage.'

The ambassador almost choked on his mirth. 'Carnage indeed, my dear Lord Chancellor.' He wiped wine from his mouth with the back of his hand. 'In Europe they are tearing each other inside out looking for . . .' his eyes widened and he brandished an imaginary pitchfork, '. . . *wolfmen*.'

It was true. Abroad, hundreds of innocents had been torn apart to see if they had fur on the inside, which was the latest theory on how to spot the atrocity that was half-man, half-wolf: the werewolf.

Such beasts had been spoken of for centuries of course. Herodotus had written of them in his *Histories*. And while there were many who thought them mythical, there were many more who believed that they stalked the land after dark, feeding upon luckless travellers.

There were but a handful of living humans who knew the truth: that the wolfen did exist. That they were shape-shifting demons sent down in The Fall. Their place in the firmament is not recorded but their earthly origins lay in Greece, in Arcadia, where Greek mythology told of Lycaon, Arcadia's cruel king, who was transformed into a wolf creature by Zeus. Thus, the wolf creatures became known as the Arcadians, the lowest ranking of the inhumans who inhabited earth, working dogs for the more powerful clans.

Which was the way it had remained, for centuries. They rarely attacked or interfered with humans, stories of them feasting upon villagers were just that, stories. There were legends that persisted: that you could become a werewolf by drinking rainwater from the footprint of the beast; that their eyebrows were joined in the middle; that it took silver to kill them.

All folk tales, of course: the wolfen could shape-shift at will. They could be killed by all the usual means, and as for spotting them, they looked like any other human when they took that form.

There was, however, one myth that was rooted in fact. The bite of the wolfen was infectious; it transmitted lycan-thropy to humans. For them to bite humans was rare, but there had been outbreaks throughout the ages, enough to make the people afraid of the werewolves in their midst, the fear like a plague, just as infectious. It spread through regions, where a credulous populace would blame attacks by wild animals on werewolves, murders on werewolves, the slaughter of livestock on werewolves. Innocents were cut open. Those whose eyebrows joined in the middle were burnt . . .

'Such a terribly superstitious lot, you humans,' Lefsetz chuckled.

'Events in Kent would suggest their superstition is well founded.' Wolsey shifted in his seat. 'Malchek is causing quite a stir, it would seem.'

The ambassador pursed his lips. 'Certainly his activities upset the order of things, yes.'

'Which makes him an enemy of us both. He must be stopped.'

'Ah.' Lefsetz steepled his fingers and placed his elbows on his knees, leaning towards the cardinal. 'Why don't you tell me what you have in mind, Lord Chancellor?'

'At this very moment I have a small squad of men awaiting my command to mount an assault on the wolfen. Their instructions are to attack, save any hostages, but kill Malchek and his followers.'

The fire crackled in the hearth. Candles flickered, casting shadows across the ambassador's face. He registered no surprise. Showed no emotion. When Wolsey finished speaking he sat back in his chair, signalled for his aide and returned his empty goblet of wine to the silver tray.

'Your request is that I should ratify a hostile act against an inhuman, a member of my own kind?'

'A renegade. Whose actions are in breach of the treaty.'

'As is the action you plan to take.'

'Which is why I require your signature.'

Wolsey stood and summoned Dudley, who came over to where the two men sat and turned to offer them his back. From him Wolsey took the quill, inkpot and scroll, which he unfurled and pinned to the writing board with tacks.

'I must sign this now?' said Lefsetz, who had stood and was looking over the parchment.

Wolsey smiled thinly. 'Time is of the essence, My Lord. His Holiness would be most grateful for your speedy cooperation.'

Lefsetz sighed rather theatrically, taking up the quill. 'Are you ready, boy?'

'Yes, My Lord,' said Dudley over his shoulder

'Poor Malchek,' Lefsetz said, as he signed, 'the first of his species to show the slightest initiative, and we're having him put down.'

Wolsey took the quill and co-signed, then bowed deeply, he and Dudley withdrawing quickly. In the corridor the cardinal moved out of earshot, then took Dudley by the shoulder and spun him round, removed the order from the writing board, rolled it and passed it to his clerk.

'Go,' he said, 'take this to Child, who waits with hot wax for the seal. He is then to convey it directly to More's cleric. He is to stop for nothing, to speak to nobody. Is that clear?'

'Yes, Your Eminence.'

'Run, Dudley, run.'

Wolsey watched as his clerk scuttled off down the hall,

still bent under the weight of the board, and he offered up a silent prayer for the men on the hill.

Then a movement caught his eye, and from the shadows appeared a figure wearing dark robes and a hood.

'Ah,' said Wolsey, 'just the person I wanted to see . . .'

IX

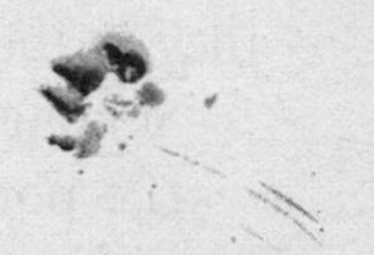

Massimo Cardinal Morante lay in the grass between two huge roots that seemed to bubble from the ground beneath him, and he closed his eyes, hoping to block the cold with sleep.

A cardinal bishop and thus the highest ranking of the quartet, Morante had until recently been attached to the Pope's bodyguard, a post he had loved dearly, but lost after a misunderstanding involving a goblet of water.

Damn that water. How was he to know it had been blessed? For that he had been banished to England, where it rained continually, and to the Observant Friary and Greenwich Palace, where it was constantly dark and draughty and the stone was cold and damp – hadn't they heard of marble, for God's sake?

Morante had let his eyes close when suddenly there was a hand gripping his shoulder and he shot upright, pulling himself from the wet grass, disturbing a mist that billowed about him, limbs stiff, chilled to the bone.

'The signal.' Barbato's gaze was directed at the hilltop across the valley, where a flame was held aloft. 'It's the first,' he added.

Morante was kicking the others awake, his eyes fixed on the hilltop where the second flame was showing.

The men held their breath. Two for go. Three for abort.

No third signal came.

The men scrambled into a crouch. With shaking hands they lit their tapers.

'Simonetti. Go,' commanded Morante.

The point man's robes swished as he went off, fast and low across the grass to the edge of the wood. The men waited. There was no sound but the lullaby of a light breeze in the trees.

Then came the call of an owl. Simonetti saying no visible activity.

Morante addressed his men. 'We know what we're going in for. You see a wolfen you kill it, understand?'

The cardinals nodded.

'Main target is Malchek. Look out for the eyepatch. We want him, dead or alive, preferably the latter.'

'Yes, Your Eminence,' came the murmur.

'Good,' said Morante, 'from now on, we're going silent, hand signals only, understood?'

'Yes, Your Eminence,' murmured his men.

'Let's move.'

Morante placed the lit taper into his mouth, as did his men. They checked swords, hefted their rifles, while Barbato notched an arrow in his bow. The men began to move stealthily over the ground until they reached the gap in the undergrowth. They joined Simonetti, nods were exchanged and the team set off through the wood, each rustle and crack making Morante wince, until they made it to the perimeter of the clearing.

Here the moon shone upon the building in the centre, so that it appeared almost luminescent. Long disused but imposing still – perhaps even more so for the cardinals who knew of its purpose – it was the church of Darenth Wood. The lair of the wolfen.

X

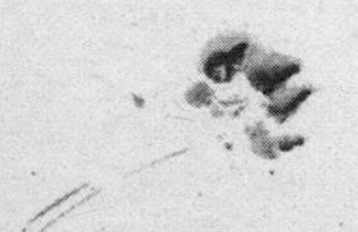

Not far away, More moved swiftly, the hem of his robes bunched in one fist as he made his way along what was a track of sorts – one used by the locals, no doubt – following the young lovers. They had been moving away from the direction of the church, at least there was that, but still the presence of this third man troubled him, and he was grateful for the feel of the sword at his hip.

Hearing a noise – voices – he stopped and knelt, putting his hand to the huge trunk of a tree, feeling the cold, knotted bark beneath his fingers and listening. He hardly dared breathe, as though the exhaled mist might give him away.

Then came the sound again. A female giggle. Next, a short sound of pleasure. More ignored a stirring in his groin and straightened a little, scanning the area around him: trees, fallen timber, hawthorn, all of it silhouetted in varying shades of black and grey.

Then he saw them. Entwined, they were in the embrace of an oak tree's roots, oblivious to all but each other.

Now – where was the third man? More felt a crawling at his bladder as he continued searching the area, looking for the hatless man who had followed them into the wood.

There. He saw the leather jerkin, the straggly, dirty hair.

He was closer to the couple but otherwise in a similar position, crouched at the base of a tree trunk, a dark irregular shape watching the two lovers. The man began to edge forward as the murmurs of pleasure intensified. From one tree to the next, until he was just feet away.

Faced with little choice, More did the same, moving silently, though stealth was hardly necessary so loud were the cries of passion. He felt a pressure down below. God, why – why be aroused at a time like this? He was being tested, he knew.

But couldn't the test wait for a more convenient moment?

He could see the young couple writhing at the base of the tree, the sounds of their lovemaking growing louder and louder. He reached below his robes and resisted temptation, grasping instead the hilt of his sword, which he drew free, moonlight giving the blade a holy, righteous glow.

The lovemaking growing louder now.

And louder. More rhythmic.

And then the other man sprang forward.

More, perhaps distracted by his own lustfulness, hesitated. Then he, too, shouting a warning, leapt forward, his sword drawn. The next moment he was sprawled on the ground, his foot caught beneath a fallen branch, just as the hatless man bore down upon the courting couple.

It turned out that the hatless man lacked more than just a hat. Neither did he wear breeches. And the moonlight shone on his erect shaft, giving it a distinctly unholy and unrighteous glow. He held a knife. That and his erect penis made his intentions all too clear.

The suitor had been roused by More's warning. He also wore nothing down below, and he came up swinging, shouting in surprise and anger, throwing a punch at his assailant, which the man dodged, replying with a blow of his own – only not with his fist. With his knife.

The suitor screamed and doubled over as the blade sunk into the soft meat of his stomach, his hands going to it, mouth an O, blood gushing quickly down over his thighs.

It all happened in the time it took More to right himself and cross the distance between him and them. He at least had the advantage of surprise, not to mention that he was the only one wearing breeches. But the men were now locked in mortal combat. Both pairs of hands were at the handle of the knife in the suitor's belly, the injured man trying desperately to remove it, while his attacker wanted to inflict more damage. Now the hatless man saw More approach and with a grunt he used his extra weight to lift the suitor and swing the body to meet More.

Never had the scholar wished more for the presence of a Protektorate member. Never had he wanted greater skills in combat. For he had blundered into battle, ready to defend the honour of a maid (though maiden she was assuredly not), only to find himself tumbling to the ground, momentarily pinned beneath the half-naked body of her suitor, blood pouring from him. More cried out in horror and terror. Above him towered the hatless man, his penis hoving into view, his ardour as yet undiminished. He brought his boot down on to More's cheek and More shouted in pain, fingers loosening on the sword, which fell from his grip and to the soft woodland floor.

Again the man kicked out. More, pinned by the body, feebly defended himself with his hands, pain flaring in his face, hearing something crack and feeling his vision blur.

He was going to die, he knew, seeing the man reach and pick up his sword – he was going to die, the victim of a half-naked man, trapped beneath another half-naked man, and the last thing he ever saw – the image he would take with him to the afterlife – would be the engorged penis of his killer. And instead of saying that Sir Thomas More was a great and learned man, a lawyer, scholar, statesman, an esteemed courtier and the author of *Utopia*, they would say, 'Sir Thomas Who? Not that rather sleazy fellow who died during some sordid encounter in Darenth Wood?'

The hatless man put the point of his sword to More's neck and grinned. Lit by the moon, More could make out his dirty jagged teeth, a face streaked with dirt, hair so filthy and thick with grease that it shone. Behind him he saw the woman, raising herself from the roots of the tree and to her he offered a silent apology that his attempts to help had met with failure.

Still smiling. The hatless man pulled back the sword to strike.

Behind him, the woman transformed into a wolfen.

More had no time to comprehend the turn of events, nor to react to them; nor even to feel emotion – fear, relief, disgust. For in one moment she was the woman he had seen on the meadow, the next she had become a beast, her clothes tearing about her, rising to tower above the hatless man.

The attacker sensed the danger behind him. Whether it was More's terrified eyes or the sound of the transformation, which was a fearful tearing and crunching, his smile faded, his penis drooped at long last, and he turned to meet his fate.

He had time for a short scream before she attacked.

She swung with one paw and sliced off most of his face, which came away from his skull with a ripping noise as nerves and membranes tore, and spun through the air like tossed dough, landing with a wet splat against an oak and sliding to its base. The impact spun him back round so that he turned to More once again, only he didn't face him, because he had no face to speak of. More saw white, bloodied jawbone, the dirty gravestones of his teeth; one dark and empty eye socket, the other wide and staring.

'Help,' managed the hatless, now faceless man. And although More was deeply religious and thus preached forgiveness, he still found it within his conscience to ignore the request, thankful only that as the hatless man sank to his knees, the sword slipped from his fingers and within his reach.

More's fingers scrabbled for it. Meanwhile the wolf woman came to the attacker, took his head in both of her huge paws and with a grunt twisted, snapping his neck with a sound like a huge branch torn from a tree until the would-be rapist was facing back to front before dropping limply to the ground.

More was still trying to grasp the sword, struggling with the corpse on top of him. He was soaked in blood. Not his own he didn't think, but even so. His hands were slick with it, his clothes soaked. He thrashed beneath the body desperately trying to work himself free.

And now the wolf woman towered over him and this, he realised, would be the image he took to the next world, of her – which, some part of his brain mused, was at least an improvement over the penis . . .

She reached to him. She pulled the corpse of the suitor, already pale in death, from him.

And now she regained her human form, only wearing fewer clothes than before. In the moonlight she looked beautiful – long, black hair, deep, dark eyes; her body golden. Indeed, her beauty was such that it eclipsed the trauma of the battle so that, incredibly, More felt desirous once again, could feel himself becoming hard.

She came to him.

Oh God.

He knew what was happening, he understood. He put up his hands to try to ward her off but was weak and she took them, grasping both his wrists in one hand, placing her feet either side of his hips. With her other hand she reached down to his breeches, and his eyes went there to see her hand change. Just that part of her became a wolfen's claw and she used it to rip his breeches and hose from him, next moving it to above his pubic area, and More gasped, expecting to feel it plunge into his stomach . . .

Instead, smiling mockingly, she touched the hem of his hair shirt, and then the claw was gone, back to a human hand – a human hand with a sensuous touch.

'No,' he moaned, '*please*,' as she sat astride him. 'No,' he repeated, as she rode him. Her hips gyrated. Still smiling, she placed her hands to his neck and began to squeeze, and he groaned, trying not to think of the pleasure at his groin, feeling himself lose consciousness . . .

'Come,' she said, baring her teeth, 'join us.'

In a moment, he understood. She meant to turn him.

Was he imagining it? he thought, distantly, as the blackness pressed in, as she bent towards him. Was he imagining the figures standing around them, who carried pitchforks and stout staffs?

XI

Henry tried to make sense of his emotions as he made his way along the halls of the palace towards the chambers of the Queen, who even now laboured to bring him a son, with God's grace, a son.

A King should not question himself, he knew. So he kept his own counsel as he walked, and he barely acknowledged the courtiers who tripped over themselves to scurry out of his way as he passed, his mouth set and his stride purposeful.

A son, he kept thinking. An heir. It was what he most wanted, wasn't it? What his father, lying near death at Richmond Palace, had commanded he do: sire a male heir and preserve the Tudor dynasty. Henry was prepared to admit that at times his need to fulfil his destiny had made him blind to reason or logic – he knew that it was foolish simply to assume the baby would be a boy, even though he still did it. But that was because, while he loved his daughter, he *needed* a son.

Protocol dictated the King could not attend a birth, so it was his habit to await news in an adjoining chamber, where he would be joined by a few confidants.

On past occasions they had sat listening to the screams; they had seen midwives hurrying from the Queen's chamber with cloths saturated in dark blood – and sometimes, in those sad instances of a stillborn, other matter too. And Henry would think of how he and his men talked of valour in the field of battle, how they toasted courage in the hunt and in sport. But the truth was, they knew nothing of bravery. That his lady could bear the pain with such fortitude, that it might end in nothing but heartbreak yet still she submitted to her duty, time and time again. That, he knew, was true bravery.

They were close to Katherine's apartments now. Ahead of them were two ladies. Of over a thousand courtiers, only one hundred were women, most in service to the Queen – or in service to those in service to the Queen. Thus it was no surprise that these two were heading in the direction of Her Majesty's quarters also.

Henry stopped before them. 'You are to attend My Lady?'

'I as a midwife, Lady Rebecca, a wet nurse,' said the older lady, casting her eyes downwards.

'And what news is there of her condition at present?' Henry asked eagerly.

'She is in pain, Your Highness,' came the reply, spoken to the floor, 'but bearing it with the dignity we have come to expect from her most gracious Majesty . . .'

Henry nodded. He considered something. Then he took the hand of the midwife, turning it palm upwards and smiling at her blushes as he did so. 'My Lady,' he said, 'I would like you to take this hand,' he bent and kissed the midwife's palm, 'and place it upon the face of the Queen, so that she may know I am thinking of her.'

'Yes, Your Majesty.'

With a curtsey, the two ladies hurried on ahead until they

came to the door at the far end of the hall. Guarded by two yeomen with pikes, this was the entrance to the Queen's apartments and was decorated with her badge, the pomegranate and arrow-sheaf, intertwined with that of the King, his Tudor rose, crown and portcullis.

The yeomen nodded them through and the door opened. From deep inside came the unmistakeable sound of screaming and courtiers – more of them in the hall than usual – perked up at the sound.

Oh dear, thought Henry. He had insisted his confidants tell no one of the Queen's condition, but perhaps had not been quite so circumspect with the information himself. Hopefully the numbers would not swell, he thought, as they reached the door to the Waiting Chamber and burst in, hanging fabrics and tapestries billowing in the force of their entry.

It was dark in the room, and cold. At the far end of the chamber was a second door, this leading into the Queen's quarters and also guarded by an impassive yeoman. A fire burnt in a huge, ornate hearth, but extra braziers had been brought in so that the chamber would be warm for the new arrival when he was presented to the King – when he would be placed in the wooden crib that now stood in the centre of the room. Henry reached to touch it as he made his way to his table, as pages sprang to their feet to pour wine and set before him a plate. Wolsey, who had been seated, his clerk at his shoulder, stood and bowed his head as the King came to him.

'Thomas,' said Henry, 'I dare say it's all happened a little quickly for you?'

The Lord Chancellor, exercising diplomacy, smiled and

shook his head no-of-course-not as Henry took his seat. Compton went to stand behind his chair but Henry waved him to sit then picked up a goblet to drink, smiling at those assembled. The Lord Steward and Archbishop of Canterbury would be present shortly after the birth, as tradition dictated, but for now it was just these four men awaiting the arrival of the heir.

All was silent in the chamber. Nothing but the fire flickering in the hearth, the occasional crackle of the brazier.

Then, from outside, came the sound of howling.

'Compton,' said Henry, when it was over. 'That howling sounded very much like that of a wolf.'

There had been a short burst of it, enough to chill the blood.

'Yes, indeed, Your Highness,' replied Compton.

'I know that we have lions in the menagerie. Do we also have wolves?'

'No, Your Majesty,' replied Compton, whose eyes went to the cardinal, who swallowed.

'Thomas?'

'Your Majesty?' the cardinal replied.

'Sir Thomas More visited me in the Presence Chamber this morning on Lord Chancellor's business. He spoke of wolves.'

At this Wolsey looked particularly uncomfortable, attempting with his eyes to remind Henry that servants were present. He leant forward, his voice low. 'Not wolves, Your Highness: *wolfen*.'

'There's a difference?'

'I sincerely hope so, Your Majesty.'

'Then I need not concern myself with this coincidence?'

'What coincidence would this be?'

'That this morning I was asked to authorise Protektorate action involving wolves; that this evening I can *hear* wolves?'

Wolsey had winced at the mention of the Protektorate, the existence of which was a closely guarded secret, known only to a select few. 'No, Your Highness, you need not concern yourself. You need worry only about Her Majesty.'

'Good,' said the King, who sat back in his chair.

The room lapsed into silence. Henry's thoughts went once more to events in Katherine's chambers, and they did not hear the wolves again.

XII

Using gravestones as cover, the cardinals made their way across the churchyard in pairs. They assembled by a side door and here they crouched, listening, but heard nothing, just the sounds of night; from within the church, silence.

Not for the first time Morante cursed the operation's lack of numbers. Before the treaty up to a hundred Protektors were stationed at every Royal house with links to the Vatican. Since the pact at the Field of the Cloth of Gold that number had been reduced to a handful, and with the required two remaining at the palace, that had left just four for the operation. It had taken Wolsey a while to convince Morante this was enough, but he'd done it with a mixture of flattery and statements of urgency; there simply was not the time to wait for reinforcements, he'd said, and anyway the Arcadians – with the exception of Malchek, of course – were not especially warlike, not predisposed to violence or aggression. Nothing that should present a problem to four highly trained Protektors.

Morante had swallowed his blandishments and gathered his team. He had accepted the picture Wolsey painted, which was of panicked hairy creatures running to and fro, before surrendering themselves to the Protektors.

Now, in the eerie silence of the churchyard, he wondered again. He wondered what it was they were about to encounter. The cardinals looked at one another, knowing what it was they were about to do.

First, Morante gave a signal, then he and Simonetti stood, placed their staffs to the ground and on them rested their rifles, taking aim at the door. Tapers still in their mouths, these were held close to the wick of the weapon.

Barbato, kneeling, fitted an arrow into his bow as Pignatelli sheathed his sword and inspected the lock of the door, then the hinges. The big man met Morante's enquiring eyes, nodded, and pulled from his pack two iron bars, flattened at either end. With exquisite care he worked the bars between door and frame, one near the top hinge and one at the lower hinge. The others watched him work as he gently and carefully tested the bars, working them further into place, until each was set. He took a step back, spat in the palm of each hand, more out of habit than necessity, then grasped the bars, one in each hand. He braced himself, looking to the commander again, awaiting his order.

Morante clenched his fist then pointed at the door, held up three fingers.

Squatting, Pignatelli tensed; Barbato readied himself; Simonetti prepared to fire.

Two fingers.

Silence from inside the church.

One finger.

Go.

Pignatelli's move was fluid. With a grunt he pulled on both bars, splintering the hinges in a single surge of strength;

then, in the same action, twisted, dipped his shoulder and hit the door.

The hinges shattered and it gave, Pignatelli going with it and rolling into the church, drawing his sword and coming up into a crouch, his robes still settling around him.

Behind came Barbato, also in a forward roll, emerging with his bow drawn, both men covered by the rifles of Morante and Simonetti.

'Clear,' called Barbato, swinging his bow from one end of the church to the other, eyes adjusting to the gloom. He and Pignatelli scuttled forward away from the door, allowing entry to the other two men who came in behind them, fanning out into the church, rifles still held.

'Clear,' confirmed Morante.

And they were in. Stage one complete. Behind them, the door, which had been hanging by its lock, thunked solidly to the floor.

None were paying attention to the door, however. They were looking at ropes that criss-crossed the nave like a spider's web, their eyes following them up – up into the roof of the church.

Pignatelli crossed himself. '*Mio dio*.'

The kidnapped peasants were hanging from the beams of the church, several feet above the Protektors' heads, suspended by ropes tied around their chests. There were ten to fifteen of them, their skin pale and waxy and shiny as though each one had been daubed with pig's fat. At first Morante thought it was a trick of the light, but then he realised that at least some of them were alive, and were swaying like a grotesque wind chime, arms swinging, hair wafting in the breeze.

And moaning. Only now did Morante hear some of them crying out in pain, and then it came to him: they had the sickness. He'd seen it in Europe, where it had killed tens of thousands. He didn't think they had it in England, but here it was, hanging above their heads in a church in Darenth: the sweating sickness was here.

Then, from over in a far corner of the church came a noise that began almost softly, ululating into a howl so deafening the cardinals were hunching their shoulders against the terrible noise: the call of the wolfen.

At the same time there was a sudden flurry of activity and a figure was running across the nave. Morante saw thick black hair swept back from an extended snout, large protruding fangs and pink, frilly gums. Though in wolf form, the beast wore clothes: a pair of loose black breeches, voluminous black doublet, silk shirt and an eyepatch. It was Malchek, no doubt about it. He carried a sword, and as he ran he used it to slash at the ropes tethering the bodies.

For a second Morante and Malchek shared a look and Malchek's good eye seemed to glitter, his snout twisted into a sneer, scars like thick fleshy worms in his fur.

'*Engage*,' ordered Morante, touching the taper to his arquebus, the wick fizzing. Simonetti did the same; Barbato swung his bow towards the fleeing figure; Pignatelli set off in pursuit, his sword held low.

Morante pivoted the rifle, tracking Malchek. He aimed ahead of the figure, timing the blast for the wolfen to run into the bullet.

And he would have done it, would have killed the wolfen for sure, such was his prowess with the rifle, if he hadn't been knocked to the ground by a falling body, a wriggling, writhing body that thumped into him, the arquebus discharging harmlessly into the air.

Bodies were dropping down all around them now, thudding to the flagstones, knocking Barbato off balance while Simonetti's bullet also went astray, the point man cursing in frustration. Through the rain of bodies Morante saw Malchek and for a second the wolfen leader seemed to be scanning the nave, as if looking for something. Then he disappeared through a door in the church floor and into the crypt. Behind him came Pignatelli, who had kept his feet throughout the shower of bodies. Then the big man too was gone.

Some bodies lay still, others were writhing and thrashing. One or two were beginning to get to their feet, unsteady and glassy-eyed. Morante crossed himself, reached to pick up his cap and dragged his robes clear of a corpse, trying to ignore the grey flesh and sightless eyes as he hurdled more fallen bodies on his way to the trapdoor.

It had shut behind Pignatelli – *impetuous idiot*, thought Morante – and Simonetti reached for it. He hefted the arquebus.

'Commander?' he said.

Morante shook his head. No, there was no time to reload. 'Quick,' he said, and he cast his rifle aside, Simonetti doing the same, drawing their swords instead. Barbato knelt and took aim. They tensed. With one hand, Simonetti dragged open the door.

Beneath them, stone steps and darkness. A thick smell of wet stone. Silence, apart from the sound of dripping water.

Then, into the nave behind them came more wolfen, alerted by Malchek's call. One of them saw the Protektors and threw back its head to howl. Saliva hung in trails from its jaws, its eyes thin slits of hate. They launched themselves towards the trapdoor.

'Go,' screamed Morante, and bundled his men down the steps, offering up a silent prayer for the good Lord to lead his fingers to a bolt as he turned, pulled the trapdoor closed behind him and fumbled in the blackness. *Yes*. His fingers touched the bolt. But too late, the door was wrenched open, pulling him with it, and for a second he found himself staring in the face of a wolfen, smelling fetid breath as a snout pressed into the gap. Then the wolfen withdrew with a yelp as Barbato came to help Morante, grasping the ring on the underside of the door, the extra weight closing it at last. Morante slammed the bolt home then turned and the men flew to the bottom of the stairs where they regrouped for a moment, catching their breath. From above them came the scratching, scuttling sound of claws on the wooden trapdoor, which rattled as the wolfen tried to lift it. It wouldn't take them long.

'Torches,' said Morante, touching the taper to his own so that it blazed and threw flickering shadows on slippery walls. He tried to control his breathing, dread churning his stomach. The oppressive blackness seemed to draw in around them and his fear-infested mind imagined it growing closer and closer until they were suffocated by it . . .

Pull yourself together.

He cast aside his fears to think – think like a Protektor, damnit, not some frightened cadet . . .

Where was Malchek heading? Was he leading them into

a trap, or attempting to escape? Either way Morante had no choice but to press on.

'Pignatelli,' he whispered, as loudly as he dared, '*Pignatelli.*'

No reply. Where the hell was he?

'Let's move.'

The three men began to edge forward, able to see just ahead of themselves. Underfoot, it was soft, a carpet of moss and lichen on the ground.

'Stop,' called Simonetti.

Ahead of them, a noise.

'I see something,' said Simonetti. He dropped into a crouch. Then called, 'Pignatelli? Is that you?'

There came no reply. Simonetti edged forward. 'Pignatelli?'

'Do you see him?' asked Morante.

'Commander, yes. It's him,' called Simonetti, darting forward to where the big man lay face down, his robes twisted, his hands trapped beneath himself as though clutching a wound at his belly. His cap was at an odd angle, sword on the ground beside him.

Simonetti knelt to him. 'Lucius,' he said, turning him over.

But it was not Pignatelli. It was another man who rolled over, and he was brandishing something he had been holding – the severed head of Lucius Cardinal Pignatelli, lion of the Protektorate.

The shock of it drove Simonetti backward even as the imposter rose, casting Pignatelli's head aside, in an instant transforming into a wolfen and leaping forward with a roar. Still off-balance, Simonetti had no time to swing before the creature was upon him, jaws locking upon his throat, which tore and burst like ripened fruit.

He screamed, arms swinging, sword falling. Twisting, he

was thrust against the wall of the tunnel by the Arcadian, which made short work of him. In one movement it raised its hind paws to grip Simonetti's stomach so that for a second it was perched on him. Its teeth were still locked on his throat, its hind paws sunk deep into the flesh of his abdomen, producing yet more screams. Then it pushed back and off, tearing both Simonetti's stomach and throat from him so that he was no longer a man but two huge holes of scarlet, pumping meat, and the wolf was landing, ragged lumps of red flesh between its jaws.

As Simonetti fell, Morante came forward with a yell, thrusting his sword into the chest of the beast. Impaled, its eyes widened, then it snarled, paws going to the blade. But Morante was already retrieving the weapon and next swept it across the throat of the animal, spraying blood to the walls of the tunnel. The wolfen gurgled and Morante ran him through again. Again. Again – even as the creature fell forward, so that Barbato had to stay his hand.

The two surviving men looked at one another. Morante knew the mission was lost. The wolfen were vicious and organised. The Protektors were outnumbered and had lost the element of surprise. *Not especially warlike*, he thought bitterly. Next time he saw Wolsey he would be showing him a few new uses for that cane of his.

Morante crossed himself and said the briefest of prayers for his fallen comrades. He looked back towards the trapdoor, as if by some miracle the wolfen there might have dispersed.

But no. As he looked at it the trapdoor splintered and broke. For an instant there was a small square of grey half-light at the trapdoor, which went dark as figures descending down the stairs obscured it.

'Here they come,' hissed Morante, who was already turning, holding the flaming torch so that Barbato could touch the tip of his arrow to it, having just enough time to draw back and let fly, the flaming arrow flying home to thump into the chest of the first wolfen, which yelped in agony. Then burst into flames.

Wolfen, it turned out, were very flammable.

Flailing, the beast turned, just as a second blundered into it and it, too, began to burn. The tunnel filled with the sound of agonised howling. Barbato grabbed an arrow blind and fired through the fire, hoping to find more. He missed. But knowing the creatures would be unwilling to negotiate the writhing fiery obstacles, the two Protektors turned and ran, once more going deeper into the lair.

The howling followed them along the tunnel as they pressed on, then came upon more steps and another trapdoor – which slammed shut as they reached it. Morante put his shoulder to the wood. From above came a scraping sound as something was dragged over the door, preventing it from being opened. Morante beckoned Barbato up the steps and together the two men heaved, able to open it just a chink before the weight slammed it down.

Again they tried. This time the door lifted further, dislodging whatever was on top of it. It was a coffin, they saw as they scrambled to the surface, for they were now in a crypt to which the entrance had been moved aside, allowing them to dash straight into the churchyard.

They arrived in time to hear a great howl tear into the night. A howl so loud and piercing it seemed to send the surrounding wood into a frenzy; birds were startled from their nest and the undergrowth rattled with sudden activity. As Morante and Barbato dropped into protective stances there was an answering call from far away. Then another, even further away.

Gravestones were silhouetted in the grey murk of dawn. A light rain fell. And there was no sign of Malchek.

The Protektors crouched, listening, eyes straining in the half-light. Just the pitter-pitter of rain on the stone now.

The wolfen leader was still somewhere close. Morante felt it. But where? He had a crawling sensation in the pit of his stomach as he cast his gaze over the irregular shapes of the gravestones, shadows in the half-light. Suddenly he was aware that they were exposed, vulnerable, had come tearing out into the open like hounds driven mad with the scent of blood.

'We need to find cover,' he hissed. '*Now*.'

From in front of them came a rustling sound. They exchanged a fearful look then began to edge back to the relative safety of the tomb.

There was a movement and both men turned to see at the wall of the graveyard a figure stumbling, dazed. It was one of the infected from the nave. Then he saw more of them – three or four – shambling away from the church. Pale, ghostly figures going into the night. *We should stop them*, Morante thought to himself. *If they reached a settlement they'd spread the disease.*

But then from behind: *whoompf* and they turned in time to see the windows of the church blown out, followed by flames that lit up the night. A sound of agonised howling. Then came a movement from behind and both men wheeled around to see a blur of animal – black fur, pointed ears, one red burning eye.

In the next instant, it was gone.

Morante, in a crouch, had his sword raised. After a moment, the threat seemingly gone, he whispered, 'By God, that was close.'

But there was no reply from by his side, just a gurgling sound and something splattering to the ground.

Turning, Morante saw Barbato drop to his knees, a pulsing cavity where his throat had been. For a moment he was illuminated by the orange glow of the burning church and his eyes were wide, the torn and ragged remnants of his trachea hanging from inside his throat, flaps of skin dangling loose, his neck a spurting fountain of blood. Then his hands went to his throat and he spent a moment pawing at it as though attempting to locate the missing parts of his body, and he was falling forward to the ground, blood turned dark in the moonlight flooding the grass, legs kicking involuntarily.

And stopped.

'Just you and me now, Cardinal,' said a voice from the darkness.

Morante jumped, his head jerking in the direction of the voice. He brandished the sword before him, every muscle in his body tense, nerves screaming. *Keep calm, keep calm . . .*

'Your headquarters burn, Malchek,' he said, trying to sound unafraid. 'Kill me and my mission still succeeds.'

He kept his sword low, swinging his gaze around the cemetery. Try to get him talking, he thought. It was his only chance. Force the wolf to give away his position.

There was a dry chuckle from the darkness. Morante squinted and for a second was sure that he saw the wolfen out there, the size of him seeming to block out the sky, moonlight glinting on the leather eyepatch. Then the figure was gone and Morante was left wondering if he had imagined it.

'You laugh,' he called into the darkness, 'any plans you had have burnt with the church.'

Just out of reach of the light of the flames was a tall grave marker. That's where Malchek stood, realised Morante. He had him. The Protektor edged forward, then pounced. Moving to the left then at the last second dodging to the right, he came to the rear of the gravestone, going forward on to one knee and thrusting forward with his sword.

In the flickering light of the fire from the church he saw that he was wrong – that Malchek was not behind the grave.

Morante tried to turn but he was too late. Something flew at him from the darkness and though he was quick with the sword he was not quick enough. The next thing he heard was a thump as his weapon hit the ground and when he raised his hand to his face he was missing three of his fingers, blood coating his hand. There was no pain, he thought distractedly. But he had been wounded in combat before and knew that pain would come.

From behind, two claws descended upon his shoulders, almost tenderly, so that strangely, he was reminded of his childhood and the touch of his father. Or was this merely his own life flashing before his eyes? He felt something warm running down his chest, realised it was blood, and in the next moment Malchek's claws turned cruel, tearing through his robes and into his flesh, forcing him to his knees. Morante moaned. The pain was here, and sheets of agony rippled through him.

'You have fought well, Your Eminence, I salute you,' said Malchek. 'But not well enough to save your King – he is about to learn that the life of a wolfen is not given lightly.'

With that the wolfen tore Morante apart.

XIII

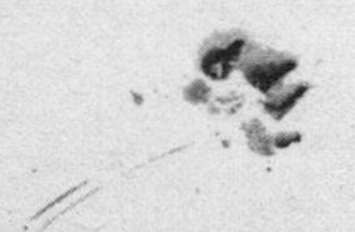

Some time later the King and his retinue became aware of a growing hubbub in the hall outside, much to the annoyance of Sir William Compton. He was about to ask the yeomen to clear the hall when Henry leant forward.

'It's all right, let them stay. It could be that I have not kept the secret as I should have done, having told a small number, perhaps after a little too much wine. They were of course warned not to divulge the confidence on pain of death, but . . .' He shrugged, helplessly.

'Then there are many who have betrayed you, Majesty, for the hall is teeming it appears.'

'Well, perhaps it was closer to a larger number that I told . . .'

The King cleared his throat, looked bashful. Meanwhile, the room lapsed into a silence that was part deferential, part apprehensive, and Henry found himself listening to the noises that came from behind the doors: from one, the screaming of the Queen, faraway and muffled; from the other, the excited murmur of the courtiers. Until, suddenly, one sound rose above all others, jerking the sleepy men in the chamber awake.

The sound of a baby crying.

Those outside had heard it, too, and a cheer went up. Then, as quickly as it had started – as those celebrating remembered that they were on oath not to communicate the secret on pain of death – it stopped. And many of those in the hallway coughed or cleared their throats, as though to cover up the sound.

Not that Henry heard or would have cared, for he had stood quickly from the table.

'Did you hear that?' he said. 'Did you hear the sound of the baby?'

Wolsey and Compton stood also. The servants straightened, the yeoman seemed to grow a little, puffing out his chest and straightening his arm on his pike. All men looking towards the second of the two doors. The door to the Queen's quarters.

Which opened.

The yeoman stood aside and into the room came a midwife, the older of the two Henry had spoken to in the corridor. She held a swaddled infant, just the pink, wrinkled flesh of its face visible. It mewled but did not cry. As she carried it to Henry an arm escaped the swaddling cloth and a miniature fist swiped at the air.

She laid it in the crib and took a step back.

'First,' said Henry, 'how is My Lady?'

'Exhausted but overjoyed, Your Majesty.'

'Were you able to give to her my token?'

'Indeed, Your Highness, and it was of great comfort to her.'

Henry smiled. 'I shall see her soon. But first . . .'

The midwife smiled. 'Your Majesty, you have . . .' with gentle fingers, she unfurled the swaddling, '. . . a boy.'

Henry felt his mouth work. Sounds were attempting to escape, though none appeared, thwarted by his brain that sang with relief and joy.

A boy. A male heir. Prince George.

The baby lay blinking up at Henry, his eyes moving, taking everything in, that tiny little fist still swiping at the air. And Henry found that he was holding his breath, and the image of his son in the crib began to swim as his eyes filled with tears.

'May I hold him?' he asked.

'Of course, Your Majesty,' replied the midwife, reaching into the crib.

Just then came a shout from outside in the hall. It was joined by others. A sound of a great commotion and running feet.

Then, from the Queen's quarters, more screams, the sounds piercing and distinct through the open connecting door. Until all around, it seemed, was screaming and shouting. Not the screaming of childbirth or even perhaps its after-effects, but of people dying . . .

Compton was the first to react. He whipped around, snatched open the door and was in the hallway. Fleeing courtiers almost knocked him sideways. He saw one lady with her face speckled in blood and his eye was drawn to a scarlet spray on the grey stone wall. Then he saw the door to the Queen's quarters – and the yeoman there. He had been opened from throat to navel and he lay slumped on the floor, half-lying, half-sitting. He held something in his hands, a dripping, yellowish-red pile of his own insides, quivering like pudding, which he was trying to replace in his gaping stomach. The reek of him filled the hall and Compton found himself gagging; his hand went to his nose and mouth but he stood rooted to the spot, horribly fascinated as the disembowelled man vainly tried to make himself whole once more.

Then Compton was pulled from his macabre reverie by more screams, these from inside Her Majesty's chambers. He stopped at the threshold, protocol preventing him from advancing further, but fresh cries propelled him inside, where ladies-in-waiting screeched and ran but not at the unseemly arrival of an unannounced male in Her Majesty's Presence Chamber, at something else – something in the Queen's room, where the screams were like that of an agonised animal, a stag torn apart by hounds . . .

In the other room Henry briefly saw the running figures of the escaping courtiers as the door swung shut behind William. Then came the second set of screams that he recognised as belonging to His Lady, to Katherine. He knew her screams, of course; he had just spent hours listening to them. But these – these were different.

And instead of following William, he ran to the connecting door, barging past the guard. Behind him came Wolsey who shouted at his clerk to wait, and together they burst into the chamber, arriving at the same time as William.

What they saw there sent Wolsey to his knees.

Two creatures were perched atop the Queen's thrashing body, feeding enthusiastically. Two small, hairy beasts, like children escaped from Hell.

Henry saw whirling claws, blood arcing from them. He saw red dripping fangs. Amid the screams were the sounds of mutilation. They were shredding her. They were tearing her apart.

It took them just seconds of frenzied work. Then the two wolf creatures jumped from the bed and landed with a moist thump on the rug. They stood on their hind legs, thick, wiry coats saturated with blood; long, bony arms extended almost to the ground. Compared to their heads, their ears were outsized and floppy; they might almost have looked endearing were it not for the blood, their slavering mouths, and the red lava pits of their eyes.

Behind them on the bed was a landscape of ragged red meat and bedsheets. Blood dripped from an outflung hand. Then her head lolled, her eyes sightless, and Henry saw that it was the wet nurse, Lady Rebecca, not the Queen, whose screams could now be heard from an adjoining chamber.

Screaming: '*The baby. The baby.*'

Henry's hand went to the dagger at his waist. It was a tiny, stupid, ornate thing. It was never really intended that it should even leave its scabbard, itself garish and encrusted with jewels. But it was all he had.

The two wolf children shook the blood from themselves, sending a mist into the air, which Henry felt on his face, like the first droplets of warm summer rain. He drew his knife and then, with a yell, came to them. An experienced, feared combatant, his judgement was clouded by his grief and he slashed wildly and ineptly, the two beasts letting him lurch towards them then easily dodging his dagger. Each moved to the side of him and in the same movement had curled into tight, bristling balls, hideous parodies of hedgehogs, and Henry swung about to see them spin away, humming over the oak boards to the connecting door.

To the Waiting Chamber, where the baby lay.

Too late Henry realised he had been outwitted. And even as he darted after the two rolling balls of blood-matted fur they had crossed into the Waiting Chamber and one of them uncurled, twisted and slammed the door in his face. The last thing Henry saw was a flash of fangs, a grin.

One of the younglings barred the door, which Henry immediately pummelled from the other side. The yeoman, who had frozen for a second, recovered and lunged with his pike. The second assassin had unfurled to meet the attack, thrusting upwards with its paw, pushing it through the jaw of the guardsman and into his skull.

The yeoman's face contorted. He gurgled. His mouth opened and something appeared from inside it, so that for a moment he looked as though he were trying to vomit a hairy parsnip. Then his eyes popped and two more claws appeared from behind his sockets as his face was gripped from within. The beast swung its arm, dragging the yeoman, his arms flailing, and released him to thump against the far wall, three bloody holes where his face had been.

More thumping at the connecting door. Shouts and screams.

The two younglings stood. Their eyes were dark slits, mouths wet red axe wounds, their chests rising and falling as they caught their breath. The servants stared at them, slack-jawed and rooted to the spot.

Then, the spell was broken. And the wolfen attacked.

A page made for the second door, too late to avoid the slashing claws of the youngling, his throat gaping as he hit the floor where he writhed for a moment then was still, dark shining blood spreading like wings around him. Another servant bravely tried to shield the baby's crib but met the same fate, while the last was knocked down, groping for the yeoman's pike as the tiny assassin straddled him to bite into the back of his neck, rummaging there then straightening with pieces of dripping spinal column dangling from its jaws, like a dog with a hard-won bone.

Finally the door gave and with a roar the King burst in, snatched up the pike and impaled the youngling.

It screeched in pain as it was hoisted into the air, its paws going to the spear through its chest, as it was sliding down the shaft. But it was strong and it twisted, so fast and so strong that the shaft of the pike snapped and in a trice the thing was upon Henry, its claws flailing, jaws snapping, shredding his clothes and tearing at his skin.

He was pushed back and to the floor desperately trying to keep the creature away from him. He saw blood, his own. The creature's claws swiped at him, its snout rose and fell. Its jaws were wide, aiming for his throat. Christ, the strength of it!

From its chest protruded the pike's blade and Henry felt it digging into his stomach. Then it was grabbed, Compton hoisting the youngling into the air and flinging it against the wall where it slid to the floor, dead or unconscious. A yeoman stepped forward with his pike raised but Henry, already pulling himself to his feet, screamed, 'No, we need it alive.'

At the same time: '*Your Majesty*,' shrieked Dudley. And Henry turned to see the second of the two wolfen reach into the cot, take the baby and clasp the bundle to its chest.

Henry shouted, blindly dashing to reach his baby, but too late, too slow.

The wolfen jumped. It leapt through the glass and into the grey, mist-cloaked morning, in its arms, the baby. Reaching the window, Henry let out a howl of frustration, pulling himself up to the sill, heedless to the glass that cut his hands and then his torso as he pushed himself through, tumbling out.

For a moment or so, everybody froze, then Dudley, Compton and Wolsey darted into the hallway, heading for the grounds. They were not the only ones. As they dashed across the lawns, there were others arriving from different directions, all running towards their King, who was now kneeling on the grass, his hands in his hair.

He was screaming. Terrible, heart-rending screams.

Then one by one, they stopped short of him. Until nobody was running any more. There was just the King, howling, and behind him, several yards away, a semicircle of yeomen and servants and courtiers. All of them gaping, horrified at what they saw in the branches of a chestnut tree: ragged pieces of torn flesh, tattered, bloody scraps of swaddling. Even as they watched, crows began to land in the tree, taking tentative pecks at the fresh meat strewn among the branches.

Part Two

THE KING

XIV

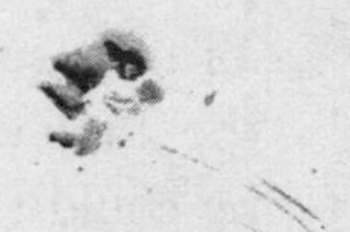

Severed heads that had been dipped in tar and placed on spikes grinned at Wolsey as he passed by the bridge on his way to the Tower, Dudley and Child scurrying in his wake.

The Lord Chancellor tried not to look at them. The heads, that was. As he walked he trembled. He gnawed on his cane compulsively. He tried not to let his imagination answer the one question insisting itself upon him: would the King blame *him* for the terrible, terrible events of earlier that morning?

Just a few hours earlier in the grounds of the Palace he had rushed to aid the King but was stopped in his tracks by a look such as he had never seen before. It was as though His Majesty had aged ten years. His skin appeared to have sagged on his skull; his eyes, sunk beneath his forehead, now burnt with something terrible and unknowable that was, for that moment, directed at Wolsey.

The cardinal had begun trembling then. He was trembling when he encountered the hooded figure an hour or so later, and hissed, 'Where the bloody hell were you?' to which the only reply had been a bowed head, a tear that dropped from beneath the cowl and splashed to the floor. He was trembling when he returned to his chamber to splash cold water on his face then regarded himself in his looking glass – was he looking into the eyes of a condemned man? And he was trembling when he left for the Tower of London. The King would be inconsolable in his grief, Wolsey knew. There was nothing he could do about that, beyond all the usual prayers. But if he could convince His Majesty the Protektorate was taking action . . . Well, then perhaps he could save himself.

He rubbed his face as he marched quickly towards the Tower, which loomed ahead of them. From the river came the shouts of boatmen, calling to one another, and for a moment he felt a pang. How he longed to spend his days in a boat on the Thames, gazing out over the river . . .

'*Bollocks*,' he exclaimed, cutting into his own thoughts. There, moored just upriver of Traitors' Gate, was the King's barge, *The Lyon*. Even in the dull grey light of the overcast morning it seemed to glitter and twinkle, a riot of gold and plush velvet seats.

He stopped and wheeled about, staring wild-eyed at Dudley and Child. 'What's the King doing here? What the *bloody hell* is the King doing here? You were sure to make it clear that the youngling is a prisoner of the Protektorate, weren't you, Child?'

He shrank back. 'Yes, Your Eminence.'

'Because all matters pertaining to demonkind are a papal concern and thus fall under the auspices of the Protektorate, don't they, Child?'

'Yes, Your Eminence.'

'*Then what the bloody hell is the King doing here?*'

As his clerks cringed away from him, Wolsey took a hold of himself.

'Right,' he said, taking deep breaths, placing both hands to his cane, 'the King is here. Let's think about this.' He carried on walking, but faster now, so that Dudley and Child had to break into a run in order to keep up with him. 'I know. The King has taken to the Tower for protection. Of course. It's the country's most heavily fortified citadel. Where else would he come if he feels his life is threatened? That's right, isn't it?'

Again he required no answer but his two clerks murmured assent.

They passed through the first gate, crossed the bridge over the moat to the second. The South Wall rose to their right, guards with pikes looking down upon them. Here, also, the guards had been doubled.

'Where is the prisoner?' said Wolsey now. 'Is he in Lower Wakefield?'

'The Garden Tower, Your Eminence,' replied Child.

'Then we'll have him taken to Lower Wakefield,' said Wolsey, who felt his nerves subside. With this prisoner he could at least regain control of the situation.

'You plan to torture the prisoner, Your Eminence?' asked Child.

'Torture him?' scoffed Wolsey. 'Of course I do, Child. I plan to torture the fuck out of him.'

They turned left, quickening their step and walking in silence, serenaded by the cawing of ravens, each man lost in a fog of deep thought and exhaustion. Presently they came to the Garden Tower, where they mounted winding steps and entered past the portcullis, a guard withdrawing his pike for them to pass. 'We will soon be transporting the prisoner to Lower Wakefield,' commanded Wolsey and the guard nodded, though his eyes shifted uneasily.

They reached the top, Wolsey out of breath, nodding to another guard who unbarred the door and gave it a push. With a creak it swung open. The cell was empty.

Wolsey looked at Child, who looked at Dudley, who looked at Wolsey. They all looked at the guard.

'It's empty,' said Wolsey. His shakes, all but gone, now returned. 'Why is the cell empty? Has the prisoner perhaps escaped?'

'No, Your Eminence.' The guard's eyes darted nervously.

'Perhaps you'd like to explain where he is, then?' said Wolsey, his voice rising, his hands shaking uncontrollably, thinking of the King's barge . . .

Moments later, Wolsey and his clerks stood at the entrance to Beauchamp Tower, the Lord Chancellor having screamed at every guardsman on his way across the courtyard. He demanded to see the occupants and after a short wait Sir William Compton opened the door a fraction. Wolsey's heart sank. In his mind he shuffled a little closer to the scaffold.

But all was not yet lost, he told himself, and he puffed himself up to full size to muster his deepest, most authoritative tones.

'You have my prisoner, I believe,' he squeaked, cursing his treacherous vocal cords.

Compton smiled thinly and pretended to think. 'No, Your Eminence, I don't believe I do have your prisoner. But if you're referring to the youngling, then I believe he is *our* prisoner.'

Wolsey turned to look at Child who spread his hands helplessly. To Compton he said, 'Listen here, Compton, all matters pertaining to demonkind are a papal concern and thus fall under the auspices of the Protektorate. The prisoner's mine. If you would return him to me, I would like to commence debriefing him.'

'I'm afraid that is not possible, Your Eminence. The King has decreed that the prisoner be the property of the crown, not the church.'

'And when was this?'

'At a meeting of the Privy Council, a matter of hours ago.'

Wolsey swallowed. 'What? What meeting? I sit on the Privy Council. There can be no meeting in my absence.'

'Your presence was not needed, as the Privy Council was dissolved, and a new council convened.'

'*What?* What new council?'

'A council of war.'

'War? Have the French . . .'

'Not against the French, Your Eminence.'

'Then whom?'

'Against the wolfen.'

Wolsey went cold. He stuttered then found his voice. 'But all matters pertaining to demonkind are a papal concern. The Pope must give his . . .'

'The King demands you secure the Pope's authority.'

'What? How am I going to get . . .? I mean . . . the Pope won't give this war his blessing.'

'It's your task to make sure he does.'

'He won't.'

'I suggest you ask.'

'Look, I want to see the King. There are certain Protektorate matters we need to discuss.'

'It is in the hands of the army and Council now. The

King will no longer be dictated to by Rome on these matters. And he will see you when he is ready.' Compton darkened. 'But if I were you, Cardinal, I would do nothing to hasten the encounter.'

On his return to his barge, Wolsey looked up at the severed heads decorating the underside of London Bridge. They were dipped in tar to protect them from the elements, and he wondered how his own head would look, impaled on a spike and oozing black stuff. Moments ago he'd been dreaming of spending all day gazing out on the river. If things went on this way, he reflected, he might well get his wish.

XV

It was a few hours after dawn, and Hob sat at the window of their lodgings, watching the villagers below build the fire. Every now and then one of the workers would glance up to award him a short deferential nod, and in return he would slowly bow his head in what he hoped was a manner both portentous and foreboding, so that the brim of his hat dipped almost to his thigh. It was the same hat that in summer he draped with a veil and wore to tend his beehives. A very versatile hat indeed.

Children picked up sticks and played swordfights until scolded by the women and chased, laughing, from the square. The men sang as they arrived with armfuls of sticks and logs, dropping them on the ground for the women to arrange around a stake that rose from the centre of the pyre. Ropes dangled from it – ready for the wolfman.

One of the women looked up, blushed and curtseyed. Hob smiled thinly and dipped his hat and did his best not to look at her breasts that threatened to spill out of her dress. She wore her skirts with one side raised and tied at the hip so that her thigh was visible. He tried not to look at that, too. He shouldn't look at other women, he knew, being a married man.

Behind him in the room, Agatha sucked noisily on her pipe, which had gone out. He could tell, because of the slurping sound it made, and he waited until she had finished knocking the saliva out of the bowl before turning to her. 'You believe, do you,' he said, 'in men who transform into giant wolves?'

She cackled and coughed. 'I believe in men that transform into large purses of silver when you burn them, Hoblet, that's what I believe. Now just you concentrate on looking grand in yer window. Give the townsfolk a show.'

When it came to burning witches there was nobody who could create an atmosphere of excitement and expectancy quite like Agatha; indeed, there was a saying: 'If you need to burn a bride of Satan, for Mistress Hoblet it's worth a-waitin'.'

And though the aphorism had been coined by Agatha at the kitchen table of their farmhouse, then repeated ad infinitum by Agatha herself until, at last, folk had caught on and were saying it almost unprompted, it did at least have the benefit of being true. Other, lesser witchfinders were content merely to torture and execute the accused, collect the purse then move on, leaving a few muddy-faced villagers in their wake. Not Agatha. She knew the value of showmanship. It was she who made sure that when Master Hoblet visited a village, it was not just a few locals who were to benefit from seeing the Lord's will carried out, but folk from far and wide.

The more that know, the better the show. That was another of her little sayings. And so it was that those building the fire had plenty of help. More and more people were arriving thanks to Agatha's insistence on sending children to inform nearby villages of the great happening to come. They were told to impress upon the villagers that this particular event was different. Not the execution of a sorceress, appealing though it was to watch a young woman burn at the stake. No, this was a different kind of abomination altogether. A wolfman.

'You'll be proving his guilt in the normal way, I suppose?' said Hob.

'How's that, then?'

'Well, by hurting them until they'd say anything to make the pain stop. Isn't that the usual way?'

'Ooh,' she mocked, 'we're quite the cynic today, aren't we, Master Hoblet? Well, as a matter of fact, I have a little surprise up my sleeve, just in case.'

She had been laying items on the bed, starting with her pricking needles. Hob noticed that she stroked them after setting them down, as other women did with cats. Now she withdrew from her knapsack something else. A square of what looked like animal hide. She laid it on the bed next to her pricking needles, hairy side up.

'What's that?' asked Hob.

She grinned. 'That's exactly what you think it is, Hoblet.'

'Oh, come on, you can't—'

'You just leave the questioning to me, you.'

Hob squeezed his eyes shut. He knew exactly what she intended to do with the square of animal hide just as he knew that inside her knapsack she would also have a needle and thread. 'Yes, dear,' he replied.

'And will you stop talking like that,' she snapped, 'all hoity-toity. What if somebody hears you? Talk like a witchfinder, man.'

'Argh, that's right, Mistress Hoblet, that's right,' he growled.

Now she stood and put her hands to her hips.

'Not like *that*,' she rasped, 'you sound like a pirate when you talk that way. You don't say, *Argh*, all drawn out like that, you say, *Aye*.'

He looked at her balefully. 'Aye.'

'That's better. And it's not *right*, it's *roit*.'

'Do you know,' he said, 'there was a time that you used to like the way I spoke. Do you remember that, dear?'

She glared at him.

He sighed. 'Oi seem to recall you loiking the way I spake once upon a time if memory serves so it be, Mistress Hoblet.'

She narrowed her eyes at him, unsure if she was being mocked. 'Firstly, if you ever call me dear again I'll shove so many needles in your arse you'll look like a pincushion. Secondly, I might have liked your hoity-toity speech once upon a time, but that's when I thought you had prospects. Why, if only I'd known then what I know now . . .'

'The feeling's mutual, Agatha, if that's any consolation to you.'

She grinned lewdly, rotted holes where teeth had once been. 'Oh, I don't seem to recall you being concerned about much besides your own ungodly desires when we first met. When you was drunk and in need of a little feminine comfort like.'

Hob felt his gorge rise; swallowing it down he turned his attention back to the activity in the square. It had been her idea that they capitalise on their lowly lodgings by establishing a presence. 'It does good to be seen, Hob,' she'd said, casting his hat towards him and bidding him sit in the window in full witchfinder's garb. 'Wave,' she urged him, 'look sinister.

Look as if you're sizing them up. Like they might be next in line to feel God's holy wrath . . .'

A villager cupped his hands to his mouth and called up, 'Have you seen the Wolfman, Master Hoblet, sir?'

Hob looked across the room at his wife.

'Have we?' he sighed. They had, but whether she wanted people to know was a different matter. She strode across the room and leant out of the window.

'Aye, Master Hoblet's seen the beast, villager,' she called, and those working in the square stopped to gaze up at the window of the lodgings of the witchfinder and his wife. 'And a more terrifying, ungodly creature has yet to be seen on God's green earth, ain't that right, Master Hoblet?'

Hob nodded gravely, trying to think about his garden at home, trying to think of his bees. Trying not to think about the frightened, half-naked young man he and Agatha had found shivering behind the bars.

'Has he confessed to his iniquity, Mistress Hoblet?' called the villager. 'Will we be able to satisfy the Lord with a burning come the new day?' He looked around at the other villagers, who murmured their approval at the thought.

'The beast has spoken nothing but *blasphemy*,' retorted Agatha, voice rising to a pious screech, an affectation of which she was fond. It had the desired effect; the villagers seemed to shrink away at the thought of the vicious and unrepentant animal straining at the chains of his dungeon.

In fact, the young man had regarded them through eyes wet with tears. On his face, disbelief and confusion. He did indeed have the sharp teeth of which he had been accused, and his employment as a farmhand might have accounted for the sightings of him communing with beasts. But otherwise he made a dismal lycanthrope. His name, they had been told, was Graham.

Graham the Wolfman.

'Tomorrow we shall begin our questioning, villager,' she called, 'and perhaps we shall have our burning on the following day.' She winked for only Hob to see. She had earned them an extra day in which to attract even more visitors.

The villager was looking crestfallen when all of a sudden came a commotion in the square. There was shouting followed by children laughing and running. Women pointed and put their hands to their mouths, rocking back on their heels. Hob and Agatha craned to see as into the square ran the cause of the hullaballoo: a man, his cheeks flushed red with either embarrassment or exertion or possibly both – for he wore nothing but a brown leather apron.

Despite the excitement and hilarity caused by his appearance, the man hardly acknowledged it save to ensure that he kept one hand at the hem of the apron and shooed away those children who came too close; instead he was trying to hush the crowd, attempting to tell them something that could not be heard above the laughter. Hob heard 'wolf' and 'murder' and eventually the crowd quietened to hear the man who repeated himself breathlessly, 'William Tanner and Paul Lundy of Bean both dead,' he said, his words wiping the smiles from the faces of the villagers, 'killed by a werewolf. We saw it – we saw the wolf change from a beast into . . . into a *woman*. We saw it with our own eyes.'

A shocked hush came over the square, the silence broken only by a clatter as Mistress Hoblet's pipe dropped from her open mouth to the ground.

'*Bloody hell*,' she said, recovering herself, then calling, 'Where is the wolf now, villager?'

The half-naked man turned to look up at her. 'Coming, Mistress Hoblet. We managed to catch the beast, plus an accomplice with whom it was engaged in . . . relations.'

'*Bloody hell*,' repeated Mistress Hoblet. Her eyes gleamed and Hob knew what she was thinking. Thoughts that could be summarised in one word: chimney.

Now there was more commotion. A woman fainted as a party of men came into the square, leading two figures tethered by rope. One of them was a man who was shouting something that Hob could not hear. Anyway, Hob had no interest in the man. It was the woman who had caught his eye, with her grace and her jet-black hair. She had been given clothes and wore a pair of man's breeches rolled up to above the ankle, as well as a man's shirt with a laced-up collar. It was oversized, it gaped at the neck and Hob had the sense of her body moving fluidly beneath it. A haughty smile played about her lips as she cast her gaze around the square, finally finding Hob and Agatha at their window.

'I'm Sir Thomas More,' her companion was shouting, to the general derision of the crowd, 'my name is Sir Thomas More, a counsellor to His Majesty, Henry the Eighth.'

Children began to throw dung at him.

The woman, oblivious to it all, smiled.

XVI

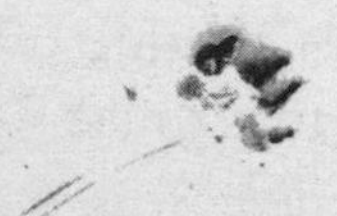

Earlier that morning, the King had stood at his window and watched as hundreds of chests had been brought out into the courtyard behind Greenwich Palace. In them, the contents of the Queen's household. The chests had been loaded on to carts and wagons and sumptermen spread boar hides over them in order to protect them from the weather. Chariots and litters had been brought. Cushions covered with golden cloth were fetched and the transports furnished. Curtains were drawn, horses saddled and harnessed. Next the stablehands and sumptermen withdrew, leaving a skeleton staff who turned their backs as the ladies of the Queen's household walked out to the convoy and took their places. Mostly they came silently, though there was some subdued snuffling.

Then came the Queen, carried on a chair, her head lolling sleepily. She had begun screaming when the beasts struck; had not stopped until physicians had administered a draught. On waking she had been hysterical until given another and she would probably be hysterical when this one wore off.

Henry saw her eyelids flutter as she was helped up to her carriage. Presently a signal was given and the carts, wagons, chariots and litters had moved off with a great rumbling of wheels and hooves clashing on the cobblestones, the convoy bound for The More, where, should anybody ask, the Queen was to recuperate after yet another tragic miscarriage.

'What will I tell Mary?' he had asked. Princess Mary was at Ludlow Castle. His voice sounded empty. As though it came from far away. As though an actor was saying his words for him.

'Nothing, for now, Your Majesty,' Compton replied. 'It is a consideration for another day. First we must see to you.'

'To me?'

'The physician has asked that I look at your wounds. If Your Majesty would be so kind . . .'

He indicated a settle chair and Henry slumped into it, raising his arms so that Compton could remove his shirt. Beneath it his stomach and chest were criss-crossed with bandaging, to cover the injuries left by the wolfen's attack plus those caused by his jump through the window.

Henry looked down at himself grimly. 'How did they get in, William?' he asked.

'In human form they are boys, just like any other. They simply blended in, Your Highness,' replied Compton.

Of course, thought Henry. There were hundreds of boys at court; rascal boys, they were called. Sometimes insolent and always dirty-faced, they were to be found darting along halls, threading their way through crowds of courtiers, or loitering in the hope of earning silver for running errands. Yes, it would have been easy to blend in. Whoever had despatched the assassins had chosen them well, this . . .

'What was his name?' asked Henry. His voice sounded hollow to his own ears. As though somebody had drained it of all feeling.

'Whose name?'

'This wolf leader Sir Thomas More spoke of . . . yesterday? Was it yesterday?' He rubbed at his brow. There he had sat, the King on his throne, his Presence Chamber golden and gaudy around him, beaming his carefree smile down upon Sir Thomas, who had battled fruitlessly to relay the import of the matter.

'He is called Malchek, Your Highness,' Compton said, 'A rebel, by all accounts. His Grace the Duke of Norfolk sent immediate word to his forces, who have begun a search of the area for him or his followers. All noblemen in the region of Kent will be compelled to give up men in aid of the search.'

'And Brandon?' asked Henry.

'His Grace the Duke of Suffolk has returned to Westhorpe Hall in order to recall his army,' said Compton. He came to Henry and began unwrapping the bandages. 'I have relayed your orders that Malchek is to be taken alive and delivered to you. Which he will be, Majesty, you can be sure of that – he cannot remain hidden for long.'

'Really?' said Henry. 'You think so, do you? A shape-shifting creature will be easily identified and captured?' He laughed drily.

'Sooner or later he will give himself away, Majesty,' said Compton, 'I am certain of it.'

Henry, certain of nothing, fell silent as Compton adjusted his bandages. Every now and then the groom's eyes flicked to Henry's face as though he wanted to convey something of great importance, until at last Henry said, 'What is it, William?'

In response Compton looked a little queasy. 'It's a matter we must discuss, Your Highness, concerning your wounds.'

'Yes, what about them?'

William's expression was intense, concerned. 'Are any of them biting wounds, Your Majesty?'

'No, William,' he laughed. 'Certainly the beast drew blood but with its claws not its fangs.'

Glad, Compton turned away. Behind his back the smile slid from Henry's face. Unconsciously, he had put his hand to his chest and to a particular wound there. One that itched more than the others.

XVII

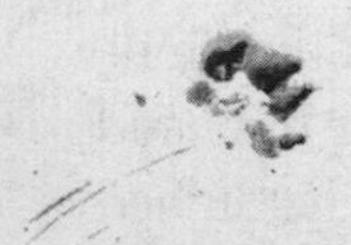

Now Henry sat at a small wooden table in a cell in Beauchamp Tower, hearing the murmur of conversation taking place at the entrance to the building, several flights of steps below him: Wolsey remonstrating with Compton.

Wolsey. Just the thought of the man darkened his mood, and he did his best to block him out, closing his weary eyes and listening to the sound of the ravens, letting sleep claim him. Slowly the sound of the birds was absorbed into a dream in which he saw crows picking at the corpse of his child. In the dream he went to shoo them away but his arms were restrained. He tried to shout but hands covered his mouth so his words were muffled. Instead he had to watch helplessly as the birds feasted on his son, as their beaks dug into his still-warm body and came away with stringy bits of flesh and sinew . . .

'Majesty, Wolsey is gone . . . Majesty?'

Compton's voice woke him with a start. Feeling the chill, Henry pulled his fur coat tightly around him. He rubbed his eyes and when he brought his hands away from his face they were wet with tears. Outside, ravens continued cawing; from the river came noises made by men who knew nothing of his bereavement and in the room stood his aides – Compton, Thomas the Duke of Norfolk, and Thomas Boleyn – whose duty compelled them to behave as though his loss was theirs. He wanted to scream at them all. He wanted to take his rage and pain and fling it at them like a truculent child flings his toys, so that they might know his hurt. Compton stood over him, and as he stared up at his groom he saw him divide and splinter through the tears in his eyes. When he opened his mouth to try to speak it was sticky and the only sound to emerge was a moan.

Compton squatted down to speak to him. 'Majesty,' he said very quietly, 'there is no need to do this now. It can wait. You know I would never presume to offer my opinion under normal circumstances. But these are not normal circumstances. Your Majesty, you need to sleep further.'

Henry shook his head. No, he thought, he did not need to sleep. For if he did that then dreams of the crows would come.

No, he had to stay occupied. He had to focus on a goal. He had to avenge his son.

But the concern in Compton's eyes merited a reply. With a sad smile he said, 'I'm touched by your concern, William, really I am. But there is no matter more important to me now than finding the creature responsible for this outrage. Now,' he took a deep breath, 'shall we meet our prisoner . . .'

Boleyn and Norfolk bowed and left for the cell next door, which, Henry knew, was even more cramped than this one. Moments later, Norfolk returned. He held one end of a chain. At the other end of it, attached to a metal collar, was a small boy, a scruffy urchin with rosy cheeks, long eyelashes and a downcast expression, the skin at his neck rubbed raw by the cruel steel of the collar.

At the sight of the young boy, clearly in distress, Henry jerked in his seat and stood, his mouth open to protest.

Compton saw. 'Your Majesty, this is one of the wolfen from last night.'

'But he is a small child,' cried Henry, 'barely ten years old.'

The boy looked at Henry with large sad eyes, tears welling in them. He snivelled a little and his bottom lip began to quiver.

'In human form only, Your Highness,' insisted Boleyn. 'Last night this boy was a wolfen, one of those responsible for the attack – the very wolfen that inflicted your wounds.'

'I don't know nothing about any attack, my Lord,' said the boy, addressing Henry. 'I'm just a boy, taken from the streets, so I am.'

'Be quiet, boy,' snarled Norfolk, 'you speak only to the King when he speaks to you.'

'What is your name, boy?' asked Henry.

'Reginald, Your Highness,' snivelled the boy.

Henry found it impossible not to be moved by the wretch. 'Is the collar necessary?' he asked Norfolk. 'Where did you get it from anyway?'

'It chafes something awful,' complained Reginald.

'Shut up, boy.' Norfolk pulled on the chain, making Henry wince. 'The collar was brought from the menagerie, Your Majesty, we had no adult restraints to fit.'

'Does it need to be so tight?'

'Your Majesty, it is tight enough that if the beast attempts to transform he will strangle himself; we have the smiths working on a more permanent device for this purpose.'

Henry crouched down so that he and the boy could stare directly into each other's eyes. 'Reginald,' he said.

'Yes, My Lord.'

'I want you to transform into a wolf, can you do that for me?'

Reginald shook his head sadly. 'I cannot, Your Highness, though I wish I was able to if it would please you. I am just a boy and not blessed with these capabilities of which you speak.'

'Really?' said Henry. Now he was closer to the boy he could smell him. He leant closer, inhaling.

'Please, don't get too close, Your Majesty,' said Compton, but Henry ignored the warning, letting his eyes close and breathing in the scent of the boy. He smelt the land. He had a sense of other paws padding alongside him, of spoor, of his pulse quickening at the sight of a grazing animal . . .

His eyes snapped open.

For a moment he rocked on his heels, feeling giddy and sick. When he looked into Reginald's eyes they no longer brimmed with tears; instead the boy's gaze held an ageless knowing. Neither did his mouth tremble. Now it had the beginnings of a smile.

The shock sent Henry backwards and over his heels so that he sat with a painful bump on the cold floor of the cell. His aides rushed to help, Norfolk cuffing the boy as he walked past him. But Henry and the boy held each other's gaze until Henry was dragged to his feet, hands brushing him down, and he felt his blood running cold: in that gaze he had discovered something dreadful.

He staggered to his seat.

'Your Majesty,' said Compton, 'perhaps we should adjourn . . .'

'*No*,' snapped Henry. Now he found himself able to look at Reginald once more. 'No, you were right, this is no time to consider niceties. This . . . *thing* may look like a child, but he is no more human than a dog.' He gathered himself, thought of the tree. 'I wish to commence questioning at once.'

Reginald was helped to his seat. His legs swung as he sat, head bowed, once again the little boy lost.

'Reginald, can you tell me the penalty for high treason?' asked Henry.

'I'm quite sure I don't know, Your Majesty,' sniffed the boy.

'Let me tell you. You will be hung, drawn and quartered. Do you know what this means? You will be taken to Tyburn, not by horse and cart, but dragged there, on a hurdle, to the famous Tyburn Tree. Have you heard of the Tyburn Tree, Reginald?'

'No, I can't say that I have, Majesty.'

'It's not really a tree, it is a very large scaffold. Now usually we hang several criminals at once on the Tyburn Tree, but a traitor's death is special, so you would have the tree all to yourself. Because you're special. Because even though we're going to hang you like the other common criminals, we won't let you die up there on the gallows. You will be hung until close to death but not quite dead. We need you alive for the next bit, you see. Because then you're taken down from the gallows, your cock and balls are sliced off, your stomach is opened, your insides dragged out and the whole lot burnt before your eyes. After which you will be beheaded and your body divided into four parts, to be gibbeted and shown as an example to others. Horrific, isn't it?'

'You'd do that to me? A mere child, Your Majesty?' whimpered Reginald.

'Yes, you're right, it would be a barbaric thing to do to a child,' agreed Henry sadly. 'I'm not sure the people would stand by and watch it happen.'

Reginald looked relieved.

'So we would have to do it behind closed doors.'

Reginald sobbed.

'Oh, I used to think it was barbaric, Reginald – until I saw my baby butchered. Now, I'd be more than happy to operate those gallows myself; in fact, I'd be first in line to wield the knife – *on you*.'

Reginald shrank back.

'I will have my revenge,' said Henry. 'Know this: I will have my revenge.' He slammed his hands to the table so that Reginald jumped in his seat. 'Now where is he?'

'I don't know, Your Grace,' whimpered Reginald.

'Where is Malchek?'

'I swear, sir, I don't know.'

With a shout of frustration Henry struck Reginald across the face, an open-handed blow that rocked the youngling on his chair. It caught Reginald by surprise, it caught Compton, Boleyn and Norfolk by surprise too, and they glanced uneasily at each other, uncertain what was going to happen next. Henry sat back, catching his breath, feeling his surge of anger subside. He looked at his hands, bandaged after being cut that morning.

Then he looked at Reginald – and he saw the boy change.

It was as though his flesh went suddenly transparent and

Henry was able to see the hide of the wolf that lay beneath it. In the same moment the boy's eyes became dangerous slits, flaring with anger, with hatred.

Just as suddenly the wolfish hue appeared to fade . . .

So Henry leant forward and slapped the boy again.

Again the beast within seemed to rise to the surface, as though the boy were unable to control it.

'So,' said Henry, 'I think we have discovered how to make your true self appear.' He looked around the room, at Norfolk and Boleyn and Compton; he sensed the shock in the air. 'We must apply pain.'

When Reginald spoke next it was with a different voice. The voice was still human but more measured, with a depth lacking before. 'You can torture me all you like, Majesty, I won't give him up. Even if I knew where he was I would not give him up. For my Lord Malchek fights for a greater cause than your silly pride; he fights for justice.'

'You think he fights for justice?' exploded Henry. 'For his kind? He fights for nothing but Malchek. He wants nothing but disorder, anarchy and death.'

Then he stopped, realising his words were not his own. He was simply repeating those of others; of More, of Wolsey. How many times had he sat stifling yawns as his earnest churchmen spoke of the demonic threat? Stories of ghosts and goblins as he had dismissively called them then.

He felt sick all of a sudden. Not twenty-four hours ago, Sir Thomas More had spoken to him of the wolfen. His mind had been on food and jousting and on the imminent birth. Unthinkingly he'd given his permission to this raid. Now he saw that it was he who had set in motion this chain of events.

He stood, putting a hand to his forehead.

'Your Majesty?' said Boleyn.

'I'm all right, Thomas, thank you.'

But he wasn't all right. He felt dizzy and his head swam. He staggered a little and put his hands to the cold stone of the wall to steady himself. For the first time he saw the graffiti etched into the walls, painstakingly chiselled there by previous occupants, prisoners of the Tower. He took a deep breath and turned back to the room.

'Norfolk, have we ever tortured a child in the Tower?'

Norfolk thought. 'Um, no children, Your Highness, no. But we have on occasion tortured dwarves.'

'Then we have apparatus of the appropriate size?'

'Oh yes, Your Highness. We have a miniature rack, and a child-size iron.'

'Excellent,' said Henry, who watched Reginald, whose lip was beginning to tremble for real now. 'Then let us repair to Lower Wakefield Tower at once, so that this wolfen will tell us all he knows.'

But Henry felt unable to remain in the chamber as they questioned the youngling. When they began strapping Reginald to the rack, his eyes met those of the wolfen and Henry was struck by a feeling that he dared not name, that he knew went far beyond mere human sympathy. He felt the call of the pack.

He took himself to another chamber but found that even there he could still hear Reginald's screams and still smell the scent of the torture chamber, which was of fire and metal and leather and suffering. He could still feel the distress.

Even when he took himself across the courtyard, Compton hurrying in his wake, pulling his fur coat about him, breath hanging in cloud, he fancied he could still hear the screams, even though it was surely impossible, them being so far away. He could still feel the distress.

The wound at his side itched and he rubbed it, feeling thick hair rasping against his shirt as he did so. That was odd: he'd never had hair there before.

XVIII

'My *name is Sir Thomas More.* Please, you must believe me, I am Sir Thomas More,' shouted Graham the Wolfman.

'No he's not!' shouted More. 'For the hundredth time, it is *I* who is Sir Thomas More.'

One thought kept occurring to More, the real Sir Thomas More: that maybe, just maybe, this was a nightmare from which he would soon awake to find himself in bed at home in Bucklersbury, to Alice's warmth, to the wood-panelled walls of his chamber and a fire still glowing in the grate, to a rug and oak flooring and the smell of beeswax candles. And he'd say to Alice, 'My love, I've just had the most unusual nightmare . . .'

Instead it was freezing in the gaolhouse, and the occupants of the cells were freezing, too, although the wolf woman seemed not to feel the cold so much. In the passage outside was a charcoal brazier on wheels, but to add to their torment it was unlit, although they still gazed at it through the bars, as though staring alone might set it ablaze.

And there was no rug or oak flooring, just the *grise*, the rushes that were strewn on the flagstones to soak up what the gaoler called 'yer leakages'. Only they served little purpose in this instance because instead of the homely smell of beeswax, there was the almost overwhelming scent of, well, of their leakages. Graham in particular seemed to have done a great deal of leaking.

And to add to the overall atmosphere of misery, hopelessness and despair, Graham – the man they called Graham the Wolfman – had begun to insist that he was not Graham at all, but Sir Thomas More. God knows why, telling all and sundry that he was Sir Thomas More had done nothing to help the real Sir Thomas More, but Graham had continued nonetheless to varying degrees of ridicule, perhaps encouraged by the attention it brought him.

The gaoler, who always carried an axe for some reason, stood before the row of three cells, regarding the occupants with a combination of boredom, contempt and resentment. No doubt he was thinking that it had been bad enough with one of the prisoners claiming to be the renowned scholar, author and humanist, Sir Thomas More. Two of them doing it was unbearable.

'*He* is not Sir Thomas More,' said Graham. '*I* am Sir Thomas More.'

'Shut up, Graham,' snapped More. Then to the gaoler he said, 'Look, do you really think that he's Sir Thomas More? Surely it should be obvious from my bearing that it is *I* who is Sir Thomas More.'

'Neither of you look no better than you should be,' growled the gaoler. He rattled his axe on the bars of the cells. 'You,' he pointed his axe at the woman. 'Are you Sir Thomas More an' all?'

She looked through the bars at More, smiling. 'Yes,' she said, 'I also am Sir Thomas More.'

'Oh for God's sake,' said More.

'*You see*,' shouted Graham triumphantly, 'would the real Sir Thomas More *blaspheme*?'

'It don't matter anyway,' said the gaoler. 'They say the King's men are searching fields and woods, going from village to village. I dare say they'll be here soon, and when they are, I expect the real Sir Thomas More will be released.'

'Excellent,' said More, who could have cheered. The King had despatched his army to look for him, his old friend. Lessons in morals and ethics had not gone to waste there, More was pleased to see.

'Look,' he said to the gaoler, 'I'm sure I can hasten things along. I want to see the Witchfinder. Bring him to me, please.'

The gaoler smiled. 'You'll have your wish. He's going to be here shortly so I hear, the questioning is to begin.'

'Questioning?' Graham paled as he retreated to the back of his cage, slid to the floor and curled himself into a ball among the piss-stinking *grise*. More looked at him, wondering if the poor wretch had lost his mind. Then he too went to the back wall of the cell, where, set high into the wall, was a tiny window. Standing on tiptoe he could just see through the bars, past some tethered horses and an emaciated ass, to the village square where a fire had been constructed, complete with stake.

He swallowed. He himself had overseen the construction of similar fires for the execution of Lutherans. Men burnt at his command . . .

'You're thinking of the men you have put to death, Sir Thomas,' came a voice from the cell at his side. The wolf woman. 'You're wondering if this is to be your judgement.'

He laughed drily and looked over at her. She sat with

her back to the cell wall, looking at him through the bars. '*You* know who I am, then?' he said.

Her full lips pursed in a smile. 'Of course. You resemble your portrait. And you have the smell of court.'

'And what is your name?' He asked her.

'My name is Aisha,' she purred, 'the mate of Malchek, the wolfen leader.'

'A wolfen?'

'Quite so.'

More must have reacted, for she smiled again. 'You expected me to deny it? You've seen it for yourself, after all. *Experienced* it for yourself.'

He indicated the window above his head. 'They'll burn you for it.'

'And if they do, then whose will shall be served, Sir Thomas? That of God, your master, or that of the Dark One, mine?'

'It is God's will,' he said, forcing an imperious note in his voice.

'Really? Are you sure? Have you never wondered, as men were burnt at the stake at your behest, as they have screamed their last in agony and their families begged for clemency? As priests have kicked on the rope and others have pulled their legs in order to try to bring merciful death sooner? Have you ever wondered if you were doing the Lord's work – or undoing it?'

'Never,' he insisted.

'Then why do you wear the hair shirt, My Lord?'

'Penance,' said More, 'of course.'

'For doing God's billing? Why would he wish you to atone for that? Or do you wear it to chafe at the guilt that lives inside you? Or because the discomfort of the garment helps you to deal with your doubt? We both must hide what's inside us, Sir Thomas.'

She raised her hand for More to see, rotating it. More found himself drawing away, then was scuttling back as the hand began to deform and warp, became not human but something halfway between that and an animal's paw, with long, curved claws that she now brushed against the bars of the cell.

'What did you mean in the wood?' he asked her, after a pause.

'When?' She smiled. 'Don't tell me you're recalling our lovemaking? With affection I hope.'

He ignored her. 'What did you mean when you said *join us*? You planned to turn me, didn't you?'

She nodded and smiled.

'Why?'

'Well, the task of demonkind is to spread evil on earth, Sir Thomas. What else would you have me do?'

'Behave according to your nature, perhaps?'

She laughed. 'You are quite right, Sir Thomas, I would have turned you. And you would have been put in service to our cause.'

'Your cause?'

'An uprising, Sir Thomas. The tyranny of Wolsey and the demon Lefsetz in the name of your King is soon to end. It won't be long before my Lord Malchek will sit upon the throne of England.'

More looked at her as though she was mad. Her mate Malchek might well have been committed to the cause, but he didn't have enough personnel to overcome King Henry's court jesters, let alone the vast armies he had at his disposal. He couldn't do. The idea was absurd.

Aisha looked across at him, an assurance about her. 'You think us fools?'

'No,' said More, carefully. 'Merely, perhaps . . . optimistic. You especially: you're to be put to death as a lycanthrope.'

'We shall see,' she said.

From outside More heard a noise and he looked out of the window. 'It might happen sooner than you think,' he said, 'for the witchfinders are on their way.'

XIX

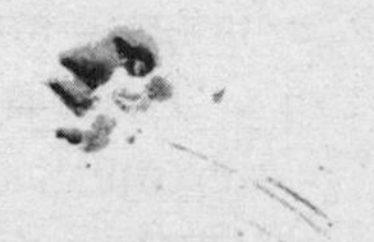

The door at the far end of the passageway opened to admit the Witchfinder General, his wife and the gaoler.

'They're all claiming to be Sir Thomas More now, Mistress Hoblet,' smirked the gaoler as they trooped in and stood before the three cells. The Witchfinder General wrinkled his nose and looked uncomfortable, his wife and the gaoler much more at ease.

'All three of them are Mores, are they?'

'Seems so, Mistress Hoblet.'

'Well then,' cackled Mistress Hoblet, 'that's more than we bargained for.'

'You mean a greater number than we expected, Mistress Hoblet?' said the gaoler, slightly perplexed.

'No.' She nudged him. '*More* than we bargained for.'

'Oh, I see,' he laughed. '*More than we bargained for*. Very funny.'

'But it doesn't matter,' continued the Witchfinder's wife, warming to her theme, 'because you know what they say?'

'What's that, Mistress Hoblet?'

'The *more* the merrier.'

She put her hands to her apron and laughed loudly.

'Oh, very good,' agreed the gaoler, caressing his axe, 'very good.'

'Look,' said More, exasperated, 'you need to release me at once. I have vital information for the Crown.'

'Ooh, hark at him,' screeched Mistress Hoblet, 'he ain't hanging around, is he? No small talk with him.'

'That's right, Mistress Hoblet,' said the gaoler, puffing out his chest a little, 'in fact you might even say it's a case of him being *more* to the point.'

'Yes, very good, gaoler.' She lowered her voice. 'But let's leave it there, shall we? We're here to do the Lord's work, remember, not make jokes.'

'Sorry, Mistress Hoblet,' said the gaoler. 'You won't hear no *more* from me.'

She narrowed her eyes at him; he cleared his throat, chastened.

'Look,' interrupted More, 'you must believe me. I really am Sir Thomas More.'

'He's been on like this ever since he was brought in,' said the gaoler. 'Mark my words, the other one will pipe up next.'

As if on cue . . . 'He's not Sir Thomas More, I am,' called Graham from the adjoining cell.

'But yesterday, you was Graham,' said Mistress Hoblet, evidently enjoying herself.

'Well, I've remembered,' said Graham.

'You see,' said the gaoler. 'In fact – you could say it's *more* of the same.'

'No more puns,' snapped Mistress Hoblet. Master Hoblet, standing beside her, looked both bored and uneasy.

'No *more* puns?' rejoined the gaoler.

Mistress Hoblet stamped on his foot.

After a short break, during which the gaoler recovered composure, picked up his axe, and finished wiping tears of pain from his face, More took advantage of the lull to say, 'Look, I am Sir Thomas More. I can prove it, I'm the author of *Utopia*.'

'*I* wrote *Utopia*,' chimed Graham.

'Graham, please,' roared More. 'For the love of God, man, still your mouth.'

'Blaspheming once more,' said Graham tartly.

'A blasphemer, eh?' Mistress Hoblet came up to the bars and looked at More, her lip curling. 'I have a very low opinion of blasphemers, sir, especially those witnessed consorting with deviants. *Especially* those who use deceit in order to try to pass themselves off as something they are not.'

'But I'm not,' insisted More. 'Look at my robes. Here.' He pulled up his shirt. 'I wear the hair shirt, a symbol of my devotion to prayer and penance. And though I know I was discovered by the villagers in a state most unfitting for a man of my stature, which gives you leave to treat my claims with suspicion, you must understand that I had been deceived and beguiled into that position.'

As he spoke, Mistress Hoblet watched him carefully, chewing the inside of her cheek a little. She glanced at the Witchfinder General who seemed to have been pulled from his reverie and looked from More to his wife, raising his eyebrows.

'I am he,' pressed More. 'I know how unlikely it sounds. I know that my ravings might sound as fantastic as those of Graham. Well, almost as fantastic . . .'

'Hey . . .' protested Graham.

'But it's the truth. My name is Sir Thomas More, I am

counsellor to the King. I found myself in Darenth Wood on the orders of the Lord Chancellor Thomas Cardinal Wolsey, for a secret operation whose details I cannot divulge, but which was of utmost significance to the Crown. In the light of that operation I have learnt information that I must impart at once.'

But just as he sensed he was making progress, Graham interrupted. 'I can prove I wrote *Utopia*,' he claimed from the other cell, and Mistress Hoblet's attention was snatched away at the prospect of further amusement.

'Oh, *come on*,' said More, exasperated.

Mistress Hoblet smirked and the moment was gone. 'How do you plan to do that, Graham?' she asked.

'Yes,' said More, 'how exactly do you plan to do that, *Graham*?'

Graham thought. 'I'll tell you how it starts.'

'Oh for the love of God . . .'

'It starts "Once upon a time, in a faraway land called *Utopia* . . ."'

'No,' shouted More, 'no, it doesn't! That's where you're wrong, because it begins with a series of correspondences, the first being a letter sent from myself to Peter Gilles.'

'I think I prefer Graham's version,' said Mistress Hoblet, 'that sounds like a proper beginning to me. Not sure I like the idea of a story that starts with letters. What kind of story starts with letters?'

'Well, it's not a story,' protested More, 'it's a speculative political essay. It's written in Latin. Did you know that, Graham? Did you know *Utopia* is written in Latin?'

'Mine isn't written in Latin, Mistress Hoblet,' said Graham hopefully.

'I should hope not, Graham,' said Mistress Hoblet, 'any book written in Latin that's got letters and essays in it ain't going to be on my bookshelf. Your *Utopia* sounds like a vision of Hell to me, Mister whatever-your-name-is; I can't see nobody wanting to read that.'

More sighed. 'It has sold in great quantities, far more than my other works. Of all my books it is my bestseller.'

'Bestseller or not, I prefer Graham's version.'

More threw up his arms in despair.

'Does that mean I can go, Mistress Hoblet?' asked Graham.

'Why no, Graham, it doesn't.' She smiled. 'Far from it. In fact, we'll be burning you at the stake the day after tomorrow.'

Graham began to cry.

The Witchfinder General cleared his throat significantly.

'My mistake, Graham,' apologised Mistress Hoblet, and Graham looked at her, his eyes wide with hope as she added, 'We'll be burning you after questioning, provided that you're found guilty of the crimes of which you have been accused. Which of course you will be. That means we'll be questioning Graham later, then having the burning on the following day after which we'll be questioning you, Your Lordship, burning you the next day, then questioning our star wolf woman here, for burning the day after that.' She turned to Aisha. 'Word's spread far and wide about you, my dear, so it has. We're expecting quite a turnout for you, ain't that right, Master Hoblet?'

'Yes, that's . . . I mean, aye, that be the case so it be, Mistress Hoblet.'

She seemed about to say something to her husband when there came a commotion from the village square. More twisted about to look from his window in time to see two figures he recognised ride into the square. They were resplendent in their finery; their strong, beautifully groomed mounts whinnied and snorted powerfully. And they had a spare horse.

'Thank God,' exclaimed More. 'Thank God. I am saved.'

XX

More was ecstatic, watching as the Duke of Norfolk and Thomas Boleyn rode imperiously into the square.

Usually he detested the pair of them. He would have hated how they viewed the scene down their noses, the manner in which Boleyn extracted a handkerchief from within his robes and wafted it at his mouth as though finding the village aroma distasteful; he would have despised the way in which Norfolk, with a peremptory wave of his hand, ordered a child on all fours in order that he could stand upon the child's back to dismount. Normally, he would have hated all that; indeed, he and Thomas Cardinal Wolsey were often to be found making merry with impersonations and satirical swipes at Boleyn and Norfolk, whose love of finery was matched only by their ambition.

Normally.

Now, though, he felt no contempt at all for the pair. Especially as they were talking to villagers, some of whom were pointing towards the gaolhouse.

'It is My Lords Norfolk and Boleyn,' More said to Mistress Hoblet, 'members of the Privy Council and confidants to the King. Here to release me.'

'What?' She looked concerned.

'Quite, and when that happens and I am back at court, my first order of business will be to see to it that your husband is stripped of his title of witchfinder and then both of you will answer for your crimes.'

The colour drained from her face.

'You may well look concerned, Mistress Hoblet, for never have I met such an evil and twisted creature as you, so totally devoid of all compassion, as ugly on the inside as you are on the outside.'

She gasped.

'That's right, you wretched old hag,' cried More. 'Never in my years have I ever encountered such irony as this before me: the wife of a witchfinder who so closely resembles a witch herself.'

Just then came a rapping at the door. The gaoler hefted his axe and went to it, opening it to admit the two courtiers who entered with a flurry of robes and colour, large feathers bouncing at their caps, ornate swords hanging from their belts. Norfolk came first; behind him, Boleyn, who carried something wrapped in sackcloth.

'My Lords,' called More, holding the bars and pressing his face close to them. 'My Lords, I am here.'

Norfolk was the first to look at him and More saw him blink, not recognising him at first then doing so, his eyes widening. But it was a tiny flame of recognition that he immediately doused, and with a gauntlet he tapped Boleyn who stood just behind him, and he, too, looked at More, his expressions matching those of Norfolk.

More felt a lurch in his stomach. 'My Lords?' His voice faltered. 'My Lords it is I, Sir Thomas More . . . I heard that the King's men have been searching the region for me so I've been expecting you.'

Both ignored him. Mistress Hoblet looked at him and her colour slowly returned. Her mouth, which had been twisted into a figure of abject fear, gradually relaxed; it became a smile instead.

'My Lords . . .' insisted More, raising his voice, 'please, this is no time for pranks. I have urgent information for the King. You must release me at once.'

Neither of them looked at him. Instead, Norfolk spoke to the Witchfinder. 'Master Hoblet?'

'Aye, Your Grace,' he said, his eyes flicking from More to the visitors, forehead creased with confusion.

'We need to take that prisoner.' Norfolk pointed towards the cells and More relaxed – until he realised the Duke was not pointing at him, he was pointing at Aisha.

'*Norfolk?*' said More, his voice edged with panic.

'Wait a minute, you ain't taking my prisoners,' protested Mistress Hoblet.

'I'm taking *one* of your prisoners, old crone,' said Norfolk.

'*Boleyn*,' shrieked More now 'Thomas, *please*, it's me.'

'You ain't.' Mistress Hoblet's voice rose. 'These prisoners are my livelihood.'

Norfolk smiled at her. 'Listen to me, aged hag, we are taking this prisoner.' He motioned to Boleyn who unwrapped from the sackcloth a pair of leg irons and handcuffs, and what looked like a scold's bridle – a metal muzzle – all of which were passed to the gaoler. 'See that the creature is restrained before we transport her.'

'Yes, Your Grace,' said the gaoler, who touched his

forelock, then with great care set about applying the irons and muzzle to Aisha.

'Now just you wait a minute . . .' said Mistress Hoblet, stepping forward. 'You're taking that prisoner over my dead—'

In a flash, Norfolk had drawn his sword and was holding it to her neck, bringing her up short. 'My pleasure,' he snarled.

Mistress Hoblet looked at the blade to her throat, then at Norfolk. Slowly she said, 'Very well, Your Grace, you may take your prisoner.'

'Excellent,' said Norfolk and relaxed, and was about to sheathe his sword when Mistress Hoblet went on.

'At least I can console myself with my two remaining prisoners, whom I shall shortly be questioning in connection with their crimes.' Her eyes shifted meaningfully to the cells. 'And who knows what might be said under questioning, Your Grace; indeed, should questioning even be necessary. For an embittered man, a man who felt betrayed by those he once considered his allies, well, he might have much to say at their expense.'

She smirked at Norfolk along the blade of his sword, and was rewarded with an appraising look from the Duke – one of admiration, almost.

'I see,' he said. 'Perhaps we should go outside to discuss this.'

'Norfolk,' screamed More, yanking vainly at the bars. 'Boleyn. I can see what you're doing here. You think with me out of the way your passage to the top becomes smoother. But you underestimate the King's affection for me. I was his tutor, his intimate.'

Still he was screaming as they left, taking Aisha with

them, Mistress Hoblet following and grinning widely as she closed the door behind her.

Left was Master Hoblet.

'This is treachery,' said More breathlessly. Once again he had that sense of being trapped in a nightmare. He addressed Master Hoblet. 'You saw that, didn't you? You saw how they reacted. This is nothing less than a conspiracy. Look, you must understand – I need to get word to the King or Cardinal Wolsey.'

Before anything more could be said, however, the door opened once more, this time to admit Mistress Hoblet only. As she came she was tucking a clinking leather purse into a hidden pocket beneath her apron.

She closed the door behind her and all in the dark passageway looked in her direction.

'Right,' she said. 'We don't need to worry about the King's men turning up. Their Lordships say we may proceed. Graham . . .'

'Yes, Mistress Hoblet?' He scrambled to his feet, hope blazing in his tear-stained eyes.

'We won't be burning you the day after tomorrow.'

'Oh, thank you, thank you, Mistress Hoblet.'

'We'll be burning you tomorrow.'

Graham the Wolfman collapsed to the floor with grief.

'Then it's the turn of His Lordship here.'

And with that Mistress Hoblet leered through the bars at More, her stare hateful. She removed her pipe from her mouth and knocked the bowl on the bars, raining dregs of tobacco and saliva into More's cell.

'*Wretched old hag*, eh?' she said, darkly.

XXI

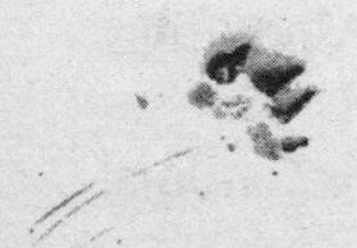

Night, and Compton had withdrawn, leaving Henry alone. And where usually the King would have gladly surrendered to sleep, now he was more wide awake than ever. How curious that was. He felt positively refreshed; his mind raced, his body seemed to fizz with energy.

Disquiet tweaked at him as he wondered why – why did he suddenly feel so vigorous? Thinking that, perhaps, he already knew the answer.

The wound at his side itched but he ignored it. Instead he raised his hands to study their backs. The hair was thicker now, he was sure of it. Standing and walking across his chamber, he peered nervously into the mirror on the wall of his bedchamber. There. His whiskers were thicker, too. He had been shaved that morning, and though it was true that a whole day had passed, his beard was already quite pronounced. Henry knew his own beard, it was often said by his barber that he was a manly man, and that his hair grew quickly but even so – it didn't grow that quickly.

He took a step back, feeling . . . what?

He wasn't sure.

Guilt, for some reason. Shame. As though he had something disturbing he needed to hide from his staff.

But then, he thought, he *did* have something disturbing to hide from his staff: this *changing*. Absent-mindedly he scratched at the hairs on the back of his hand. Would he get fleas? he wondered, and he made a mental note to stay away from the palace dogs. Then again, they stayed away from him these days; they tucked their tails between their legs and slunk away when he passed.

They were not the only ones to have noticed the change in the King. Compton was asking him how he felt so regularly that Henry had threatened to have him immersed in boiling oil if he asked again. He'd smiled, of course, and Henry had assured him that if he felt at all unwell he would call for the physician, and that any change in his mood was purely as a result of the shock, and his desire for revenge, nothing else.

He knew he wouldn't call a physician though. Physicians you called upon when you felt unwell, and Henry didn't feel unwell. Quite the reverse.

He moved to the window, peered out at the darkness, and at the moon that flooded his chamber with white light.

In fact, he realised, as he stood lit by the rays of the moon, he felt really well. He felt a surge of vitality that took him by surprise, making him feel giddy and leaving him out of breath. He blew out his cheeks, riding the wave of energy as it rolled through him, gathering more force and filling him.

Something in his cheek moved of its own accord, as though he'd been prodded by an invisible source, and he touched it, feeling the skin ripple beneath his fingers, sending him rushing back to the mirror, pressing his face close to the glass.

He was smiling, he noted, though nothing had amused him. He was smiling but not aware of doing so. Smiling without wanting to. And there was something odd about his smile, as though his lips would not quite seal. He noticed his breathing quicken. At the same time there was a crunching sound and a pain in his mouth, almost unbearable at first, but then he seemed to adapt to it instantly, as though the pain somehow belonged in his body. And as it coursed through him he saw his face change. It grew.

It grew so that suddenly his skin felt too small for his skull and his hands went to his face as he panicked. Was his flesh to split? It seemed to stretch and bulge. His breathing was harsh and he fought to control it, finding that as he did, his skin seemed to grow to accommodate his swelling features, even as extra hair began to push through, prickling him.

Yes, the breathing helped. If he relaxed then the pain reduced. It was like flexing muscles, and for a second he concentrated on that. He caught a glimpse of himself in the mirror and saw his facial features, screwed up in concentration, shift and transform. The old Henry face was replaced by a new one, a snout forming, matted with thick, black hair; his ears disappearing beneath more hair and growing into long points. He felt his chest expand, pushing against his nightshirt, thankfully big and baggy enough to accommodate his new form. He looked down to see hairy pectorals, expanding thighs.

And he began laughing. It sounded like growling, he thought, but was laughter. He was laughing with the pleasure that was pulsing through his body, waves of it crashing into him. The power he felt.

Next he was pushing out his chest, throwing back his head, arching his entire body to accommodate his transformation. From his hands came a tearing sound and he felt his fingers lengthen. He twisted his head to look along the length of his arm and what appeared from the end of his fingers, pushing through with crackle, were claws, pointed and curved and razor-sharp. He thought of the paltry weapons he normally used: swords and arrows. Now he had weapons of his own, deadly weapons at the end of his fingers. And he felt a kind of delirious happiness at their arrival, as if he had been waiting all his life for them without knowing it. He had claws. He laughed to think of his normal self (his normal self) and his obsessions with hunting, with being a hunter. For he knew now that he was truly a hunter, not a silly man on a horse, accompanied by dogs, but a predator. He knew it because along with his physical transformation came a kind of primal knowing, an ancient instinct. His senses, which had been sharpening before, well, now they were alive. They sang and danced and he could smell everything. How fusty his bedchamber was, how vibrant the tang of the burning wood. Hear things, too: people moving about in hallways, the murmur of distant conversations. All of his senses at their fullest height.

Suddenly he could see with a clarity he had never thought possible; he could taste the night – taste it. More than that, he could feel it, as though it belonged to him and he to it. He felt the call of it now and returned to the window to look upon it. There hung the moon, full and glowing, and he felt it drawing him, calling to him like a lover cooing to him from her bed, and he was about to answer her when he had a second thought, and went again to the mirror.

What he saw there made him gasp (that sounded like a growl, of course, simmering in his throat) because he was now no longer himself. He was the wolfen version of himself. He recognised his nightshirt, of course, and he saw something of his old self when he looked into his eyes. They were threaded with livid red veins, but they were his. Elsewhere, though, all that was Henry had disappeared beneath the beast: pink flesh replaced by black leathery hide and thick hair, mouth by a protruding snout.

He bared his teeth and chuckled in appreciation. Ordinarily his teeth ailed him. They were discoloured and possibly rotting and there were often occasions he had to submit to the barber-surgeon who would pull them out with pliers.

Now look at them. No longer stubby and crooked, they filled his mouth. Four in particular were huge: his fangs. He found himself moving his jaw, opening and closing his mouth, enjoying the feel of them, clenching them together.

The action made him feel hungry so he cast his eye around the chamber then lolloped across to a large table where food had been left.

Wait a minute. He stopped himself. He had *lolloped*, he realised. His walk had been halfway between a run and a walk and his limbs had felt fluid and loose, his arms longer than he was used to. They seemed to swing as he walked. There was that sound, too. When he'd stepped off the rug his claws had rattled on the wooden floor. He swung around and did a short run across the boards, chuckling at his gait, the sound his claws made, the way his arms swung as though not properly attached to his body.

He did that for a while. Until he got bored. Then he

returned to the table to inspect the fare. As he did so he noticed something wet on the tabletop then realised it was him, drool hanging from his jaw. He brushed it away with the back of his hand then lifted the lid of a silver platter, then another, looking for something tasty to eat.

His claws scratched the silver as he lifted lids. Claws were not at all practical for this sort of thing, he decided, stopping as he came to a hunk of whale meat. He jammed it into his mouth but just as quickly was spitting it out again. It was . . . fishy. And roasted. And not at all appetising.

What else? Beaver's tails. No. Here was a boar's head, cooked rare, just as he had requested. He raised his paw, flexing his claws a little, realising he was about to use his new additions for the very first time. He took a step back and addressed the boar's head as though it were moving prey and not a static piece of meat. Then he struck, sweeping his claws across the meat and coming up with a ragged chunk of meat that he brought to his face and sniffed, his snout wrinkling.

And he stuffed the boar into his jaws.

Seconds later he was spitting that out, too. It might have been rare enough for him in his day-to-day form, his *usual* self, but not as a wolf. It tasted burnt, over-cooked. It was like trying to eat a charred lump of wood. He reached for a goblet of wine and knocked it back in one gulp, hoping to wash the taste out of his mouth and doing it before it had even occurred to him that wine might disagree with him in his wolf form.

He braced himself for the worst, expecting, what? Vomiting? But there was none. In fact it seemed as though the wine agreed with him, so he reached for the jug to pour himself some . . .

Ah. He fumbled with the jug for a moment, trying and failing to slide his claws through the handle. Eventually he gave up and brought his two paws to it, and instead of pouring it into a goblet, tipped it directly into his mouth, until it was flooding down the back of his throat, escaping his mouth and soaking his fur. But he didn't care, because by the time he had replaced the goblet to the table he was feeling even better than he had been before, and that was *good*. He turned, the wine still dripping from his fur, and he shook himself to be rid of it then dashed across the chamber, back to the window, dropping to all fours as he did so – which brought him up short.

Oh, this was new. He stood up, on two legs. He dropped to all fours.

Up.

Down.

On all fours he had a sensation, another of those ingrained memories of running with the pack across vast plains.

He jumped to the windowsill, deciding to hunt now, leaping from the window to the ground below, setting off across the grass on all fours, hunting for meat.

He was drunk. He was a wolf. Life was good.

XXII

Several hours later, Henry awoke, his head throbbing, mouth dry, something hard and crusted on his lips.

And something wet on the sheets beside him.

The shock of waking sent him tumbling from his bed and he lay on the rug, disorientated but not so much that he called for William, who slumbered next door. Because something was wrong, wasn't it? Something was terribly, terribly wrong. He pushed his hands to his temples, wanting to rub away the pain living there. At the same time, he tried to recall the events of the night.

He had drunk a lot, he knew that. Through the legs of the bed he could see the discarded jug of wine lying on the wood. A whole jug, indeed. No wonder he . . . oh, and in one go, of course. More of the evening was returning to him. Why had he tipped the jug of wine into his mouth? What on earth had possessed him to do that?

Of course. It was because he couldn't pour the jug properly. Because . . .

His claws had got in the way.

There was a whimpering sound in the room that Henry realised was him. Everything came back to him. The changing. The elation he'd felt. He put his hands to his face, feeling for a snout that thankfully wasn't there. When his hands came away from his face there was something red and flaky on them and he knew instantly what it was. He had dry blood around his mouth.

Now he remembered being on all fours, streaking through the forest, fangs bared, a skittish stag ahead of him, trying to weave and zigzag and escape him. And you almost did, didn't you, deer? Because Henry had never hunted this way before and though he had the scent of blood in his nostrils the stag had the scent of survival in his. But Henry was too swift and too strong and too hungry and had brought the animal down. He had straddled its thrashing body; he had grabbed its antlers and torn off its head for a trophy and then he had fallen to his knees and used those new claws of his to part the belly and take warm meat from the stag until he was fully sated, when he had sat back on his haunches and looked up at the moon and howled at it, the blood on his fur black in the moonlight.

And he'd felt alive and maybe for the first time ever, truly free.

But it was wrong, and it should never happen again, and . . .

Trophy?

Henry pulled himself to his knees, raising his head to the level of the bed. Slowly, slowly, he brought his gaze to it, seeing first the bloodied sheets, then the mound of something beneath.

There was another whimpering sound in the room. He stood, took hold of one corner of the sheet and pulled it away to see the sightless eyes of the stag staring up at him.

Only it had no eyes. Now he recalled plucking them from

their sockets to chew upon like grapes. He gagged. Hand over his mouth, he backed away, trying to control his nausea until he was certain he wasn't going to be sick. Then he took stock, looking at himself in the mirror.

He was fully human again, thank God; a hairy human, but a human nonetheless. His shirt hung in tatters, splashed with mud, and as he'd thought, his face was covered in gore, blood forming a hard crust around his lips. His hair was in disarray and flecked with bits of twig and leaves.

Now he cast his eyes around the chamber, looking for a basin. There was one with water still in it. But what did he do now? What did they use to use wash him?

At a loss he balled up his shirt, dipped it into the water and began scrubbing his face until almost all of the bloody crust was gone. Next he tossed the wet shirt to the bed, gathered up the blood-soaked linen and the severed head of the stag and bundled it up. Antlers jutted from the wrapping so he reached to them. Grimacing he snapped each one off then hurled them on the fire. Embers glowed red beneath them and he dropped to his knees, blowing on the ash to try to speed up the process. Didn't they have some kind of device for puffing up the fire? He was sure he'd seen them do it. Yes. There they were, the bellows, standing by the side of the fire, and he reached for them. *There was this to be said for turning into a werewolf*, he thought grimly, fanning the fire, *you had to learn to fend for yourself*.

Unfortunately, the other thing he was learning this morning was that burning antlers have a most distinctive odour. Unique, in fact, and quite noxious. So much so that he found himself gagging once again and rushed to the window, throwing it open. On the wall was a large hanging tapestry depicting the story of Abraham and he grabbed it, wafting it to try and break up the revolting scent.

There came a knock at the door. 'Your Highness,' called Compton, and Henry felt a surge of annoyance. Though it was a routine that took place every morning of his life, he suddenly found it irritating and intrusive. Plus he had a chamber full of poisonous antler fumes and the severed head of a stag on his bed.

'Wait,' barked Henry, 'just wait, Compton, will you?'

'Oh,' came the bewildered reply, years of routine suddenly broken. 'Of course, Your Majesty.'

Henry snatched the bloody bundle and took it to the Chamber of the Close Stool, the room where he vacated his bowels. Inside it was the close stool, a wooden armchair with a hinged seat that concealed his chamber pot.

In here? No. His last bowel movement had been particularly violent and Compton would need to see to the chamber pot. Henry's furry souvenir would soon be discovered. He wheeled about. How on earth did you hide the severed head of a stag?

Swiftly he crossed his bedchamber to the closet, which was supposed to be used for private reading and contemplation, but now – now he dropped the stag's head inside and kicked it to the far wall, slamming the door and wafting the air as he dashed, naked, across the bedchamber, grumbling loudly about people always barging in on him and how he was never afforded any privacy, and, 'I think from now on, you should first knock but then not enter until I say so. Is that understood?'

There was a pause and Henry could picture his groom's confused face. 'Yes, Your Majesty.'

'And be sure to tell the rest of the staff. No more bursting in on me, is that clear, Compton?'

'Yes . . . Your Majesty.'

Well, thought Henry, running fingers through his hair to dislodge foliage, they were just going to have to get used to it. He needed a little more privacy.

Especially if he was going to continue transforming into a wolf and eating the wildlife. He looked at himself in the mirror, tutted and scraped off a bit of dried blood, then stood in the middle of the room.

Took a deep breath.

'Come,' he said.

The door opened and in walked Compton. If he wondered about the smell of burning antlers, or why Henry was standing naked in the middle of the room, or why he was banned from entering the closet, then he said nothing. After all, it would have been a breach of protocol.

XXIII

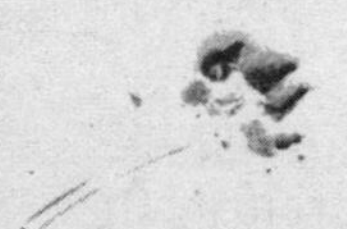

Later, after a breakfast of black pudding, for which Henry was most appreciative, the King left Greenwich Palace, accompanied by Boleyn, Compton and Norfolk.

They rode in a state of great anticipation, for the previous evening Boleyn had come with news from his family seat, Hever Castle in Kent. The county was abuzz with news of a great occurrence in Darenth, he said, where a wolf woman had been captured and was to be questioned then burnt by the Witchfinder General. Entire villages were making the trip. Not since the Peasants' Revolt had there been a mood of such excitement.

The news tallied with something told to Norfolk and Boleyn by the youngling – in between his screams of mercy on the rack, this was. After toiling for an hour, and having increased the wolfen's size by at least an inch and dislocated both of his arms, the two inquisitors had come to believe that the creature had no idea of Malchek's location. Instead, they had extracted from him that Malchek had a mate: Aisha, who was missing after the raid. Her description matched that of the wolf woman in Darenth.

'Your army is in the region?' Henry had asked Norfolk.

'Yes, Majesty,' he said, 'conducting thorough searches and making arrests'.

'Though no sign of Malchek?'

'None yet, Majesty.'

'They will reach Darenth before long then,' said the King.

'Certainly, Your Grace. Then we shall have the wolfen.'

'No,' said Henry. 'I would feel happier if she didn't fall into the clutches of our army. Can we reach her before they do?'

'We can but try.'

So it was that the King and his three aides arrived at Hever to find extra troops patrolling the ramparts. Inside, meanwhile, it was almost eerily quiet. Norfolk and Boleyn left for Darenth immediately, promising to return with the creature. Compton went to prepare the King's chambers. Which left Henry to brood and then to sleep, where once again the nightmare came, until he surfaced, letting out a startled cry as he awoke.

'It's all right, Your Grace,' said a voice he did not recognise. 'You are safe.'

He sat up, finding himself in a settle chair along one wall of a room dominated by a long dining table. Vast windows were luminous with bright, unseasonal afternoon sun and chandeliers hanging from the ceiling sparkled like summer sea. The owner of the soothing voice stood before him, given a silver aura by the light behind her, smiling down at him with her lips pursed prettily and her hands clasped in front of her.

She looked like an angel, he thought, casting his eyes up

and down the figure in her black velvet dress, its neck scooped low. A dark angel.

'Be still, Your Grace,' she said, a little colour appearing in her cheeks beneath his appraising look. 'I shall have Sir William fetched to you.'

'Thank you,' he croaked, 'please excuse me, but I don't think I . . .'

'I am Anne, Your Grace.' She curtseyed. 'Anne Boleyn, sister to Mary. Please be still, I shall return presently.'

Of course. The other of Boleyn's daughters, the one not yet at court. He watched her go, her back straight. Memories of her sister Mary came to him and he cleared his throat, adjusting himself down below.

Not long later she returned, curtseying. 'Sir William is tending to the prisoner, Your Majesty,' she said. 'He asks that I convey you to the cellar where it is being held.'

'You know about the wolfen?' asked Henry, sharply.

'Indeed,' she said. 'Because the wolfen takes female form and will need tending to, father considered it proper that she should be attended by a lady. He has impressed upon me the need for total discretion and secrecy.'

'Quite, quite,' said Henry. 'She's here then? Or *it* is here. For how long?'

'Long enough only to bring her in and see her secure, Your Grace.'

He stood, and was able to take a good look at Anne Boleyn. She was not as pretty as her sister, yet it was apparent that she had a certain quality: a playful charm that lit her eyes and touched her smile when she spoke to him. She had dark hair, worn long. She had large, wide eyes and these were dark, too, so that he found himself entranced by them. He couldn't help but notice that her dress was cut low in the French style. Of course it was; she had spent time at court in France. Curtseying a second time she afforded him a view between her breasts and he looked and felt guilty for doing so, dutifully casting his thoughts to The More and Katherine.

But he could smell Anne, he realised. He became aware, in fact, that her scent was rising, growing stronger. Somewhere inside him a longing made itself known. A longing that was not human, he knew.

One he should ignore.

She led him out of the withdrawing room and into a wide hall with views out on to the gardens.

'Where are your servants?' he asked as they reached a door which opened on to a flight of stone steps leading down, light dancing on the walls.

'All confined to quarters, Your Majesty,' she said, 'on my father's orders.'

'None have seen the beast?'

'Nor have they seen you, Your Majesty.'

'And you, Lady Anne. Have you set eyes on the creature?'

'Indeed I have, and was most struck by her.'

'You were not given fright, my lady?'

'Indeed no, Your Grace. She has human shape.'

'Even so, with your knowledge of its natural form . . .'

'I marvelled at the grace and dignity of the thing,' she said, adding playfully, 'I find myself most in admiration when confronted by such elegance and power.'

Now they came to the bottom of the steps. Here, iron cressets on poles had been set out to light the way to a door. Anne knocked, and the door was opened by her father, who bowed to the King as they entered a damp chamber with stone walls so dark they were almost black. Was it a trick of the flickering light, or did Henry see Anne and her father exchange a secretive smile as they passed through? Either way he did not dwell on it. His attention went to Norfolk and Compton who both bowed. And then to the wall . . .

Slumped there was a woman, unconscious, her hands and feet manacled, chains attached to metal pins driven into the wall. She half sat, half knelt, and her head lolled with the weight of a metal apparatus she wore over her head and face, which was a branks – or scold's bridle as they were known – a mask made of rusty metal strips locked at the neck. They were used to punish women said to be nags or gossips, but the blacksmith must have made some alterations to this one because there were spikes on the inside, too, so that if she transformed she would impale herself upon them.

Quite what he'd been expecting, Henry wasn't sure. After all, he knew the wolf creature was a woman. Had he imagined her with big ears and sharp teeth and hairy elbows? He'd pictured an ugly creature, certainly. At least in the sense of seeing the evil within. Yet he found himself admiring her; he knew what Lady Anne had meant. Wolsey had always told him that Malchek and his rebel Arcadians were evil manifest; that they claimed oppression at the hands of demonkind in order to pursue their real agenda, which was advancement and the acquisition of power.

Again Henry found himself wondering what was the truth. Because his first instinct was not to hurt this creature or see her kind defeated, it was to rush and release her from her chains.

'Is this . . .' he started. He looked around himself, Boleyn, Norfolk, Compton and Anne watching him. 'Is this necessary?'

The prisoner stirred. Moved her head. She made a groaning sound but it was muffled and Henry realised that the branks had a mouthpiece. Designed to stop tongues wagging they were often spiked, too. This particular mouthpiece would be spiked, he'd wager.

She was coming round now, her eyes flickering open and closed, rolling up into her head, everything about her so human. Then she was gagging and spluttering in distress at the unfamiliar piece of metal forced into her mouth.

'Undo it,' ordered Henry.

'But, Your Majesty,' protested Boleyn.

'Where's your humanity, man? Undo it now.'

'We lay ourselves at risk if we do, Majesty,' warned Norfolk. 'The creature may transform . . .'

'She is manacled. You are armed.'

'Even so . . .'

'*Do it.*'

Norfolk's eyes flashed momentarily but he obeyed. He and Boleyn approached the prisoner and Boleyn drew his sword to hold at the creature's neck as Norfolk unlocked the metal mask and lifted it from her. He did it gingerly, the thing being covered in spikes designed to inflict maximum damage. They had already, Henry saw: her face bled from where it had knocked against the spikes in transit.

With the mask off, her eyes closed and she savoured the feel of being released from the apparatus, like an animal freed from a trap. When she opened her eyes she gazed at Henry from beneath strands of black hair and her mouth hung open, panting slightly.

'Lady Anne?' said Henry.

'Your Highness?'

'May you fetch the prisoner water?'

'Yes, Your Grace.' She left.

'I don't want that thing used again,' Henry said, indicating the branks that Norfolk held.

'As you wish, Majesty,' said Norfolk, 'but if I may say, it's a mistake to underestimate the creature. The villagers we spoke to described her transformation. How she killed a man.'

'You went there personally?'

'Yes, Your Grace.'

'And did you ask after Thomas More?'

'We did, Your Majesty. Of him there was no sign.'

There came a dry, strangulated sound from the prisoner, almost like a laugh, and Norfolk stepped forward and struck her with the back of his hand.

'I thought I made myself clear,' he boomed. Spittle flecked his beard. '*You* are not to make a sound.'

Her eyes blazed. For a moment it looked as though Norfolk was about to strike her again and Henry was about to move and restrain him when Anne returned, studiedly oblivious to the atmosphere in the room. Approaching the prisoner with a bowl, cup and muslin, she offered her a drink then began wiping blood from her face.

For some moments there was near-silence in the chamber. Just Anne murmuring instructions to her patient, working quickly but tenderly, disregarding the danger. In return, Aisha watched her intently, a half-smile on her face.

The men, meanwhile, waited too. Until it became apparent that all were expecting His Majesty to speak. So he did.

Without ceremony he said: 'Where is Malchek?'

Aisha tore her gaze from Anne and moved her head to regard him, smouldering eyes taking him in.

Did she know? he wondered. Did she guess his secret?

And if so, would she say?

'So you can take your revenge?' she said.

'Quite so,' he said.

She smiled sardonically.

Norfolk charged forward. 'Then we shall force the information out of you, just as we did the youngling,' he exclaimed.

'Information I do not have, My Lord,' she sneered at him.

'Thomas, prepare the adjacent chamber, please,' ordered Norfolk. 'Bring braziers, pokers and tongs. We shall *burn* Malchek's whereabouts from her.'

But Henry could tell from her scent that she was telling the truth.

'No,' he said to Norfolk, 'there will be no more torture. It would do us no good anyway. She tells the truth.'

'As you wish, Majesty,' said Norfolk, bowing and throwing a puzzled look at Boleyn.

Henry and the wolfen looked at each other. *She knows*, he thought. *She can smell it on me, just like the youngling in the Tower. She knows I have the curse.*

She fixed him with her gaze, drawing him in. 'Let me tell you about our people, My Lord,' she purred.

Henry felt a stirring inside.

'Go on,' he said.

'My forefathers were banished in The Fall,' she began, 'along with the rest of demonkind. Clans were left on earth to do our father's work . . .'

Henry sneered. 'His *work*? You mean the devil's work. The spread of evil?'

'For good to exist there must be evil, My Lord. Each has its worth dictated against a measure of the other. Our kind is as necessary to the Kingdom of Earth as yours.'

'So you say. And then what happened?'

'Clans rose and fell. In the early centuries warlords battled constantly. The Baal became the most powerful of all the demonic dynasties. They ruled over us. They also harboured the most bitterness at being left on earth plain; they felt they should have taken their rightful place at Father's side down below. And though they did the master's bidding and continue to do so, they were unable to direct their resentment towards him. Instead it was directed downwards and just as in your society, My Lord, the lower orders were ruled over with brutality, and lowest of them all were our people – the Arcadians. From the dawn of time our clan was forced into slavery by the Baal. We were stripped of rank and forbidden to mix with either humankind or demonkind. All across the earth, Arcadians were forced to live as outcasts. In the wilds. In the deserts and forests. We were hunted for sport by the Baal, our packs slaughtered. And over the centuries our numbers dwindled. The persecution continued, but with less frequency than before. Humankind had risen by then and the Baal had fresh sport: they hated humankind and brought plague and warfare and misery upon them.'

'*Hated?*'

'Hated in the past, My Lord,' the wolf woman said sardonically, 'because of the treaty, remember?'

The treaty? Of course, the treaty. It had been signed at

the Field of the Cloth of Gold, so named because the fabric had been in such plentiful supply. When the sun lit upon it, everything had glittered; fountains dispensed red wine for over two weeks.

And at the centre of it all, Henry, sportsman by day. A peacock at night. And as he'd pranced and strutted, Wolsey had been working tirelessly behind the scenes, drawing up a pact between church and demons. For Henry it was a chance to create a legacy as peacemaker. Or so he was told by Wolsey.

But had Wolsey been aware that by signing the treaty they were creating other, disenfranchised parties? The wolfen.

'Why?' he asked now. 'Why did the Baal sign the treaty if their hatred of humankind is so great?'

'Because they were instructed to. Our fathers agreed on Natural Order, and that it should be preserved via a truce. Pontiffs were instructed.'

'And your clan?'

'We sought to rise. Our leader Klarek was the strongest of us and he called upon Arcadians to shake off their imprisonment and go forth. Word went across earth plain and the wolfen began to emerge from their hiding places, going among humankind and demonkind, becoming stronger. But Klarek was killed by a Baal assassin, and most of his pack slaughtered. His brother survived, and so did his mate.'

'His brother?'

'Malchek.'

'His mate?'

'Me.'

Henry started.

'Is that so strange?' she said, eyes mocking him. 'You, too, took your brother's mate on the occasion of his death. Just as it was your brother, Arthur, who was due to reign and you became King in his stead, so it was with my Lord Malchek. He became wolfen leader, and vowed to continue his brother's struggle. And just as it was that you took Katherine, your brother's *virgin* bride, so it was that he took me, although I wasn't a virgin, we deviants being less strict about that kind of thing.'

She smiled. 'So you see, My Lord, you have made the mistake of believing this is a conflict that involves you, when it is not. You are a mere diversion, your child a casualty of a battle started not by you, but by the Lord Chancellor and his ally, the demon Lefsetz.'

Henry, his thoughts dark, said, 'Your Malchek gained an extra adversary when he staged his attack. Perhaps he underestimated me. For my revenge will be terrible.'

'Oh yes? And how are efforts to find My Lord proceeding?' she asked, light dancing in her eyes. 'Your men currently scouring the countryside, what success have they reported?'

She laughed at Henry's scowl. 'You and your forces will never be a match for us, My Lord,' she replied. 'You may have the numbers, you may have the means, but our kind has something yours does not. We have resolution and will. We have heart.'

'Then you underestimate me, wolfen.' Henry's smile was thin and joyless. 'My desire to see Malchek dead is greater than you can possibly imagine. He has only himself to blame for that.'

XXIV

Henry awoke. Suddenly. Not the way he normally did, feeling bleary and disorientated, but focused and sharp, aware immediately of . . .

A need.

It was pitch-black in the chamber. The embers of the fire glowed in the grate, the smell of the logs hung in the room. He cast aside sheets and put his feet to the rug, feeling the tuft of it between his toes. It was really quite luxuriant, and he made a mental note to praise Boleyn on his choice of rugs although for some reason he found it irritating that Boleyn had more sumptuous rugs than he, the King.

A log in the fire crackled and it startled him. Then he found himself listening to the wind outside, hearing tree branches rustle and sigh. At the same he became aware of his body, and of an aching feeling.

The same feeling as the previous evening.

No, he thought. He was going to resist it this time. There would be no more stags' heads, no more beards of crusted blood and tattered nightshirts.

But at the same time he knew that he couldn't resist it. He went to the window to see the moon, and of course it was full and beckoning to him. He reached to open the window and admit the night, but it was sealed. He went to others. The same. Now his breathing began to quicken. Tomorrow he would fight it he decided; another time he would fight it, but not now – now his body ached to be wolf again. He felt the sensations flowing through him, hastened by the rhythm of the moon. He needed to change.

But just change, that was all, he pledged. Just change and run free. No hunting, no killing, no stags. Nothing for which he might feel shame the next day. No, he would simply enjoy it, the feeling of it. The freedom.

But how? He needed to be outside. He needed to be with the land.

Trying not to panic, he tiptoed over to a door and opened it gently, peering inside to see an adjacent chamber; from within it, the sound of snoring William. Then he went to another door, this one opening on to reveal – aha! – hanging garments, his clothes. Success.

He pulled a selection out and cast them on to the bed.

Several minutes later, he had still not managed to negotiate the intricacies of the jerkin. Now he wished he had paid more attention in the mornings when he was being dressed, instead of staring out of the windows or indulging in trivial banter.

Then again, did he need a jerkin? He felt his body shift, and a powerful wave of desire passing through him so that he felt invincible and alive. No, he thought, he did not need clothes. Clothes belonged to his normal self, his mundane self.

The wave passed, leaving behind the certainty that his wardrobe was of little consequence. So – sorry, jerkin. His nightshirt would have to do.

Some moments later, having crept through William's chamber, he found himself in the hallway, unsure where to go next. He tried to recall the last time he had been awake and alone for so long, and could not, and he considered returning to his chamber.

Then there was a crackling sound and he felt the needles, his fur pushing its way through the skin. And his decision was made for him.

He walked along the dark hallway, the only light that of the dying torches. At the end was a door. Here, perhaps? Opening it, he peered through, hoping to see steps. Instead, he was greeted by the warm scent of the bedroom – a lady's bedroom. Too late, he realised he had opened the door to Lady Anne's bedchamber and before he could close the door again a shadow at the bed shifted and a voice said, 'Your Majesty?'

'Lady Anne,' he whispered 'my most humble apologies, but I hoped this was the door to below stairs.'

She was already getting out of bed. He heard the swish of her nightgown and saw a shape move to a dresser, plucking from it a robe. As she came forward and into the meagre light, he breathed in her scent. It was strong, primal and he found himself drawn to her, all of a sudden having to resist the urge to gather her up in his arms and bury his head into her so that he could breathe her in.

'Majesty,' she said quietly, 'I'm sure that I can fetch you wine if your throat is dry. Or is there something else?'

He crackled slightly and hoped she didn't hear. He felt hairs growing against his clothes and his feet in his boots began to expand, becoming uncomfortable.

'Lady Anne,' he managed, his voice a growl, 'perhaps you could help me find my way below stairs.'

'You wish to visit the servants' quarters? I'm sure they would be most honoured, though their appreciation would only be matched by their bemusement at the lateness of the hour, not to mention Your Majesty's attire. They might be forgiven for wondering if His Majesty was . . .' and here she moved her head to study him carefully, 'sleepwalking?'

He looked down at himself, then at her. Her eyes sparkled, a smile at her lips.

'No,' he chuckled, 'I assure you I'm not sleepwalking. And the servants can sleep easy in their pallets. I merely wish . . .'

He crackled again, and there was a brushing sound of hair extending. It dawned on him that she couldn't hear it, of course. The sounds of transformation were only audible to him. She might *see* it, though. He felt his feet grow some more.

He pressed on, 'I merely wish to reach the outside so that I may take some moon.'

'Some *moon*, Your Highness?' She smiled.

'Some air,' he corrected himself.

'In that case, I can lead you there,' she said. 'Wait one moment.'

Anne returned with a candle and led them to another door. He made sure to remember the route back as she led them downstairs, across the main hall and to a huge front door inset with a smaller door, which she opened, bending slightly to go through then beckoning Henry to do the same.

Now they stood at the top of the main entrance steps, overlooking the grounds, the lawns and hedges swathed in mist which bubbled on the river, rippling over a footbridge. Henry reached to his face and felt hairs there, knew he needed to be alone but at the same time wanted to stay close to Anne, to drink in her scent and luxuriate in the sense of her nakedness beneath her nightclothes; he could hear the rustle of the material as it rose and fell with the heaving of her breasts and before he knew it he was bringing his face close to her, sniffing her animalistically – he couldn't help himself.

Crackle.

But he must. He must help himself.

Crackle.

Must be alone, too, before it was too late.

'Thank you, Lady Anne,' he said, his voice now noticeably deeper than normal.

'That is quite all right, Your Majesty,' she curtseyed. 'But excuse me, isn't this a little . . . irregular. Shouldn't you be with your staff, a guard?'

She indicated above her where the guards patrolled. Of course, he thought, the guards. And silently he blessed her. But now he really needed to be alone.

'Oh no,' he insisted, trying to hide the new timbre to his voice by passing a hand over his mouth at the same time. 'I often take the night air at Greenwich Palace alone. In truth, Lady Anne, it is because I like to run.'

'You run, Your Majesty?'

'It is excellent exercise.'

Crackle.

'In your nightshirt?'

'Indeed. It is most bracing to feel the wind in the nethers.'

She blushed a little.

'Now I need detain you no longer, Lady Anne,' and Henry made a deep bow just as one of his boots split its seams and out bulged a hairy foot. Quickly he hid it behind the other as he took her hand to kiss then with a series of flamboyant waves left her standing on the steps as he descended them two at a time, reaching the grass and breaking into a run, glancing behind him to see her watching him, his nightshirt bouncing around his knees as he ran.

Crackle, crackle.

At the same time as Henry was exercising at Hever Castle, his Lord Chancellor, Thomas Cardinal Wolsey sat in his office at Hampton Court many miles away, vexed.

'What on earth am I going to tell the fucking Pope?' he raged at his clerks. 'Either I need a reason why we should declare war on the wolfen, for His Holiness, or I need a reason we shouldn't, for the King. What the bloody hell is he up to anyway?' He looked at Dudley. 'Hever, you say?'

'Yes, Your Eminence.'

'What's he doing there? I need to know. I need to know anything that will help my application. Are we keeping an eye on Compton?'

'Yes, Your Eminence. He is watched all the time by Frank and Walters. They never let him leave their sight.'

'Boleyn?' He spat the name.

'At Hever.'

'Norfolk?'

'Stays with his brother-in-law, at Hever.'

Plotting his downfall, no doubt. Meanwhile at court, Thomas Cromwell, that fucking traitor, would be worming his way into the King's affections.

'And why haven't we heard from Sir Thomas More yet, for God's sake?' he snapped. 'You did send somebody to look for Thomas?'

'Indeed, Your Eminence,' said Child.

'Who, Child, who? Not one of the clerks, I hope? Not his cleric, the one who's blaming himself?'

'No, sir, it was a task requested by a Protektor – one who holds a particular affection for Sir Thomas.'

Wolsey nodded, knowing who was meant. 'Then if he's alive Sir Thomas More will be found, we can at least be assured of that.'

XXV

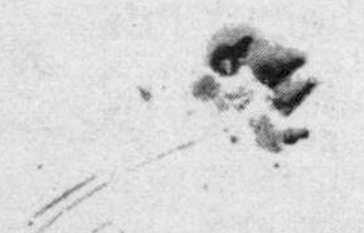

It was dark and smoky in the Butchered Cow, as it always was, the gloom oppressive, despite the noise of the place. The smell of ale seemed to hang about the damp boards like mist; it was ingrained in the walls and in the woodwork and the tables at which the drinkers sat stank of it – not that they minded. Some were hunched over their tankards, so low that the brims of their hats were almost touching the tabletops, talking in low voices and whiling the evening away with grumbles and gossip; others were in groups, rattling dice in cups or laughing and joking. They banged their empty tankards on the table and called for more ale, brought to them by the only woman in the room, a smiling barmaid who was as practised at dispensing ale as she was of dancing out of the way of the men's grabbing hands. She would do even more dancing as the night grew older.

Talk was mainly of the soldiers who had descended upon the region. The King's men were abroad and conducting searches, though for what was unclear. So when the door to the tavern opened to admit a blast of cold air, the men turned and they half expected to see a uniform in the doorway.

Instead it was a solitary figure, wearing dark, expensive

robes that almost reached the floor, with a hood pulled up to hide the face: a stranger, not known around these parts.

Conversation was apt to die down at such moments and sure enough the loud chatter in the tavern was suddenly hushed, replaced instead by a low murmur. The brims of hats dipped lower; the men watched the newcomer turn, close the door, then stand in the shadows for a moment, a silent, dark figure. Now the stranger moved across the room, boots clacking on the boards, and to a counter where stood the owner, the barmaid and two regulars clutching tankards, one of them regarding the floor, the other watching with flinty eyes and a set mouth. This was Pearson – Pearson had something of a reputation in the village.

At the counter the stranger stopped, reached to the hood and drew it back to reveal blonde hair that she shook loose a little, her beauty greeted by an audible gasp; even the barmaid pursed her lips a little, and almost reflexively her hands went to her hips.

The woman looked carefully around the room, not at all intimidated by her surroundings. The men regarded her back with watchful eyes, no longer studying the table tops, fascinated and entranced by the new arrival. Some licked their lips and there was much nudging, some sniggers. Ribald remarks were exchanged.

She took it all in, the blonde woman. A smile touched her lips, then she turned to give the room her back, moving up to the counter, where one of the regulars shifted away to let her in. Pearson, however, remained where he was, so that he was standing close to her, deliberately looking her up and down.

'Good evening,' she said to the barman, 'I'm hoping you might be able to help me – I'm looking for a man.' She said it loudly enough for the entire tavern to hear.

'Looks like you've come to the roit place then, m'dear,' said Pearson, although he said it to the room, which roared with laughter.

She smiled, ignored him. 'He's a peasant, he goes by the name of Norman,' she added. 'He has some information I require. I was told I might find him here.'

All eyes turned to a corner of the tavern, where Norman sat, his eyes wide,

'Thank you,' she said. 'Norman, perhaps we could step outside for a moment in order that we can talk.'

Norman stared but didn't move.

'Come on, Norman, I won't bite.'

Then Pearson stepped away from the counter so that he was in front of the woman, facing her. His stare grew harder, if such a thing were possible, but his grin was sloppy and he swayed slightly as he stood.

'Now you just wait a minute, girlie,' he said, with a sneering tone. 'Norman ain't going nowhere, especially not till you tell us what's on your mind.'

She frowned a little. Looked him over. 'And how are you related to Norman?' she asked politely.

'Well, it looks like I've just become his guardian,' replied Pearson. 'Protecting him against a little slip of a thing who seems to be getting a bit above herself if you don't mind my saying so.'

There was a chortle from around the tavern.

'I come from the office of the Lord Chancellor Thomas Cardinal Wolsey himself,' smiled the woman. 'To be honest, if you don't mind me saying, it's you who's getting above himself.'

Pearson snorted. 'I doubt that to be the truth, that the Lord Chancellor sends pixie blondes to do his bidding.' He threw the last words over his shoulder, slurring them slightly.

'You would be surprised,' she said evenly, 'we pixie blondes have a habit of getting the job done, the job in this case being to speak to Norman. I intend to get it done. So I suggest that you go back to your ale and leave me to my business.'

'And what business might that be? Far as I can see, the only business a lady has in a tavern is serving the ale, and I'm afraid that position is already taken.' More titters, this time led by the barmaid.

'Or perhaps you have come to entertain us. Is that right Norman, have you paid for a singer for the evening?' Pearson licked his lips that were already wet. 'Or perhaps another kind of entertainment?'

'Look, you're drunk, you're forgetting your manners, so I'll forget you said that on condition you stand aside.'

But her voice was steely, the men in the tavern noticed.

Not Pearson, though. Oblivious to the sudden shift in atmosphere, enjoying himself too much. 'Perhaps you are here to entertain us with a dance,' he said loudly. 'What is it you're hiding under there?' And with that he reached forward to pluck at her robes.

He froze. Her hand went to his. Her eyes narrowed. Then Pearson was pulling back and snatching a dagger from his belt.

'Well, well,' he said loudly. 'It looks as though blondie is carrying a sword.' He waved the knife. 'Now what you be needing with a sword, my lady?'

She sighed. 'Oh, I don't know. In case I need to cut some cheese? Why would it matter to you anyway? '

'I'll take it if you don't mind,' he said, '*then* you can be on your way.'

Behind, the other customers watched wide-eyed. Some of them began to edge away, sensing that their visitor was unlikely to give up her weapon willingly.

Instead, after a moment of seeming to consider, she reached a hand to her robes. Pearson jabbed threateningly with the dagger but she held her palms out and moved slowly, drawing back the robes.

Below she wore a leather tunic. At her waist was the hilt of her sword. She reached across herself towards it, her eyes never leaving those of Pearson.

'Other hand,' said Pearson, grinning at his own cleverness, insisting with the knife.

She obliged. With finger and thumb she used her other hand to gently remove the sword by its handle. It slid slowly from the scabbard. All held their breath.

Now, with a sudden movement of her wrist she flicked the sword up and out of the sheath so that one moment it was in her fingers, the next gone.

It happened in the blink of an eye. For a fraction of a second Pearson gaped at the spot where the sword should have been, then his eyes flicked up in time to see it slice down towards his knife hand.

Which he snatched out of the way, the sword thunking to the wood, where it stuck, vibrating slightly.

A smile of victory had already begun to gather at Pearson's

mouth before he realised he had left himself exposed, his knife pointing in the wrong direction, giving the blonde woman enough room to step forward, twist and smash him across the nose with her forearm. There was the unmistakeable sound of metal meeting face. A sword was not all she had hidden beneath her robes it seemed.

Blood fountained from his nose, his eyes rolled upwards. His knees met the boards as he sank downwards then seemed to wobble as she stepped forward, put her boot to his chest and was about to push him gently backwards when she thought better of it, took a step back and kicked him in the face.

He dropped face first and lay still, blood spreading from beneath him.

There was silence in the tavern as the blonde woman beckoned Norman then retrieved her sword. Norman was already scrambling obediently over as she sheathed it.

'Don't worry,' she told him as he stood some feet away, adam's apple bobbing. 'You're in no danger – unless you're planning on calling me a blonde pixie.' She looked at him. 'Are you planning on calling me a blonde pixie?'

Norman, younger, taller and more spindly than Pearson, shook his head vigorously.

'Good, then let's take this outside.'

She glanced around to check whether or not there were any more challengers – the customers, owner and barmaid all found something of interest to study at their feet and satisfied, she ushered Norman outside.

'Right,' she said, once there, 'I'm told you may know something about the whereabouts of a friend of mine – he goes by the name of Sir Thomas More.'

XXVI

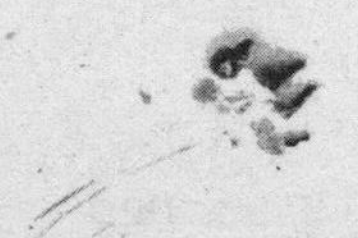

Rain sluiced down in sheets, turning the village square into a seething lake of mud, making it treacherous for Master Hoblet the Witchfinder General as they came tramping across to address the crowd gathered around the pyre. There were two to three hundred folk in number, all standing stony-faced in the torrent, hats plastered to heads, hair hanging in thick, wringing wet clumps, shoulders drooped. Some sat on upturned baskets, others leant on pitchforks – even as they sank into the mud. Still others had climbed aboard carts that had been brought in to afford onlookers a better view.

Yesterday word had swiftly spread about the nobles who took the wolf woman, and there had been much grumbling about the cancellation of what most considered to be the main attraction. However, Agatha had assured them that there would be a burning the following day and had retired that evening comfortable in the knowledge that sufficient people would remain to watch the burning, even though it was not quite the spectacle originally promised. She would receive her dues from the taverns and she would collect the money from two executions if not three – though this had been more than compensated for thanks to the gift given to her by the Duke of Norfolk.

Hob had been reading as she counted her money on the bed, burbling as she did so, about her new chimney and how she was going to ask Master Brookes the builder to make changes. They would be having chequered brickwork, that much was certain. Perhaps some tiles, too.

Hob had stood, walked over to her and placed his book on the bed next to the money.

'You'd better get that thing off this bed, Hoblet,' she warned, 'I'm trying to count here.'

'No, Agatha, look,' he said, 'read the title.'

'"*De optimo rei pubic . . .*",' she read, then looked up at him, eyes narrow. 'Pubic? What's this you got here, Hoblet? If this is one of your erotic texts you can put aside any deviant designs you have on me, for such ungodly things are behind me.'

'No.' Hob fought nausea. 'Not "*pubic*", "*publicae*" – "*publicae statu deque nova insula Utopia*".'

'Talk proper,' she said, almost distractedly, for the word *Utopia* had jumped out at her, and now she looked closely at the cover. 'This is it, is it?' she said. 'This is the bestseller. This yours?'

'Yes,' said Hob.

She looked at him.

He sighed. 'Aye, that it be. Look, Agatha, it's written in Latin and it begins with a series of correspondence between Sir Thomas More and Peter Gilles. Do you know what this means?'

Her mouth dropped open. 'All my saints, Hoblet . . .' she exclaimed.

'Exactly.'

'You can read Latin. *You?*'

He sighed. 'Yes, I can read Latin.'

She had guffawed, slapping her hands to her thighs. 'Well, I've heard it all now. Master Hoblet, a scholar, reading stories in Latin. No, forgive me, Hoblet, not stories, but "speculative political essays" no less.'

'No, Agatha, look,' he tried, 'don't you know what this might mean. That he's the real Sir Thomas More. That he's telling the truth.'

'Oh, right, that, yeah. I know.'

'*You know?*' he said.

'Of course I know. You only have to look at him to know he's of good stock. Don't you see his hands, the cut of his hair? What about the way he speaks? He speaks the way you do, ain't that right, Hoblet?' She dug him in the ribs. 'Plus, he was very familiar with *Utopia*, wasn't he? And how he was when the duke and his friend turned up, well, you just can't fake a thing like that.'

'The Duke of Norfolk told you, didn't he?'

'Now steady on there, Hoblet . . . yes, he did. But not in so many words, like. He didn't actually say that man in there is Sir Thomas More, but he sort of did.'

'I knew it,' said Hoblet.

'Aye, you catch on fast, Hoblet.' Agatha raised her eyebrows ironically.

'So what are we to do?' asked Hob.

'We'll do what's right and proper, of course,' said Agatha and Hob's heart sank, 'we'll burn him.'

It was not many moments later that the windows had begun to rattle from the force of the rain. Hob had sat at the window and looked out on to the saturated pyre and said, 'Do you remember Brasted?'

She mumbled something.

'You do, don't you?'

'I tell you what, Hoblet, you're always bringing up Brasted. How would you like it if every time we saw someone drunk in the street I reminded you of your past mistakes, eh?'

'My past mistakes didn't result in a poor girl—'

'A *witch*, Hoblet—'

'A *poor girl* taking so long to die, and dying in such agony that even the countryfolk who had gathered to watch her suffer had begun to plead for mercy on her behalf.'

Agatha pretended to study something on the boards, grinding it with the toe of her boot.

'She used witchcraft to delay the onset of the flames, Hoblet, we both know that.'

'No, the wood was wet. I have told you time and time again, we cannot proceed with burnings when the wood is wet. You ignored me that time, and we made enemies in Brasted for our supposed cruelty. We should have had a hanging that day, Agatha. Rainy day burnings are a recipe for disaster.'

She pushed out her bottom lip. 'But hangings are *boring*.'

'Better to have a boring hanging than the crowd turn against us.'

'And?'

'Well look at the weather, Agatha. We can't do a burning, not in this weather.'

'It might ease off . . .'

'Even if it does, that wood is wet through.'

'We'll see,' she said. But Hob knew one thing about

Agatha. For all her faults – and these included greed and sadism, so some of the worst faults it was possible to have – she knew the value in keeping the crowd happy.

It didn't stop her being most glum that morning, though, when she had looked out of the window to see that not only was it still raining, but that it had worsened overnight; it had become torrential. It was a deluge.

Now they stopped a short distance away from the crowd, their backs to the goalhouse which was barely visible behind them such was the density of the rain – rain that had smudged the world a charcoal grey.

Hob stood and tried to look sinister, which was somewhat difficult given the weather, but still. Agatha cleared her throat. 'It grieves me to say this, oh yes it does, good people,' she said, and never was anything more true, for Agatha loved a good burning. 'But there will be no burning today.'

It took a split second for the information to sink in, during which the only sound in the square was the slapping of wet upon wet. Then the village folk began to shift and grumble. Agatha turned and scowled at Hob, as though the rain was his fault.

'But instead,' she continued, her hands on her hips, emphasising her point with a wagging finger, 'we will be hanging one of the accused, up on the hill, so join us, won't you, to see God's vengeance carried out, and a terrible beast despatched to meet his maker, wherever his maker might reside.'

Agatha's proclamations were not met with the usual gasps or a fainting or two, however, they were met with tuts and disgruntled looks.

'And we will be starting today, with the hanging of a most fearful lycanthrope,' continued Agatha. 'Then tomorrow we will be hanging the one who calls himself Sir Thomas More, who was apprehended by the plucky men of this here village after he was seen consorting with a werewolf in a most disgusting manner.' She wiped rain from her nose and spat.

'Mistress Hoblet?' came a call from within the crowd.

'Why yes, villager.' Agatha squinted to locate the source of the query.

'I wonder if we might hang Sir Thomas More today, Mistress Hoblet?'

'And why might that be, villager?' said Agatha. She pursed her lips and put her hands to her hips, not used to having her decisions questioned in such a way.

'I merely mean that I think I speak for everybody here when I say that we'd prefer to see this Sir Thomas More hanged. For there is a rumour going around that it is the real Sir Thomas More, and there are many here that have to return to our work and families on the morrow and would rather not have to sit through the hanging of a less prestigious sinner.'

'Step forward, villager,' commanded Agatha. At her side, Hob swallowed nervously.

The man stepped out of the crowd, rain coursing from his wide-brimmed hat. He regarded the witchfinder and his wife with fearful eyes.

'Just who do you think is in charge here?' asked Agatha.

'Master Hoblet?' ventured the villager.

Agatha was momentarily taken aback before remembering herself. 'Why, that's exactly right, it's Master Hoblet who's in charge here, and don't you forget it. And Master Hoblet has decided that Sir Thomas More is to die tomorrow.'

The villager turned to look at the crowd, shrugging his shoulders. In return came shouts of disapproval and pointing fingers as he was urged to continue negotiations.

'I think, Mistress Hoblet,' he gulped, 'those of us here would prefer to see Sir Thomas More hanged today.'

'Is this right?' called Mistress Hoblet over his head. There were murmurs of assent from the crowd. She scowled. Under her breath she said, 'You better not be finding any of this funny, Hoblet, or woe betide you.'

Hob said nothing, just hoped that the bristles of his beard were not quivering with the effort of suppressing his smile.

Agatha sighed heavily. 'But the weather might have improved by tomorrow,' she argued, 'we might be able to have our burning after all.'

There was much shaking of heads. The village spokesman drew back and there were some moments of consultation. He looked a little braver and his voice contained a little more authority when he returned to face Agatha. 'If it's all the same to you, Mistress Hoblet, we'll hang the noted cleric today and the farm boy tomorrow.'

He had overdone it, Hob knew. Gone was deference, replaced by confidence – confidence that slowly ebbed away as Agatha fixed him with one of the most awe-inspiring and punishing looks he had ever seen her give, which made it the leader in an overcrowded field. Her eyes narrowed to dangerous slits, her mouth worked around the shaft of the pipe. Even with mud flats of the square between them; even with the massed countryfolk at his back, nothing could quite protect him from the stare.

'I look at you,' she said quietly, 'and you know what? I wouldn't be at all surprised if at some point in the future I find myself questioning you on charges of lycanthropy.' The villager paled. But even so, Agatha knew when she was beaten. 'Very well,' she said, 'I shall ask Master Hoblet what he thinks.

She turned to Hob. 'Right, there's only one thing for it, Hoblet,' she said, 'we're going to have to get his Lordship out here.'

She turned back to address the crowd. 'Very well,' she called. 'We shall hang Sir Thomas More. Summon the priest!'

XXVII

On the hillside overlooking Darenth three men in leather jerkins heaved upright a gallows, which stood silhouetted against the charcoal sky. One of the men placed a three-legged stool beneath it as the other two went to work on it, the rhythmic knock-knock of their hammers carried by the wind to the village below.

There the villagers stood in a quiet, respectful knot, watching the work on the hillside above. The rain had eased and was now a steady drizzle; but a bone-chilling wind had blown up, and they wrapped shawls tightly around themselves or clasped shirts at their necks.

From the gaolhouse came a noise and the spectators turned to see the priest emerge. He wore a black hat and robes and read from the Book of the Revelation of John, his voice rich with solemnity. Behind him came the Witchfinder General, face set. Behind him came Agatha and the gaoler, who was grasping a length of rope, the other end of which tied the hands of Sir Thomas More, who wore a hood and who staggered, blindly shouting protestations in the direction of no one in particular. 'When His Majesty discovers what you've done here today, he'll have you executed,' he called, attempting to address the crowd, though his comments actually went in the direction of the well, '*all* of you,' he told the well.

The priest ceased his reading, looking irritated at the disruption. All looked at More.

'Your guilt has been proved,' called Agatha.

'Proof? There hasn't been any proof!'

'Now you listen here,' said Agatha, 'we need to hear from this man of the cloth, not sinner talk from the likes of you.'

'I'm not a sinner, I'm Sir Thomas More.'

'Now hush your mouth or it's the turnip for you,' warned Mistress Hoblet.

'Oh, for God's sake. You're going to hang me, I hardly think stuffing a turnip in my mouth will make any diff—'

Agatha had taken hold of his head with one hand, using the other to feel for a mouth beneath the hood. Then inserted a turnip. More, unable to open his jaw sufficiently wide to discharge the vegetable, lapsed into silence and Agatha gave a nod to the priest, who continued his reading: 'Come, gather yourselves together to the great supper of God that you may eat the flesh of kings . . .'

Above them on the horizon was a black smudge. Here a figure on horseback watched the procession winding its way towards the gallows, which stood further along the hillside. The rider wore a black hooded garment, its hood down and lying across her shoulders to reveal long blonde hair and features that entranced all who gazed upon them – including the peasant, Norman, who stood by her side.

'Here they comes, m'lady,' said Norman, 'just as I promised they would.'

'And that's definitely him, is it?' she asked.

'Aye, so it is, m'lady,' said the villager. 'Why, it's been said that he quotes from his books.'

'Then you may have your payment,' she said, 'and not a word of this to anyone.'

'Ah,' he grinned nastily, altogether more confident than he had been the night of their first meeting at The Butchered Cow. 'You didn't mention keeping quiet about it all. I'm afraid to say that I shall be wanting extra for that . . .'

His grin froze. From nowhere, she had drawn a sword – so quickly that her robes were still settling about her as she held it to his throat.

'If I were you, villager,' she said, not unkindly, 'I would keep quiet about helping me today; I don't think your neighbours will be happy to learn that you have aided the escape of today's entertainment.'

Further away along the hillside, on the opposite side of the gallows and unnoticed by all, was the lone figure of a man. He had a pale, pasty pallor, and shone as though he had been rubbed with pig's fat, and he shambled slowly, weaving slightly as he came, his arms out slightly in front of him as he approached the gallows.

Where the noose swung in the wind.

'And the beast was taken,' the priest was reading as the procession congregated around the gallows. A line of barren women formed, ready to touch the hand of the hanged man in order that they should conceive, 'and with him the *false prophet*,' and here he pointed at the condemned man, 'who wrought signs before him, wherewith he seduced them who received the character of the beast . . .'

The gaoler and Mistress Hoblet brought forward the false prophet in question and helped him up to the stool, his hands still bound. One of the carpenters donned a hangman's mask – being multi-skilled as he was – stepped up to the stool and was there to receive him. The stool wobbled dangerously for a moment as the hangman placed the noose around his neck, tightened the knot then stepped down.

'. . . and all the birds were filled with their flesh . . .' finished the priest. He shut the Bible with a snap. All looked expectantly in his direction. The wind whipped his robes. He nodded and the hangman acknowledged, reached down and yanked the stool away.

The body dropped. The turnip shot from his mouth . . .

'The *escape* of Sir Thomas More?' said Norman to the blonde rider, further along the hilltop.

'That's right, villager.'

'Well,' he said, looking over at the gallows, 'you'd better get a move on, then.'

She swivelled in the saddle in time to see the stool yanked away, More's body fall then be snapped tight by the noose, something shooting from his mouth.

'Jesu,' she snapped and pulled round her horse, digging in her heels – 'yah!' – and setting off across the hillside, low in the saddle, brandishing her sword, blonde hair flowing behind her.

More jerked and writhed on the rope.

'Yah!' she urged her horse. 'Come on, Griffin!' thundering

towards the gallows. The crowd were all staring at something and she saw a peasant moving slowly towards them looking disorientated, arms held out and rivers of sweat sluicing from him. At the same time somebody screamed, '*Sweating sickness! It's the sweating sickness!*' and suddenly the crowd was dispersing, mindful more of the infected man than the horse bearing down upon them.

More's dangling legs pumped.

Just the hangman at his post, the barren women still desperate for a touch of the dead man.

She dropped the reins and sat upright in the saddle, a matter of yards from the gallows now. She tossed her sword from her right hand to her left, brought the weapon across her body then flung out her right arm. She leant to the right, dangerously low in the saddle.

His legs gave one last convulsion.

She swept the sword across herself, cutting the rope and scooping up the body with her right arm, with a shout heaving it on to the neck of her horse, hoping that forward motion, God's grace and maybe just a little bit of luck would keep them upright.

Come on, Griffin.

But the sudden weight was too much. For her, for Griffin, whose legs buckled, and they all came crashing to the floor.

In a trice she was on her feet, sword held. Almost upon her was the sweating man and she swivelled on her haunches to sweep his legs out from under him, sending him sprawling to the ground where he remained motionless as she scuttled away. Perhaps she should have left him standing; he was at least an effective deterrent. For though most of the crowd were already halfway down the hillside, screaming, 'sweating sickness, sweating sickness,' the witchfinder, his wife and six or seven braver men remained, and they surged forward now, ahead of them the hangman. He met her boot as she pivoted and kicked, choosing to stun rather than hurt him, sending him reeling back. The others collectively thought twice and came to a halt.

Sir Thomas More had scrambled to his feet and immediately set off in a run. Still hooded, and panicking, he tore off in the wrong direction, returning to the gallows, his hands still tied, the severed noose dancing on his back.

'*Sir Thomas, watch* . . .' she tried to shout, but too late. With a solid thump the noted thinker ran into the gallows, rebounding with a yell of pain and falling to the ground, coughing.

'*Get her*,' shrieked an old crone who had a pipe in her mouth. That would be the Mistress Hoblet she had heard about, no doubt – she was bawling at the man who was obviously the Witchfinder General, who stood with his mouth open, deaf to her screams.

As were the men, thank the Lord. Brave they may have been, but thanks no doubt to their visitor's sword skills, not to mention her prowess at hand-to-hand combat, they shrank back as she flipped back her robes and sheathed her sword, then led Griffin to where More lay.

'Sir Thomas . . .' She bent to him, keeping one eye on the men who stood at bay. 'Sir Thomas . . .'

There was no response but the fabric of his hood pulsed in and out at his mouth so he was breathing at least. She went to remove the hood when something caught her eye. A swarthy-faced young man was almost upon her, lunging forward with a pitchfork. She sidestepped, taking hold of his pitchfork and snapping him forward, meeting his face with her forearm to send him sprawling. Another, with similar looks – a brother perhaps – stepped up. Rising, she flipped back her robes, part-drew her sword and stared hard at him from beneath her fringe. Daring him.

The villager gulped, then shrugged and backed away.

'Clever boy,' she said. Then she bent to the first peasant.

'You,' she said, 'you look like a big strong lad.'

Using the sword she prompted him to take the unconscious body of Sir Thomas More and lay it over the back of Griffin then climbed on too and grasped the reins. She caught Mistress Hoblet's eye, winked, then took off.

She rode for miles. There were many people abroad, but they paid her no mind. They were either hurriedly leaving the area, or helping to build the pyres to seal it off, to try to stop the spread of the epidemic. Until there came a sound from the prone body in front of her, and she stopped, pulled him from Griffin and laid him on the ground, then reached for a water bottle, knelt to him.

'My name is Lady Jane Seymour,' she said, pulling the noose over his head and discarding it, then reaching for the hood. 'I'm a member of the Protektorate assigned to the Royal Household. We have met, very briefly. We were introduced by Cardinal Wolsey. I'm very pleased to meet you properly, Sir T . . .'

She tailed off, the hood dangling from her hand. 'Who are you?'

'But you know who I am,' said Graham the Wolfman. 'I'm Sir Thomas More.'

She sat back on her haunches, aghast. On the horizon, the pyres had started to burn.

Part Three

THE QUEEN

XXVIII

Four months had passed since the outbreak and London's surrounding counties had been ravaged by the sickness. Rings of fire raged and soldiers had slaughtered thousands trying to escape the diseased areas, but even so – it had spread: in London, supposedly outside the worst-hit area, there had been forty thousand cases alone; tales from within the contaminated zones, meanwhile, were of widespread death and of barbarism.

Henry had been brought news of the sweating sickness the morning after his arrival at Hever Castle – after his night of hunting when he'd changed back into human form, scraped the blood from his face and retired fretfully to bed, worrying about fleas and rotting stags' heads – the kind of things a King might worry about, in fact, if he was also a werewolf.

When he awoke later, morning sun streamed through the window and Lady Anne Boleyn was standing at his bedside.

'My lady,' he said, sitting up and snatching at the sheets, hoping he didn't have foliage in his hair, or mud – or, worse, *blood* – still on his face. He itched and he wondered if his biggest fear had finally been realised: that he had finally caught fleas.

'My Lady, if William finds you here . . .' he started, though he didn't feel at all prim; it seemed natural for her to be there somehow. She was pale and wore a dress with a high neck. It rustled as she bent to him and held a finger to his lips. With her close, he had inhaled her, knowing at once that he must have her. He must have her.

'Sir William will be here in a moment, so I must not linger,' she whispered. 'You are to leave at once and I have a gift for you.'

'We are to leave?' said Henry, dismayed. He sat up in bed.

'At once, Your Majesty. Sir William is preparing your departure now. There has been an outbreak of the sweating sickness. The epidemic is spreading, the region is to be confined, roads and tracks sealed . . .'

'Lady Anne,' he said, his words tripping out of him, 'I want to thank you for your aid last night. It was most unorthodox of me to want air at such a late hour . . .'

She took a step back, curtseyed and blushed. 'I was pleased to be of service, Your Majesty,' she said. She fixed him with a meaningful gaze. 'And how do you feel this morning?'

Had she seen him change? No, of course not. Women don't pay werewolves early-morning visits, even those women with the obvious inner fortitude of Anne Boleyn. They screamed and ran. They alerted villagers with pitchforks and stout staffs.

'I feel well, thank you,' he replied carefully.

'So do I, Your Majesty,' she said. She bent to him and very gently, with the breath of angels, she kissed him.

Then she straightened and turned on her heel.

'Lady Anne,' he called, short of breath all of a sudden. She turned at the door, a hand to the frame, gazing back at him.

'Yes, Your Majesty,' she said.

'May I write to you?'

'I will await your letters, Your Majesty,' she said.

'And then perhaps see you again?'

She nodded, her eyes downcast. 'With luck the epidemic will be over swiftly,' she said.

With that they had parted; her to her quarters, he back to Greenwich Palace, where he'd been faced with the problem of the stag's head in his closet. He'd eaten most of it in the end, finding that its two days in storage had given it a certain gamey quality he did not at all mind.

Some days later the fever arrived at court so that Henry had been forced to dismiss most of his staff and flee Greenwich for Waltham Abbey. At Waltham Abbey, staff had also fallen ill, and within hours of the symptoms appearing, in the dead of a freezing night, Henry and his diminished court – now around a hundred of them – had taken flight. They next set up home in Hunsdon. There Henry had spent much time in the tower, taking pills and supping potions of treacle and herbs, watching the fires on the horizon, demanding daily reports of the worsening situation. He thought of Anne's kiss and his frustration made him ever more intemperate, his desire for her growing by the day.

At night the urges came but he had learnt that they were controlled by the moon; indeed, those close to him had remarked on His Majesty's sudden interest in astrology. When the moon was on the wane, he could resist The Change; when it was full, on the other hand . . .

When not thinking of The Change he would think of Anne, and he'd spend hours poring over her letters or composing his replies. He had discovered that she liked music, was a poet and loved to dance; that she had a mischievous sense of humour, but could also be resolute. In his last letter he had proposed to her that she be his mistress – his one, true mistress – but in her reply she had rebuked him for asking, reminding him of his vows to Katherine, who in truth faded a little more from his mind every day.

Court had moved to Tyttenhanger, where Henry's letters to Anne became even more ardent.

'Give yourself up, body and soul, to me,' he wrote.

Court moved to Ampthill, then to Old Moor Hall in Sutton Coldfield.

'Wishing myself, especially an evening, in my sweetheart's arms,' he wrote, 'whose pretty dukkies I trust shortly to kiss.' Bit risqué, that one, but even so.

Then back to Tyttenhanger and finally back to Waltham Abbey, where he wrote letters and brooded and on those occasions when not thinking of Anne, he grieved for George. Thoughts that led inevitably to Małchek, who was at large, out there somewhere, growing stronger, while he, Henry, was forced to hide away at the mercy of an illness.

And the worst of it all was this: of everybody at court Henry was the least likely to catch it. He took the medicines and potions as directed by his physicians and apothecaries but never for one moment thought he would contract the sickness; somehow he knew that he was stronger than the virus.

Instead, he sat and he brooded in his cold chamber. These days no fire burnt in the grate. Lately, he had taken against them.

XXIX

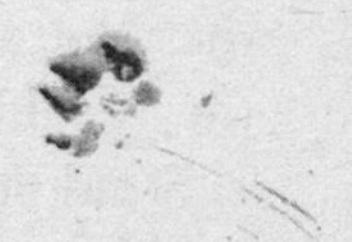

Young Billy Brookes, thirteen years old, stood at the well for the first of what would be many times that day, dangling the bucket over the lip of it and staring down into the hole, where the only sign that water lay there was the reflected light of the morning sun overhead.

'Hello,' he called.

His words came back to him. 'Hello.'

The bucket thunked woodenly on the side of the well as it descended, Billy lowering it hand over hand until it reached the bottom with a small splash and the rope went slack.

Would it ever run dry? he wondered. And if it did then what of Father, who lay desperately ill with the sickness, tended to by Billy's mother and sister? The sweat poured off him, soaking his bed linen, filling the room with its reek. His eyes were wide and wild and they stared at his family as if he did not know them. Sometimes he would sleep, whimpering and thrashing. Sometimes he would go still, so that Billy would worry he had been claimed by the sickness and call his mother, who would press her ear to his chest then nod to Billy: he was still alive, just.

Days ago she had sent his older brother Hugh into town,

a day's ride away. She had instructed him to bring a physician or apothecary, and to spread word that Master Brookes the builder lay very ill with the sickness and that he needed treatment at once. There were rich landowners who relied on Master Brookes for his craftsmanship, she said. Once they got word of his condition they would surely do all they could to hasten his recovery.

She'd smiled wearily at her family, gathered around the kitchen table, wincing at the sound of Father's suffering from the room next door. 'Prayers and faith, and with the help that Hugh brings, Father will live,' she told them, though none of them were reassured, because the certainty of her words was not matched by her eyes.

They expected Hugh back that day.

'Keep your eyes peeled,' she had told her children earlier that morning and as Billy wandered out to the well he cast his gaze over the horizon, praying to see his brother in the distance, waving at him, his horse laden with flasks and bottles.

He grunted as he retrieved the bucket, every spill making him flinch. His arms were strong from the work, but even so he found it exhausting, and having pulled the bucket to the rim he took a moment to catch his breath, resting his forehead on the stone for a minute.

The sound of wheels roused him and he looked up to see a covered wagon in the yard of their house. Men were getting down from it, but they were too far away to see properly. There were three of them, large men wearing outsized robes, despite the heat. One wore a wide-brimmed hat. One was taller than his companions and he could see this one gesturing to the other two.

And there was something about the way they carried themselves. The way they looked around. They spread out in the yard, as though to acquaint themselves with the Brookes' homestead. Instinctively, Billy ducked down to avoid being seen. At the same time he knew that these men had not come here to help them. They had not brought a cure for Father.

Still spread out, the men approached the home. Billy wondered if his mother and Grace were aware of them yet. Perhaps not if they were tending to Father. Especially not if Father was screaming and thrashing. He pictured them both on Father's bed, trying to restrain him, dabbing at him with wet cloths and wondering where Billy was with the water from the well, unaware of the danger in the yard.

Danger? he thought. Was there danger? Yes, he realised, knowing it now. There was danger. He wished for an axe or even a hoe. But Father insisted that all tools were kept in the barn when not in use. A workman always cared for his tools, he would tell them, that way the tools would look after you.

But the tools weren't looking after anybody in the barn, which was on the other side of the yard. To get to it he'd need to pass the house.

The men's backs were turned. They were moving cautiously closer to the cottage. They seemed to be inspecting it, as though unsure who might be inside.

Billy held his breath, then, keeping low, ran from the well to an enclosure which lay about halfway between the house and the well. There he crouched with his back to the fencing, catching his breath and steeling himself for a shout from the visitors. But none came and when he once again felt brave, he twisted around in the dust and peered through a slat in the fencing.

They remained where they were, still facing towards the house. As he stared, one of them turned to look his way, and he was too late to duck down. Rather than risk the movement he remained stock-still, praying the man wouldn't see him at the slats. He had squinty eyes and he seemed to be sniffing at the air, like a dog might do. He looked towards the enclosure, almost as though he sensed Billy might be there, and Billy held his breath, feeling a pressure in his bladder that he dearly hoped would disappear.

Then there came a noise, the sound of someone groaning that came from one of their wagons, and the leader was turning to the squinty-eyed man.

'Shut them up,' he said.

'Aye, My Lord,' said the squinty-eyed man, who cast one more suspicious look in Billy's direction then moved over to the back of one of the wagons. He spoke harshly to those within, who fell silent, then returned to join the other men.

The leader spoke to his men, his voice low. 'I smell two women and a man with the sickness. This must be it.'

They murmured in reply.

'We just want the sick man,' said the leader. 'I want no unnecessary deaths. I'm talking to you, Solly.' He indicated the squinty-eyed man. 'Any more carnage like yesterday we risk widespread panic. I need hardly tell you how much this would displease me.'

Solly gave a rather sickly smile in response.

'Keep human form,' he commanded, 'no matter the

provocation.' He pointed at another of the men. 'Strode,' he said. 'Perhaps you would like to introduce us, so that our hosts may know our business.'

'Aye, My Lord,' said Strode, who wore a brown felt hat with a wide brim. He hitched up his breeches, spat, then marched up to the front door and rapped on it.

They mean to take Father, thought Billy, panicking. He glanced towards the barn, then back to the house, where now the men had gathered more closely around the door. Events there had their full attention, so Billy swallowed and decided to make a run for it. He crabbed around the side of the enclosure then, once more bent low, darted across to one of the wagons, using it as cover. He found himself at the rear and peeked in to see the contents, catching his breath at the shock of what he saw: men, mostly, though he thought he saw women, too, fifteen or twenty of them, lying cramped on the boards or propped up against the sides. They were chained but it hardly seemed necessary, all were in what seemed like advanced stages of the sweating sickness. Most were wearing nightclothes as though pulled directly from their sick beds. Some thrashed and sweated; others lay semi-conscious, heads lolling and hair hanging in thick, sodden clumps. As he looked, one of the men moved his head to regard him. His face was pale, he had dark rings beneath his eyes and he appeared to be having trouble focusing on Billy, almost as though the boy were a mirage. Then he did, and seemed to brighten, and was about to call to him, when Billy held a finger to his lips, shushing him.

'Please,' he whispered, 'please say nothing. I will set you free. But say nothing to alert your captors.'

I will set you free, he thought. How was he to do that? He, a boy, against three dangerous men.

He didn't know. All he knew was that he was going to try. To do nothing, to let the infected be taken away by the men in their wagons would be wickedness.

But still the prisoner was trying to form words, until, with Billy desperately trying to silence him, he said, 'Wolf.'

Wolf? What did he mean? Billy had no time to dwell on it. Once again he tried to impress hush on the man, then glanced around the back of the wagon at the front door of his home in time to see it open, just able to make out his mother through the huge, hulking forms of the men, their filthy jerkins.

'Yes?' he heard her say.

'You'd be the wife of Master Brookes the builder, is that right?' asked Strode.

'I am,' she replied, and though she was trying to sound calm he heard the fear in her voice.

That decided him. Though he longed to step forward to help his mother, he opted instead to find arms, and that meant getting to the barn. The last thing he saw before he set off was his mother's eyes scanning the yard for him.

He stealthily made his way first to the side of their cottage, then around the back to where the barn stood. He eased open the door, thankful that his father insisted on keeping the hinges greased. No wonder his mother had faith that the local noblemen would want him in the best of health: he was much in demand. And the reason Billy's father was in demand? Because he only ever worked to the highest standard. Sure enough, on the wall hung all of his tools, and Billy spent a second making his selection. A large wood axe looked tempting but he didn't think he was strong enough to wield it effectively. Instead he eyed a pair of sickles. With those he had plenty of experience. He reached for one and tucked it into his belt. The other he held. Then he let himself out of the barn and dashed back to the cottage where he edged along the wall until he was able to peer around the front of the house. The doorstep was empty; the men had gone in. Suddenly he was assailed by nerves. He found himself scanning the horizon, looking for Hugh.

But Hugh was gone and Father was ill. They were relying on him now.

He hefted the sickle in hands wet with nerves and made his way to the front door. He heard raised voices now, his mother shouting, '*No. You're not taking anyone anywhere*,' in a tone he recognised. Her telling-off tone.

'Now then, Mistress Brookes, we have been commissioned by the Crown,' he heard Strode say. 'We've to remove all the sick and dying to a safe place in order to limit the spread of the disease.'

'That's roit,' he heard Solly say. 'Now let us take him, if you please, Mistress Brookes, and we'll be on our way. God willing you will see your husband again, and who knows, he may be twice the man he was.'

He gave a dry chuckle.

'Commissioned by the Crown, my foot. You're taking him nowhere,' said his mother. There was anger in her voice now, noted Billy. You didn't want to make Mother angry, he knew, not where her family was concerned. Plenty of times he had heard her say how she would gladly die for her children, and it was never just talk with her.

He prayed she wouldn't have to die for them today.

'Mistress Brookes,' said a third voice, the leader, 'we intend to take your husband. We'll use force if we must.'

'You don't scare me,' she said. Billy pictured her squaring up to the leader. He was close to the threshold of the door now. He heard feet on the boards of his kitchen and had a sense of the strangers moving around his mother, trying to frighten her, no doubt. Where was Grace, he wondered. In with Father, most likely.

'Really?' said the leader. 'We don't scare you? It would be better for you, Mistress Brookes, if you were scared just a little. It would be . . . safer for you.'

Billy swapped the sickle from his right hand to his left hand. He wiped the sweat off his right hand. Swapped the sickle back.

'Get off my property now,' he heard his mother say. 'You're trespassing. You've got no right even being here.'

There was a sudden movement that Billy found difficult to place.

'That was the force you were thinking of, was it?' laughed his mother. 'I'm afraid you'll have to do a bit better than that.'

Whatever they had done it had not had the desired effect and there was a moment of silence.

'Fetch the daughter through here,' said the leader.

'*No*,' shouted his mother.

'There was more movement, scuffed feet, a door opening and a cry: Grace. He tensed, gripping the handle of the sickle hard, waiting to . . .

Waiting to do what, he wasn't sure. For a moment when their attention was arrested by events in the house, he supposed. When he had the element of surprise. Fight them, Gracey, he thought. Keep them occupied. I'm coming.

He took deep breaths.

From inside, Grace screamed. Billy's mother was still shouting, 'Leave her be, just leave her be.'

'Get the husband,' commanded the leader.

'Aye, My Lord,' said Strode.

There was a defiant cry from his mother, the sudden pounding of feet on boards, then a slap and a scream followed by a thump, his mother hitting the floor with a cry. Grace shouting '*Mother!*' at the same time.

Billy did not see it, the sounds were enough, and an anger descended, so that before he knew it – before he'd even had a chance to think about it – he was charging over the threshold of the front door and into their kitchen.

The scene was just as he'd pictured it: his mother was on the floor, aprons twisted around her, Grace cowering in the restraining arms of Solly, the leader impassive.

It took a split second for the strangers to recover. Then Solly was tossing Grace aside like a wooden toy and advancing on Billy, saying, 'I thought I could smell *boy*,' and grinning. His teeth, Billy noticed, were unusually sharp.

'Solly,' warned the leader.

Everything happening fast.

'*Billy!*' screeched his mother.

Solly bearing down on him.

Billy screwed up his eyes and swung the sickle, more to ward off the attack than in the hope of doing any damage.

But he hit home and opened his eyes to see the sickle embedded in Solly's arm, just as the man screeched and twisted, his scream becoming a howl.

And changing. Billy's eyes widened in horror as Solly became something else – a beast, a creature even more vicious and terrifying than the man he had been.

'Solly,' warned the leader, but it was too late. He had changed. He was a wolfman.

Blood spurted from his arm, which was no longer human; had sprouted hairs and grown and featured claws where his fingers had been. He reached for Billy who was still trying to wrest the sickle free, even as his mother sprang up to his defence, Grace still screaming.

Strode looked at the leader, at Solly, now fully transformed.

'Kill them,' said the leader, shaking his head almost sadly, and Strode changed, too. One moment he was human, the next he was wolf and he bore down on Grace, cuffing her across the head, flaying off a chunk of her face and grabbing her ankles as she tumbled, screaming, to the floor. She hung there, shiny white cheekbone showing, skin torn, teeth exposed, but still screaming and trying to pull free of Strode who easily lifted her, swinging her by her ankles. He'd completed one circle before she even had time to react, swinging her so fast that she was a blur – then dashing her against the door jamb. Her head disintegrated, just a spurting jumble of bone and windpipe at the top of her shoulders, bits of her skull flying off in all directions, her brain hitting the boards with a mushy slap.

Strode let go of her body, still moving with such force that it slammed in a tangle of arms and legs into a far wall, all trace of the girl Grace had once been gone. Just meat now.

Billy's mother shrieked and went for Strode who smiled and met her attack with his claws that he slid into her belly, lifting her so that she was level with his face. She gasped and spat blood, writhed and gagged. Strode spun her and jammed his claws into the hardened mud of the wall so that she was pinned there, still struggling, trying to get free, her eyes going over Strode's hairy shoulder to find Billy.

'*Run*,' she managed.

It was her last word. Strode grunted and twisted his claws and with a final cough she died, her head hanging forward.

The tears were streaming down Billy's face even as he turned to try to run, but was stopped by Solly, who dragged him back into the room and tossed him to the floor, where he landed among the blood and skin and shards of skull. He saw Grace's decapitated body. He saw the sightless eyes of his mother slumped against a wall, her front red with blood. Above him Solly at last pulled the sickle from his arm with a shout of pain and frustration and moved over Billy, bringing up the sickle and slicing it down over his neck.

Thunk. It hit the board without touching Billy, the blade creating an arch over Billy's neck and trapping him. Terrified, he watched as Solly stood over him, growling, his lips pulled back from his fangs.

Billy knew now why the man had said 'wolf'; he knew what the leader had meant when he had spoken about remaining human.

'You're going to die slowly, little boy,' said Solly, and was about to bend to Billy when the leader stepped forward to stop him and knelt, his features swimming in the blur of Billy's tear-stained eyes.

He wore an eyepatch, Billy saw.

'No,' the leader said, 'this little boy has fought well.'

'He will join us?' grinned Solly.

'No,' said the leader reflectively, 'we owe him better than that.' He reached to tenderly brush some hair from Billy's forehead, and as he did so his hand transformed to become a claw.

'Safe journey to the other side, brave warrior,' he said and slashed Billy's throat.

Solly griped about his hurting arm. Strode thought it funny and ridiculed him. 'Bettered by a teenage boy,' he shouted, much to Solly's disgust. Malchek reproached them both: Solly for being unable to control his transformation, Strode for his violence. He would not always be with them, he scolded. He needed to be able to trust them. 'Especially you,' he said to Strode, who had been about to put Grace's flayed face against his own and do a humorous impersonation of the girl. Instead he dropped it to the floor, where it landed with a smack. Both of the wolfen transformed to human form, regarding Malchek with penitent looks – from wolfish to sheepish. In return he frowned and bade them collect Master Brookes the builder from the bedroom, watching them pick their way through the remains of the family to the builder's room. They brought him through, his feet dragging along the boards, making bloody tracks. When they reached the outside, Master Brookes groaned but the two wolfen paid him no mind; they slung him in the back of the wagon with the rest of the infected then dusted themselves off and joined Malchek at the reins.

He looked at them. 'We're just going to leave that for travellers to see, are we?' he said testily, indicating the house.

They gulped, knowing what he meant: fire.

Reluctantly they got down and dragged hay bales into the cottage. Out of sight of Malchek they took quick, surreptitious bites from the bodies, knowing that he'd never approve of them enjoying their kills like that. The girl tasted best, they decided as they checked each other for tell-tale bloodstains or meaty breath, then – with infinite caution – set light to the bales and flew out of the house.

It was already burning fast as they trundled away from the cottage. Malchek could smell the girl on their breath and once again found himself reprimanding them. He was so intent on doing so and they so intent on providing him with the right amounts of contrition, that none of them sensed the presence of another, a young man who had ridden back from town that morning bearing various potions and medicines, who had hidden and seen the strangers take his father out to the wagon and bundle him inside. He had watched the men set fire to his home and when he dashed there as they were leaving, he was able to glimpse the bodies of his family burning.

Wasting no time, young Hugh Brookes got back on his horse in order to follow the mysterious wagon men.

XXX

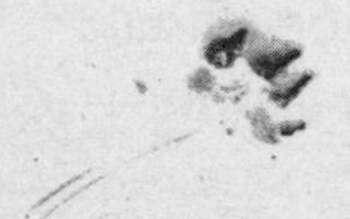

The moon was full and calling to Henry, silver and round in the sky, mottled with grey cloud. It looked good enough to eat and he was powerless to resist its pull so he didn't even bother trying. He threw open the curtains and stood before it naked, bathing in its rays, his wolf side coming out to play.

Then he was running, the moon singing to him, warm earth humming beneath his paws. He felt the wind in his fur and his tongue lolled as he ran. Waltham Abbey was close to town and he had to be careful, so he kept to the banks of the Lea, galloping on all fours until the town was a distant collection of dancing fire lights behind him. He thundered through the long grass caring nothing for the noise he made, alive with speed and freedom.

This was why he didn't want it to stop. This feeling. And he ran until his thoughts turned to his stomach, when he slowed to a halt, settling back on his haunches and searching the horizon for a treeline, where there would be prey.

The night was still. By his side the river, calm, boats pulled up to the bank. Absent-mindedly, he scratched.

Then he heard something. Shouting. Making himself low in the grass he raised his snout to sniff at the air – the air, his hunting companion – and on it he smelt human: ale, sweat, excitement and fear. Two men. And still that shouting, someone in pain. Henry moved closer, the noise louder now, until he came to the rotting shell of a rowing boat and hid behind it to watch them. One of them wore a hat and waistcoat and stood over the second, kicking him and beating him with what looked like a club. The second man writhed in the filth of the riverbank. He begged for mercy as he tried to ward off the fierce blows raining down upon him, yelling in agony. The moonlight illuminated the face of the attacker, giving it a pale, waxy glow. A look of evil.

Henry watched them for a second, a growl building in the back of his throat, an impulse forming.

Then pounced forward.

'*Oh my God*,' screeched the attacker, whose voice was so unexpectedly high that it almost stopped Henry in his tracks. And for a second the man seemed to catch himself, his fear temporarily absent, as though thinking his eyes deceived him, because – *didn't that werewolf just look surprised?*

But if Henry's features had registered shock at his prey's screechy voice, then they very quickly rearranged themselves, for the terror instantly returned to the man's face and he screamed, '*Monster*,' just as the man on the ground caught sight of Henry and he too shouted in terror, though with not such a high pitch.

Henry bounded past him on all fours. He saw the moon reflected in the water. He saw fountains of mud sent up by his paws as he streaked across the riverbank, jaws wide, the scent of the high-pitched robber in his nostrils. He was used to hunting beasts, both as King and wolf, but this was the first time he had ever made man his quarry and already he could sense that this was something new and exciting.

A few feet away from the man Henry's hind legs bunched and he sprang, his claws reaching around his victim and across one another. The impact brought them both to a halt on the mud flats and for a second Henry was on the robber's back, the man squealing as Henry dug his claws into the man's chest then whipped them back, turning him like a human spinning top, opening his chest at the same time.

The screeching man spun so that he faced Henry, split like the carcass of a pig, his entire torso open for inspection. Above the ragged hole his eyes went wide and he gazed down at himself. Henry stared, too. And for a moment both man and werewolf stood fascinated by the contents of the cavity, which quivered slightly then, with a squelch, spilled out of the robber, slippery intestines unspooling to the mud.

Henry inhaled the sudden stench of the man's open gizzard and was immediately transported, a slave to his senses, which sang. They *sang* as he sprang forward, knocking the dying man to his back, then crouched on top of him, first ripping warm flesh from his throat, twisting to drink in sprays of blood, then nuzzling into the warm and welcoming insides of the man.

After some moments of feasting he became aware of movement behind him and a low tremulous voice said, 'Please, Mr Wolf, please don't hurt me.'

Henry felt himself bristle at the interruption, and he growled as he stepped off the body, turning to face the second man who now stood before him. The man bled, and one eye was almost closed. He'd collected his hat which Henry saw was not a cap as worn by men of the town, but a round, embroidered skullcap. He wore a large and colourful shirt, gathered at the waist.

The gypsy shook as he stood before the wolf.

'Sir,' he managed. His voice, as deep as his attacker's had been high, quavered. 'I see that you have good in your heart, that you saved me from the robber.' His knuckles were white as he clasped his skullcap. His face was brown and lined, eyes kindly.

Henry growled a little more. He stepped off the body and rested back on his haunches. Blood dripped from his jaws, splattering to the mud below.

'I wonder, sir,' continued the gypsy, 'if I might ask that you don't eat the money he took from me.' He reached out a hand. 'The robber took the takings from our show tonight, meagre as they are in these days of the sickness, and I fear that with them gone our family of travelling performers will be lost.'

Henry went to all fours and padded a little way away from the torn corpse of the high-pitched robber. He settled back on his haunches, allowing the gypsy to go to the body. The old man put his skullcap to his nose, averting his eyes as he went through the dead man's pockets, eventually locating a fabric purse in gaudy colours and palming it.

'There must be much torment within you,' said the gypsy. He looked at Henry who regarded him with interested eyes.

'Our people have many ancient ways,' continued the gypsy, 'many wise elders. We could find a cure for your condition. Perhaps you could stay with us, travel with us. In return we would ask only that you let others witness your incredible gift.'

Henry watched him. The gypsy turned to face him and he crouched a little. He offered a hand. 'People are frightened of you when they see you, aren't they, wolf?' he said, gently. 'You're shunned in that state because they see only the beast in you. But tonight I've seen the humanity within you, the goodness. Creature, I am not afraid.' He tapped his chest, he smiled, the skin around his kindly eyes creased. 'In me you have a friend.'

He brought his hand forward to stroke Henry, at which point Henry discovered that he didn't like being stroked. Hated it, in fact. Whether he felt indignation that a commoner should presume to stroke the King, or simply that as a werewolf he wasn't partial to being stroked he wasn't sure. All he knew was that one moment he was bristling and rearing back as the old man began stroking him, the next he had the old man's hand in his mouth – just his hand.

The gypsy screamed and fell back, blood spurting from the ragged stump at his wrist. Henry tossed aside the severed hand. 'Don't touch me,' he said and went for the man's throat, his favourite bit he was finding, tearing off meat and gulping arterial spray.

From not far away came the sound of running feet and he saw flaming torchlights bouncing on the horizon. The other gypsy folk, no doubt, joining the hunt for the robber. He stood then bent again and located the colourful purse of money, placing it carefully next to the body. He stared down at it for a moment, taking no pleasure from the kill – not like he had with the screeching robber. Then he set off back across the mud.

Join the circus, he thought as he ran – ran past the rotting shell of the boat then scrambled up the bank and into the high grass where he dropped to all fours, taking off across the land, his ears pinned back with the speed of his run, tasting the blood and meat in his jaws, feeling the wind in his fur, exulting in his freedom. Why would I want to join the bloody circus?

XXXI

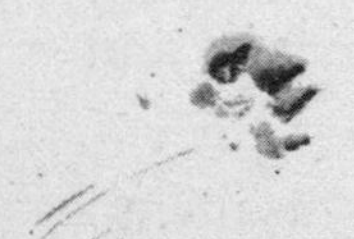

He usually had difficulty remembering the events of his changes. And unlike the lapses in recall he experienced after a night's heavy feasting, there was no William to remind him of his deeds. Instead he had to remember them for himself.

Normally, that is.

Last night, however, something had happened that was seared into memory, and standing before his mirror that morning, Henry expected to see himself covered in blood. After all, he'd butchered two men, not to mention eating bits of them. But then he also found a memory of sitting on the steps of a crypt in the grounds of the Abbey cleaning himself, licking off the last of the offal clinging to his fur.

That was clever of him, he thought, reaching to scratch at his scalp, dislodging fleas.

He picked a bit of gristle from his teeth and regarded it on his fingertip. Either it was a bit of high-pitched robber (he'd deserved to die), or gypsy (he hadn't). Henry dabbed at it with his tongue to see if he could tell: it was the gypsy, he decided. It had that matured old-man flavour to it.

He hadn't deserved to die, though, the old gypsy. In his own way he'd been trying to help the wolfman; and how could he know that the wolfman was really the King and that he hated being stroked. Henry didn't even know it himself until the attempted stroking occurred.

Fretting over the ethics of his kills put him in a state of anxiety for the rest of the morning, and he was irritable as the Gentlemen of the Privy Chamber – those who had not either been dismissed or excused, that was – entered the chamber to begin his morning ablutions. He sat in his night-shirt, broodily submitting to their attentions, catching sight of the barber as the man grimaced, probably at the fleas hopping about. Henry smirked inside, knowing the man would never dare raise the subject of His Majesty's fleas. What would it take to break the barber's silence? he wondered. A tick? Still, whatever the barber found in Henry's fur – his *hair*, he meant – it disturbed him, for the man was most ungentle.

'*Damn it, you oaf*,' he snapped at the barber, pulling away, 'why must you yank on my scalp so?'

The barber stepped away, bowing his head. 'My deepest apologies, Your Majesty,' he said, 'I have been having problems with my tools. They seem to blunt easily.'

'Well have them sharpened.'

'Indeed, Your Majesty, and so I have. Household has sharpened them daily now for some weeks. I had new instruments commissioned for Your Highness. They, too, appear to have blunted. Your Majesty is blessed with unusually luxuriant hair.'

That's not the half of it, thought Henry. You should see me when the moon is full.

'Do you know why I have more luxuriant hair, barber?' he asked with a smile.

'No, Your Highness, I can't say that I do.'

'Well, shall I tell you?'

'If it pleases you, Your Highness.'

'What do you mean if it pleases me,' he said, exasperated, 'I'm asking *you* if it pleases you. Well, does it?'

The barber coloured and nodded.

'I'll tell you, then,' bellowed the King, laughing raucously. 'It's all of these blasted potions and medicines I am forced to drink on a daily basis. Gentlemen, I do declare I have found a cure for baldness. Sir Francis?'

'Yes, Your Majesty?'

'Are you thinning on top?'

The groom touched a finger to his crown. 'A little, perhaps, Your Majesty.'

'Then you know what to do,' he laughed, and chuckled inwardly at the thought of his Gentlemen furiously imbibing all manner of vile liquids in order to combat their hair loss.

'Indeed,' he continued, warming to his theme, 'I do declare these potions have been having a most advantageous effect on me. He pulled himself from his chair, sending servants scuttling backwards. 'Am I not the picture of health?'

At first he had lost weight, but now, perhaps due to his increased appetite, and due also no doubt to the effects of The Change, he had gained more bulk. He patted his chest proudly, strutting before his men. 'Am I not the picture of virility?'

'Yes, Your Majesty,' they said, bowing their heads, and Henry nodded approvingly, turning to admire himself in the mirror . . .

Where he saw the face of a killer.

A gypsy, he thought, suddenly scared. He had eaten a gypsy. Would he now be cursed?

What was he thinking? He already *was* cursed.

He swung about. 'Now go,' he commanded his men.

'But, Your Majesty?' said Compton, indicated the clothes laid out, the grooms waiting to do their duty.

'I can dress myself,' snapped Henry. 'Do you think me helpless? Like a child?'

'No, Your Majesty.'

'Then dismiss them.'

Compton did as he was told and moments later the chamber had emptied and Henry had regained his seat.

'Will Your Majesty be wanting boar for breakfast?' asked Compton.

'Thank you, yes,' said Henry, staring at his hands. 'And rare, Compton, yes?'

'As you wish, Your Majesty.'

'I like it very rare, Compton.'

'Yes, Your Majesty.'

There was a pause. Just the sound of Henry's breathing, surprisingly loud in the room. 'I need to see Wolsey,' he announced at last.

The groom's eyebrows arched in surprise. 'The Lord Chancellor will be most grateful, I'm sure,' he said carefully. 'As you know he has been petitioning for an audience daily, wanting to atone, no doubt, for the catastrophe of his decisions. Certainly, he will be hoping to talk you round and regain your favour.'

Henry watched Compton from beneath lowered lids.

'Well, I need to see him at once,' he said. 'See to it, will you?'

'Yes, Your Majesty.'

'And when are you to leave for Sevenoaks?' Henry asked next.

'Shortly, Majesty.'

'You will bring Lady Anne's reply directly to me?'

'Yes, Your Majesty.'

Henry sighed. 'Good. If it's night-time, you only need post it beneath the door. Now leave me if you don't mind, so that I may use my close stool.'

'Yes, Your Grace.'

The King was some time on his close stool that morning, filling his chamber pot and emitting a series of groans and loud complaints followed by a most noxious odour that seemed to linger in his quarters for most of the day.

In that way, at least, the gypsy really had cursed him.

XXXII

Master Brookes the builder was only vaguely aware of what happened to him after he was taken from his cottage.

Which was, no doubt, a blessing.

He found himself in a covered wagon, manacles on his wrists, a chain at his ankle, jolted on bumpy roads. His companions were like him, in nightshirts mainly, hands in cuffs and all attached to the same chain at the ankle. Like him they were pasty and unwell. Some moaned and thrashed with the sickness. Most lay dazed, sliding in and out of consciousness. One or two tried to talk.

'They say we're to be cured,' coughed one in the darkness. 'They're taking all of the infected.'

'It must be nice where we're going if they have to drag us there in chains,' answered another with a dry laugh that became a cough.

Every so often the wagon would stop and more of the infected would be pushed aboard. Brookes became aware of a commotion at one point, one of the infected fighting to be let out, but the man with the squint came to the back of the wagon and silenced the man with a club.

They travelled further. Then were going down a steep

incline. From the back of the wagon, Brookes saw fields and hedgerows as far as the eye could see, no sign of any settlement.

The wagon drew to a halt. Vaguely, Brookes was aware of being taken down from the wagon, the chain dragging at his feet, a line of them shuffling across sun-parched dirt and coming to what looked like a large barn. Around them the guards were bullying and cursing any infected who tripped or fell or held up the line, and in front of him, the other men on the chain cowered beneath the blows raining down on them. Men were pushed and shoved, sworn at. Master Brookes looked behind himself to see that he was almost at the end of the chain. The last was an old, white-haired man, who prayed and mumbled as he was pulled forwards, bare feet shuffling in the dirt. Next, Master Brookes became aware of a sound: a great clamour, of screaming and frantic moaning and any distant hopes of a cure evaporated. Now there was just danger.

Trying to focus now Brookes became aware of one guard in particular. This one seemed to be the leader. Like the others he wore breeches that were too large for him and an oversized shirt, but he had an eyepatch. His hands were clasped behind his back and he smiled cruelly as his guards kicked and punched the infected towards the barn, herding them inside. Brookes grunted, feeling a punch to his kidney, almost losing his footing as he stumbled into the barn.

The stink hit him first. Of urine and sweat and fear. The barn was full of infected men packed in like cattle, the noise of them intense all of a sudden, panic coming off them in waves. Despite his weakness Brookes reared back, thumping into the old man behind, the two of them nearly losing their footing. Then Brookes was gasping as he caught sight of the guards, who seemed to change as they came into the barn. He saw them grow and darken, their faces bulge. He saw them snarl, attacking the prisoners with a gusto to match the rising frenzy in the cavernous space, the noise deafening now, as Brookes and the old man were thrust forward into the group. For a second he found himself almost suffocated by the stale bodies pressing in on him, kept upright only by the pressure. He stumbled over those who had fallen, who were writhing on the floor left for dead, trampled by the others. He struggled for breath, carried forward.

And only then did he see what it was they were being pushed towards. The men were funnelling through fencing to a raised platform at the far end of the barn on which stood two wolfen on their hind legs. The beasts gnashed and growled and paced the platform, adding to the great cacophony in the barn as though plagued by a great frustration – as though the job they were doing caused them great pain. And perhaps it did, because other wolf creatures were passing prisoners up to them – some squirming and terrified, some limp – and the wolfmen were taking the prisoners, lifting them like dolls, then biting into their necks, but only a little, a small wound considering how huge were their jaws. And after each one they would roar with the pain of denial, cast the bitten man aside, shake blood from their snouts and take another.

Many of the discarded men remained on the floor, a pile of bodies growing. Some had passed out, others were too weak to have even survived that one restrained bite. Some would stagger to their knees clutching the wound, expecting perhaps another attack, instead finding themselves pulled to their feet and dragged out of a door.

Brookes tried to find the strength to scream but found he could not as he was dragged along with others on his chain – dragged inexorably towards the platform which ran slick with blood.

Every instinct shrieked at him to run but even if it weren't for the restraints he was too weak. The chain was yanked as a man in a nightshirt feebly tried to pull away but was slapped and pulled back into line. And now the men were being fed between two wooden gates, forced to go single file as they moved towards the platform. Some of them screamed, some of them moaned. Some tried to run, some fell to the floor, some merely shuffled glassily to their fate.

Paws grabbed at his shoulders, pushing him along. Then he felt movement at his feet and he was released from the ankle chain.

Then Master Brookes felt paws propel him to the platform where for a moment he stood looking up at the wolfen, blood and saliva pitter-pattering down on him as he was passed up.

He felt hot, rancid breath. His skin was scraped by wet, wiry fur. He tried to raise his cuffed hands to stop it, but couldn't, and he sobbed, thinking of his family as the jaws bit into his neck, robbing him of his humanity.

XXXIII

Sir William Compton stood at the crossing and let his eye follow the line of the border until it disappeared over the horizon: mile after mile of burning pyres interspersed with gallows and gibbets, motionless bodies hanging from them. On one side, the safe zone – so-called – on the other, the contaminated area.

To call it a crossing flattered it. In fact, it was a pallet on wheels operated much like a river ferry from posts driven into the ground. It was used to pass supplies or messages in and out of the contaminated zone, the occasional body. It was manned by soldiers and an operator, and was blessedly free of the crowds that thronged the larger crossings, families hoping to escape the diseased zone, soldiers with covered faces dispersing them. Those caught trying to escape were shot, hung or gibbeted – perhaps all three if they were especially unlucky – their bodies left to dangle and decompose as a warning to others.

Even so, the border was a useless measure by and large. It was true you *might* be seen by one of the guards who kept watch in hastily erected towers every mile or so. You might be spotted by one of the soldiers who patrolled between the pyres, which were at such irregular interludes and with such long gaps between them as to be virtually useless. You *might*. But only if you were unlucky. And most of those who wanted to cross simply waited until dark or took their chances, and were usually successful. There was no such thing as a safe zone in England any more. Not where the sweating sickness was concerned.

Compton almost envied those who simply made a run for it. Being an ambassador of the King he had no option but to obey the rules, which meant coming here every day to the same crossing, the same ferry operator, a grizzled old cove called Brian who liked to lean on his crossing post and either swap shouted pleasantries with the ferryman on the other side, or banter with the guards, or just smoke his pipe and be glad of the warmth provided by a nearby pyre.

Compton waited now, one hand on the hilt of his sword, a handkerchief held to his mouth. Behind him was his carriage. Not far away three soldiers crouched playing dice. Brian stood smoking his pipe, squinting through plumes of smoke at his opposite number, some two hundred yards away on the other side of the crossing.

'He's not long for this world,' said Brian in a low voice.

'Who?' said Compton, who had come to enjoy the man's company.

'Ferryman on the other side,' said Brian, indicating with his pipe at the man who waved back. 'He's got it: the lurgy.' Brian gave a phlegmy chuckle. 'He don't know it hisself yet. Look at him, smiling and waving like that. He gots the reaper sitting on his shoulder, you mark my words.'

'How can you tell?' said Compton, amused. He glanced back at his coach. The driver sat staring off into the distance; while sitting in the carriage was the court minstrel, Godfrey, whose services were so rarely required at court these days that he was able to accompany his lover on his assignations. They shared a smile. It amused Godfrey that his lover enjoyed his conversations with Brian the ferryman.

'Well, My Lord,' exhaled Brian, 'it's more of a feeling with me if I might say so. I've seen them come and go, I tells you, so I tends to knows it when I knows it.'

He smiled and cupped a hand to his mouth, calling to his opposite number. 'Ahoy, any sign of that Boleyn standard in the valley?'

The ferryman turned to scan the area below then turned back and waved, shouting. 'I see it. My Lord, your message approaches.'

Compton cupped his hands to his mouth. 'Thank you,' he called.

'My pleasure, My Lord, happy to help.'

'Besides,' said Brian from beside Compton, his voice low, 'you only needs to look at him. He's sweating like a vicar with a conscience.'

Not long later, the standard-bearer had arrived, his face covered with a scarf. He had shooed away the ferryman before placing the letter on the trolley, weighting it down with a large stone and stepping away.

Brian set to his business and for a moment there was no sound apart from the squeak of the trolley wheels as the pallet was recovered to their side of the border. Compton fetched the letter, disinfected it by wiping it with a handkerchief dusted in oregano, and placed it inside a leather case.

'Farewell to you, ferryman,' he said, making his way back to his carriage, 'I shall see you tomorrow, no doubt.'

'Aye, you'll see me tomorrow,' said Brian, 'me, you'll see. Him over there, I wouldn't be so sure.'

Compton climbed back into the carriage and grimaced at Godfrey, the two of them bracing themselves for what would be a very uneven and uncomfortable journey home.

As it began, Godfrey was doing his usual: wanting Compton to open Anne's letter. He had removed the letter from the case and was turning it over in his hands. He held it up to the window but night was falling, the fading light doing nothing to help him see its contents. Not that this stopped him pretending otherwise.

'I can see the name *William*,' he teased. 'Now why would Lady Anne be discussing you in her love letters, do you think? Perhaps she has taken against you, William. Court is abuzz with the notion that the Boleyn girls are as devious as they are ambitious.'

'In common with their father, then,' frowned Compton.

'Oh? A bad word for your allies?'

'All we share is a common goal, Godfrey. Boleyn's desire for advancement sickens me. Norfolk, too.'

'But?'

'Wolsey sickens me more.'

'Then the King's new romance must be a turn of events that pleases you?' Godfrey brandished the letter. 'After all, Lady Anne's feelings for Wolsey are no secret. She has hated him ever since he banned her from marrying Henry Percy. They say, too, that she is a Lutheran.'

'Indeed.' Compton scowled at his well-informed lover. 'If anyone can seal Wolsey's downfall, it is her.'

Godfrey seized at the doubt in Compton's voice. 'But . . .?'

'But when I think of Wolsey, I think of a silly, vain man who wears his ambitions on his sleeve. He wants two things: wealth and the papacy. And he is prepared to use the King to achieve both. That is why I collaborate with plans aimed at his downfall.'

'And Anne?'

'Where Wolsey is stupid, she is clever; where he is open, she is guarded.'

'Then let us open her,' pressed Godfrey, proffering the letter.

'It is not worth the risk.'

'Who would see us?' Godfrey indicated the tiny carriage.

Compton shook his head. 'Wolsey has spies everywhere. Two of his clerks follow me. They think I don't know but they're as stupid as he is.'

'Well, they're not in here, are they?'

'No.' Compton looked at the letter in Godfrey's hands. Of course it would be beneficial to know the Lady Anne's thoughts. She had already snared the King, of that it was certain. What now did she ask of him? She would surely want to remove all competitors for the King's affection, he among them.

And now Godfrey, seeing the indecision in Compton's eyes, pretended to inspect the seal and at the same time pretended he had accidentally unsealed the letter.

'By God,' exclaimed Compton, 'please tell me you haven't broken the seal?'

'Hush, Will,' said Godfrey, 'the letter is open now, and Oh, Will.'

'What,' said Compton, 'what is it? What have you seen, Godfrey?'

'Well, My Lord,' said Godfrey, smiling, 'I think we now know why His Majesty had requested to see the Lord Chancellor . . .'

XXXIV

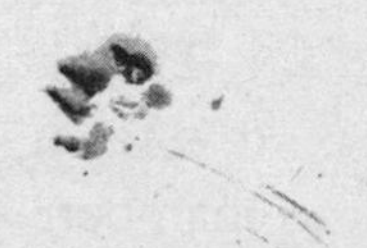

'A divorce?' said Wolsey, who, though shocked, was at least relieved that he wasn't to be put to death. Not yet anyway.

Usually the Presence Chamber would be thronged with servants, members of the Privy Council, ambassadors, ladies, clerks and attendants. Whispering and gossiping, they would crowd the room's edges, blocking the windows but lightening it with their presence, giving it life. Now, however, it was empty. Where once there were people, unfamiliar spaces had been revealed, bare boards and walls. Dust had gathered. The King's palaces were famously short of furniture; there was barely enough room for all of the courtiers. But in the absence of people the rooms looked empty, this one being no exception. Empty and light it was, though the King gave it a darkness.

He sat slouched in the grand chair. He wore a crown at a crooked angle and had a hand to his mouth. He looked unshaven, though it was certain he had been attended to by the barber. Wolsey wondered if he had got the sweating sickness, and he found himself edging back just in case. If he did it surreptitiously perhaps his Majesty would not notice. He glanced upwards to see Henry gazing out of the window and used the opportunity to scuttle back another foot or so.

'Yes, Thomas, a divorce,' Henry said finally.

'That might be . . . difficult.' Wolsey smiled his thinnest smile. 'On what grounds, Your Majesty?'

The King reached a hand inside his chemise and began to scratch, the coarse noise uncommonly loud in the empty chamber.

'On the grounds of . . . that I want to take another wife.'

Seymour, thought Wolsey hopefully. Please let it be Jane who has taken his fancy. If so, Wolsey's troubles were surely at an end.

'Who might that be, Your Majesty? I had heard that you have formed an affection for the Boleyn girl, Mary, but there is another perhaps . . .?'

Jane, Jane, Jane.

'Yes, there is another,' growled the King, 'but not Mary. The other Boleyn girl.'

'*Anne?*'

'That is correct.'

Wolsey blanched, frantically trying to dredge up what he knew of Anne: not as pretty as Mary, very ambitious, and – oh no – a Lutheran.

'I see,' he said sweetly, 'indeed the Boleyn sisters are both most fair. I wonder, though, whether . . .'

'She can grant me a son.'

'Well, the Queen can . . .'

'*The Queen?*' roared Henry. 'The Queen is ageing. And now she is crippled with grief. The Queen is no more likely to bear me a child than you are, Thomas. And are you likely to bear me a child?'

'Indeed not, Your Majesty.'

'Quite. Besides, I have grown most attached to Lady Anne. There is a . . . bond between us.'

He gazed out of the window again. Wolsey used the opportunity to edge back further, saying, 'But, Your Majesty, I fear that talk of a bond, affecting though it is, may not be enough to persuade the Pope to agree to a divorce.'

The King gave Wolsey a sneering look. 'Then use your diplomatic skills to see to it that he is persuaded.'

'He gave you special dispensation to marry Queen Katherine, Your Grace. It will not be easily rescinded.'

Henry leant forward in his chair, glaring at Wolsey.

'Thomas, between you and me, I don't give a fig what the Pope says. I'm having my divorce. If he grants it, fine, we'll remain allies. If he doesn't, I'll just make the necessary decrees myself and there are plenty of clerics who will support me. Your former colleague Thomas Cromwell and the Archbishop of Canterbury Thomas Cranmer among them.' He stopped, reflecting on something. 'Everyone's called Thomas, have you noticed? One Thomas falls, another rises.'

Wolsey gulped. *Cromwell.* That fucker.

Henry leant forward, looking at the Cardinal from beneath his brow, his eyes dark and full of threat.

'Do not think I have forgotten your role in the wolfen attack, Thomas. There were plenty who would have been overjoyed to see you sent to the scaffold as punishment. You should count yourself very lucky to be alive, Thomas, by my grace.'

'Yes, Your Majesty.'

'But luck can run out.'

'Yes, Your Majesty.'

XXXV

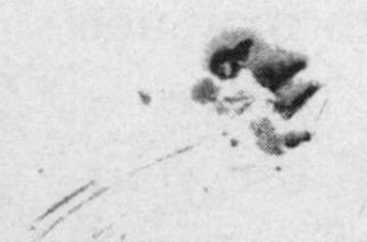

Just as it was in the King's Presence Chamber, so it was with the Protektor's Chamber at Hampton Court. Once, it would have teemed with life. Now there were just the three of them: Lady Jane Seymour, still fatigued from her journey, who sat with her feet on the table, her blonde hair light against the dark robes she wore; Lorenzo Cardinal Campeggio, the eldest of the Protektors, once feared, but now little more than a mascot, his beard long, eyes wise but tired; and at the head of the table, Thomas Cardinal Wolsey, glumly observing the empty seats now before him. No Morante, Barbato, Pignatelli or Simonetti. Just Campeggio and Seymour left.

Cardinal Campeggio opened his mouth to speak but Wolsey silenced him with a hand. Campeggio, he knew, was about to insist upon fulsome prayers for their departed comrades, but Wolsey really couldn't face it today, so instead he recited the shortest prayer decency would allow, and the elder Protektor harrumphed a little and settled his beard into his chin, the matter, thankfully, at a close.

'Right, let's hear it,' said Wolsey. 'Lady Jane, how were things in Rome?' He smiled thinly at Seymour. *Get your feet off my table*, he wanted to say, but was too weary. Too close to the edge of human endurance. She could vomit on his table for all he cared. Just as long as her news was favourable.

'Things in Rome were in order, Your Grace,' she replied, twisting a lock of hair in her fingers. 'His Holiness was saddened to hear of our defeat at the hands of the wolfen and concerned to hear that our wolfen are refusing to abide by the terms of the treaty . . .'

'Oh, they're being well-behaved in Europe are they?'

'It would seem so.'

'I suppose he thinks this is my failing, that our wolfen are playing up.'

'That I couldn't say, Your Eminence.'

'Very well. What else?'

'He did not think our wolfen uprising grounds to declare war on them fearing it might spark more hostilities between human- and demonkind.'

Wolsey's shoulders slumped. 'Oh, that cunt,' he sighed. 'Of course. I mean, the day that the Pope helps me out will be the day hell freezes over, won't it?'

Campeggio frowned. Jane put her hand over her mouth to stifle a laugh. Wolsey looked at them both.

'Well it's true,' he said. He took a deep breath. 'Okay, what else? Please tell me he's sending more Protektors at once. I'm looking at a lot of empty chairs here.'

'Your Grace, His Holiness says he will send a cadre of Protektors once the worst of the sweating sickness has passed.'

'*You see?*' exploded Wolsey, 'how he delights in seeing me disadvantaged? They have the sweating sickness in Europe, do they not?'

'They do, Your Eminence.'

'You were able to sail there and back unmolested?'

'Yes,' she grinned.

'Don't laugh, Seymour. The point is that the Pope could have sent Protektors here if he had wished. He wants me to fail. I wager that when the Protektors arrive they will be old like Campeggio or disgraced like Morante. I negotiated the fucking treaty for the Pope and still – *still* – he treats me like a serf.'

'Perhaps he knows you desire his job, Your Eminence,' said Seymour.

'Fat chance now,' spat Wolsey.

'Might I say something, Your Eminence?' she said, pulling her feet down from the table at last. Her chair scraped on the flagstones as she pulled it forward.

'Yes, go on,' he said.

'I should still be out there.' Seymour gestured towards the lead-pane windows. 'I should be out there looking for Sir Thomas More. He may well be alive and stranded by the sickness. Perhaps he has information of use to us.'

'Not during the sickness,' said Wolsey. 'I can't risk having you out there.'

'I'm as likely to catch it at Greenwich or Hampton,' she said. 'You own staff has been decimated.'

'But you're less likely to be hanged for crossing into the contaminated zone.'

She looked at him disbelievingly and Wolsey had to admit that the idea of her being caught by lumbering border guards was rather fanciful. Nevertheless.

'No,' he insisted. 'I need you here. You will be the only Protektor at court once Campeggio is gone.'

'Gone, Your Grace?' croaked Campeggio.

Wolsey raised his voice, though Campeggio could hear perfectly well. 'That's right, Your Eminence. You are to go to Rome.'

Jane leaned forward. 'But I've only just returned from Rome.'

'Quite, but things have changed. The King has a new request he wishes to make of the Pope, a matter of such delicacy, I fear it would be instantly dismissed coming from anyone lacking the dignity, wisdom and long-time service of Cardinal Campeggio. The King wants a divorce.'

Jane's mouth fell open.

'Exactly what I thought,' said Wolsey.

'Why?' said Jane.

'He wishes to take another wife.'

'Who?'

Wolsey looked at her.

'Me?' she said, shooting up straight.

'No,' he snapped, 'not you. More's the pity. Had you used your charms more efficiently, we wouldn't be having this conversation. No, the lucky lady is Anne Boleyn.'

Jane sat back. 'Anne Boleyn,' she said, eyebrows raised. 'That's . . . not . . . the best of news.'

'Indeed not,' said Wolsey. 'Indeed it is not.'

XXXVI

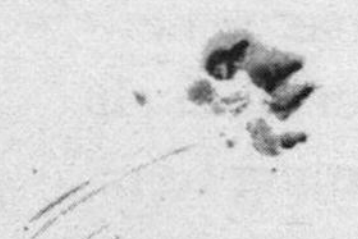

Never had the onset of a deadly epidemic been welcomed with such enthusiasm as the Hoblets had greeted the outbreak of the sickness that afternoon, for they had used the pandemonium as cover to make good their escape from Darenth.

Rushing down the hill, Agatha and Hob had gone to the gaolhouse.

The bestselling author of *Utopia*, Sir Thomas More, had opened his mouth to protest as Agatha pulled a hood over his head then gagged him for good measure. Together the Hoblets had tied the wriggling humanist's hands and feet and Hob slung him into a stolen cart. Next Agatha bound his feet to his ankles, so that he was curled, foetus-like in the bottom of the cart.

'Check his bindings,' she snapped at Hob.

As he did so, Hob slipped a small knife into More's hand, whispering, 'The journey is some twenty miles, Sir Thomas. Do not leave it long to make your move.' More nodded and Hob had pulled a blanket over the cart, tethering it to Agatha's horse.

He mounted his ass. Around them was running and shouting: 'The sweating sickness, the sweating sickness.' And, relieved to be out of it, they trotted quickly away, leaving Darenth behind them, the soaking wet pyre still in the village square. All they had to worry about was the theft of the cart; nobody cared that the witchfinders were leaving town, or that there would be no wolf burnings that day. Not now the sickness had come.

They began the slow journey back to the farmhouse. More than once they saw soldiers, at one point holding their breath as a column marched past them going in the same direction. What the soldiers were doing in the region, Hob had no idea. He knew where they were going, though: anywhere out of reach of the sickness.

Sir Thomas More, meanwhile, seemed to be asleep. Once, Agatha bid them stop then she had poked More in order to ascertain whether or not he still lived, getting a groan in response to her prodding. Satisfied, she regained her horse and waved them on. Hob relaxed. If she lifted the blanket she might see Sir Thomas sawing through his bonds. What was taking him so long anyway?

'What are we doing, dear?' Hob asked, after some more miles. He bobbed up and down in the saddle. They were closer to home now and he was becoming concerned about the lack of activity on the escape front. On the horse beside him sat Agatha, puffing on her pipe and squinting into the distance.

'Don't call me *dear*,' she grumbled. 'Don't think I haven't noticed you calling me *dear* cos you know it winds me up something chronic. That's why you're doing it, I know.'

Hob pushed his fingernails into his palms in order to keep from smiling.

'I'm sorry, darling,' he said.

'One more time,' she said. 'One more time and I'll knock you so hard you'll be picking teeth out of your turds.'

'Charming.'

'You think sitting on this here horse won't stop me?'

Hob decided he had pushed his luck far enough and mentally called a halt to his goading. 'Which still leaves us with the question . . .' he said.

'"Which still leaves us with the question",' she mimicked. 'If you mean why the bloody hell did we save him back there, I'll tell you.'

'Go on.'

'So's we can execute him.'

'Oh, Agatha, really . . .' he protested, although he hoped More had heard that and that he was even now redoubling his efforts to get free.

'Don't you, *Oh, Agatha* me,' said Agatha, 'Look, you've proved he's the real Sir Thomas More. Them noblemen practically admitted it anyway. See, I got to thinking, Hoblet. This is Sir Thomas More we've got back there. You don't waste an execution like his on a shithole like Darenth. We got to think big, Hoblet, big. This is something half the country will want to see. We'd need to advertise it far and wide, and stage it on a hill. We'll have to have Sir Thomas beheaded, of course. Burnings are exciting but there's no getting round the smell, and anyway, there's something really classy about a beheading I always feel. On the day we'll let everybody think there's going to be a last-minute pardon. We'll hire a messenger to dash up to the scaffold and hand a letter to the executioner. That's you, that is, Hoblet.'

'Oh no, Agatha, come on . . .'

'Well, I'd do it but once again I find myself the victim

of our patriarchal society. Do you know how many women executioners there are, Hoblet? None. So it's you that's going to have to decapitate him, despite your squeamish ways. Besides, your particular talent will be needed for the next bit.'

'What's that?'

'You takes the letter. You open it and read it. Now you look out over the crowd with the gravest of faces and you tell them there has been no pardon. The crowd will have gone silent and there'll be a moment of shock. The next sound is the crying of his servants and staff, because they're too unrefined to keep their emotions in check. While his family stand there all stoic, like, giving him strength. And he should stand on the scaffold holding his wife's gaze, even as I come up behind him and blindfold him and he goes to his knees. Then you step forward and in one clean stroke off comes his head, at which point his wife will finally break down and be comforted by her children. And at that moment a second messenger will arrive on the hill and just like the first he'll dash up to the scaffold and hand you the letter, and the crowd goes silent and you read the letter, and you cross yourself and say, "May the Lord have mercy on all of our souls, Sir Thomas had been pardoned," and you'll drop the letter, which will flutter to the floor, landing near a spreading stain of blood.'

She took a deep breath.

'What do you think?'

From the cart came a muffled clap as Sir Thomas More applauded with his bound hands.

'Why thank you very much,' cooed Agatha, genuinely pleased, and More said something that was too smothered to make out, but was probably, 'my pleasure,' then lapsed back into silence. For his part, Hob had to admit his wife's scenario certainly sounded interesting, and at the very least there was a refreshing absence of torture. They would of course stand to benefit financially. She'd already made enough to complete her chimney but this might set them up for good; he could go back to his bees and gardening while she could do something sadistic as a hobby; she'd always talked of one day opening an orphanage.

He liked Sir Thomas More, of course he did. From what he'd read of his bestselling book *Utopia*, the man had one of the finest minds in the land. But his execution could be worth a fortune. It could be worth a thousand accusations.

Yes, that was it, he thought. By executing More they would be saving the lives of others. Surely he, as a man of God, would understand and encourage such a decision?

Of course he would.

Right, thought Hob. The knife. He had to get back the knife.

Lying in the cart, More had been using the knife to saw through the ropes. His entire body ached, his head ached. He was shivering, too. And whatever the type of knife he'd been given, it was most assuredly not sharp.

But hearing Agatha's plans he had redoubled his efforts and when she had spoken of his wife and children he had pictured them in the crowd, their upturned faces as he said his final words from the scaffold.

What would those final words be? he wondered. He would need to say something nice about the King, of course. Forget to do that and your whole family might be following you to the afterlife. Nevertheless, he would like to make it clear that he had served God before anything else, so perhaps he should say something about serving the King and God and being devout. This, of course, providing it didn't somehow emerge that he had been raped by a wolfen.

The wolfen.

He remembered her talk of raising an army.

He'd gone back to sawing at the rope, bounced around in the cart, listening to the Hoblets' conversation.

There. Finally the ropes at his ankles parted, and he was able to uncurl his body a little. Even so, how was he going to cut the bindings at his wrists? He couldn't even see. His next task was to use the knife to cut into the hood, a job he finished with his hands, ripping a hole through which to see. In the gloom he stared down at his hands, concentrating as he tried to manoeuvre the knife around his fingers, when he felt them draw to a halt.

Oh God, I've failed, he thought. I've left it too long, we've reached our destination.

But no. 'What the bloody hell are we stopping for?' he heard Agatha say.

'I just need to check the bindings,' said Hob and More tensed. The blanket was pulled back and he could feel Hob leaning in towards him, feel the other man's hands searching for something.

'I'm going to need that knife, Sir Thomas,' he whispered.

'No,' More whispered back, harshly.

'Just for now,' insisted Hob.

'*No*.'

'It's for the best, Sir Thomas,' pressed Hob, feeling for the knife.

'What are you whispering about back there?' called Agatha.

'Just give me the knife,' whispered Hob.

'*No way*,' hissed More.

'Give me the knife.'

'I must get free. I must raise the alarm at once.'

'*What?*' screeched Agatha.

'Give me the knife!' shouted Hob.

'What knife?' shrieked Agatha.

More twisted to be on his back and kicked upwards, catching Hob in the chest and sending him sprawling backwards.

'Hob!' screamed Agatha, and the Witchfinder General began scrabbling to his feet just as More jumped out of the cart, twisting to thump into Hob shoulder first, knocking him to the ground a second time then springing up.

He couldn't see. He rocked on his feet a little. He brought his bound hands up to rip the hood further off then ran to the edge of the track, finding a gap in the hedgerow and plunging into the woodland.

'Come back here, you,' screamed Agatha.

'Goodbye forever, old hag,' shouted More triumphantly as he waded into the forest.

He ran deeper, the Hoblets now way behind somewhere. Finally he stopped and let the wood settle around him, straining his ears to listen. There was nothing, just the creak of trees, chirrups and birdsong. He pictured Mistress Hoblet, hopping mad, warts lit up like beacons. Stick that in your pipe and smoke it, wizened crone, he thought. Ha!

He shivered, his head throbbed. He set to work freeing himself, first removing the hood then with more difficulty sawing through the ropes at his hands.

It was dusk by the time he had finished, and the temperature had dropped. He stood and began to make his way forward, not wanting to be trapped in the wood when darkness fell.

But when darkness fell, however, he was indeed still trapped in the forest, and he ached all over, and he pulled his robes around him, shivering now, and sweating. This, despite the chill in the air.

He continued, blundering through the undergrowth, barely able to see, until he at last spotted patches of grey light and walked towards them, the forest thinning out. He found himself at the edge of it, looking out over a shallow valley, at the bottom of which was a house, with lights in the window, what looked like a half-built chimney protruding from the roof.

With perspiration pouring from him, he made his way across the field and in the direction of the farmhouse. By the time he reached the front door he was barely able to keep to his feet, and he sank to his knees before using both fists to hammer on it.

There was movement inside. The door opened. He looked up, blinking.

'Ah, Sir Thomas, how very nice of you to drop in.'

He collapsed on the floor of the farmhouse, sweat pouring from him, his breathing shallow.

XXXVII

It was now months later, and the sun shone on the Hoblets' farmhouse, bathing it in a glow so generous that Hob found it difficult to believe there could be anything wrong in the world, let alone the sickness that had wrought such widespread devastation.

Their land lay just inside the contaminated zone, so in the early weeks they were bothered often by travellers. Those who ventured along the track to the Hoblets' door were either begging for money or shelter, or attempting to steal the livestock.

The stealing stopped soon after Agatha had caught one lad trying to make off with Hob's ass. She had cornered him at the fences. Coming up from the garden, snatching his hat and veil from his head, Hob saw them facing off: Agatha and the thief, a strapping young man of about twenty years old, in his prime.

Poor lad didn't stand a chance. Especially not as Agatha was carrying her washboard. Hob knew from painful experience that she was expert in its application.

So it proved. As the thief moved forward, the not-unreasonable expectation of easily overpowering this tiny washerwoman written all over his face, Agatha took a step to the side and swung her washboard.

Whap.

For a second his face disappeared beneath splintering wood then was visible again, bristling with shards of washboard and already pouring blood. Agonised and disorientated, he was in no position to defend himself as Agatha reached to her broken washboard, tore from it one of the upright legs and jammed it into his chest. He coughed, ejecting a dark glob of blood and fell, his eyes rolling to the back of his head, legs convulsing. Agatha stood over him, withdrew her washboard stake then jammed it into him again. With the tip of her tongue protruding from her mouth she did it again, until his legs stopped convulsing and he was still on the dirt.

'Oh for crying out loud, Agatha,' said Hoblet, arriving, 'couldn't you just have knocked him unconscious or something. Must it *always* be death?'

'It might seem harsh to a man of your delicate sensibilities, Hoblet.' She was already dragging the bloodied body across the yard. 'But this young fool will serve as a warning to others.'

Quite literally, she meant. She lashed the corpse to their front gate, testing it to make sure that it would open and close with the body still tied to it. Within moments she had found a wooden panel, painted the word 'Thyfe' on it and pinned it to his chest with the stake.

They were not bothered by thieves again, and only the most desperate of honest folk needing shelter dared come down their path. When the body got ripe, visitors were virtually non-existent.

Those who braved the threat of death and stench of decomposition brought tales of horror from across the infected countryside: of bodies in piles, of the sick herded together like cattle. Families were burnt out of their homes for harbouring the diseased, they said; those who were infected were being rounded up and taken away on wagons which roamed the countryside. Taken away by men who wore long flowing robes and oversized shirts and breeches. Sometimes they had a leader, who wore an eyepatch. Sometimes not.

Where these wagons went nobody knew, but it was said the infected were kept like livestock somewhere, waiting to die. The men in wagons had become the scourge of the land.

She won't like that, Hob had thought, on being told that particular tale. Sure enough, when the itinerants had been given short shrift – Hoblet preferred to tell the needy that they already had a sufferer in their home; Agatha simply shooed them away – she had jammed her pipe between her teeth and with rounded shoulders stalked off towards the farmhouse.

Hob raised his eyes heavenward and later found Agatha in the kitchen, her eyes red from crying. 'Did you hear that?' she wailed. 'Did you hear what they said? "The scourge of the land". Some men in wagons. *We* used to be the scourge of the land, Hoblet, not men in wagons. Now look,' she gestured at the unfinished chimney. Money was no longer the issue, of course, but of Master Brookes and sons there had been no sign, and finding another builder during a time of plague was always going to prove problematic, so the chimney remained half built. 'I tell you this, Hoblet. As soon as his nibs in there gets better we'll be back. *We'll* be the scourge. Not men in wagons. I ask you.'

Sir Thomas More lay in their guest room and had done since the night he had lost consciousness on their doorstep. He would have had no recollection of being brought in and put to bed, and little of the weeks that were to follow, for he had the sickness, the same sickness killing thousands across the land; the sickness that would have killed him, too.

But for Agatha's determination to keep him alive.

Because, as she often pointed out to Hob, there was no point in executing Sir Thomas More if he was already dead now, was there? Oh no.

'If this is going to be done proper we need him up on that scaffold in the best of health. Unshaven, of course, and maybe a little malnourished, but otherwise fit and well.'

As ever, her logic was faultless.

So it was that Agatha had turned apothecary. She had found a new passion: making Sir Thomas well. Every day she mixed Hob's honey with herbs and made thorough notes on ingredients and quantities. And she hit upon a formula of sorts, because Sir Thomas's condition improved, the fever began to subside – and his sweating came under control.

Still he remained delirious, though, and would babble about armies of wolves and somebody called Malchek, who was a danger to the King. The Hoblets paid his rantings little mind, although they did wonder what had become of the wolf woman, and one night after Sir Thomas had been yammering about wolfmen building an army, Hob had joked that there were enough folk going missing to build an army.

And they looked at one another, and wondered if they'd ever see these fabled Wagon Men.

As it turned out, they didn't have long to wait.

XXXVIII

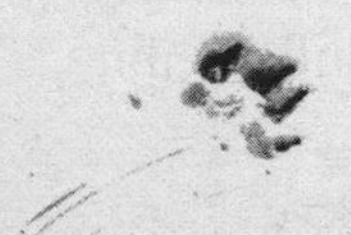

'Is everything all right?' asked Compton.

'Indeeds it be, sir,' called Brian the ferryman, who was standing some distance away, and had been since Compton had arrived.

The groom yawned and rubbed his aching head. He'd had too much wine last night. Worse, his whole body felt bruised from the constant daily jolting inflicted upon him by this accursed journey. Oh for the disease to pass so that Lady Anne could come to court and his messenger role be a case merely of ambling along hallways and knocking on doors.

Or maybe not even that. For it was becoming clear that Anne Boleyn was not to remain Henry's fancy for much longer. She had resisted his attempts to be his mistress, crafty operator that she was, and if the contents of the letter Godfrey had opened were anything to go by, had been persuading the King to ask Wolsey for a divorce. Anne's letter had been a study in innuendo and implication, leaving the King (and Compton and Godfrey, who had both pored over it on the journey home) in no doubt as to the Monarch's rewards for divorcing Katherine and marrying her: everything from having a Queen less in thrall to the dictates of

Rome, to certain sexual techniques Anne had heard of in France, and was most eager to try out with her 'one true love'; to inevitably, the successful production of a male heir.

Ending her letter, Anne had requested that the King inform her of his progress in the matter; there was a confidence she wished to share, she said.

The next day Compton had taken the King's reply, making the journey to and from the border alone. Brian the ferryman had been right. His opposite number had been replaced.

'Been up and died, just as I said he would,' Brian had advised, with a wink. 'Soon as the sweating sickness gets you it don't take long.'

Today, though, Brian was less garrulous. He seemed to be keeping his distance, puffing on his pipe and staring balefully at Compton who waited impatiently for the arrival of the blasted standard, his head throbbing, limbs aching.

When the standard was at last raised and the letter placed on the trolley, Brian had been forced to approach Compton, though such was his demeanour that the groom felt obliged to give him a little more space than usual, and moved away. Brian seemed to go red in the face as he pulled the squeaking trolley towards them. Then redder and redder – almost as if he was holding his breath – until the pallet arrived at last and he indicated the letter and moved away with a great explosion of breath.

Puzzled, Compton reached for the letter, disinfected it then returned to the carriage. As they pulled away he glanced out of the window. The ferryman was making the sign of the cross.

'By God,' he paled. 'I have it.'

'The letter?' said Godfrey.

'The sweating sickness. Did you see the ferryman? He avoided me like the . . .' he whispered, '*plague*.'

'Come, Will,' said Godfrey, whose eyes widened anyway, perhaps thinking of his own proximity to the sickness. 'The sickness comes on quickly. What symptoms do you have?'

'I ache,' wailed Compton, 'all over. I took it to be from the demands of the daily journey. Do you ache, Godfrey?'

'No, Will, I do not.'

'Good God. Do you have a headache from last night's wine?'

'No, Will. But even so. You are not . . . I mean, those with the sweating sickness, well, they sweat, don't they?'

Compton passed a hand across his forehead and it came away wet.

'Look,' he said, '*look*.'

'Will, listen to me,' said Godfrey calmly, 'it's the fear making you sweat. The symptoms you describe may well have their root in last night's over-indulgence. Please, close your eyes and try to sleep.'

Compton nodded and sat back, closing his eyes. He did indeed feel tired. My God, was that another symptom of the sickness? No, he didn't think so. He controlled his breathing, calming himself, letting sleep claim him.

When he opened his eyes it was almost dark. The carriage thundered on through the countryside. The moon was a crescent in the sky.

And on the seat next to him sat Godfrey, wearing a bemused expression. Compton jerked upright. 'What is it?' he said. 'What's wrong?'

'It's this,' said Godfrey, showing him Lady Anne's letter, deftly unsealed and lying open.

'What about it?'

'They've gone mad, the pair of them.' He shook his head with a smile. 'Lady Anne says she's seen the King turn into a werewolf.'

XXXIX

The morning the men in the wagon came to visit, More had been sitting up in bed for the first time, sipping from a cup of warm potion Agatha had prepared for him and tentatively asking questions. Questions like: 'Where am I?' And, 'Are you still planning my execution?'

'Oh, tish, Sir Thomas,' exclaimed Agatha, colouring, 'don't you be worrying about that now. Any plans for your execution were made in jest, you should know that, just Agatha's little joke was all it was.'

'We have a rule in this house,' chuckled Hob, 'we never execute the guests.'

'We've tortured a few of them, though,' laughed Agatha.

'And that was just the cooking,' said Hob.

'All right, Hoblet, don't take it too far.'

At that, Hob went through to the kitchen and there had gazed out of the kitchen window.

And his eye had followed the line of their land. To the gate where the corpse of Thyfe was now rank with decomposition. To the meadow then to the track at the top of the hill. There, he saw two large-wheeled covered wagons turn off the track and on to the lane that ran down to their farmhouse, and he went into the yard to watch them approach.

Two men sat up front on each one. Their features were indistinct in the distance but they were strangers to these parts. They wore dark robes, even though the sun was hot. These were the Wagon Men of whom it was spoken, coming to collect the sick. The fearful Wagon Men.

It would be a bloodbath, thought Hob. Poor souls.

'Well, well, well,' said Agatha, joining him, 'if I'm not very much mistaken it's the scourge of the countryside.' Her eyes were bright. 'The scourge of the countryside coming to see little old Mistress Hoblet.'

'What do you think they want?' asked Hob.

The wagons trundled slowly down the lane, bright sun behind them.

'Him in there,' she said, thoughtfully, jerking a thumb back at the house. 'Word must have got out that we're harbouring a sick one.'

'They know he's Sir Thomas?'

'Maybe. Doubt it, though. More like they just want him cos he's sick.'

'What are we going to do?' asked Hob.

She gave him a withering look. 'We're going to tell them to sling their hook is what we're going to do.'

The wagons had now arrived at the gate and Hob became aware of a sound. A low, pained moaning that came from the rear of the wagons. One of the men jumped down from the leading wagon and moved to the gate. He looked down at Thyfe, then shouted back to his colleagues. He said something they could not hear. He pointed to where

Hob and Agatha stood. There was laughter. No fear or hesitation. Just the laughter.

'A look of disquiet flicked across Agatha's face. 'Hoblet,' she said, calmly.

'Yes, dear.'

'Firstly, don't call me dear. Secondly, run into the farmhouse and let His Holiness know what's going on and tell him to keep his trap shut. Thirdly, when you come back, make sure you're holding a couple of axes.'

'Yes, dear.'

'Oh, and wear your witchfinder's hat.'

'Yes, dear.'

He dashed off. It was at times like this, he thought, that Agatha really came into her own.

The lead wagon man spat on his hands and opened the gate. What was left of Thyfe's head lolled. With the gate open, the two wagons passed into the Hoblets' yard. They came past where the Hoblets had planned to put an orchard one year, past their barn where they kept the horse and Hoblet's ass, and since their trip to Darenth a new cart, too. Until they came to the well, fifty yards away, where they stopped.

Agatha hawked some phlegm into her mouth and chewed upon it thoughtfully as Hob reappeared by her side. He brought with him a two-handed wood axe and a smaller axe, keeping both of them out sight.

'Here,' he said. Surreptitiously, he handed her the larger of the two weapons, which she concealed behind her skirts, the head of it on the dirt, handle resting against her thigh. She wiped her hands on her apron, removed the pipe from her wet mouth and licked her lips, folded her arms across her chest.

The men had come down off their wagons. Two were craning their necks to look down the well and seemed to be debating which of them should be in charge of retrieving the bucket. Meanwhile, two more approached the Hoblets, hitching up their breeches and adjusting their jerkins. One wore no hat and had a weather-beaten face, eyes no wider than slits; the other wore a felt hat, his eyes only just visible beneath a wide brim. He was in charge, decided Hob. If there was dying to be done, he would die first.

The two visitors stopped a few feet from the Hoblets. Hat man spat, squinting man squinted; Agatha's lips moved around her pipe and Hob tried to look sinister and distinguished. He held his hands in front of him, the hand axe hidden inside the folds of his robes.

'You'd be Mistress Hoblet then?' said the hat man slowly.

'Aye, that's right, countryman,' said Agatha, 'and this be Master Hoblet, Witchfinder General, who stands at my side. You'll be the feared Wagon Men I hear so much about?'

'That's right. Travelling the countryside bringing in the infected so that the disease should not spread.'

'Oh we've heard much about you,' said Agatha, 'you've been making quite the name for yourselves, so you have.'

Hat man grinned and dug his toe into the dirt. 'Well, that's very kind of you to say, Mistress Hoblet, very kind indeed. Certainly coming from you, for your own reputation is known far and wide. Why, we hear about it most everywhere we go.' He addressed his companion. 'Ain't that right, Solly?'

'Aye, that be right, Mr Strode. That be right.'

Strode put his hand to the crown of his hat, shifting it

back on his head so that for a moment Hob could see his eyes, and the sight startled him because there was something red and feral about them. Something wild.

And he thought of Sir Thomas More's babblings. Found himself wanting to shake the ridiculous thought from his head.

'Well, that's most flattering to hear,' said Agatha, 'perhaps you might tell me what it is that people are saying about Mistress Hoblet.'

His hat back in position, Strode grinned once more, showing rows of black, uneven teeth. 'Well, they say of Mistress Hoblet that she's holed up on her farm with the Witchfinder General and that she's been turning folk away on account of a sufferer she's trying to cure of the sweating sickness, right there in her home.'

'Folk should talk less,' answered Agatha, evenly.

'Sweating sickness is declared over,' rasped Solly. 'We've been commissioned to pick up the last of the sufferers.'

'Well it's lovely to know the operation is in safe hands, lads,' declared Agatha, cheerily.

'So we'll be taking your patient, then.'

Agatha smiled. She took the pipe from her mouth and indicated the wagons with it. 'You have plenty already by the sounds of things,' she said.

'Room for one more,' quipped Solly. Behind him the other two wagon men had finished their tasks: the infected folk checked, water distributed among them. Now the pair of them had moved apart and were coming forward stealthily. Their progress made Hob nervous, they were disappearing out of his eyeline. Hoping to make their way around the back of the farmhouse no doubt.

He gripped the handle of the axe more firmly.

Agatha chuckled. 'I tell you what, if you take your men and your wagons and your cargo of the infected, and you get off my property right now, closing my gate behind you, then I'll be prepared to forget this.'

Strode laughed, looking at his companion, who smiled. Hob thought he heard a rustling sound. Was it a trick of the sunshine or did they both seem to shimmer, so that for a moment they were like a pair of mirages?

'There was something else we heard on our travels, Mistress Hoblet,' said Strode.

At the same time Solly took a step forward. Perhaps he expected Agatha to flinch away but then he wouldn't be the first person to underestimate her. The last to do it was rotting at the front gate.

'Now what would that be, countryman?' said Agatha to the leader, who remained still.

'Why, they said that you and yer husband was in Darenth, and you were about to interrogate and burn a wolf woman.'

As Strode spoke Solly came even closer and his face seemed to change and seethe. Even Agatha flinched a little. Hob found he was holding his breath, gripping the axe handle so tightly his fingers ached.

The two others had now moved further up the yard and were about to vanish from the periphery of Hob's vision; plus they'd see Agatha's axe, he realised.

If Agatha remained unnerved by the shifting physique of the man she made no sign.

'What of it, countryman?' she said.

Solly was now even closer. Agatha stayed stock-still.

'It *was* you, then?' asked the other.

Agatha spat. 'You better call off your friend here,' she said.

'Oh. I'd prefer him there if you don't mind,' smiled Strode, 'just while we're having a natter like, if it's all the same to you.'

'Now why would that be?' asked Agatha.

'Well, it's so he can tell if you're fibbing to me, see.'

Solly was now inches away from Agatha and moving his face up and down, inhaling her. Rather him than me, thought Hob. Neither Agatha nor Solly gave ground.

'Why would matters in Darenth concern you, then?' said Agatha.

'It's my master, Mistress Hoblet. He has a personal interest.'

'I see,' said Agatha. She eyed Solly. 'And who might your master be, countryman? I don't suppose it would be this – now what is his name? – *Malchek* we keep hearing about, would it?'

Beside her, Hob willed his face to remain impassive while Strode's mouth dropped open and Solly jerked back to look at Agatha.

'Now that is an interesting thing,' said Strode. 'Very interesting indeed. Perhaps you might like to tell me how you come to know of my Lord Malchek.'

'Oh, his name is known far and wide,' said Agatha breezily, 'everybody knows Malchek.'

'She's fibbing,' sneered Solly. 'Lying through her teeth – what's left of 'em.'

Oh she's not going to like that, thought Hob.

Sure enough: 'I beg your pardon?' said Agatha sharply.

'I said you're lying,' grinned Solly.

The two stared at each other for a moment.

Hob could no longer see the two remaining wagon men.

'Let's try again, shall we?' said Strode. 'Who has spoken to you of Lord Malchek?'

Agatha took a deep breath.

Hob recognised that deep breath – it was the sort of deep breath that meant she was about to hurt somebody.

And he realised something. He realised that ever since the Wagon Men had arrived, his faith in his wife's ability to kill their way out of the situation had barely wavered.

'You say he can tell if I'm lying?' she asked Strode.

'Oh yes.'

'Well how about this, then?' She addressed Solly. 'Any moment now I'm going to bury an axe in you, my boy,' she said. 'Am I fibbing about that?'

Squint straightened, puzzled. He turned to his leader.

'She's not fibbing,' he said.

Then came a warning shout from one of the other men: '*She's got an axe.*'

Strode's mouth dropped open as Agatha reached behind her, grabbed the weapon, hefted it in two hands and swung it, *thunk*, embedding the blade in Solly's back.

For she was nothing if not a woman of her word.

Solly screamed, but not like a human. Instantly he changed, thick, brown fur burst out of his skin. His back arced. His face, upturned and in agony, seemed to grow.

Hob resisted the impulse to run, suddenly knowing that everything Sir Thomas had told them was true as he saw the two remaining visitors shape-shift from human to wolfen. He saw wiry brown fur, large, pointed ears and snouts dripping saliva. He wheeled about in time to see one of them come running across the yard, at first on two feet then on four. Bearing down on . . .

'*Agatha*,' he warned, and she tugged the axe from the body of Solly, which even now seemed to ripple and change as though the transformation had been interrupted. Then with a grunt, Agatha swung, sinking the axe deep into the wolfen's stomach, stopping the animal in its tracks, a bright red stain flowering on its white shirt.

'*Oof*.' For a second it was lifted off its feet and bent over the shaft of the axe, then was falling back to the dirt still impaled on the blade of the axe.

Agatha glanced up to check they were no longer in imminent danger. The second of the two wolfen had come to a halt. Strode remained in human form.

Satisfied, she put a foot to the wounded wolfen's stomach and with a grunt of effort pulled the weapon free. In response the creature moaned and writhed, its paws at its chest which was soaked with blood. Agatha regarded him a moment.

'Now that,' she said, 'is what I call a hairy axe wound.'

With that she stood over the wolfen, raised the axe and slammed it into the creature's face, cleaving open its skull and exposing grey brain matter that shone in the afternoon sun. She stepped away, spat then used her sleeve to wipe blood and brains from her face. She glanced over at Hob who remembered himself and withdrew the hand axe from his robes to brandish menacingly; Agatha gave him a withering look.

'Now you look here,' she called to Strode, 'you want to have another go, you just try it, but I don't go down easy, I go down hard, and if and when I do, people will want to know why, because this here is Master Hoblet, Witchfinder General, commissioned by His Majesty. We ain't no weak infected you can just cart away to your master, wolfen. Folk know you're here. Kill us and you'll have them hunting for wagon men high and low.'

Strode still had not changed, but seethed nevertheless, his eyes blazing. His sidekick looked to him, angry and slathering, desperate to avenge their companions.

Strode seemed to decide something. He barked an order at the remaining wolfen who reluctantly obeyed, slinking back to his wagon, the two of them taking their seats, swinging the wagons around in the yard and leaving.

Only when the convoy was halfway up the lane did the two Hoblets allow themselves to relax a little. They turned to one another.

'Bloody hell, Agatha,' Hob exploded with nervous laughter at the same time as she did.

'Bloody hell, Hoblet.'

'You were . . . fantastic.'

'Oh, *you*.' She blushed. 'I hardly did a thing.'

'"Hardly did a thing"! You killed two of them.' He indicated the hairy, bloody corpses in the dirt of their yard.

'Aye,' she said reflectively, staring up the valley where the wagons had reached the main track and were now bumping back in the direction they'd come from. 'We'll see who's the bloody scourge of the countryside.' She sighed. 'Now,' she said, 'we'd better get inside and tell Sir Thomas More that he's right, the buggers are everywhere and if what we've seen today is anything to go by, they bloody well are forming an army.'

'And then what are we going to do with him?'

She took a deep, regretful breath. 'We're going to have to let him go, aren't we? So he can warn the King. There's not much point in us being rich if we're going to be overrun by bloody werewolves? Godless creatures that they are. No, we need to get Sir Thomas well, then see to it that he gets to London.'

XL

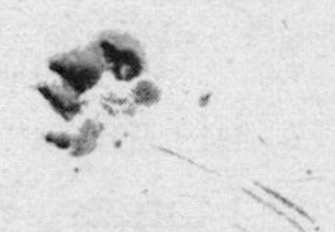

Henry was feeling the pull of the moon more strongly than usual – than he had for some time, in fact – so he avoided the window. Instead he angrily dashed empty plates and meat bones from his dinner table. He slopped wine from a jug into a goblet and drank it in one long draught then wiped his beard with the back of his hand and tossed the goblet away, the clatter it made almost unbearably loud. On the table he unfurled the astrological charts and stared at them trying to focus but finding they were just a series of shapes and drawings. How was he supposed to make head or tail of these, for God's sake?

Compton. No, he couldn't try Compton. His groom was ill, so he was told, and had repaired to his family home in Warwickshire, curse the man. Fulbrook Castle, it had been called, when Henry gave it to him.

'I didn't give it to him so he could hide away when I bloody need him,' the King raged, to nobody in particular.

There came a knock at the door.

'Majesty?'

'What?' he snapped.

'Are you all right, Majesty?'

Sir Francis Bryan opened the door and stepped in,

surveying the chamber, dishes and remains of food on the floor, the dishevelled King in its centre, scratching, which was something he seemed to do a great deal these days. It was cold, and the groom ruefully regarded the empty fire grate.

'I'm hungry,' said Henry, indicating the devastation of his dinner table. 'Bring me more food. More meat. And, Sir Francis?'

'Majesty?'

The King picked up a plate on which was something that looked much like a slab of cake.

'What is this?'

Bryan looked from the plate to Henry, looking, perhaps, for some trace of playfulness or mockery; some of the old King. Finding none, he eventually stammered, 'It's . . . it's marzipan, Your Highness.'

'Marzipan?'

'Your . . . favourite?'

Henry looked at it in wonder. It had been his favourite? Had it? Really? He searched within for some trace of a man who had once counted marzipan among his favourite foods. In vain, he searched. The new Henry did not enjoy marzipan. The new Henry liked meat. Fresh, bloody and off the bone.

Human meat.

His thoughts went to the high-pitched man and the gypsy. He remembered the squelchy sensation of pressing his muzzle into the still-warm wet meat, how it pulsed as life ebbed away. He imagined the texture of it in his jaws, thick hunks of it sliding down his throat.

Inwardly, he cursed. Why hadn't he brought some of it back with him? He could have hidden it in his closet. There was such disarray at court his stash might well have gone unnoticed and he could have torn off strips and added them to his food while nobody was looking. Instead of boar he could be feasting on tasty gypsy.

His stomach did a hungry flip at the thought. He felt sick at the memory of all that meat he'd left by the riverside. What a waste.

But then, *no*. He caught himself, revolted by his own thoughts.

'Your Majesty?' came Bryan's concerned enquiry and he turned away with a hand to his head.

'Get out, Bryan, get out,' he ordered.

'Majesty.'

Bryan began to withdraw.

'Wait,' said the King.

'Majesty?'

'Go to the window. Quickly. Tell me the phase of the moon.'

Bryan did as asked. Henry heard the swoosh of the curtain being brought back and felt rather than saw moonlight flood the room. To him it was like sunlight warming him, promising life and rebirth, power and freedom.

Bryan hardly needed to say it: 'The moon is full, Majesty.'

'Leave me now,' said Henry, 'and do not disturb me until morning, however important the matter.'

But why had he said that? he wondered as Bryan left. He had already decided that tonight he would fight it. He was going to prove that he was stronger than the curse; that The Change belonged to him, not the other way around.

He fumbled for his locket with its portrait of Anne, a lock of hair curled into the lid.

If she were here she would help him. She knew about The Change. She could help him, he thought. She could help him stay Human.

Bryan had left the curtain open a little and Henry rushed to close it, resisting the impulse to scream an insult through the door for the man's incompetence. As he drew the curtains he saw the moon bright and baggy with promise and he felt its rays upon him. Even when he stood away from the window they seemed to hang in the room like fumes, making him light-headed. He felt the call of the pack. Had a sensation of the wind in his fur. He felt his skin prickle.

But fought it, and his skin returned to normal.

He should do something to take his mind off it. Read a little of *Utopia*, maybe, gaze at a wall hanging. Because it was increasing – the need – it was growing stronger. He felt his body tighten and contract, felt slithery then brittle. And at the same time little waves of warmth and pleasure flooded through him.

Perhaps, he thought – now here was an idea – he could change but not hunt humans. After all, he was still the same Henry inside. He could just hunt another rabbit; no, a stag.

Yes, that was it. What an excellent solution! Feeling decisive and in charge, he let The Change come, let it flood through him with a feeling of great relief, until he stood, fully transformed at the window. He took off his clothes and allowed the moonlight to flood over him. Turning, he padded over to the table, enjoying the smells, the sounds – he could hear Bryan snoring next door – snatched the jug of wine from the table and finished it.

Now he was set and he yanked back the curtain, pulled

open the window and gathered himself on the sill, enjoying the chill air on his fur, wishing he could howl but choosing not to. Instead he jumped to the grass below and set off across the lawns.

Soon he dropped to all fours and was flying across the land, keeping the lights of the town to his left. He wondered about returning to the same spot as last time. But no, the bodies would be long gone and anyway he'd vowed not to eat human.

Even so. He was drawn there, and found himself padding along by the riverside, leaving the forested areas behind. There would be no stags here, he knew. No rabbits or wild boar. Here there was only the likelihood of encountering a human.

He continued his progress, knowing that he was coming closer to where people lived. The Henry bit of him was thinking that as King he was never allowed to see his kingdom like this. The realm he saw was groomed and clean: armies of people built whole estates in preparation for his visits and his progresses around the country were accompanied by furious campaigns to cleanse the towns and villages on his route.

No, he never saw it like this: the weather-beaten houses by the riverside, broken-down mud walls, shabby lean-tos, clothes hanging on lines in small, dirty yards. Here there was some livestock, a chicken coop he contemplated destroying: a pig tethered to a post saw him as he passed and reared back squealing, so that he hurried on in case its cries alerted the home's occupants.

Still he ran, on two feet now, sniffing at the air, feeling hungry and drooling as his stomach growled. Now he came to a churchyard; there inside was the low stone building of the church and gravestones at odd angles, silhouetted by the full moon.

He stopped. Raised his snout and sniffed at the air.

People.

And they smelt of something that was familiar to him; they smelt of grief.

He vaulted the churchyard wall and crouched beneath it for a moment, his nostrils twitching. Then in hunter's stance he weaved his way through the gravestones until he could see them properly: a man and woman. Wearing little more than rags, they knelt in the mud in front of what looked like a makeshift grave. Now he was closer he could smell the freshly turned earth, the corpse still fresh. The *small* corpse. Because the mound of earth before which they knelt was large enough only for a child.

The couple held hands. The only sound they made was a snuffling, this coming from the woman, the mother. She held something at her face as she cried, a keepsake of some kind, while the man clasped his hat to his chest, his eyes red-rimmed from tears.

And the scent of grief rolled from them. It transported Henry just as surely as that of a slaughtered stag. It took him to his own bereavement and he tried to remain there, but found he could not, for his thoughts insisted on returning to food. He thought of George to try and stop himself. Then he thought of the gypsy, how badly he felt after he killed him, to try and stop himself. But then he thought of *eating* the gypsy . . . And his stomach rumbled again, but this time so loudly that the grieving man looked over to where he crouched.

Henry's eyes glowed. Moonlight glinted from his fangs.

With a gasp the father scrambled to his feet, grabbing his wife by the arm and yanking her with him so that she yelled in pain and surprise. 'Who is it?' called the man, sounding braver than he looked and peering into the darkness – just as Henry emerged from behind the gravestone.

Henry's shoulders were hunched; his head was low. There was a splattering sound as his saliva dripped to the muck. On seeing him the woman gasped and the man moved in front of her to shield her as Henry gave a low snarl. A hungry snarl.

'Please,' started the man, 'we just . . .'

But he never finished his sentence. Henry pounced, clamping his slavering jaws to the man's throat and ripping it out so savagely that he tore bits of spinal cord with it, death cutting off a scream that had barely begun.

The woman screamed, turned and ran, slipping in the mud, regaining her footing, barging painfully into a gravestone. Warm blood on his fur, Henry bounded after her. He snagged a trailing hand, shook his head, and took off most of her arm, leaving a ragged stump just below the elbow and she stopped, blood spurting from the wound.

She turned, as though in a daze, as if deciding that it was the final straw. First her child, then her husband, now her arm: she no longer wanted to live.

Henry obliged her, finding the warm meat at her chest and ripping into it with his jaws, her screams of agony ringing around the graveyard.

And when she had finished writhing and was still, Henry dragged the corpse back to the graveside so he could work on them together, growing more and more frenzied as the smell of blood and innards hung in the air.

Marzipan? he thought as he ripped them apart. *Marzipan*. He had a new favourite food now.

Moments later he found himself on his knees in the mulch of the graveyard, tears streaming down his hairy face.

Around him was carnage. He'd ripped the head from the mother and forced it on to a stone crucifix, her jaw smashed by the impact and hanging at an odd angle. From there her sightless eyes had watched his repast and now they watched his regret too – as the blood mist subsided and Henry stared around himself with revulsion.

Strewn in the muck were intestines. Body parts. Torn flesh everywhere. He saw a slick-looking hunk of liver. A portion of face. He saw torn-off legs, the flesh ragged where he'd bitten into it. He saw arms, part of a flank, bloodied and torn. There were torsos, open and messily disembowelled, ribs like the abandoned hull of a boat. And there were three torsos because he'd been drunk with blood lust, so when he'd finished tearing apart the mother and father, he'd decided he wanted dessert and gone to work on the tiny grave, digging in the mud to reveal a miniature coffin, home-made by the looks of things, constructed by the father perhaps, which Henry tore from the ground with a triumphant roar, setting it down and getting to work on the lid.

He made short work of it. Inside was a little boy, pale but recently dead, and gratefully Henry had plucked the corpse from its box, torn off the head then sunk his snout into the torso and fed, eventually pulling off the limbs and stripping the meat from them, working on the belly last.

Then he had stopped, as horrible realisation dawning. He stood, looking around himself, and he felt over-fed and nauseous. The decapitated head of the mother leered at him. The bits of meat stuck in his fangs repulsed him. He could smell the family's blood on his fur.

The family, he caught himself thinking. Not a thief but a *family*, hurt and bereaved. *They're together now*, he tried to tell himself, pathetically: *I've helped them be together*.

He threw back his head and howled in anguish, grief and shame.

So he ran from the churchyard. He dropped to all fours and sprinted, knowing exactly where he was going. He ran until he saw a figure on the horizon, silhouetted by the moon, and there came a howl. He stopped, rose, threw back his shoulders and sent an answering call.

His heart sang.

Both dropping to all fours they ran to meet one another, and as they came together they reared up and pawed one another for some moments, slavering, delivering tiny affectionate nips, batting at each other with their paws.

'My love,' she said.

'You too?' he growled, and she nodded.

Next they began to run, and all the exhilaration Henry felt as a wolf was multiplied as they tore across the plains together, the wind rippling through their fur. Wordlessly they knew they both wanted food and so they ripped apart a muntjac for a light snack then ran together before finding a larger stag for a main meal. *Does she eat human flesh, too?* wondered Henry. But he decided it didn't matter and he didn't care as she set off across the moon-dappled meadow with him in pursuit, her protruding tongue pink against the black of her fur.

She was the same as him.

Oh, but quicker, he soon discovered. More lithe. And when they raced each other – whether on two legs or four – she would pull ahead, turning to gently mock him. She had greater cunning, too. More than once they chased a rabbit and it was she who caught it, astonishing him with her expertise in the hunt. A match for him. Maybe even more than a match for him. He goaded her and together they went in search of a deer and this, he knew, was what they meant about the thrill of the chase.

They found a deer. They ripped it to bits but discovered they didn't have an appetite, so they played in it for a bit, then left it, running some more, making the countryside their playground.

When he came to, he was still naked and he lay on the bank of a stream, a cool breeze on his body. He awoke with his head in the lap of his love, Anne, who had balled up the hem of her skirt and was dipping it into the water to gently clean the blood from his face and body.

Everything was going to be all right, she told him, smiling. The sweating sickness was over. Now they could be together, for ever.

XLI

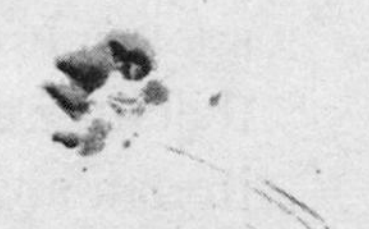

Godfrey was tired, having not long returned from Compton Wynyates where Will lay dying of the sickness. His lover had been roiling hot, twisting in his sheets, perspiration pouring from him, and Godfrey had held his hand, a disinfected scarf over his own mouth. When Godfrey had called for water no servants appeared, and when he tried to release Will's hand in order to find help, Will had gripped him even tighter, his eyes imploring Godfrey not to leave.

Godfrey waited. He watched Will's face, which bore a permanent sheen of sweat; he listened to his shallow breathing; he watched his eyelids flutter, and he arranged his bedclothes so that his lover would be more comfortable. Around him the estate was quieter than usual. Where once there were footsteps in the hallway, the sound of maids and housekeepers exchanging banter, now there was an eerie stillness. Gardeners had called to one another on the lawns, strutting peacocks brayed. Now there was silence. Sickness and scandal had come to the estate.

Later, with William asleep, Godfrey went looking about Wynyates. The house was bright with sunlight, but empty, and it echoed to the sound of his footfalls. He located a housekeeper, the only one left, she said, the others having left, not wanting to catch the sickness. Looking around he could see that they had not left empty-handed.

'Sir William is to die, Master Godfrey,' she wailed, her bottom lip quivering. 'What will become of us?'

She held the bottom of her apron to her mouth as she spoke. It had been liberally treated with disinfectant so that little clouds of oregano, marjoram and rosemary puffed from it as she spoke, dancing in shafts of light. Everywhere, it seemed, stank of the herbs. Godfrey found the smell of it oppressive and depressing. What's more, the blasted stuff had found its way into his chemise, where it itched terribly.

He persuaded the old woman to stay, pushing money into her trembling hands, then returned to William's chamber, where he pulled the oregano-impregnated scarf up over his mouth and set about making his lover as comfortable as possible.

'Godfrey,' managed Will. He grasped the minstrel's hand.

'Yes, Will,' said Godfrey.

'You have told no one of the contents of Anne's letter?'

'No, Will, of course not.' Even in these dire circumstances, Godfrey had to suppress a smile at the very thought of wanting to share that particular bit of fancy. He longed for the moment when he and Will would laugh about it; he hoped there would be one.

'You know what you must do, should I die?'

'You're not going to die, Will.'

Will fixed him with watery, rheumy eyes. 'You know what you must do, if I die?' he insisted.

Godfrey lowered his eyes. 'They have the best physicians and apothecaries still attached to court, Will. I plan to return with one.'

'Have you heard anything of the King?'

'No, William. He has just the few in attendance. He has withdrawn from all public life. Whether this is for reasons of the sweating sickness or . . . another reason, I do not know.'

'He needs me.'

'Not in this condition, Will. You must get well.'

Not long later, with William once again sleeping, and having gained the housekeeper's promise to care for Will until he returned the following day, Godfrey set off for Waltham Abbey and there to his chambers. He sat on the bed, pulling his riding boots from his feet and lost in thought when there came a knock at the door. For a moment or so he waited, expecting his page to answer before remembering that he no longer had a page. So he stood, one boot nearly off, and went to the door, dragging the half-removed boot as if it was a wounded leg.

'Who is it?' he called through the door.

'It's Frank and Walters, My Lord, clerks to the Lord Chancellor,' came a young voice in reply. The voice held an impudent tone.

Wolsey's boys, he thought. Were these the two Will had referred to when he spoke of being followed?

'Yes, well, what do you want?'

'To speak to you, My Lord, if you wouldn't mind opening the door.'

'I'm afraid it will have to wait. I am indisposed.'

There was a snigger from the other side of the door.

'The Lord Chancellor requests to see you, My Lord. He wishes you to play for him and his company. He asks that you accompany us and bring your accursed lute.'

'My *what* lute?'

'Your accursed lute.'

'Did he say that? It's not an accursed lute, it's just a lute.'

'My apologies, sir, I considered it to be a type of musical instrument, like a *bass* drum.'

'Well, it's not, he was just being rude about my lute.'

'A slip of the tongue perhaps, sir, for the Lord Chancellor is keen to hear it now. He wishes you to come at once.'

Godfrey screwed up his eyes. It was not a request he was able to refuse, or even defer.

'Wait there, then,' he snapped.

His footwear changed, his lute retrieved, Godfrey opened the door to his chamber to find the two clerks on his doorstep. They wore the embroidered livery of the Cardinal's household and smiled in a too-obsequious way.

'Would you like to come with us, My Lord?' smiled one of them. Either Frank or Walters, he did not know which, never having bothered to differentiate between the two. They strode off ahead of him and he followed, furious not only that they had interrupted his mission, but had also been rude about his lute. He was apprehensive, too. What did Wolsey really want? To hear him play? He doubted it.

They led him to a courtyard where a carriage stood, and they all boarded before either Frank or Walters gave a signal and they began their journey. Another blasted bouncing journey, he mused, though he was of course accustomed to using the journeys to sleep, and soon found it overtaking him, despite his worries.

When Godfrey awoke the carriage was at a standstill. He heard Frank and Walters outside, opened the door to the carriage and stepped out into a cool, evening breeze and a smell that it took him a moment to place. Then he was looking around, trying to make sense of what he saw: the Thames, sailboats, the bank opposite where the city lay, fire-lights twinkling like stars.

London. They were in London.

He spun about. There behind him was the Tower.

Godfrey gasped, a dreadful realisation dawning.

'Why are we here?' he asked, hoping not to betray his fear. 'I expected Hampton Court or Greenwich Palace . . .'

'The Cardinal's gathering is in the White Tower, My Lord,' grinned either Frank or Walters. That is where he requests the pleasure of your company.'

'Are you sure?' said Godfrey.

'Of course. Please follow us.'

They handed him his lute then took him to the bridge over the moat, across it and inside the Tower walls. Every step of the way, Godfrey felt less safe. His questions – What was the gathering? Who was present? Were other minstrels in attendance? – were all rebuffed with increasing degrees of disrespect.

Until Godfrey stopped.

'The White Tower is to our left,' he said, pointing through the arch that led to the Inmost Ward.

'Ah yes, that's right, My Lord,' smirked either Walters or Frank. 'However, we have a small bit of business we must first attend to in Lower Wakefield.'

Godfrey went cold. He knew exactly what happened in the bowels of Lower Wakefield; walking along the banks of the Thames at night, he had heard the screams.

'Gentlemen,' he said, 'this is no time for jesting. Now let

us repair to the White Tower at once, or otherwise part company.'

'I'm afraid not, My Lord,' said either Frank or Walters, voice hard, all pretence now evaporating.

Godfrey swung his lute at the two clerks to send them off balance then tried to make a run for it. But they were ready. And quick. And strong. One of them nipped ahead of him, stuck out a foot and he tripped over it. On the ground he rolled just as the other was looming above him and stamping his stomach. Godfrey shouted in pain, the breath whooshed from him and he found himself fighting for air, curled up on the stone of the Tower courtyard. His lute was grabbed from his hand and the next he knew hands were gripping him in the armpits and he was being dragged, gasping, in the direction of Lower Wakefield.

Lower Wakefield, where they took traitors and heretics. The most feared of all towers inside the great fortress.

Godfrey was still gasping for breath as they took him down a long set of spiral stairs.

He was still gasping for breath as hands stripped him of his robes, and then of his jerkin. He began struggling when his breeches were pulled down, but by then other hands were holding him, those of a gaoler. As he struggled he saw a low ceiling, the beams black with soot. He saw slimy stone bathed in a flickering orange glow, filthy metal instruments hanging from the walls.

There was another man there, too, who wore a black leather apron and a mask. This man had thick rubbery lips that glistened with sweat, the chamber being almost unbearably hot, braziers filled with roaring fire lining the walls.

There was yet another man, in a far corner, his face obscured by shadows.

Next Godfrey was dragged over to what looked like a bench and thrown over it, so that he was bent at the waist. His hands were grabbed and shackled with cuffs fixed to the oily wood and there was a clanking sound as a chain was tightened and he was pulled to the bench, able to smell the sweat and pain of others trapped here before him. His ankles, also, were manacled.

Now the men stood back, gathering their composure following the struggle. Godfrey moved his head, trying to find breath that when it came was hot and rancid. His exposed buttocks quivered.

In front of him on the wall was a collection of evil-looking instruments. The masked torture master approached the wall now and stood with his hand on his hips, searching the hanging metal, mumbling something that sounded like, 'Arse hooks, arse hooks, arse hooks . . .'

Godfrey, the gaoler, Frank and Walters all watched him.

'Is it me?' said the torture master. 'But I can't see these wretched arse hooks up there.'

Godfrey snivelled. He tried to think of Will, to give himself strength. He tried to think of his family. He began to pray.

'Jones?' asked the torture master over his shoulder. 'Come and give me a hand, will you? I've lost these blasted arse hooks again.'

Jones the gaoler walked over and picked them out immediately, handing them to the torture master who slapped his forehead. 'Well, I never – can't see for looking.'

He turned to bring them over and Godfrey saw them properly: two hooks, wickedly sharp, each attached to a short chain at the other end of which dangled a weight. The torture master came over to Godfrey, looked him over and said, 'Jones, we'll need more weight for this one,' and Jones went to fetch two more weights as the torture master disappeared behind him.

Godfrey's lips moved in prayer. Sweat poured from him.

In front of him came Frank and Walters. They both smiled. One held his hands clasped piously, as if overseeing a matter of much religious importance; the other held Godfrey's lute and observed him with his head tipped to the side a little.

Godfrey blinked tears from his eyes. 'What do you want?' he said, his mouth wet with anguish. 'What do you want from me?'

'As Sir William's lover, we were hoping you might be able to help us with our enquiries,' said Frank, or Walters.

'I don't know anything.'

'Ah, we think you do.'

'I don't.'

Jones the gaoler came back into view bearing two weights and glancing down at Godfrey as he passed, his face grave. Then he was at the rear and talking to the torture master as they added more weight to the arse hooks.

'All right, Jones, get the cheeks,' said the torture master.

'Cheeks again,' grumbled Jones.

'Don't you worry. I separated many a cheek when I was just a gaoler.'

'*No*,' cried Godfrey. He felt hands grip his trembling buttocks and pull them apart. He heard the drag of chain. Something nuzzled between his cheeks. Something cold and hard.

Then a searing pain as the hook penetrated flesh. On one side and then the other, the weights dropping, pulling the chains taut, hooks slicing into his cheeks and dragging them open at the same time.

His whole body jerked with the shock and pain, hands pulling at his restraints, thumping down on the bench like a fish ready for gutting, screaming, his eyes screwed up and tears spilling from them.

After some moments, there was silence in the chamber. Just the roaring of the braziers, the soft splattering of blood on the stone and Godfrey mumbling a prayer.

Either Frank or Walters cleared his throat. 'My Lord,' he said, 'you've been spending a lot of time with Sir William lately, am I right?'

'We're in love,' mumbled Godfrey.

'Oh, I know, I know, and His Eminence wants it to be known that despite what you may have heard regarding the prejudices of the Catholic Church he makes no judgements in that regard.' Frank or Walters leant forward. 'He just wants to know what you read in the letters. Something in particular you read that got you most excited. Something about wool? Or was it Wolsey? Or was it even woll, I wonder? What was it you read in Lady Anne Boleyn's letter, that got you all hot under the collar, My Lord?'

'I don't know what you're talking about,' repeated Godfrey. 'I know nothing of Royal affairs. I've read no letters.'

Either Frank or Walters tut-tutted then gestured to somebody. Now, a figure stepped out of the shadows, the other man who had been in the chamber when they arrived. He stood with his head bowed, the wide brim of his hat hiding his face.

Prompted by the clerks, he raised his head. It was Will's driver.

'I'm sorry, Master Godfrey,' he said, close to tears, 'I should never have been eavesdropping to hear you read those letters, and I felt so guilty for my sin that . . .'

'He went to confession,' finished Frank or Walters.

Godfrey groaned.

'I'm so sorry, sir,' wailed the driver.

'That's all right' Godfrey felt a twinge of guilt at not remembering the man's name, 'that's quite all right. Please – won't you do me this favour? Please will you tell Will what you saw here tonight. How I suffered but never betrayed his trust.'

The driver cleared his throat uneasily. 'Well, I can't really do that, sir. They'll kill me if I do.'

'Of course,' said Godfrey. 'In that case please visit Compton Wynyates as soon as is possible and see to it that he is cared for.'

'Well, sir,' said the driver uncertainly, 'I'll try, but I must admit I am a little bit busy over the coming days. Plus there's the sickness to think about. Obviously I don't want to be in danger of catching it.'

'Of course, of course. When you can then, perhaps?'

The driver brightened. 'Thank you very much, My Lord, thank you very much.' He hovered. 'I suppose this is goodbye then?'

'Yes, I suppose it is,' managed Godfrey.

'Well I must say, you and Sir William have been a pleasure to work under, always most generous with your tips.'

'Oh get out,' said Frank or Walters, ushering the driver away.

He shuffled away.

'So you see, My Lord,' said the other, leaning towards Godfrey when the driver had gone. 'We already know that you've been reading the King's correspondence. You will be executed on that charge. You and Sir William.'

'No,' shouted Godfrey, 'not William. Please. He had nothing to do with it. I insisted that we open the letters. I pretended the seal was broken. It was me, not him. He should not be held accountable.'

'Either way your own execution is beyond doubt,' smiled Frank or Walters, 'All that remains to be seen is whether you endure hours of painful torture beforehand – or you tell us what was in that letter.'

Godfrey groaned. There was silence in the chamber, broken only when Godfrey at last raised his head and smiled up at Frank or Walters. 'You'd better go and fetch more weights,' he said, 'because I will never talk.'

Either Frank or Walters straightened, sighing. 'Right,' he said, 'it's about time we made some use of this accursed lute we've been carting across the land.'

Godfrey shook his head, moaning. 'No, no,' he cried, becoming louder as either Frank or Walters passed his lute to unseen hands that reached over him.

'This?' said the torture master.

Frank or Walters nodded grimly. The other one tilted his head to stare at Godfrey, whose eyes were closed, his lips moving in prayer, sweat pouring from him, tears running down his cheeks.

'Are you sure?' queried the torture master.

'Quite sure,' said Frank or Walters.

'It's just that we normally use something a bit more – I'm not sure what word you'd use, really – something a bit more rounded. Pokers are very popular. We can heat one up for you . . .'

'The *lute*, torture master,' insisted Frank or Walters. His companion with the tilted head smiled at Godfrey.

'As you wish, My Lord,' said the torture master. 'Right, Jones, this is going to be interesting. Let's get those cheeks as far apart as we can, shall we?'

The two men got to work on the two arse hooks, and Godfrey started to scream.

Those walking along the banks of the Thames heard the minstrel's shrieks as the torture master inserted the lute.

XLII

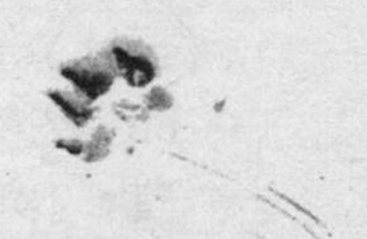

'You did *what* to him?' Wolsey was apoplectic with rage.

'It was as you ordered, Your Eminence,' said Walters.

'What? *What?* It fucking well was *not* as I ordered,' screeched Wolsey.

'But, Your Eminence,' said Frank, looking worried, 'you said that if he refused to talk we should take the accursed lute and . . .'

'Yes, yes,' Wolsey spluttered, his face going red, 'I know what I said. I know what I fucking well said, but it wasn't "an order", it was a mere fancy intended to convey my distaste for his instrument. A turn of phrase. It was a joke, Walters, a fucking joke. What on earth happened? I mean, I take it he was of no further use during the session.'

'No, Your Grace, he was not.'

Wolsey raised his cane to his mouth and chewed on the end of it. 'Well you better hope for your sake that he's not too injured to talk.'

Walters cleared his throat. He looked at Frank, who tilted his head to return the gaze. 'Well, Your Eminence, there may well be a problem there, too.'

Wolsey froze, still gnawing at the cane. He stared at his two aides, enunciating each word carefully. 'What – problem – is that?'

'The minstrel died.'

'He died.'

'Yes, Your Eminence.'

'How?'

'The torture master thought something to do with the shock of the penetration,' said Frank. 'He mentioned about it being a foreign object.'

'Plus,' said Walters, 'if you recall the shape of the lute, Your Grace, it has a strangely shaped neck with what they call a pegbox—'

'I know what a fucking lute looks like, thank you.'

'Well Jones the gaoler had to remove the pegbox prior to the procedure, which he did by snapping it off.'

'And neither of you thought to wonder if the broken and jagged neck of a lute wasn't the best thing to push into a prisoner when we want to hurt him enough to extract information but not actually cause sufficient trauma to kill him?' said Wolsey.

Frank and Walters shuffled. 'No, Your Grace.'

'And what happened next?' said Wolsey, resigned.

'What happened next, Your Eminence?' said Walters. 'Well, there was a great deal of screaming and really quite vast quantities of blood.'

'Oh, a lot of blood,' chimed in Frank.

'Fair gushing out of him it was,' added Walters. 'Torrents of it. And it was the sheer amount of it made us realise that perhaps the lute had inflicted greater damage than we had intended, at which point the prisoner gave a great jerk, a final agonised scream, ejected even more blood from his mouth, then died.'

Ripe with defeat, Wolsey nodded slowly. He seemed to have lost the energy to rage at his two idiotic clerks. With the minstrel dead he had nothing: no information, no bargaining chips; bugger all but accusations against dead men, which amounted to naught. He closed his eyes. He began to formulate a prayer then abandoned it. What was the bloody point?

'Right,' he sighed at last, retrieving from somewhere a tiny reserve of strength. 'You two, get out of my fucking sight. Fetch Dudley and Child. Tell them to prepare the carriage. We're to leave for Compton Wynyates in the morning.'

XLIII

Waking up in Anne's lap that morning, she dressed in a long chiffon dress and cleaning blood from him, Henry realised that he had never really known love before. Not until now anyway. Not like this.

For the King had the sudden realisation that love wasn't just feeling kindly towards a lady or getting his breeches in a tizzy; he'd been stupid to think otherwise. It was this: this feeling that was like being in a giant embrace. It was lying with Anne knowing they shared a great secret: that they were hunters.

She had discovered his secret the night he came to her chamber, she explained. Worried for him alone in the grounds of Hever, she'd gone to find him – and saw his transformation from man to wolf. She'd screamed and ran but Henry, fast, had bounded after her. She felt the hotness of his breath, heard his slavering jaws. But when she tripped and fell into the dewy grass, she was not devoured as she feared – feasted upon, eaten up for dinner – instead, 'your bite felt like a kiss, Your Majesty'.

Then he was gone, running towards the trees, and she had picked up her skirts and fled for home.

There, however, rather than raising the alarm or retreating

petrified to her chamber, she'd taken a torch and descended the steps to the cellar to see Aisha – Aisha had told her what she would become, had helped her to understand it, even welcome it.

Now Henry looked up at her. He heard the tinkling of the stream, the birdsong. 'Anne,' he said, 'do you have the fleas?'

She laughed. 'No, I *do not* have fleas. Do you?'

'Yes,' he said, ashamed. 'Also, I hunger for human flesh. Do you?'

'Aisha told me about this, also,' she said, stroking his forehead. 'You must use the moon, my love. Learn to absorb the moon's power, store it and channel it so that you release it only when you wish to do so. Use the moon and you can control the urges.'

'I want to,' he said, thinking of the family in the graveyard.

'Of course,' she agreed, 'but don't resist it, Your Grace, you shouldn't fight what you really are.'

Then they made love, the passion of it taking Henry by surprise, even after the months of desire and longing. In the moments afterwards they lay in the grass and all of the darkness was gone from him. For the moment at least, he wanted nothing to change.

They dressed and rode back to Hever. There, of course, a great pandemonium had ensued, the King being an unexpected guest. Messengers were sent to Waltham Abbey to reassure court the King was safe; Sir Francis Bryan was to be informed and return with staff and supplies.

As ever, his subjects moved quickly to accommodate the sudden, unorthodox behaviour of the King.

Which was fortunate, as there was more to come. Hever was next rocked by the King's announcement that he and Anne were to be married, 'Immediately on our return to court', he said, and Thomas Boleyn had all but messed his breeches with excitement, his efforts to make the King comfortable suddenly taking on a no-expense-spared air.

Meanwhile, makeshift thrones were set up in what was summarily renamed the King and Queen's Presence Chamber: ornate wooden chairs draped with the finest gold-spun cloth Elizabeth Boleyn was able to provide. Henry and Anne spent the day receiving those who wished to pay their respects as the news made its way across the region. As they received gifts and good wishes from visitors on bended knee, Henry found himself repeating the same statements over and over again: that Anne was to be the prettiest bride in Christendom; that he was sure the people would take her to their hearts, for they would see in her the same remarkable qualities he did, that had made such a happy prisoner of his hearts; that he cursed the sickness, not only for the death it had brought to the land, but also for keeping him away from his Anne.

Sitting, her back was arched slightly, chin tilted a little. She had sharp, intelligent features, mouth so plump and perfect.

He was in love now, Henry knew. Anne had made him the happiest werewolf in the land.

XLIV

Thanks to the injudicious rectal insertion of a lute, Thomas Cardinal Wolsey found himself at a great disadvantage, a situation worsened by the latest news.

The King was to return to court with his bride-to-be, Anne fucking Boleyn. Word was that the confounded woman was already starting to behave like the Queen, while Henry was telling all and sundry that his marriage to Katherine was illegal, apparently on the grounds that she had consummated her marriage with his brother.

Wolsey sighed the sigh of the eternally damned on being told. 'We went through all of this at the bloody time,' he complained to anyone who would listen. 'It was precisely *because* she had been married to his brother that we had to get the Pope's permission – which, incidentally, Campeggio is on his way to get rescinded.' He sighed again. 'I need to see the King, tell him of our plans. Perhaps he can be persuaded to reconsider.'

'The official word is that the King will not be dissuaded, Your Eminence,' said Child apologetically. 'He is to marry Anne at once. In the meantime an Act of Supremacy is to be drawn up declaring him the head of the Church of England.'

'Oh, fuck off: *the Church of England*?'

'Yes, Your Eminence.'

'Whoever heard of a Church of England? Christ, what next? Before you know it, everyone's going to want their own bloody church – next we'll have the Church of *Wales* rearing its ugly head.'

His clerk was dismissed to prepare for their forthcoming trip, while Wolsey ran over what he knew, which was this: that the recently departed Godfrey and the seriously ill Compton had been reading the King's letters from Anne. And just that knowledge would have been enough – *if* Wolsey had been able to put a culprit before the King. Unfortunately, he had decided to find out what was in the letters first, because whatever it was it involved either wolfen or Wolsey and he was very interested in any mention of either. Unfortunately, he had put his worst men on the job.

Now all he had was a dead minstrel clenching a lute.

Which left him with Compton. He couldn't very well have Compton tortured. Not with his rank. And anyway, who the hell would he get to do it? Christ only knows what instrument the terrible twosome would try to insert next. He hardly dared think.

No. What he had to do, he'd decided, was speak to Compton. And so he, Dudley and Child left Hampton Court in a carriage, bound for Compton Wynyates.

As they travelled they were able to see some of the devastation wreaked by the sickness for themselves: the roads thronged with wagons and families, rows and rows of gallows, dangling bodies. The epidemic had created grievances and scores to be settled. Either that or a desire to use the fresh pandemonium as cover for crime was the reason for the many beatings they saw; in one instance, as they passed by the outskirts of a small town, they saw what looked like a mob burning a family from their home.

'Should we stop?' asked Child. He and Dudley exchanged a brave look.

'Don't be stupid, Child,' snapped Wolsey, who had more important matters on his mind.

Eventually they arrived at Compton Wynyates. What they'd been expecting there, Wolsey wasn't quite sure, but one thing was certain: he'd assumed Compton would have retained some staff.

It appeared not. Their carriage sat in the courtyard unattended until it became apparent no footman was going to appear and Wolsey looked impatiently at Child, who knocked upon the ceiling of the carriage.

'Driver,' he called.

'Yes, sir,' came the muffled reply.

'You've driven Sir William before now?'

'Ah, yes, sir, rather a lot in fact.'

'*It's him?*' mouthed Wolsey to Dudley who nodded.

'Then perhaps you might be familiar enough with the layout of his home to venture inside in search of his staff?' added Child.

'Oh no, sir, I've never been here before. All of my journeys involving Sir William were to and from court.'

The horse snorted and whinnied. Wolsey, Dudley and Child looked at one another. Wolsey began to go red. Child shrugged then said, 'Perhaps you would be kind enough to venture inside anyway . . .?'

'Uh, I'd really rather not, sir. You know, being as Sir William is infected with the sickness.'

Wolsey could take it no longer. He threw open the door, dragged his huge bulk out into the courtyard and screamed at the driver. 'Get the fuck in there and find us a servant, before I have you taken to the Tower.'

He had barely finished his sentence before the driver was scrambling down, 'Yes, Your Eminence, certainly Your Eminence,' and was heading inside the deserted-looking house.

After long moments he returned with a housekeeper who explained that she was the only one remaining, and that all the other staff had left, and how she was surviving on the generosity of those who came to visit the master.

Wolsey sighed and told Dudley to give her some coins. Standing nearby, the driver shuffled, cleared his throat and coughed and Wolsey recommended he visit an apothecary on his return to court.

'Right,' Wolsey said to the old woman, 'you – take me to Sir William. Dudley, strap on the writing board and come with me . . .'

A few moments later, Wolsey was standing in the chamber of Sir William Compton, Dudley in the hall outside. Wolsey pulled at his collar and fanned himself with his free hand, the room hot and stuffy. Dust danced in thick shafts of light let in by gaps in the thick curtains and the scent of herbs hung heavy in the air.

He looked around. As with the rest of the house, the chamber was sparsely furnished, just the bed, occupant: Compton. And next to it a chair. Compton lay still, Wolsey was pleased to see, having heard a lot about patients of the sweating sickness thrashing in their beds. Then again, he thought, wasn't that in the early stages of the disease?

Now he pulled a disinfected scarf from his pocket and wrapped it around his mouth before stepping forward and clearing his throat.

There was no reply. No movement, no sound.

What a wasted trip it would be if Compton was dead, thought Wolsey, dragging the bedside chair back a few feet and sitting down, leaning his ravaged cane against it and arranging his robes around him. When he looked up, Compton had moved his head and was looking at him. His face was drawn, pale and expressionless, in his eyes, resignation.

'Hello, Sir William,' said Wolsey.

'Wolsey,' managed Compton.

'May I say how sorry I am to see you in such ill health,' said Wolsey. He waved a hand around him, 'And in such reduced circumstances, too.'

Compton chuckled without humour.

'No, My Lord,' said Wolsey, 'you may have considered us opponents, but it was only ever the Duke of Norfolk and Thomas Boleyn whose downfall I hoped to see. They seek only power and advancement. You and I, on the other hand, have the King's welfare at heart.'

Again a dry, hoarse laugh.

'I do, My Lord,' insisted Wolsey. 'At least, you must admit, to a greater degree than Norfolk and Boleyn.'

Compton's eyes conceded the point.

'My Lord, ' said Wolsey, pressing home, 'if the worst was to happen and you were to die . . .'

'I *am* dying,' drawled Compton. 'Look at me, for pity's sake.'

Wolsey bowed his head. 'And in that sad event, those to worm their way into the King's affections in your absence would be Norfolk, Boleyn and Thomas Cromwell.'

'Cromwell?' said Compton. 'Your hatchetman?'

It was true. Cromwell had been most useful to Wolsey in carrying out some of the more distasteful acts of the Lord Chancellor. If you needed a monastery dissolving, Cromwell was your man. Perhaps, thought Wolsey, it was only ever a matter of time before Cromwell directed those ruthless instincts towards usurping him.

'He has made himself useful to the King in my absence,' said Wolsey. 'It is Cromwell who has drawn up the Act of Supremacy. His support for the Reformation has brought him in line with the King's own desire to break with Rome.'

He was gambling that Compton's inbuilt distrust of Cromwell would outweigh his dislike for Wolsey. 'Cromwell is not of noble blood,' he pressed, 'and supporting the Reformation . . . well, who knows what new ways he will introduce to court; indeed, to the whole land . . .'

'And what would you have me do about this?' said Compton.

'Write to him,' said Wolsey. 'Urge him to take me back into his favour.'

Compton laughed. 'And you think I would do that in order to prevent Cromwell's ascension?'

'Yes, My Lord,' said Wolsey earnestly.

Compton regarded him with a dead stare. 'Wolsey, you've used your position to amass a wealth that is greater than the King's. You have used your position as a means of currying favour with the King *only* so that you may also curry favour with Rome. Thomas Cromwell may well bring in new ways that I might disapprove of – if I was alive to witness them, that is – but I know this: I could never disapprove of him more than I disapprove of you. I would sooner die than write your letter.'

Bollocks, thought Wolsey, and he leant back in his seat. He stared morosely at the gap in the curtain.

'Look, Compton,' he said, playing his trump card, 'we happen to know that you and Godfrey read the King's correspondence. We have a witness, and I'm afraid that if you don't do as I ask I will be forced to give the King this information.'

Compton gave a wheezy snort of derision. 'So? I shall be dead.'

'But not Godfrey.'

Compton's eyes flickered.

'I've taken the precaution of bringing him into custody, My Lord.'

'No, please.'

'We have the testimony of the driver, and not a mark on him. Which is, I'm afraid to say, more than could be said for Godfrey.' Wolsey brushed a flake of oregano from his robes.

'You're torturing him.' William tried to move but had no strength – rising just an inch or so off the bed before flopping back.

'Just a few questions to soften him up, My Lord. He told us that it was he who insisted on opening the letters, not you. Is that true?'

'No,' said Compton, 'it was me. All me. He begged me not to.'

'How funny, that's exactly what he's saying. Tomorrow we plan to ask him what you read in the letters. Your driver reports the two of you whispering about something in a state of great excitement. We're most keen to find out what it was.'

'Don't, please. Let him go.'

'Now why would I do that?' said Wolsey. 'I might learn something to my advantage. It might help – in the absence of a letter from you.'

'You have it,' said Compton. 'Fetch my writing board and ink and I shall write it now, anything you desire. Just please let Godfrey go.'

'That would be most kind,' smiled Wolsey. 'Certainly I would find myself prepared to overlook Godfrey's crime in return for your endorsement to the King. However . . .' he paused, slyly, 'my appetite has been whetted by all this talk of the letters' contents. And though I would be prepared to release Godfrey on his charges of treachery, I may still find myself keen to discover what he knows. As I already have him imprisoned, why it would be only too convenient to continue my questioning. The torture master is most keen to try out some new methods . . .'

'No,' said Compton, resignedly, 'that won't be necessary. I shall tell you the contents of the letters.'

'Wolsey drew his chair closer. There was a clatter as his cane was disturbed and fell to the floor. He ignored it.

'It is the King,' said Compton, 'though his wounds were so numerous it was impossible to tell at the time, he was infected by the wolfen on the night of the attack.'

'Christ,' said Wolsey, who had been imagining all manner of things in the letter, but not that. Though of course it made perfect sense now he recalled the events of the night, the King's subsequent behaviour. *Yes*. His temperament. All this talk of splitting from Rome. Certainly he'd developed a rather feral instinct of late.

He thought for a moment. 'Who else knows? You. Godfrey. Presumably . . . *Anne*?'

'Yes. She witnessed him change one night at Hever.'

'He changes?'

'Isn't that what werewolves do?'

'Yes, but . . . he's the King. Shouldn't someone notice if the King is becoming a werewolf? Don't we have people paid to take care of the King, whose duties should rightly include preventing him turning into a fucking werewolf? You, for example?'

'He was different,' admitted Compton. 'Looking back it should have been obvious, but at the time I thought it was the shock of the attack and the death of his son that affected his temperament. But there were physical changes, too. You must have noticed, Wolsey?'

'I suppose,' agreed Wolsey, thinking back. Yes, the King had been much hairier the last time they met.

'And did *you* suspect the King was a lycanthrope?' asked Compton.

'No, of course not. Not for a second. Does he go out when he's changed? Is he dangerous?'

'According to the letter, his changes seem to be controlled by the moon. He mentioned no details of attacks or diet.'

'And Anne *saw* him transform, did she? Yet she still wants to marry him. Christ, she must be desperate to be Queen.'

'You know what's amusing?' chuckled Compton, 'Godfrey didn't believe a word of it. He thought it the most fanciful thing – all part of some fantasy woven by the King and Anne.'

'He has a point,' said Wolsey thoughtfully. 'Why would Anne want to marry a werewolf? Not some kind of new perversion she picked up in France, is it?'

Compton coughed. 'At Hever we have imprisoned an

Arcadian. A she-wolfen called Aisha. She is Malchek's mate. The King seemed keen that she should be treated humanely. Since the outbreak Lady Anne has been caring for her. From her letters it seemed that Lady Anne and the wolfen had become acquainted . . .'

'Oh, it gets better,' said Wolsey, going cold. 'A wolfen has the ear of the future Queen? Jesus Christ . . .'

'That's how it would appear.'

'And the King either so in love or infected beyond repair has allowed this situation to develop?'

'So it would seem.'

'Christ, Compton, you should have raised the alarm.'

'I hoped to somehow reverse the King's infection. Find a cure that I could present to him.'

'Oh yes, and he *wants* a cure, does he?'

'He said so in his letters.'

'Did he?'

'Yes,' wheezed Compton.

'And that's it, is it?' said Wolsey. 'That's what I would have heard from Godfrey?'

Already his mind was racing. The King was a werewolf. How could he, Wolsey, benefit from the King being a werewolf? Not at all, he thought. Far from it, the new werewolf King was going to see him defrocked. In fact, what Wolsey needed was a return to the status quo.

'Yes,' sighed Compton, 'that is exactly what you would have heard from Godfrey. Sorry if you were expecting something a little more scandalous.'

'Not at all. Let us write this letter.' And with that Wolsey summoned Dudley.

* * *

It had begun to get dark by the time the endorsement was finally written. Wolsey bid Dudley back out to the carriage. He stood over Compton, whose eyelids flickered, sleep about to carry him off. *He has a couple of days in him, if that*, thought Wolsey.

'Wolsey,' managed Compton, so quietly.

'Yes, My Lord.'

'When you see Godfrey, will you tell him not to come? Tell him that I died. And that I said I loved him.'

'Yes,' said Wolsey, 'it would be my honour.'

'And you'll see that no more harm comes to him?'

'Absolutely,' said Wolsey, 'you have my word that he will remain untouched.'

Godfrey had, of course, been slung out of the Tower and into the Thames, and would have drifted downstream to an area they called Dead Man's Hole, where bodies tended to gather, and where it was said that some unsavoury types were based. The sort who would be doing more than just *touching* Godfrey . . .

'Thank you, Wolsey,' croaked Compton. 'I know you are a man of honour.'

'I can do that much at least,' said Wolsey, and he turned to go, hoping that Compton wouldn't ask him to deliver the last rites. He'd be there all bloody night.

'Wolsey,' said Compton, just as Wolsey was reaching out a hand to the door, 'I wonder if you'd . . .'

'Ah, God, well I would, Compton, only I've forgotten . . .'

'. . . finish me.'

'Finish you?' Wolsey turned. 'What, you mean kill you? Look, Compton, I really am in rather a hurry. Couldn't you get the housekeeper to do it?'

'Please.'

'Wouldn't you like to make the most of your final moments? Look out of the window, commune with nature, that kind of thing?'

'Please . . . Thomas.'

'Oh God, all right then.' Wolsey sighed and returned to the bedside. 'Did you have any particular method in mind?' he asked testily.

'Smother me,' said Compton. 'Please. Use a cushion.'

Wolsey looked around the room. Didn't Compton know that his servants had taken everything? Including cushions it seemed. In the end he gave up looking, but had a better idea.

'You will tell Godfrey I love him, won't you?' said Compton.

'Don't you worry about that.' Wolsey turned and sat on Compton's face. 'You'll be able to tell him yourself.'

The groom began to thrash beneath the Lord Chancellor's huge bulk. Wolsey supposed that thrashing was the natural reaction, even if you wanted to die – you'd try to fight for life. Gradually, though, the thrashing decreased then stopped altogether.

With the room silent once more, Wolsey remained atop Compton's face, gloomily pondering his problems.

XLV

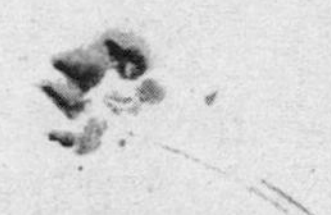

'How do you feel, Sir Thomas?' said Agatha, pulling open the curtains of More's chamber and letting sun flood the room. She placed a tray on a short table by the side of his bed as he pulled himself upright, yawning and smiling at her.

'I feel well, Mistress Hoblet,' he said. 'I feel very well indeed, thank you.'

She clasped her hands in front of her apron, glowing with an almost maternal pride.

'Well, I have to say I am pleased with your progress, Sir Thomas. There's not many that recover from the sweating sickness.' She gestured out of the window. 'Most of them's that had it are dead and gone. Makes you something of a miracle, so it does.' She gazed at him adoringly.

'The miracle is you, Mistress Hoblet.'

'Now listen, you, if I've had to tell you once it's a thousand times, don't go calling me Mistress Hoblet. It's not every day I get to save the life of one of the country's greatest thinkers. The least I can do is let you call me Agatha in return.'

'Well thank you . . . Agatha.'

'Don't think nothing of it. Well, no, that ain't quite right.

You should think *something* of it, being as it's only Hoblet that's usually allowed to call me Agatha. But don't think *too* much of it.'

'Well I think a great deal of it,' More reassured her. 'I consider it an honour.'

'Why, thank you,' blushed Agatha. 'I'm just pleased to have you alive and well.'

And if either of them thought back to a few months ago, when Agatha had been planning More's execution, and was even bemoaning the fact that she wasn't allowed to perform the act herself, they both chose not to say anything now, for fear, perhaps, of spoiling the moment.

'Well, it's your miracle cure, Agatha,' said More.

There was movement from the door and Hob was standing there, removing his hat and veil.

'Well hello, you two,' he said. 'Did I hear talk of Agatha's miracle cure?'

'Indeed you did, Hob,' laughed More.

'Well it wasn't all her own work, you know,' said Hob. 'She did have a little help from me.'

'I must admit, Sir Thomas, he's right. Hoblet has long spoken of the life-giving properties of honey. Lot of poppycock if you ask me, I just added it to make the medicine that bit sweeter for you.' She winked.

'Who knew it would have been such a tasty concoction, Agatha,' said More.

'But I have to say,' she relented, 'that I do believe the honey added a certain something to the medicine. There's no doubting it's done you the absolute power of good, Sir Thomas. Why, you're positively glowing.'

'Which means . . .' said More, almost sadly.

'That you'll be on your way,' said Hob, coming forward.

'That's right.'

Hob looked at Agatha, who was studying the floor, her hands fretting at the hem of her apron.

'I dare say I won't be the only one who'll be missing you,' said Hob.

'Oh don't be ridiculous,' said Agatha. 'I've become attached to Sir Thomas, that's true, but it's no different than tending to sick livestock, no disrespect intended, Sir Thomas.'

'None taken.'

'When Sir Thomas has gone,' she said, 'we'll get back to doing what we do best, which is burning witches and wolves.'

'Will we?' said Hob, unable to hide his disappointment.

'Yes, we will,' she snapped. 'That's what we do, Hoblet, and don't you forget it.'

She stomped off.

Hob and More shared a sympathetic look, before Hob departed, too, leaving More to dress.

Later, he bid farewell to the Hoblets, thanked them for the horse and departed for court to tell them what he had learnt: that somewhere in the countryside Malchek was gathering an army of wolfen, ready to march upon the throne.

On the track leading away from the Hoblets' farmhouse he came upon a cart driven by a grim-faced teenage boy, who stopped and touched the brim of his hat, asking, 'Sor, can you tell me if I'm on the right track for the farmhouse owned by Mistress Hoblet, the wife of the Witchfinder General?'

More smiled. 'Indeed you are, boy. I'm acquainted with

the witchfinders. May I ask, do you have business there? If not I might advise against an unannounced visit.'

'Well, sir, I am Hugh, the son of Master Brookes the builder. I have some news regarding my father.'

'Very well, then,' said More. 'I should imagine they will be most keen to see you.'

XLVI

Henry had recalled court to Greenwich, installed Anne Boleyn, and was now receiving well-wishers. All were to pay their respects to the King's new consort.

His new consort. Anne fucking Boleyn.

At home in Hampton Court, Wolsey had awaited word that his presence was required. When it came his heart had sunk even further. He knew that his duty was to protest the engagement on behalf of Rome, and in return Henry and Anne were going to insist he abide by the Act of Supremacy, which effectively farted at the Pope and left him, Thomas Cardinal Wolsey, looking very expendable indeed. No doubt about it, there was not a lot to look forward to at that particular meeting. In fact, when was the last time he'd seen Anne Boleyn? Oh yes. She'd been in tears as he told her that she was not permitted to marry Henry Percy. Hadn't she mentioned something then about making an enemy of her? Wolsey was used to that, of course. Lowly courtiers hating him went with the job. Those lowly courtiers then ascending to higher than him in rank, the grudge very much still intact – that was most unfortunate.

As if all that wasn't bad enough, there was an elephant

in the room. A hairy elephant with sharp claws and big teeth.

Because all the time they were discussing matters of state or those concerning the King's marriage, Wolsey would be standing before them thinking, The real issue here is not about the church or Anne, it's about you, Henry Tudor, being a werewolf.

But of course there were issues of protocol to consider and Wolsey thought it prudent to ignore the wolf thing, at least for the time being. Until after he'd seen Lefsetz.

So upon arrival at Greenwich he dispatched word that he was present and awaited his summons, organising a summit with the Belgian ambassador in the meantime. The King would want to keep him waiting, he guessed. One sure way of knowing whether or not you were in his favour was by the length of time you had to wait after a summons. As predicted, Wolsey received word that the happy couple were seeing a series of unimportant nobles first, and so he made his way to the ambassador's chamber.

On his way, he was joined by Jane Seymour, who appeared at his side and hurried to keep up with him, harried at having stolen away from the Presence Chamber.

'You've been chosen as one of Anne's ladies?' he asked her.

'Yes, Your Eminence,' she replied. 'I am one of the Queen's ladies.'

'Well thank God for that,' he hissed, then stopped. 'What did you just say? One of the *what's* ladies?'

'One of the Queen's ladies.'

He raised his cane to his mouth. 'Tell me this isn't happening.'

'They exchanged secret vows this morning, Your Eminence,'

she said, 'in a service performed by Archbishop Thomas Cranmer. The only other person present was—'

'Let me guess: Cromwell?'

'Yes, Your Eminence.'

'Bollocks.'

'There is also a rumour . . .'

'If you say she's with child I will throw myself in the river.'

'I'm sorry, Your Eminence . . . As though wishing to confirm the gossip, my Lady Anne often passes a hand across her stomach before gazing lovingly at the King.'

'Christ, how sick-making.'

'She is the picture of a devoted wife and mother-to-be, Your Eminence.'

'I don't bloody doubt it. Being ingratiating runs in the family. What of the King? How does he appear in character and temperament?'

Wolsey had decided to keep his discovery secret from the Protektorate for the time being. He should feel guilty about that, he knew, essentially sending an operative into the field without all of the necessary intelligence. But he judged it the best thing to do for the time being. With any luck the Protektorate need never know, which meant Rome need never know – which meant the Pope need never know . . . what a complete balls-up he had made of the whole situation.

'It's difficult to say, Your Eminence,' answered Jane. 'He alternates. One moment, irascible and ill-tempered, the next distracted, the next unable to take his eyes from Anne. He is not himself. His Gentlemen say he has been this way for some time now; that they had hoped his engagement to Anne might soothe his temper.'

It would take more than that, Wolsey thought. Some fresh meat dripping blood at the very least.

But what *would* it take for the King to return to his normal self? As Jane hurried off, to return to the Presence Chamber where no doubt she would be busy curtsying to the Earl of Wolverhampton or some such, Wolsey arrived at the chamber of the Belgian ambassador, Lefsetz, who received him with his usual irritating air of amusement.

It occurred to Wolsey, as he took his seat, that recent events had very much favoured demonkind, who must have enjoyed the outbreak of the sickness, the untold misery it had wrought.

'How are things going with the wolfen, Thomas?' asked the ambassador sweetly.

'Shall we take it that you already know exactly how things are going?'

Lefsetz conceded. 'Let's do that then. Should I be concerned?'

'Not at all,' said Wolsey, 'with the sweating sickness over, our troops will resume the search. Malchek will soon be located and the rebellion quashed.'

'Excellent news.'

Lefsetz grinned. Wolsey grinned back. He wondered whether Lefsetz ever tired of this pretence.

'Will there be anything else?' asked Lefsetz, after a pause.

'Indeed there is – it seems that Malchek or his followers may have bitten some people. Infected them,' said Wolsey.

Lefsetz nodded sadly. 'It happens.'

'Yes, well. In view of that, I need more information. What can you tell me about . . . werewolves?'

'Werewolves,' said Lefsetz, as though the word were a fine wine. 'Are we talking about anyone in particular?'

'Purely hypothetical, My Lord,' Wolsey assured him.

'Well now,' said Lefsetz, 'what do we know? In the eyes of demonkind, an abomination, obviously. Unnatural. A hybrid of demonkind's lowest caste with a human? Ugh.' He shuddered. 'Against the established order.'

'Yes, yes,' said Wolsey testily. 'We humans tend to take a dim view of it as well. And I rather suspect those infected find the whole experience somewhat traumatic. But I ask again: what do we know of them? What characteristics do they display?'

'The ability to shape-shift, obviously, but without being able to exercise the control that the Arcadian has. Arcadians use the moon's power instinctively. But a hybrid won't have that ability, so when changed the wolfman would find himself overridden by ancient instinct and bloodlust. In effect, he would become the most savage Arcadian.'

'So can a werewolf control it? In much the same way as an Arcadian?'

'Yes, though there are no known cases of a werewolf successfully doing so. In theory they ought to be able to do so with quite some success since they are by definition half human.'

'I see,' said Wolsey thoughtfully, 'and what of a cure?'

'A cure?' Lefsetz smiled. Light danced on his earring. 'By God, he wants a cure. Are you sure this is nobody you want to tell me about? I do hope nothing is happening that might be considered in breach of the treaty.'

'Most assuredly not, My Lord,' oozed Wolsey.

'Well there are two methods known to remove the curse. One is to have the infected person kneel on the ground . . .'

Kneel on the ground, thought Wolsey. That sounds fairly simple.

'. . . for one hundred years.'

Wolsey looked at Lefsetz. 'What's the second one?'

'He must kill up the bloodline.'

Wolsey's eyebrows knitted. 'Go on.'

'The Arcadian clan is a series of packs, its members each descended from its leader. In order for a werewolf to be cured he must kill further up the bloodline than himself, not forgetting to taste the blood of the victim. Very important, that bit. To be *absolutely* sure, the wolf should kill the one who bit him . . . Failing that, the pack leader.'

'Really?' said Wolsey. He was thinking of the youngling, the one they had in the Tower. Was he the one who bit His Majesty? *Yes, he was*. That being so, then surely a cure could not be far away? It was just a case of persuading His Majesty to take that course of action.

'Absolutely,' said Lefsetz. 'It's important to drink from the blood at its strongest. 'Another option would be to kill the leader of the pack.'

His Majesty would be more than happy to kill Malchek, thought Wolsey, and was still thinking about that as he made his excuses and left the ambassador's chamber – as always with the feeling that Lefsetz knew more than he acknowledged – and was joined by his two clerks, both of whom were in a state of great excitement.

'Sir,' said Child.

'Yes, Child.'

'We bring news of great importance.'

'And what is that?'

'Sir Thomas More has returned to court.'

Wolsey stopped. 'Really? Thomas is back?' He clasped his clerk's shoulders. 'Then let us go to him, at once.'

'Thomas.'

Wolsey burst into the Chamber where Sir Thomas More sat awaiting his audience with the King.

'Thomas,' said More, standing, his face breaking into a grin. And for a moment the two friends regarded each other, only now realising how much they had missed one another. When they came together for an embrace, each found his eyes brimming with unexpected tears.

'Look at you,' said Wolsey, coming apart and holding More by the shoulders to take him in. 'You look as if you haven't seen a meal in months.'

'Well, believe it or not, I haven't,' laughed More.

'Where have you been?'

'A prisoner, first of witchfinders, then of the sickness. At which point I then became *a patient* of the witchfinders, which is a long story.'

Wolsey scuttled away. 'You've had the sweating sickness?' he said with an uneasy smile.

'Indeed, I have, but I'm now fully recovered, Thomas,' said More. 'I'm the picture of health.'

'Well that won't last, not now you're back here. Have you been informed of the news?' asked Wolsey. 'I've got to warn you, there's a lot to tell.'

'Since I announced my arrival my only companions have been these yeomen,' said More, 'so I know nothing more than I've already gathered.'

'Which is?'

More looked bemused. 'Well, apart from the fact that the King has grown . . .' he puffed out his cheeks and held his hands around an imaginary stomach, 'I am told that he has a new bride?'

'Indeed so.'

'By the name of Anne, more than that I don't know. He is divorced, I take it? Surely the quickest divorce ever, if so.'

'Therein lies another tale.' Wolsey lowered his voice. 'In your absence Cromwell has wormed his way into the King's affections and drawn up for the King an Act of Supremacy. In effect, the King has declared his own divorce in order to marry Anne.'

'Oh . . .' said More.

Wolsey saw his friend's face fall. More, being the devout sort, wasn't going to like that, he thought. Good. Ever the voice of calm reason at court, More had long been the King's confidant and the two shared a great bond. If anybody could talk the King round it was him.

'I have disturbing developments of my own,' said More, his voice dropped. He took Wolsey by the arm and with a meaningful look at the yeomen, steered the cardinal into a corner of the room. 'I was worried I might have to break it first to the King,' he said, in a low voice, so that Wolsey had to strain to hear him. 'The wolfen rebellion continues. Malchek is readying an offensive against us.'

Wolsey pulled away, his eyes wide. Both men stole sideways glances at the yeomen. 'Malchek has used the sweating sickness as cover in order to build an army,' continued More. 'During the outbreak his men have been roaming the rural areas and taking the dying, my guess is to infect them for his militia.'

What little colour there was in Wolsey's face drained at More's words.

'Christ,' he said, at last.

'Exactly. We should be recalling all our men to protect the palaces, and send armies out to find the wolfen base immediately.'

'Quite,' said Wolsey, who was trying to think how such a situation might benefit him, and coming up with very little. At least he was allied to More, who was the bearer of what could be a vital forewarning. That ought to count for something.

Moments later, the door to the Presence Chamber opened, and they were ushered inside for an emotional reunion between the King and his old tutor and friend, Sir Thomas More.

Shortly after that, to the surprise of all those gathered, Sir Thomas More was sentenced to death.

XLVII

In the Presence Chamber, with Anne by his side, Henry sat and brooded. His thoughts were of William, his friend and Groom of the Stool, dead and already in the ground at Compton Wynyates, yet another victim of the sweating sickness.

It was one of the highest-ranking posts in the land, yet the groom's task was not on the surface an enviable one: it was to wipe Henry's bottom for him, to see that 'the house of easement be sweet and clear'. It was by far the most contested position in the Privy Chamber, for the sole reason that the house of easement in question belonged to the King – and there was no finer arse-wiping job in the land.

Even so, the best-kept secret was that Henry had never allowed Compton or indeed anyone else for that matter to wipe his arse. Like being dressed in the morning he hated relinquishing control of it to someone else. He wanted to be the King of himself.

During their last months together he had been unpleasant to William, he knew; since the bite, after he'd let the beast take over. There had been no more stories after that. No more late nights in the chamber. The only light in his life was the light of the moon.

Who was that Henry? wondered the King. Where had that Henry gone, who was merry with wine and dance? The one who hated to relinquish control.

Now the last of what felt like a never-ending line of noblemen had left the room and he glanced across at Anne, who fairly glowed with her new status, the colour high in her cheeks. She looked at him, smiled, and he smiled back, finding that he was having to force it a little. She passed a hand over her stomach and he made sure to increase his smile. But when she looked away again, he felt it slip, his eyes wandering across the room where Anne's ladies stood in a group. One in particular caught his eye, looking at once attentive yet distant.

Jane Seymour.

Of course. What was it William had said? Or – no – was *going* to say? How Henry had wanted to 'see more' of her. Henry had replied that his thoughts were reserved for his lady.

Now he wondered: when was the last time he'd thought of Katherine? He couldn't remember. He thought of her now and he imagined her pain. Her baby killed and now this: disowned, husband taking another wife.

Those he loved, he hurt.

A shadow must have passed across his face at the thought because he became aware of a look of concern on Lady Jane's face so he tried to smile to put her at ease, but only one half of his mouth would obey the order so he ended up grimacing, like the victim of a bad beating.

In return she laughed a little, bowing her head in order to hide her giggles, and for a moment he was entranced with her hair. A hypnotising shade of blonde, it seemed to shine as though there was another source of light in the room.

Perhaps there was.

Then, Anne's hand fell to his knee and he was pulled from his reverie. She squeezed his leg. She leant towards him so that only he could hear her.

'Tonight,' she said, 'we hunt.'

He smiled and brought his lips to her cheek, the thought of the hunt sending a thrill through him with a warm shiver. *The hunt*. He wanted to do it more; every night he wanted to run out with her, but she rationed him. It was too sweet, she said, why spoil it through familiarity? When they hunted together it was like they were joined. Like they were one mind, one heart.

But as humans, though – as humans Henry wasn't quite so sure, and he found his gaze wandering to Jane when he thought Anne was otherwise occupied, rewarding himself with stolen glances in her direction.

Behind him stood Thomas Cromwell, black robes and simple dark hat in sharp contrast to Wolsey's finery. He leant forward now.

'Your Majesty,' he said into Henry's ear, 'next to see you: Cardinal Thomas Wolsey and Sir Thomas More.'

Thomas, thought Henry and he sat up in his seat. *Sir Thomas More*. 'Bring them in,' he commanded, waving impatiently to Cromwell, who in turn indicated to a page who went to the door.

Then Henry was on his feet as his old friend and tutor entered the chamber. Wolsey and his two clerks came with him but Henry barely saw them, and as the visitors knelt before the King, he left his seat and strode lithely from the raised platform on which the two thrones were placed, went straight to More and grasped him by the shoulders, so that More rose from his knees to his feet and raised his head to look at Henry.

'Thomas,' said the King. 'Thomas, you're a sight for sore eyes. What there is left of you, I should say. What on earth have you been eating during your absence?'

More laughed and picked at his robes. 'A period of enforced starvation, I'm afraid,' then picking up on Henry's concern added, 'Nothing that need worry Your Majesty too much, though you may find some of my tales a little hair-raising.'

'I look forward to hearing them in great detail,' said Henry, 'I've missed your stories. While you've been away I've contented myself with *Utopia*, it's a real page-turner, Thomas.'

More smiled and bowed his head in thanks.

'I do declare,' continued Henry, 'that we have missed your wisdom and piety around here these past months.' Here Henry threw a look at Wolsey, a look that sent the kneeling cardinal's gaze towards the floor. 'Truly there have been some trying times since we last saw you.'

'I look forward to being of service, Your Majesty.'

'Henry, to you,' said Henry, at which there was an audible intake of breath around the room. 'And now you are back at court, Thomas, I plan to keep you with me,' he added, throwing his arm around More's shoulder with such force that More almost lost his footing. 'I need advisers with level heads, Thomas. I need men around me who understand me.'

'There would be no greater honour,' said More, almost bent double under the force of the King's affection. 'However,' he managed, twisting his head so that he was speaking into the King's jerkin, and hardly needing to lower his voice for this reason, 'we must convene a meeting of the Privy Council at once.'

Just then, Anne cleared her throat loudly. Henry spun. 'Thomas,' he recovered, 'may I introduce you to my Queen – Queen Anne?'

More and Anne regarded each other. Wolsey, on one knee, watched them. So did his clerks. Anne's ladies looked on. Bryan and three of his men watched; Cromwell watched; the yeomen watched; pages by the door, their hands clasped behind their backs, watched; and servants standing by a long, food-covered table, awaiting their orders, watched.

The whole room watched Sir Thomas More and the Queen look each other over.

'I am overjoyed to welcome you at court, Sir Thomas,' said the Queen insincerely. Nor was her insincerity lost on More, who was regarding her intently.

'Your Majesty,' said More at last, his face still puzzled, 'you look most familiar to me. Won't you tell me, what is your family name?'

'Boleyn,' she said, smiling.

More's face fell.

Henry smelt a change come upon him. Suddenly More was angry, he knew, the anger directed at Anne. Henry's eyes narrowed as he looked at More. He felt a noise building in his throat and realised it was a growl, moved closer to his lady, his gaze not leaving More.

'Yes,' she said imperiously, 'I believe you know my father.' She indicated to one of her ladies who glided towards the rear of the room and to a door there.

More's face darkened. 'Yes,' he said, 'indeed I am acquainted with your father.' His voice rose a little. 'I met your father recently, in fact, in a small village called Darenth in Kent, just before the outbreak.'

'Goodness,' said Anne, 'what a small world.'

The lady-in-waiting opened the door and into the chamber strutted the Duke of Norfolk and Thomas Boleyn. Both were laughing as though enjoying the punch line of a joke as they came to the side of the thrones, standing near Cromwell and presenting themselves. They bowed first to Henry then to Anne, with Boleyn reserving a special smile for his daughter before acknowledging her ladies and lastly, bowing to the room. Henry saw Wolsey bristling at the sight of his two arch-enemies. The Lord Chancellor's reaction, though, was as nothing compared to the change in More, who had darkened, pulling himself up to his full height.

'*Boleyn*,' he said.

'My Lord?' replied Boleyn, affecting to look both surprised and perplexed.

'And you – Norfolk,' snapped More.

'My Lord?' said Norfolk. He and Boleyn shared an amused look.

'Perhaps you would like to explain to the assembled company where we last met,' demanded More.

'Well, My Lord,' said Boleyn, 'I'm quite sure I couldn't say. At Richmond Palace, perhaps?'

'Sir Thomas says he saw you in a village called Darenth, Father,' said Anne helpfully.

'Well I know of Darenth, of course,' said Boleyn, 'but I don't believe I have been recently, and certainly not to see Sir Thomas. Perhaps Sir Thomas might expand.'

'You left me there to die, Boleyn,' said More.

He turned his attention to Henry, who sensed the danger in the air.

'Your Majesty,' continued More, his voice vibrating with emotion, 'you want to know where I've been, simply ask these two blackguards. Not only that, but they paid – they actually *paid* – two witchfinders to execute me.'

Boleyn chortled, then put a hand over his mouth to excuse himself. 'From this are we to deduce then that you are a witch, Sir Thomas?'

'Oh no,' said More, 'the charge was one of lycanthropy.'

'You're a werewolf?'

More cleared his throat. 'Actually the charge was of consorting with a lycanthrope.'

'Consorting?' said Norfolk, pretending great confusion. 'And was there any truth in this, Sir Thomas? Had you had *relations* with a werewolf?'

More reddened. His voice rose. 'That's not the point. The details of my supposed offence are insignificant compared to the act of treachery that took place that day.'

'Treachery?' Now it was Boleyn's turn to darken. 'That is a most serious charge, sir.'

'Indeed it is, and it is not lightly used. I can and will present witnesses who will state that these two are traitors to the Crown.'

'You would do well to temper your speech, sir,' said Norfolk, his own voice rising.

'Thomas,' said Wolsey from behind them, 'perhaps we should leave this for another time.'

'I would have died,' shouted More, pointing at Norfolk and Boleyn, his arm shaking with emotion, 'if the wicked plans of this pair of plotters had come to pass.'

'I shall stand for no more of this,' roared Boleyn in return, 'you, sir, are a liar.'

'A liar am I?' screeched More. 'You left me to die and now you call me a liar?'

'I do, sir: liar, liar, liar.'

More could take no more. He flew forward, throwing himself at Boleyn, swinging a fist. Even after his enforced diet he was still larger than Boleyn, who fell back with a cry, and for a moment there was a flurry of robes on the stone floor as though a pile of laundry had come alive, a glimpse of Boleyn's ginger beard as he tried to twist away from More's attack, shouting in pain and shock.

'Liar?' screamed More. 'You call me a liar?'

'*Argh*,' replied Boleyn.

'You left me to die then call me a liar!' screeched More again, fists pummelling.

'*Argh*,' said Boleyn.

Anne was the first to recover. 'Father,' she called, jumped from her throne and dashed over to the fighting courtiers where she grabbed More's arm, yanking him off her father with a strength that took all by surprise, not least More, who in his fury and little knowing that it was Anne who had taken him by the arm and not Norfolk, blindly threw a punch at his new assailant, catching the Queen on the chin and sending her skittering back, falling over the hem of her dress.

The Queen crashed to the stone.

'Anne,' roared the King. He made to dash across the chamber to her but she had already righted herself and stood, chest rising and falling, pointing at More who remained with his fist still clenched, his mouth open in shock. Behind him, Boleyn, still spread-eagled on the floor, looked as triumphant as it was possible for a man spread-eagled on a floor to look.

'Guards, arrest this man,' shouted Anne, 'take him to the Tower. He will be hung, drawn and quartered for this. Prepare the Hill. Send word we are to *execute* Sir Thomas More for the crime of high treason.'

Henry had reached her side by now. He watched as the yeomen rushed over to More and grabbed him by the shoulders, already manhandling him to the door. More's eyes were beseeching as they met his.

'Your Majesty,' he said, 'you must believe me. I am the victim of a betrayal.'

'Thomas . . .' said Henry, his feelings a riot of indecision and torn loyalties. He felt the presence of the wolf inside and it pulled him to Anne; meanwhile, his humanity called for Thomas.

'Your Majesty, I must tell you my matter of urgency,' More called over his shoulder, almost at the door now. 'The wolfen are building an army, they plan to march against you. Your Majesty, please . . .' They had reached the door now. '*Please*,' shouted More as it was opened and he was bundled through. 'Henry . . .'

Still kneeling on the floor, Wolsey watched More go. As the door slammed behind him, he looked at Child, mouthing a single four-letter word to him.

Part Four

THE BEAST

XLVIII

Crouched in a ditch in a remote part of the region – Betsham was the nearest village, and that a good hour's ride away – Agatha and young Hugh Brookes applied a mixture of grease and flour to Hob's face as the Witchfinder General fidgeted nervously.

'Will you hold still, Hoblet,' she said testily. 'If you hadn't spent so much time in the garden you wouldn't have caught so much sun and we wouldn't have to go through all of this.'

With that she reached her fingers into the pot she had brought and slapped a great dollop of the mixture on to Hob's forehead, rubbing it in until his skin had a shiny, pasty glow

The trail by their side had been baked hard by the sun It led down the hill to a collection of three barns in a field. There, the Wagon Men were at work. They took human form while out of doors, but it was them: it was the wolfen. Their clothes were baggy and oversized on them, and the Hoblets knew why – for the transformation.

The day before, squatting in their vantage point on the hill, Agatha, Hob and young Master Brookes had watched them go about their business. They saw a wagon arrive and sick men in chains herded off it; the infected, mostly docile or semi-conscious, many in nightshirts, were dragged like reluctant cattle towards the entrance of the first barn.

At the rear of the barn was yet more activity. Here, an almost constant flow of the infected were shepherded towards the second barn. Where before they had been slumped or were being dragged, now they walked. A little dazed perhaps, but they walked. Whatever was happening in that first barn, it was a miracle cure to put Agatha's potions to shame.

What's more, it left large bloody marks about their necks and shoulders.

Hob and Agatha had looked at one another. They thought they knew what the wolfen were doing. They were turning them. They were taking the infected and making them . . . disinfected? Perhaps. Making them wolfen, almost certainly.

What wasn't so clear was the buckets that were brought out of the second barn. The first time Hob saw a wagon man walking from the barn with a bucket in each hand, he wondered what could be inside. Then he saw the creature approach a patch of what looked like tar in a corner of the yard, set down a bucket and slosh the contents of the other on to the patch. It hit the ground, bright red. The wolfen did the same with the other bucket, then hefted the two buckets and returned to the barn.

Not long later, the same guard reappeared. Again, he carried two buckets of blood that he sloshed on to the ground, the last lot already hard and dry, having been baked by the sun.

'What do you suppose that's all about, Agatha?' asked Hob.

There was a click-click sound as she chewed thoughtfully on her pipe. 'Not long after we got started in witchfinding

I was trying out some new techniques. You ever hear of exsanguination, Hoblet?'

'No, I can't say that I have.'

She chortled. 'And you with all your book lurnin. It's draining blood, Hoblet, removing blood. I tried it out a few times and it was a bit like the sleep deprivation, you remember that? They got so sleepy they were good for nothing. Same as when you remove large quantities of blood from a person. They get all weak. Might be just what you need if you wanted to keep a large amount of people docile.'

Every so often bodies were brought out of the first barn, and these were slung on to a wagon, which, when it was full presumably, was driven back up the track and away from the camp.

The witchfinders and young Master Brookes had watched two wagon-loads of infected arrive, and had counted about fifteen wolfen in attendance at any one time, most of whom seemed to be milling around in the yard.

Only once did they see the activity cease, and this was when a cart came down the track, causing a shout to go up. At that the infected were swiftly herded inside the first barn. Left in the yard was one man who approached the cart to point the driver back up the track.

Despite being some distance away, the Hoblets could see he wore an eyepatch.

So . . . Agatha and Hob looked at each other. What to do? Even with Agatha's superior combat skills, an attack was out of the question. Anyway, was Master Brookes even there? Perhaps the builder had been one of the bodies they were carting away.

What they needed, they decided, was an inside man, so

reluctantly they returned home, where Agatha mixed a pot of gloop designed to give its wearer the pallor of an infected person. Just what was needed for Hugh to pass into the camp in order to locate his father.

Or so Hob had thought.

Agatha had other plans. Although young Hugh was desperate to take on the mission – having been tortured by guilt since the massacre at his home – Agatha had told him no. He was too emotionally involved, she said. No, Hob would have to go, and no amount of him protesting would change her mind.

'Have you tried getting a decent builder round here?' she screeched. 'When you find a good craftsman like that you hang on to him.' She gave a dramatic pause. 'You don't throw him to the wolves.'

'Now we know about the existence of the camp we could alert the Crown,' argued Hob. 'We could get word to Sir Thomas.'

'Might be too late by then,' she said, firmly. 'Who knows what's going to happen. Sir Thomas spoke of an army, did he not? And what have we seen today if not that army's base? Who knows when it will be on the march?'

'But if the builder's there he will have been turned.'

'We'll cross that bridge when we come to it, Hoblet.'

The following day they took the cart back to Betsham, pulled it off the track behind hedgerow and regained their position. Hob was now shaking with nerves, finding it difficult to see as Agatha applied soot to his under-eyes then helped him off with his clothes and slipped a nightshirt over his head.

'Listen, Hoblet, listen to me – you hold it together,' said

Agatha, looking deep into Hob's fretful eyes. 'Now – you remember the plan?'

'You'll be right behind me.'

'Right behind you.'

'You'll be right behind me and when the yard's empty and you have Malchek's attention, I make my move.'

'Don't you get sent into that barn, Hoblet. You get put in there you're dog food. What you have to do is get to that second barn.'

'And then what?'

'Well, then you look for Master Brookes. With any luck you'll be able to pass word through the slats.'

'And if he's there?'

'That's another bridge we'll cross when we come to it. Make it to the hedgerow at the back and return up here. Got it?'

'You'll be right behind me?' he repeated.

'Right behind you. You needn't even see a wolfen.'

'Right.' He looked down at himself. 'Then why am I dressed like this?'

She shrugged. 'In case – in case one of them looks in the wagon. You've got to look the part, that's the thing.'

She and Hugh fetched the cart, keeping it out of sight behind the hedgerow but close to a short bridge crossing the ditch, little more than a few boards laid out. She prepared to board and was stopped by Hugh.

'Let *me* go,' said Hugh now. 'Let me take this duty. So I can look into the eyes of the creature that killed my family.'

'No, young Master Brookes, you're to remain here,' she said, firmly, and the young man's eyes flared, but he said nothing. They waited, until at last they heard the trundle of a wagon. Nodding to Agatha, Hob moved forward and crouched in the ditch, out of sight beneath the wooden bridge, waiting for the wagon to pass. He thought he might wet himself with the tension as the wagon slowly trundled overhead and he readied himself. As it passed he shifted, ready to spring from beneath the bridge and scramble up to it.

Any second now.

Almost . . .

Now.

He sprang. Then immediately was pulled backwards, his nightshirt caught on one of the boards of the bridge. Desperately he yanked away the nightshirt, dislodging the board but letting him free, so that he was able to run on to the track and – *hup* – pull himself on to the tailgate of the wagon, twisting so that he fell backwards, encountering not the hard wood of the wagon floor but a soft body, his landing accompanied by a groan.

'Sorry,' he whispered, 'sorry,' but was already turning to peer over the tailgate. He was just in time to see the cart come over the bridge, Agatha in the driving seat wielding her crop.

And he was just in time to remember the board he'd dislodged with his nightshirt.

Dislodged enough to upset the cart?

He held his breath.

The wheels of her cart were on the bridge now. No, just *one* of the wheels was on the bridge. And suddenly the cart listed violently to one side, dipping almost out of sight and throwing Agatha off, Hob powerless to do anything, but . . .

Get out. He had to get out.

Except now the wagon had browed the hill and had picked up speed. Hob saw hardened track blurry with the pace. Hit it at this speed and he was likely to end up resurfacing it. Plus he'd be seen by those in the yard.

But he had no other option he decided, and was about to climb up to the tailgate when it became clear that the matter was out of his hands. The wagon was passing into the compound. The last thing he saw before he ducked down behind the tailgate was the track stretching up the hill. Empty. No sign of Agatha's cart.

Oh God.

For the first time he looked around him in the cart. Gazing back at him were the infected, all in advanced stages of the illness. Most just stared listlessly, some groaned, some writhed; some sweated, some shivered. Hob, not being sure of the etiquette in such a situation, tried to smile encouragingly while simultaneously holding his breath. He was going to need plenty of Agatha's cure if he got out of this.

If he got out of this.

A big if.

He yearned suddenly to be back on the farm, standing at his hives, hearing Agatha in the kitchen, singing as she polished her torture equipment.

But now the wagon was at a standstill and he heard footsteps coming to the back so lay down, trying to look as if he'd been there for hours. He pushed his feet beneath the buttocks of a man lying unconscious on his side, to hide his chainless feet.

The latch on the tailgate clicked. Hob saw the figure of the guard as he moved to the latch on the other side. He saw the track, still no sign of Agatha.

The second latch clicked and the tailgate came down.

Hob felt a hand grip his arm by the armpit and pull so he affected a stupor, wearing his best glassy stare and going limp, his head hanging as he was dragged out of the wagon and to the dirt, where he landed painfully, drooling a little in order to complete the effect.

A foot jabbed at him. 'Hey, this ain't roit. This one ain't chained.'

'Well you must have forgotten to chain him,' said a second voice. 'It don't matter either way. Just get him inside. There's one more batch to turn before we break for lunch.'

'Oh, aye. What's for lunch?'

'A fat butcher and his wife.'

'Perfect.'

'Well get a bloody move on, else there'll be nothing left but hair and fingernails.'

This is it, thought Hob. They were going to turn him. They were going to make him into an inhuman. A deviant. A beast. Who would look after the garden? As hands reached down to him, he cast one final look up the track – the empty track.

That wasn't empty any more.

Barrelling down it came their cart, the rear of it on fire, flames licking around a hay bale. Driving the cart was Hugh, the reins in one hand, in the other a pitchfork.

The guards saw it at the same time: '*Fire*.'

One of them rushed to try to close the gate, but it had become stuck in the baked earth, the guard desperately yanking at it to free, even as Hugh passed into the yard and with an angry shout jabbed downwards with his pitchfork, stabbing the man in the chest, the man yelling as he fell away, chest wound spurting blood, but already dead.

Into the yard came the cart and Hugh was aiming it

towards the second barn, the horse rearing up as it realised the driver's plan. It turned and the cart skidded sideways, smashing into the rear of the barn and sending young Hugh Brookes flying from his seat and to the ground, where he rolled then scrambled to his feet in a cloud of dust, teeth bared and wielding his pitchfork. A brave gladiator.

His eyes found Hob. Just for a second. And something passed between them. Something that was gratitude and courage and resolve.

Then the men around Hob were making their way over to where Hugh stood, his back to the flaming cart, the fire now licking at the barn. From the barn ran terrified wolfen, no longer paying any mind to the infected who followed, streaming out of the barn, dazed and disorientated, smoke billowing behind them.

Meanwhile the other captors were making their way over to the conflagration. They were transforming. All the guards, Hob realised, were no longer guards. They were Wolfen now. But they were nervous of the flames so gave Hugh a wide berth and stood growling, all kinds of hatred in their eyes, but too scared of the fire to approach him further.

'Stay human, stay human,' came a shout, too late. 'You're less vulnerable to fire if you're human.'

Meanwhile, most of the wolfen were either unwilling or unable to obey the command not to change, except Malchek, who strode forward now, shouting commands. 'Fetch water, put the fire out. See to it the troops cannot escape.'

Now the yard was also teeming with the infected, who shambled about, dazed and disorientated. Some instinct had driven them away from the flames; there, however, all thought ended.

Hob was now scrambling to his feet. He'd seen his chance; every wolfen in the compound was now occupied with events at the barn.

He crouched by the wagon, eyes darting this way and that. He had the perfect opportunity to escape now, he thought, he could make a dash for it; he'd be halfway up the hill before anybody saw him. He looked towards his escape route. Looked back to where Hugh stood bravely facing the wolfen, the fire raging at his back.

Then: '*Father*,' shouted Hugh, and Hob's mind was made up for him as he turned to see Master Brookes the builder among the evacuees. Like the rest Master Brookes was milling about, his expression blank as though just waking from the deepest sleep; like the rest he appeared to have a wound about his shoulder. Agatha had been right: they were turning them then taking their blood to keep them weak and docile, stop them escaping.

'Master Brookes,' he started to call but then the words died in his throat. The builder was too far away to risk shouting and he didn't want to alert the wolfen.

He'd have to make a run for it. It meant going out into the open. It meant praying none of the wolfen turned or even looked to the side, because he'd be seen if they did. But if he was going to do it, then it had to be now. Malchek was striding forward, shouting for water. He was trying to break the hold the fire seemed to have over his men, a kind of fearful trance that rooted them to the spot.

And the way he decided to break it was by seeing to young Hugh.

Hob had taken a deep breath and started running, met

Hugh's eyes once more, the boy nodding almost imperceptibly. A look of gratitude.

Hob was just a few feet away from Master Brookes now, running stealthily, his nightshirt flapping around his ankles, keeping an eye on events at the barn, willing the wolfen not to turn. He saw Malchek come forward, his hand fishing beneath his black robes for something.

A knife. Long handled, the blade curved. It flashed in the sun.

Hugh saw it too, his eyes fearful, Malchek still striding forward despite the fire. He twirled the knife then put both hands behind his back, approaching Hugh like a friend in the street.

Hob reached Master Brookes.

Now the wolfen were howling, encouraging their leader, who danced to the side, out of reach of Hugh's pitchfork. He was smiling, Hob could see, mocking the boy by easily dancing away from him. The knife remained behind his back at least.

Hob grabbed Master Brookes, taking him by the arm and pulling him towards the hedgerow that lined the far side of the compound. If they could reach it. If they could just reach it . . .

He'd blundered into the reservoir of blood before he even had time to register it there. He slipped and slid, the bloody mud squelching beneath his feet, pinwheeling one of his arms for balance while trying to keep hold of Master Brookes with the other.

The howling from the wolfen increased and Hob turned just in time to see Malchek finish his game. Hugh came forward with the pitchfork and instead of dodging it the wolfen leader grabbed it from his hands and snapped it.

Hugh's eyes widened in shock. His hands were frozen in place as though he still held the pitchfork. The knife flashed as Malchek jammed it into the side of his neck, forcing him to his knees.

Master Brookes stared glassily as his son died. If he was aware of it then he didn't show it.

'*No*,' screamed Hob, who instantly regretted his outburst as the wolfen guard nearest to him turned and saw him. The guard wore a hat. A felt hat with a wide brim that looked a little ridiculous but must have simply remained on his head, forgotten about in all the excitement.

Hob recognised that hat. It was the same hat worn by the one they called Strode, who had come to the farmhouse that day.

Hob turned and ran, but too quickly and he lost his footing in the thick oily blood and fell with a splash. He flailed, panicking, beached in the blood, his nightshirt instantly soaked red, blood on his hands and face. By some miracle, Master Brookes had remained standing.

Hob found his feet, gagging but standing, bloody, churned-up mud all around him. Once more he took Master Brookes's arm and led them through the stretch of scarlet quagmire, Strode coming up behind them, splashing through the slough, claws ready, a snarl on his lips; looking terrifying – apart from the hat.

And Hob was thinking that the chimney had better be good as he found an opening in the hedgerow and dived through, pulling Master Brookes with him.

Behind him Strode burst through, too, the creature gnashing its teeth, barking with anger. Hob pressed on, pleading with Master Brookes to speed up, too, but the builder was weak; he could hardly walk let alone run.

The wolfen was almost upon them now. Did Hob feel the breath of it upon his neck, or did he imagine it?

A paw reached out to grab him. Over his shoulder he saw claws, the brim of the hat. He heard the sound of it as it was almost upon him, and he could have wept – for himself, for Master Brookes and young Master Hugh. Dimly he recalled a moment many years ago, when he had been drunk and weeping in a town square, the rain soaking his clothes, and a woman had stopped to speak to him; had picked him out of the street. Literally picked him out of the street. He was grateful for her then. She had appeared to him and offered him her hand.

He'd been grateful to see her then.

But not as grateful as he was now – when she stepped out from behind a tree, said, 'Duck, Hoblet,' and swung the axe two-handed, a blow that should have taken off the wolfen's head in one clean cut.

Except that Agatha had used the flat end of the axe, so instead of scything through the wolf, metal met snout with a crunch of crushed bones and Strode was swept off his feet, crashing heavily to the forest floor. Fluttering prettily down in its wake came his wide-brimmed hat.

'You see,' she screeched, as the wolfen collapsed to the forest floor. 'Perfect. I'd be just as good an executioner as any man. It's not fair, Hoblet.'

But Hob wasn't listening. He was trying and failing to speak. He was pointing at Strode, who was already trying to get up. The beast was hurt and unsteady. But it wasn't going down that easily.

Agatha tutted, hefted the axe and spat on each hand before moving to stand over it. She twizzled the axe so that the blade was pointing up to the sky, and brought the flat of it down on the wolfen.

The wolfen twitched a little, tried to get up. Hob thought of wasps, like when you were trying to kill one and you gave it a good thwack with a trowel but it just kept on wriggling. Mind you, he thought, Agatha wasn't trying to kill this one. That much at least was clear. If she'd wanted to kill it, it'd be dead by now.

Thunk. She hit the beast again. It whined piteously. But was still moving.

'Come on, you hairy bastard,' she mumbled, 'time for sleepies.' *Thunk*.

At last it fell still. Agatha slung her axe over one shoulder and bent to feel for a pulse.

'Still alive,' she said. 'But out cold. How long for is anyone's guess. We'd better get a . . .'

She looked over to Hob, who had sunk to his knees. Beside him Master Brookes the builder had also folded to the ground but Hob didn't care. He was fighting an attack of hysteria.

Agatha bent to her husband, put a hand to his back and rubbed it gently as he sobbed.

'Hey,' she said, her voice gentle. 'Hey, Hoblet. You did well in there. You got Master Brookes out. And there was nothing you could have done for the boy. If his luck had matched his bravery he'd be alive, but if not for his bravery, you'd be dead and so would Master Brookes. You did what you could, Hoblet. You did as much as anybody could have asked of you. You made me very proud today.'

XLIX

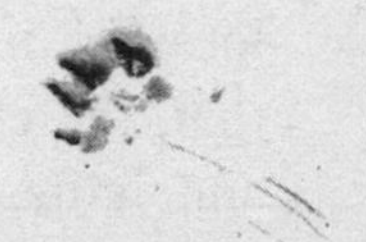

Sir Thomas More was to be hung, drawn and quartered at Tower Hill in two days' time, and still Henry could barely make sense of his feelings on the matter. Yet again, events seemed to move ahead regardless of him. Out of his control.

It was night-time and the moon was half full. That meant The Change soon. Even with the curtains closed he could feel its rays, not strong but like the early drops of rain before the downpour, the first pangs of hunger mid-morning. He could expect its temptation to grow stronger over the next few days. Until it became irresistible. When he would have to obey. And then: watch out, gypsies, stay in your home, grieving families, the King would be going hunting.

'Bryan,' he called, and Sir Francis approached his table.

'Majesty,' said Bryan, casting a sideways look at the plates piled high with meat, all of it nearly raw and wrinkling his nose a little.

'What news of the Tower?'

'The Tower, Your Highness?'

'Of Sir Thomas at the Tower, Bryan. What news of him?'

'There is little to report,' said Bryan. Like most of the King's Gentlemen, Bryan liked More. Sir Thomas shared their occasionally bawdy sense of humour; he lacked the pomposity of Wolsey, he had been a man after their own hearts. 'Nobody is allowed to see him apart from Thomas Cromwell, on orders of Her Majesty. To Cromwell he talks of a wolfen army incessantly but says he has no idea of its location, making it difficult to verify his claim. Other than that, the chief warder reports that Sir Thomas prays often and writes a devotional, and has spoken of beginning a sequel to *Utopia*, though he fears he will never be able to finish it.'

'Does he write letters?'

'Indeed, Your Majesty.'

'To me?'

'Queen Anne has ordered that all his correspondence be taken and destroyed,' said the groom with a pained look.

'Really? Has she?' said Henry.

'So it would seem.'

'Anne has shown quite a vindictive side to herself in her treatment of Thomas,' said Henry reflectively, 'don't you think?'

'I cannot say, Majesty,' said Bryan, but his eyes told the true story.

'But the fact is, she has.'

Bryan cleared his throat. 'I wonder, Majesty, if there might be a precedent.'

'For vindictive queens? I should think so.'

'No, Majesty, for a monarch pardoning an act of high treason.'

'Why would I want to pardon him?' said Henry crossly. The image of his lady shoved across the room by the force of More's blow was still fresh in his mind. 'You saw what he did – to the Queen?' His voice rose. 'Why, I would gladly carry out the execution myself.'

'Pardon me, Your Majesty,' simpered Bryan, 'I took your observation about the Queen to mean Your Majesty's fury at Sir Thomas had abated.'

'Well, it hasn't,' said the King crossly, even as he felt his fury doing just that – abating – and he sighed. 'If my forefathers pardoned traitors, Bryan, they did so because those traitors had done pardonable things. I'm willing to wager that nobody pardoned bodily harm against a Royal person – when that Royal person was the Queen. *Even* if I wished to pardon him, I couldn't.'

'Your Majesty, if I might say,' began Bryan, 'it has been decided, has it not, that Sir Thomas More's assault on the Queen is to be kept a secret, known only to those present during the incident; that officially his treachery lies in his denial to recognise the Act of Supremacy.'

'Well, he's doing that, too, apparently.'

'He probably feels he has nothing to lose, Majesty. I wonder, though, if this situation makes granting him a pardon a less scandalous proposition.'

'Just a few would know the truth?'

'Yes, Majesty. History would see you as the gentle and merciful King, who refused to let one of the era's greatest thinkers go to his death on a matter of principle. Some of those in the room might well think the same.'

'With at least one exception?'

'Yes, Your Grace,' conceded Bryan.

'Queen Anne – the very person whose honour we find ourselves forced to satisfy?'

'That does indeed present a problem, Your Majesty.'

Henry waved a hand, exasperated. 'Thank you, Bryan, that'll be all. You can leave me now.'

The groom retreated into the shadows.

'No, leave me,' said Henry. 'Alone, please.'

With Bryan gone, Henry poked at his food. Then from the side of the table he took a letter, the seal broken. More's letters might have been denied to him, but Wolsey's had not, and in this one, the Lord Chancellor begged to meet him. He had an urgent and grave matter he needed to discuss with the King, he said, in person and alone.

Wolsey had underlined these last two requests and Henry read them again now, brow furrowed in thought. Rightly, Henry should discard the letter – the impudence of the Lord Chancellor being enough to see it thrown on the fire. Something stopped him. Something human.

He placed the letter at the side of his plate. Now he raised his hand to look at it, holding it palm forwards. He twisted in his seat to look at the door that connected his chamber with Bryan's chamber. Satisfied, he looked back. Candlelight flickered so that the skin of his hand seemed to move. Just a trick of the light.

But could he do it for real? He took a deep breath and closed his eyes as he tried to reach something that was inside of him, as though attempting to recall a memory or isolate a feeling, looking for the wolfen inside – and finding it now.

A crackling sound. He opened his eyes to look at his hand, and saw it change. He felt the scrape and prickle of hairs pushing their way out of his skin, saw the fur slowly spreading down his forearm. He inhaled and exhaled, concentrating on that part of his arm so that the sprouting fur now stopped, just above the elbow. He smiled, having stopped it. Was he controlling it now? His hand became a paw, talons sprouted from it, but that was the extent of the transformation. He was able to dam The Change somehow, prevent it enveloping him – for even though part of him had transformed, the wolfen instinct was absent, his strength and senses remained human. He could feel The Change straining at him, wanting to claim him, but now found he was capable of resisting it.

He admired his paw, even speared a little meat to eat with his claws, then put it to his cheeks, stroked it with his other hand to feel his own fur, placed them next to each other to look at: his human hand, his wolfen paw.

Another deep breath and he returned the hand to its usual state. Again he looked at his two hands. Then, deciding something, he called for Bryan.

'I need two things doing,' he said, when the groom appeared.

'Yes, Majesty.'

'Firstly, I am commuting Thomas's punishment. He isn't to be hung, drawn and quartered, he will be beheaded, as befits his station. The Queen will have to be satisfied with that.'

'Yes, Majesty.'

'Secondly, get a message to Wolsey, tell him I'll see him.'

'When shall I say you can see him, Majesty?'

Henry thought. 'When does the Queen leave for Hever?'

'Tomorrow afternoon. She plans to stay overnight and remain there during the execution of Sir Thomas.'

'Not wanting to be seen as savouring his execution, perhaps,' the King said with an ironic tone.

'Quite.'

'She will be one of the few at court not to attend.'

'And you, your Majesty?'

'I will not be attending, either,' he said wearily, 'I shall use the opportunity to slip out with no official accompaniment. Just you and I. Tell Wolsey that is when I shall see him.'

L

Getting home from Betsham had been hard for the two Hoblets. Standing in the forest that afternoon they had been faced with the problem of how to transport the wolfen and Master Brookes the builder back home: Strode, unconscious; Master Brookes in a state of stupefaction; at least one of them a fully fledged wolfen, the other well on his way.

So Hob had fetched his ass down the hill then Hob had taken Strode's shoulders, Agatha his feet and they slung him over the ass. They gave the compound a wide berth as they climbed back up, trying to stay hidden by trees and hedgerow, bearing the limp body of Strode, still in wolf form, as well as Master Brookes the builder, dazed and pallid and thankfully with no idea that the last surviving member of his family was now dead.

Somebody was going to pay for that, Agatha had said, casting a dark look at their prisoner. Oh yes, somebody or some *thing* was going to pay for the death of young Master Brookes.

'Young lad took me by surprise, Hoblet,' she said. 'One minute we was lifting the cart out of the ditch, next thing I know he's chucking a hay bale on the back. "What you playing at?" I says to him. He said you'd be discovered if he didn't make his move.'

'He was right, Agatha,' agreed Hob, 'they had me out of the wagon and on the floor. Another second and I would have been found out or sent into the barn. God knows, I'd be turned by now. He saved my life, Agatha; saved his father's life, too.'

'Aye, that he did.'

At the top they collected Agatha's horse and were able to get a better look at the scene.

'Bloody hell,' said Agatha.

'Bloody hell,' echoed Hob.

While it was true that smoke poured from the barn and the Hoblets' cart still smouldered, in every other respect the wolfen had returned the compound to a state of normality – whatever that was for an operation that involved turning humans into werewolves. The last wagon had now been emptied and as the Hoblets watched, a line of infected entered the first barn. With the operation resumed they were already exiting from the far door, now being herded past the smouldering barn and into one at the end. Buckets of blood were already being transported to the pond. The wolfen doing it paused on seeing that the area had been disturbed, then continued anyway, depositing his buckets.

They looked at each other and Hob blew out his cheeks with relief. Then they turned and hurried back to where the horse was tethered. Strode seemed about to stir and Agatha looked at him for a moment, chewing her lip and weighing up the options.

'They're mighty strong when they're transformed, Hoblet,'

she said, 'we need him in human shape. Besides, he was an ugly bloke, he's an even uglier wolf.'

'How do you plan on forcing him to change?' asked Hob. 'I'm not sure a polite request will work.'

She frowned at him. 'You're right. Gimme your belt.'

Then she put the belt around Strode's neck, tightening it a little, at the same time coaxing him awake with light slaps to the face and dousing him with water from a flask. Until his eyes snapped open and he began to struggle. At which point, Agatha tightened the belt.

She braced her feet on his shoulders to do it. The tip of her tongue protruded from her lips, she went red with the effort. Strode's grunts became strangulated gasps then ceased altogether. His eyes bulged, his tongue lolled from his mouth as he tried to take in air.

'What are you doing? He'll die,' said Hob.

'Aye, that he will,' replied Agatha. 'He'll strangle himself to death.'

Strode could only manage a sound – a sound that was a lot like, '*Gurk*.'

Strode had no choice. Unable to breathe, he was forced to change. Working together, the two Hoblets rushed to tighten his ropes. Agatha then spent several minutes rendering him unconscious with a mallet, and then they were ready. Lashing him as tightly as they were able to Agatha's horse, they made the journey home as swiftly as possible, Agatha with her mallet at the ready in case he woke up.

But luck had been on their side: Strode remained unconscious. And back at the farmhouse, after Master Brookes had been put to bed, Agatha had been able to call upon her vast collection of shackles and restraints to truss him up. They passed chains through the restraints, tautening them, and lastly lashed him to a chair.

'Did you notice what they really hate, Hoblet?' she said.

'Couldn't really miss it, could you, Agatha?' said Hoblet.

'Come on, let's move him over to the fireplace.'

After that, they dragged the kitchen table closer to Agatha's workspace. Agatha set about arranging her instruments. Out came the pricking needles, of course, and a set of pliers was laid out. She disappeared then reappeared with her special copper bowl that she also placed on the table.

'The bowl?' said Hob. 'Oh, Agatha . . .'

'I know, Hoblet, I know. But this is a matter that calls for barbarism – and it's a call I feel minded to answer.'

Strode sat with his head lolling, arms fastened, clothes hanging off him. Every now and then his eyelids began to flutter and as Agatha stoked up the fire, he began to sweat, too. A stranger coming into the kitchen would have seen the maltreatment of a battered-looking young man, his clothes too big for him.

Hob saw that, too. And he stood looking at the prisoner, full of doubt, until Agatha came to him and put a hand to his arm.

'Fetch me a rat, then get to the garden, Hoblet. Don't you worry, I'll shout you in when it's all over.'

Hob agreed and trudged out to fetch a box for catching the rat. By the time he returned with the rodent, Agatha was working on waking Strode using water and slaps. The wolfen's eyes opened and widened when he saw the fire. Agatha took his chin and angled his head to see the kitchen table at his side. His eyes widened even more.

She thanked Hob for the rat, then he went out to the garden, where he spent a couple of hours tending to the hives, hearing the screams from inside the farmhouse. Every so often the screams would stop, but he knew that Strode had passed out. When the screams had been over for some time – when Hob was sure it was over – he trudged back to the farmhouse, and entered to find Agatha kneeling on the floor, scrubbing off blood. A rat, covered in gore, was perched not far away, sniffing the air.

'You used the bowl then?' he said.

'Don't get squeamish on me, Hoblet,' she said. *Scrub, scrub, scrub.* 'He deserved it.'

Hoblet looked over to her workspace. The chair was empty. Agatha had transferred Strode to the kitchen table, presumably during a period when he had not been conscious. He lay dead, his mouth open in a final scream, dried blood around his lips. Strapped to his chest was Agatha's special copper bowl. She rarely used the bowl; as a method of torture it was a little unpredictable, involving, as it did, fixing it on to the stomach of the victim with a live rat inside, then placing hot coals on top of the bowl.

This of course, created an unpleasant situation for both rat and victim, and each would be considering their means of escape. For the victim this was not an option, especially with the likes of Agatha around. The rat, on the other hand, would soon reach the only conclusion: it could burrow its way out. And would usually commence doing so, eating its way through the insides of the victim and appearing from within the body; out of the side if the rat had a good sense of direction. Agatha reported seeing one emerge from between the legs once, which had caused Hob to feel slightly faint at the thought.

Here Strode had been lucky, it seemed, for he had a gaping, bloody hole in his flank. It was an ignominious death for a werewolf, thought Hob, to be eaten by a rat.

'You avenged Master Hugh to your satisfaction?' he said.

'I did,' she said, scrubbing furiously. There had been a lot of blood. Looking at the rat again, Hob wondered if he was imagining the sated look it wore.

'You were able to ask your questions.'

'Indeed, I was, Hoblet,' she said, kneeling up. 'And I got the answers to them as well. And you and I are going on a journey.'

'Where to?'

'We're going to court, Hoblet. We need to see Sir Thomas at once.'

LI

'This isn't the handwriting of Sir Thomas,' frowned Wolsey, closing the edition of *Utopia* with a snap and pushing it back across the desk.

On the other side of it sat the Hoblets, who shifted uncomfortably in their seats. They had decided not to mention the fact that they were witchfinders, just in case any misunderstandings occurred but guessing their word might not be enough, Hob had set about inscribing their copy of *Utopia* with a testimonial, signing it 'Sir Thomas More' with a flourish.

Not, as it turned out, a successful strategy.

'Perhaps,' continued Wolsey, 'you should start by telling me the truth.'

'Tell *us* the truth,' corrected Cromwell, who stood by his side.

'Yes, us,' said Wolsey, through gritted teeth, cursing his luck. The yeomen at the gates had despatched runners to send word to the Privy Council that there was a couple at the gatehouse. The couple had requested to see Sir Thomas More and they bore an inscription from him. But Wolsey and Cromwell had both been given the message, thus Cromwell had insisted on being present in Wolsey's chambers.

'The truth is that we are acquainted with Sir Thomas, sir,' said the woman, Agatha Hoblet, who was quite one of the most unpleasant things it had ever been Wolsey's misfortune to gaze upon.

'Really?' said Wolsey. 'It would seem not, or why bother going to the trouble of forging his testimonial? You could have just asked him himself.'

'Well, he had just recovered from the sweating sickness,' said Agatha, 'and keen to return to court. He had urgent news.'

Despite himself, Wolsey traded a look with Cromwell, then sat forward in his seat. 'Did he say what this news was, by any chance?'

'Well, of course,' she said, 'we had first-hand experience ourselves. The wolfen have been building their army. They plan to march on the Crown.'

'Oh, Christ,' said Wolsey. God, soon the whole country would know.

'And you say you've seen this army?'

'With our very own eyes, Your Holi . . . ness.'

'Just Your Eminence will do. If I was Your Holiness I'd be the . . . doesn't matter. Look, if you've seen the army, you know where it is?'

'This is one of the things we had to tell Sir Thomas, Your Eminence. Plus we have since learnt something else.'

'What might that be?'

The Hoblets shifted uncomfortably. 'We were hoping to relay it directly to Sir Thomas, Your Eminence. I must say we've been looking forward to seeing him actually, having nursed him back to health.'

'Sir Thomas is in the Tower,' said Wolsey, with a sadness

that was entirely genuine. 'He is due to be executed on a charge of high treason.'

'Sir Thomas? Treason? *Never*,' said Agatha.

'It's a long story, and not very pretty. I'm afraid there is nothing that can be done for him.'

The Hoblets looked at one another, downcast, and Wolsey almost felt sorry for them.

'I'm afraid, with Sir Thomas indisposed, you're going to have to tell me what you know,' he said.

Master Hoblet nodded at his wife, who took a deep breath, and told them about the secret wolfen army at Betsham, leaving nothing out – although she neglected to list the chimney among her list of motives for wanting to rescue Master Brookes the builder. Then she told them about kidnapping Strode and here she omitted a little more, claiming that the information had been extracted via the method of her husband 'giving that old wolf a good duffing up'. But that, 'perhaps Master Hoblet got a little over-zealous and not knowing his own strength and that' because the wolfen had subsequently died.

'And what did the creature tell you before he died?' said Wolsey.

Mistress Hoblet looked grave. 'That the army is ready to move, Your Eminence. The attack is to happen any day now.'

LII

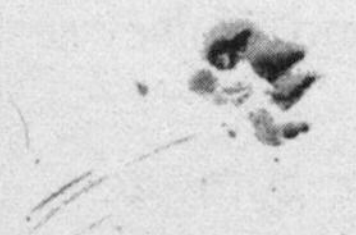

'We need to mount an offensive as soon as we are able,' said Wolsey to the Privy Council.

The days of taking Protektorate decisions behind closed doors were over it seemed. Once upon a time they had simply discussed the matter at Hampton Court then Sir Thomas informed the King or the Privy Council. They were going to seem like the halcyon days under the new system, Wolsey feared. The King had made it plain that there was to be no Protektorate action without his involvement at all levels, which meant involving the Privy Council too. Which meant Wolsey now sat with the likes of Norfolk and Boleyn grinning openly at him, enjoying seeing him squirm beneath the interrogation of the King. At least the Queen wasn't here, he was grateful for that. Then again, he thought, looking across the table at Cromwell – she might as well have been.

'Now, I think we can safely assume the old Hoblet woman has the wrong end of the stick,' he said. 'Malchek cannot yet have enough troops for his army. Plus he will need time to ready his troops, who he has deliberately kept languishing in a state of ill health.'

He looked around the table. Frowns or sneering grins greeted his logic.

'Nevertheless,' he said, 'we need to move as soon as the new members of the Protektorate arrive,' said Wolsey. 'We know that Malchek has been removing blood from the infected in order to render them weak and soporific. We need to catch them in this state.'

'He'll be training them,' said Henry.

'Training them, Majesty?' said Wolsey.

'To channel it,' said Henry distantly.

Wolsey winced and was almost grateful for Norfolk's interruption when it came: 'My Lord,' he sneered, 'isn't this all rather fanciful. How can this Malchek be expected to control all these wolfmen?'

Wolsey opened his mouth to reply that he had no bloody idea but Malchek seemed to be doing a fair job of it so far, when Henry said, 'The pack.'

If Wolsey had been closer to the King he might have tried discreetly kicking him.

'The pack, Your Majesty?' enquired Norfolk.

'Yes,' said Henry, and he looked at Norfolk as though only just focusing on him. 'The pack. It's all about the pack.'

Of course, thought Wolsey, his mind going back to the meeting with Lefsetz. The wolfen, be they pure Arcadian or hybrids, were bound by the bloodline of the pack. The King knew this. He knew it by instinct.

Even so, at Henry's talk of the pack Norfolk looked at him as sharply as it was possible for a member of the Privy Council to look at the King. Henry returned his stare blankly. Then Norfolk was nodding vigorously. 'Of course, Your Majesty, of course, the pack.' Wolsey squirmed. He cast a look around the long, rectangular table and saw the other members of the Privy Council nodding too, as if they knew precisely what the King was talking about. Only Bryan and Boleyn looked a little perplexed.

'Perhaps so,' agreed Wolsey. 'But I think we can safely deduce that they will be building up the troops' strength . . .'

'With red meat,' said the King a little wistfully.

'Yes, probably, Your Majesty.' Wolsey cringed, wishing the King would hold back a little on the insights before a member of the Council started asking awkward questions.

'They would recover far faster than a normal man,' said Henry, dashing Wolsey's hope in that last regard.

'I'm sorry, Majesty?' simpered Wolsey, hardly daring to think what the King might say next: 'Hey, everyone, I'm a werewolf!'

'I mean that your logic is flawed, Wolsey. They are not waiting for their troops to recover physical strength; they've got no need to. Nor will they need to add to their numbers. You say there was at least one barn housing the wolfen force.'

'At least, perhaps two, but still not enough to—'

'It would be enough. They have superior strength and speed. They have . . . instincts.'

Wolsey cleared his throat. 'Yes, quite, Your Majesty. Certainly these things would appear to be true from what little we know of the wolfen. And this being the case, we should strike as soon as the new members of the Protektorate arrive.'

From Norfolk came a disgusted sound. 'Protektorate,' he scoffed, 'Your Majesty, we don't need to wait for a squad of Italians to come over here and show us how to fight. As is well known, Italians might have some skill in culinary matters, but when it comes to fighting they are as feeble as the French. We have our own armies. We can despatch men immediately.'

'But, Norfolk,' smiled Wolsey, 'as we are all aware, this is a Protektorate matter.'

'We are at *war* with the wolfen, remember, Wolsey,' said Boleyn and Wolsey looked at him sharply.

'I would appreciate it if you would address me by my correct title,' smiled the Lord Chancellor, 'the last time I looked I was higher in rank than you.'

Boleyn gave him an insincere smile. 'I do apologise, *Your Eminence*.'

'Pimp,' sniped Wolsey back.

'Incompetent,' returned Boleyn.

'Which reminds me,' said Wolsey, 'I'm having Holbein paint a scene and I wonder if you might consider posing for it. It shouldn't be too taxing for you, My Lord. I'm hoping to recreate a scene in the Presence Chamber for a piece entitled "The Homecoming of Sir Thomas More". All you would be required to do is lie on your back and screech like a little girl as Sir Thomas More kicks your arse.'

'Certainly, Your Eminence,' replied Boleyn, 'though I'm afraid I am busy the day after tomorrow, when I shall be at Tower Hill. It's a beheading, I recall that much, but I can't quite remember who is due to be beheaded.' He wrinkled his brow. 'Perhaps you could remind me?'

Wolsey was about to respond when: '*Gentlemen*,' snapped Henry, 'that will be all. Thank you. Wolsey, when are you expecting your Protektorate to arrive?'

'The day after tomorrow,' said Wolsey.

'What a shame nobody will be there to meet them,' interjected Boleyn, 'everybody being too busy at Tower Hill.'

Wolsey shot him a withering look.

'Majesty,' protested Norfolk, 'we don't need to wait for the Protektorate and their stealthy attack. Picking off the leaders is a strategy fraught with difficulty. We should mount a major offensive, amass an army to wipe out the Arcadians *and* their army. We can have a force ready tonight. We could attack tomorrow.'

'And innocents would die,' said Wolsey, making sure to sound as though he cared.

'Casualties of war, Wolsey,' Boleyn said. '*War*.'

'Majesty, please,' said Norfolk, 'if we leave this to the Protektorate we waste time. We declared war on the wolfen in order to avenge the Prince George . . .'

Henry flinched a little at the mention of his name.

'Norfolk, your bloodlust is matched only by your ambition,' said Wolsey. 'Only the Protektorate can mount the operation we need, which is to neutralise Malchek and his lieutenants.'

'Leaving us with an army to defeat.'

'An army without generals,' said Wolsey, thinking, Not bound by the blood of the pack.

'Majesty,' he said, appealing to the King now.

They hung on his reply, all members, especially Wolsey and Norfolk, agog as they awaited the King's answer.

'We shall wait,' said Henry at last. 'We shall await the new Protektorate then launch the operation recommended by His Eminence.'

When the meeting was over, Henry found himself alone in his chamber, night approaching. Already he was feeling the lure of the moon, and he knew it would be strong tonight. The following night, it would be full and at its strongest.

That would be the night of Malchek's attack, he knew. When the moon granted his army its greatest strength.

He knew this.

So why, he wondered, hadn't he mentioned it at today's Privy Council?

LIII

The next day, Queen Anne arrived at Hever Castle, in a procession of carriages and wagons.

The staff rushed to the windows to see her – the first time that 'Lady Anne' had returned to Hever since she became 'Queen Anne'. They, too, had heard the rumours that she was pregnant. When the carriage came to the end of the castle's approach road and swept on to the Hever courtyard, the staff were already straining their eyes to see whether Lady Anne – 'hush my mouth, *Queen* Anne' – showed any signs of being with child.

She showed signs of being Queen, that much was certain. When the carriage drew to a halt, Queen Anne gazed out of the window in a studied manner, as though admiring a beautiful Winter Wonderland, but – and this was the surprising thing – as if she was admiring it for the very first time. Nothing had altered at Hever since she last set foot on the grounds – it had been only a matter of days, after all – and she had been born and brought up in the castle, her family seat. Yet she gazed about the place as though waking up from a dream.

She greeted the servants in the same manner. When a footman helped her down from the carriage and bowed deeply, and said, 'It is good to see you back, Queen Anne,' she had smiled at him as though she were indulging an impertinence. Her ladies-in-waiting were also helped down from their carriages; servants began to disembark. The Queen looked around at her ladies and smiled.

'Shall we?' she said, and with a swish of skirts and a flash of the exciting new French neckline that she had introduced to court, she and her ladies glided towards the huge front doors of the castle, leaving the staff of Hever to exchange bemused glances in their wake.

The Queen Mother was there to greet her. Her sister Mary curtseyed and gave her a sardonic smile. Queen Anne's eyebrows knitted together a little and mother and sister both remembered themselves and knelt. Members of her company went in search of castle staff: to ensure that Queen Anne's quarters were sufficiently equipped; to ensure that Queen Anne's dietary requirements were met; to ensure that Queen Anne was treated in the manner to which she had been accustomed in her few days as Queen of England.

After greeting her mother and sister, Anne spent as short a time as she could with those valued staff who had gathered hoping to be able to pay their respects to the new Queen.

The Queen in question motioned to three of her ladies and set off along a hallway of the castle, her back straight, her chin jutting out and the light flashing from the pearls and jewellery she wore, until she reached a certain door. Here she told her ladies to wait, that she would be continuing alone. At this the ladies were terribly flustered, but the Queen fixed them with a glare and told them not to be so stupid.

'After all,' she said, a little more gently, 'until a few days ago, this house was my home. Did you see how they greeted me outside?'

The ladies, who were lined up along the wood panels, nodded agreement.

'Therefore, do I need accompanying on a personal task that involves going about my own home?'

Lined up, the ladies shook their heads, and with the matter at an end, Queen Anne took her skirts in one hand and with the other reached to open the door for herself, grinning at the horrified faces of her ladies as she let herself through the door.

On the other side, she stood and enjoyed her moment of freedom for a moment, then skipped down the remaining steps to the bottom and, still with her skirts clasped in one hand, dashed along the passageway to the door, iron cressets on poles set out to light the way. She felt into a crevice on the wall and found the key, pushed it into the lock and turned, and let herself into the vast chamber.

Torches on the wall provided the only light. From somewhere there was the drip-drip of water. The sights and sounds were familiar to Anne, though, as familiar as the layout of the cellar, and she wasted no time in dashing across the damp floor, her shoes splashing slightly in the moisture that collected there, deep underground, and went to Aisha.

Aisha had been expecting her – had sensed her – and sat up with a rustle of straw to greet the Queen, who dropped to her knees to take Aisha's face in both her hands and leant forward to kiss her.

They came apart. Aisha clasped the Queen.

'What news, Anne?' she gasped. 'What news?'

'My love,' said Anne, 'the Crown is to move against you.'

Aisha took her at arm's length and looked searchingly into her eyes.

'To move against *us*,' corrected Anne.

'That's right,' purred Aisha. She grinned, her teeth grew. 'The King sends his troops, does he?'

'He is minded to send a Protektorate force. On the advice of Wolsey he expects they shall be able to kill our Lord Malchek and save the countryfolk who make up the army.'

Aisha chuckled. 'And what do we think, my beautiful Anne?' she said.

'That we must warn our Lord Malchek.'

'And how shall we do that?'

'The howling, Aisha.'

'Not tonight, Anne,' said Aisha, 'tonight you must set me free so I shall be with him.'

Anne crumpled a little. 'Then how shall I see you?' But already she was standing and she went to the far side of the chamber to reach for the key.

'We will be together again soon,' Aisha reassured her as the cuffs came open and she brought herself from the wall. She stood and let Anne drink in the sight of her, then gently indicated the far end of the chamber, where there was a delivery hatch.

'Shall we?' she said.

At the hatch she turned. 'Go back to court at once, Anne. The King continues to waver; it is clear that he has not fully embraced his Arcadian side. He may be vulnerable. Your job is to see that his loyalties lie with the pack.'

'His hatred of Malchek is what anchors him,' said Anne.

Aisha nodded. 'Be with him, Anne, show him the way.'
And with that she was gone.

Glumly, Anne watched her go. She watched as Aisha ran down the lawn towards the bridge. She watched Aisha cross the bridge then change, become wolf and run, free, dropping to all fours, running to Malchek.

LIV

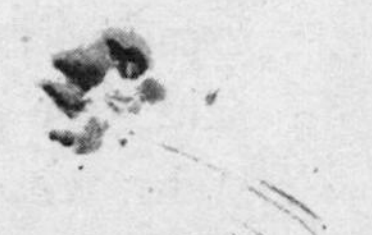

The tradesmen had begun to arrive at Tower Hill. More could see them from the window of his cell in the Bell Tower. 'For crying out loud, they're not executing me until three,' he wanted to shout at them, but he supposed they knew their business. Executions were popular; people came from far and wide and would arrive early to get the best vantage points. He could hardly blame tradesmen for setting up if there was custom to be had. He might as well blame the workers, who yesterday had built the scaffold, whistling and calling to each other all day, singing and swapping jokes, every bang of a hammer reminding More that he was due to die.

He could hear them working during his short clandestine meeting with Alice, where she begged him to sign whatever Act it was they wanted him to sign, and he had been forced into the role of a martyr, a fact that ailed him, having to lie to her like that. But then again what choice did he have? What else could he say? 'I punched the Queen, Alice; they're beheading me because I threw a right hook at Her Majesty, a punch so hard that I actually knocked her to the ground, an act of High Treason.'

No, he could not bring that upon his family. He had

to play the martyr. Hopefully history would see him that way, too.

He looked at his candle, the flame moving gently in the breeze from the window. It had been provided to him by the chief warder, a kindly old man of whom More had grown fond during his stay. The candle, the chief warder said, one grimy fingernail indicating indentations along its stem, would count the hours. Some of the prisoners found it of comfort.

More had thanked him, then, after he was gone, he had lit the candle. As the first hour burnt down, he watched two figures in hooded robes busying themselves around the scaffold, seemingly checking it for stability. The scaffold was surrounded by a thick fabric skirt that dropped from the stage to the floor, and the two figures disappeared inside to inspect underneath the structure. This, he thought, was the executioner and his assistant. Hopefully their thoroughness would be matched by a skill with the axe. He had seen for himself the damage inflicted by an inexperienced axeman; it was not unusual for them to need many attempts.

Now more people began to arrive on to Tower Green, vendors selling ale, a stall for the provision of pies. Sightseers began to drift into the square, women mainly, who wore aprons and pinnies and bonnets and coifs. They carried baskets they used to sit on in order to reserve a good space at the front. As the candle was burning down to the second hour, more people were arriving, and workmen were busying themselves around the scaffold. Two sweating men carried the huge block on to the scaffold, dropping it down and wiping their brows. One of them went to his knees and placed his head on the block so that the other could walk around him and determine the views. The one with his head on the block made an *urk* sound, then a plop sound. The two of them laughed.

Sir Thomas More looked at his candle. Six more notches to go.

LV

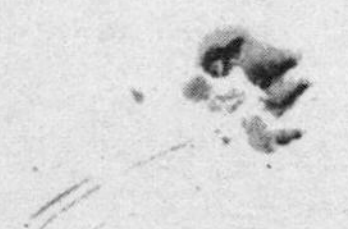

Meanwhile, the Protektorate was readying itself.

Yesterday a ship had arrived, bearing the excitable, jabbering and resentful members of the Protektorate, having sailed from Naples, braving scandal and a near-mutiny along the way.

Not at all happy to be setting foot on English soil, they were greeted by Wolsey and his clerks. When they had made their way from their ship to the observatory, they were introduced to Lady Jane Seymour, the operation commander, who joined Wolsey in the briefing room of the observatory to outline the next day's mission: the attack needed to take place during daylight hours, they were to move in, take out the wolfen leaders using deadly force, withdraw and let the army move in to deal with the hybrids.

There were ten new Protektors, not all of them old or disgraced as Wolsey had feared. However, the next morning had found them only partially refreshed after a night's sleep and they were disgruntled as they made up backpacks for the mission, sheathing swords, secreting tinderboxes and blades. They moaned in Italian, thinking Wolsey couldn't understand. They complained about the food and the weather, about their lack of rest and preparation; they complained about the horses and the equipment and they were indignant that their first mission involved something so unprestigious as merely despatching a few wolfen. But most of all they were offended that a woman was to take command of the mission. The Pope was going to hear all about this, they were muttering darkly. Wolsey understood perfectly well, of course, and it was all he could do to hide his glee; he'd put his best man on the job. The fact that she was a woman? Quite frankly, he was beyond caring what they thought.

With the cardinals' preparations complete, they repaired to the courtyard, which rang to the sound of their horses' hooves. Not long later, at midday, the squad, led by Jane Seymour, rode out, grim-faced and combat-ready, a three-hour ride to Betsham ahead of them.

Thomas Cardinal Wolsey watched them go. He tried to cross himself, but became slightly confused with the sequence of the motion, and ending up whirling his finger at his chest in case anybody was looking.

God speed, he thought.

Then Wolsey turned and collected his clerks for the journey along the Thames to the Tower. Travelling along the river on the cardinal's opulent barge they could see processions of people and carts making their way towards the Tower, and Wolsey frowned to see the baskets full of food, the children playing with hoops, a family day out for most for them, the vultures. Instead he tried to focus on what lay ahead. His meeting with the King in Beauchamp, but first to the Bell Tower, where he arrived to find More watching the crowds, the condemned man brightening a little when Wolsey walked in.

'Ah, the Queen has given you leave to see me?' he said. 'It makes a change to see a friendly face.'

'She could hardly deny me the chance to give you the last rites.'

'You've come to give me the last rites?' said More, his eyebrows raising.

'Well, no,' said Wolsey, 'I mean, I could, but I'm a bit short of time.'

'It's all right, Thomas,' chuckled More, 'I'd wager you don't even remember the words.'

'An outrage. Of course I do,' said Wolsey, mock offended.

There was an awkward moment, neither really knowing quite what to say.

'Will you be out there today?' said More, waving at the window, through which Wolsey could see activity on Tower Hill.

'No,' said Wolsey, 'I have urgent business with the King.'

'He won't be there, either, then?'

'He will not be far away,' said Wolsey. 'But he's using your execution as an opportunity to meet me – in private.'

'Oh?' said More. 'Then I'm pleased to be of service. What is the nature of the business?'

Wolsey went to the cell door and peered out of the small viewfinder to verify that the guard wasn't eavesdropping. He lowered his voice anyway as he returned to More. 'Normally I would say, "You're not going to believe this", but I think you will: His Majesty is a werewolf.'

More laughed drily. 'You're right, I'm not surprised. And now you come to mention it he does have more hair than previously. And his girth . . .'

'He does, doesn't he?' agreed Wolsey, chuckling. 'And do you notice a wild quality to the eyes?'

'Now you come to mention it.'

'It is my belief that the King is not fully reconciled to his condition. My hope is that he can be cured.'

'Oh yes. How?'

'By killing the one who bit him. The youngling we have in Beauchamp.'

'Ah,' laughed More, 'You're seeing him over the way.'

'Quite. With most of court watching your execution, he has a chance to slip away.'

'If it works then my death will not have been in vain, Thomas,' said More. He looked at his candle. There were three more notches to go.

'Yes, Thomas, yes,' agreed Wolsey reflectively, but looking out of the window and seeing the sightseers patiently awaiting the beheading, he wasn't so sure.

When the two men had said their goodbyes, Wolsey tried to say a prayer for Sir Thomas, but was a bit rusty on the old words, so he gave up. It wouldn't do Thomas much good anyway, he reflected ruefully as he left the Tower, Dudley and Child in his wake. Coming to the bridge over the moat he saw a commotion there. A knot of people he recognised: Alice, More's wife, and their children were being barred from entering by soldiers, Alice almost hysterical, the children's faces streaked with tears. They were imploring the soldiers, who remained stony-faced.

Wolsey stopped. 'What's going on here?' he asked a yeoman.

'Queen's orders, Your Eminence' bowed the head yeoman.

'Nobody is allowed to see Sir Thomas apart from on religious business.'

Wolsey looked at Alice, her eyes wide, beseeching him. He looked at Dudley and Child, both of whom knew that with a word Wolsey could have them allowed through, and they could exchange their final words, say their goodbyes.

But when the Queen finds out I will be next, he wanted to say.

He looked back at Alice and the children. Margaret, John, Elizabeth and Cecily.

Then thought: bollocks to the Queen.

'Let them through,' he told the yeoman. 'The condemned man has a right to see his family. I will answer to Queen Anne.'

'You,' he indicated to the head yeomen, 'after you've apologised to Sir Thomas More's family, take them to him at once.'

'Thank you, Thomas,' Alice curtseyed, 'thank you.' And the family hurried through, following the yeoman who gave Wolsey a look as he went. The kind of look you might give a man who had just signed his own death warrant.

Wolsey watched them go, Alice and the children, then turned to make his way to Beauchamp.

Would there be anyone there for him, he wondered, when it was his turn?

Now he went right, leaving the gateway behind him, and on his way to Beauchamp Tower. There he was compelled to wait at the doorway and this wasn't a command he was about to challenge, coming directly from the King.

LVI

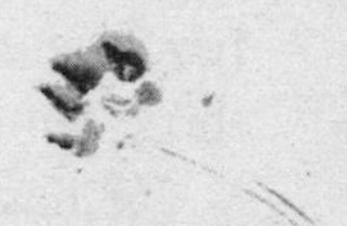

'I had hoped to be greeted by His Majesty,' said Anne imperiously, as she was helped down from her carriage by a footman.

Thomas Cromwell bowed deeply. 'I can only offer my humble apologies, Your Majesty, but the household was not expecting you back today. Most of court has gone to the execution. All are most keen to see your honour satisfied, Your Majesty.'

She smiled thinly. She detested the smell of Cromwell. He stank of desperation, always.

'Those not attending are preparing tonight's banquet,' continued Cromwell, joining her as they crossed the courtyard towards the entrance. Behind them her ladies disembarked from their own coaches, stiff from the journey. Pages and footmen approached to begin removing luggage, all of them flustered at the Queen's unscheduled appearance. 'It is sure to be a sumptuous feast.'

Something was not right, she could tell. Apart from the fact that there were fewer staff around than usual, apart from the fact that she had flustered them by appearing early – some instinct told her something was not right.

'And the King?' she asked tartly. 'Where is the King?'

'Has left court with Sir Francis.'

Anne stopped, gravel crunching beneath her feet. She wore the same alluring clothing as usual: her dress was purple, the Royal colour, with a scooped, decorated neckline; she wore a tiara now, instead of the French hood, and it glittered and twinkled in the sun. But for all her finery her face had hardened and she regarded Cromwell with those famous dark eyes.

'He has left court?' she said icily.

'Yes, Your Majesty.'

'I trust *you* know where he has gone?'

'Indeed – though he gave express instructions that no one was to know.'

Anne smiled. She reached to Cromwell's shoulder and brushed a bit of dust from it. 'Not an instruction that applies to the Queen, though,' she told him.

'Of course not, Your Majesty.'

'Then where has he gone?'

'To the Tower.'

Anne's eyes narrowed. Aisha had been right. 'Alone?' she said carefully.

'With Sir Francis.'

'Just Sir Francis?'

'Yes, Your Majesty.'

Something nameless stirred within her. A sense of the pack under threat. 'Where is Cardinal Wolsey today?' she added, then remembered she had given him permission to visit More.

At the Tower.

She wheeled, marching back to the staff at the carriages. 'Prepare my horse immediately,' she called, taking off her tiara and shaking out her hair as she strode across the courtyard. 'I am leaving for the Tower at once.'

LVII

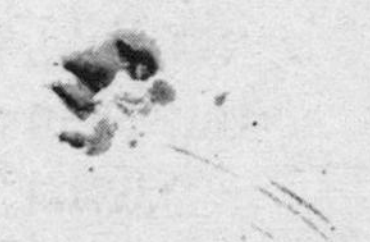

There, in Beauchamp Tower, Thomas Cardinal Wolsey and the King were watched by Reginald the youngling, who regarded them with baleful eyes partly hidden behind his scold's bridle. He was chained and sat on a chair that was too big for him so that his legs swung. Just him, Wolsey and the King in the cell.

He looked calm, the youngling, for one whose death was being urged.

'You must kill him, Your Majesty,' said Wolsey. 'In order to lift the curse, to rid yourself of the infection, whatever it is that makes the wolf live inside you. You must kill the youngling.'

He held out the dagger to Henry. An expensive, ornate thing, he had taken it from a wall at Hampton Court, thinking that the more opulent the weapon, the more enthusiastic the King might be to use it.

But Henry merely looked at the dagger in Wolsey's outstretched hand. He took a deep breath.

'How did you know?' he asked Wolsey.

'I had my suspicions,' lied Wolsey. 'I had it confirmed to me by Sir William, who confessed to me on his deathbed that he and Godfrey had been reading your letters from Anne.'

'William had been reading my letters?' said Henry sadly, a great look of betrayal coming over his face.

'Yes, I'm afraid so, Your Majesty,' said Wolsey. 'If only you could have trusted me more fully, I could have helped you sooner.'

'I held you partly responsible for the death of George,' said Henry.

'Now I hope to redeem myself in your eyes, Majesty,' Wolsey held out the dagger by the blade, urging Henry to take it. 'I have found the cure. You need to kill up the bloodline, kill the pack leader or the one who bit you. All you have to do is kill it, then taste its blood and you will be free, Majesty. Free. You will be human again.'

Henry regarded the dagger. He looked from that to Reginald, who still looked calm – perhaps because he wanted to believe that he was protected by the safety of the pack; that Henry wouldn't take the knife and kill him for that reason.

Henry could smell him, though. His scent was of uncertainty. Despite his pretence the young wolfen *hoped* the bonds of the pack would save him; he didn't *know*.

And neither, Henry realised, going to the window, did he.

He looked out across the Tower and to Tower Hill, thronged with people now, More's execution imminent.

More saw the same thing from his cell in the Bell Tower, his lips moving in constant prayer. His candle had burnt to a stub now, the flame dwindling, and without ceasing his prayer, he licked a finger and extinguished the fire. It was time now, he knew. Time to die.

As if on cue there was the familiar jangle of keys at his door, then the chief warder appeared, stooping under the low rounded ceiling of the doorway to enter. He regarded More with apologetic eyes.

'It is time now, My Lord,' he said, 'the executioner and his assistant are here. They desire a few words alone with you, in the hope that you will give them your forgiveness.'

'Thank you,' said More, coming forward to hand the warder a leather pouch, coins clinking inside.

'Thank you, My Lord,' bowed the gaoler. 'May I say, from me and everybody here, what a pleasure it has been to have you with us.'

'I only wish I could agree,' smiled More.

The warder bowed once more, withdrew and was replaced by the executioner and his assistant who came in wearing hooded robes, their gaze cast downwards.

'Just a few things to go through, Sir Thomas,' said the executioner, raising his head and pushing back his hood . . .

'When The Change comes I feel free, Thomas,' said Henry softly.

Wolsey cast a look at the youngling, who smiled. 'I'm quite sure it must be a most energising experience, Your Majesty.'

'Energising? Thomas, I feel stronger and more powerful than any King. I feel like the most powerful creature that ever roamed the plains. The hunt during a transformation, Thomas, imagine the greatest exhilaration you have ever felt then multiply that feeling by an infinite number and that is how it feels. And when in human form, I feel stronger and more robust than ever, wiser and more decisive. A better

King, Thomas. You call this a curse? How can these feelings be a curse? Why would I want to lose them?'

'Your Majesty,' pressed Wolsey, 'these feelings you describe, I'd wager Malchek feels them, too, because what you're describing is what it feels like to be a wolfen, an animal, ruthless and savage, capable of the worst atrocities. If you give yourself to the wolf inside, you relinquish your compassion and fair temper, you become an animal. You sacrifice all that makes you human and all that makes you a good and just King. When history is written do you want it said that you ruled with the fist, or with the head and heart? For that is the choice you must make.'

Outside on Tower Hill, a roar went up as Sir Thomas More was brought on to the hill in a procession led by the executioners and flanked by yeomen. Henry couldn't quite make out his features but he walked with a straight back, staring ahead, ignoring things thrown by the crowd: insults and rotten vegetables. Henry had a memory all of a sudden, of being a child and sitting at a wooden desk in the middle of a cavernous room filled with bookshelves, Sir Thomas teaching him the scriptures. Sir Thomas had seemed big, then. Big and kindly and with a gentle humour, wise and all-knowing, tutoring him in the ways of a King and of a Christian. Back then, Sir Thomas had been his whole world. Sir Thomas had taught him right and wrong.

He walked across the room. Reginald gave a whimper, only just audible from within the branks. He tried to squirm away and the stool fell but he remained chained to the table, on his knees now. He flexed and pulsed as though he was trying to change – or trying not to.

Still Henry paused, ripped apart from within. Warring

instincts wanting different things. Torn apart by loyalty to the pack and to his country.

'Do it, Your Majesty,' urged Wolsey. 'Do it.'

He glanced outside and saw the two executioners ascending the steps to the top of the scaffold. They took up position. The taller of the two, the axeman, picked up his axe and leant on it. Now they were in place it was More's turn to climb the steps.

'Do it,' said Wolsey again.

Just then there was movement outside the door. A scuffling of feet and jangling of keys.

At the scaffold, More had started to speak.

From the door of the cell came a rattling of keys and all three of the room's occupants, startled, looked as it swung open and a yeoman entered, taking in the scene but showing no reaction.

'Your Majesty,' he said, 'Her Majesty the Queen is here. She requests—'

'Yes, thank you, that will be all,' said Anne, bustling in and standing with her hands on her hips, looking furiously at Wolsey and Henry.

Fuck, thought Wolsey. *Fuck, fuck, fuck.*

LVIII

As the guard withdrew, bowing and closing the door behind him, a great roar went up outside and Wolsey again glanced out of the window, where there was some sort of commotion at the scaffold. He strained his eyes to see. It seemed that More had either fallen or been pushed off the scaffold. Either that or he was making a run for it. Wolsey actually saw More disappear beneath the skirt of the scaffold, the taller of the two executioners in pursuit, a yeoman with him. Christ, thought Wolsey, that is a turn-up. Then the yeoman reappeared and the crowd hushed to hear him calling to the executioner's assistant, who reached to the boards and passed a length of rope and what looked like a black hood to the yeoman.

He must have broken, thought Wolsey. They did that when the condemned became hysterical: they hooded them, tied their hands and feet, bundled them screaming and squirming and begging for mercy to the block.

He hoped Alice wasn't there to see it; that the painters laid down their pencils out of respect.

Then he remembered himself, turning his attention back to the cell and bowing deeply to the Queen, who was glowering at them both.

'I let you out of my sight for one day,' she said, 'and I find you with *him*.' She indicated Wolsey.

'I'm sorry,' said Henry blankly, 'I'm sorry, but it has to end.'

'Queen Anne . . .' said Wolsey, stepping forward. 'I know His Majesty's secret.'

'You know nothing, Wolsey,' came her retort.

'I know a great deal more than you might think, Your Highness.'

'*That* is where you are wrong,' said Anne, whose dark eyes suddenly burnt red and her face became a snout upon which fur appeared, fangs sliding into sight. Reginald rattled at his chains triumphantly as Anne, staring at Wolsey, growled . . .

Wolsey stood open-mouthed in shock and fear. He began to redden.

'Anne!' shouted Henry.

Then, as quickly as it had appeared, the head was gone and Anne was back to her human state. But by the window Wolsey's jaw was working as though he was trying to form words but could not. He gripped his chest. Anne took a step back, her hands on her hips again, laughing merrily.

'Thomas,' shouted Henry and he leapt over to where Wolsey had now dropped to his knees and was gasping for breath, face going red to match his robes. His mouth worked up and down. One hand gripped the King's arm as Henry bent to him. Henry raised his head about to call the guards when suddenly Wolsey's hand gripped his arm so hard that he called out in pain and looked down to see the Lord Chancellor looking up at him.

'If I had served my God as diligently as I did you,' gasped Wolsey, 'he would not have given me over in my grey hairs.'

'No, Thomas,' cried the King, 'you served us both diligently. Please Thomas, stay with me.' Wolsey shook his head. Though he struggled for breath, his eyes were sad.

'Thomas, I need you,' pleaded Henry.

But Wolsey's eyes rolled into the back of his head. With a sigh his grip, finally, relaxed – and he died.

At the same time there was a great roar from the crowd outside, and Henry looked in time to see Sir Thomas More's slack body fall from the block, head rolling on the boards, a dark stain spreading.

There was silence in the cell for a moment. Henry's eyes went from the body of Sir Thomas More, to that of Thomas Cardinal Wolsey. His two advisors. His two friends.

'God forgive me,' he said, 'what have I done?'

'You did what had to be done,' said Anne, the growl still in her voice.

'Thou are the cause of these men's death,' snarled Henry. 'Now I will do what has to be done,' and he sprang up, towards the youngling, one hand transforming to become talons, ready to rip at the youngling's throat, drink his blood, rid himself of the curse.

But Anne, always the most efficient hunter, faster and with sharper instincts, was there first. Like him she came with a transformed paw, only her claws met their target. The youngling cowered at the wall as she opened his throat then danced away to avoid the spray of blood.

'No,' screamed Henry. But the youngling wasn't dead, not yet. He thrashed on the stone like a stranded fish, the metal branks thunking on the stone, chains clanking around him. There was a blur of skirts, a flash of talons. A final gurgle and thrash.

And now the youngling was dead.

'And what was I supposed to do, with you cured?' she shouted, wheeling to face Henry, shaking blood from her talons and returning her hand to its human form. 'You were just going to leave me? Leave me with *your* curse?'

'Drink it,' said Henry.

'What?' she said.

'Take some blood. You will be free of it if you taste the blood.'

'No,' she said, 'I don't want to be free of it. Why would I want to be free of it, my love. Our army is ready to march, Henry, soon our kind will rule.'

'Not *our* kind. Taste the blood, Anne. The Protektorate will defeat the army.'

'The army have been warned, my love. They will slaughter the Protektorate. They're ready and you know why: because they've been awaiting the right phase of the moon.'

'You warned them?' he said, aghast, 'This is treachery.'

'To whom? And who is guilty? You allowed the Protektorate to move knowing they faced an army strengthened by the moon's rays. You *knew*, Henry. You see how strong is your wolfen side?'

'Not strong enough,' he said, and he reached for her arm, catching it, and taking her by surprise, pulling her to her knees. Instantly she tried to transform, her clothes bulging, snout appearing. But while she was more lithe, he knew from their hunts together that he was stronger physically, and he too channelled The Change, his power increasing to cope with her struggles. And before she'd had time to marshall her own force he had slapped his hand into the pool of wolfen blood and pushed it between her jaws. She bit, he screamed, yanked his arm away and thrust her back at the same time, so hard that she thumped into the far wall and slumped there, her head lolling, dazed.

Around her lips the youngling's blood.

There was no time to waste. Henry called for the guard. Told the yeoman that there had been a great fight and the Queen was hurt; that she shouldn't leave this room. Then he was dashing down the stone steps of Beauchamp Tower, taking them three at a time, already exhausted by the time he reached the bottom. There was a guardroom where Bryan and Wolsey's two clerks sat with a group of yeomen, seemingly playing cards. All scrambled to their feet.

'Bryan,' called Henry, who trotted out to meet him, and the two left the Tower, Bryan breaking into a run to catch up with the King as he made his way across Tower Green and to the gatehouse.

'I need your robes,' said the King, and as Bryan, still half-running, half walking, took them off and handed them over, added, 'and you need to keep an eye on the Queen. She has had . . . a turn. She must see a physician at once, and is not to venture anywhere unaccompanied, is that clear?'

'Yes, Majesty.'

Henry pulled the robes on, buttoning them up as he strode through the gates. You,' he called to a yeoman, 'bring the Queen's horse at once.'

Then, turning to Bryan he said, 'Give me your sword.'

Bryan went to unbuckle his belt. 'Why, Majesty, where are you going?'

'To Betsham. The Protektorate are walking into a trap.'

Plus, he thought, if he could reach Malchek, the pack

leader, and kill him and take his blood, he, too, could be free of The Change. He had made his choice now.

The horse arrived and he climbed on.

'Majesty, do you know the way to Betsham?' asked a perplexed Bryan.

'I'll follow my nose,' said Henry, and with that he spurred on the horse, clattering away.

LIX

The Protektorate sat at the top of the hill out of sight, looking down upon the wolfen compound, seeing nothing. They had been watching it for over an hour, Jane keeping an eye on the sun. They had to move during daylight hours. She knew they had no idea what to expect from the army – indeed, they'd seen no evidence it even existed – but if it was ready then it would be even more ready in the light of the moon. Not to mention stronger, hairier and more vicious.

But of the army, hairy or otherwise, there was no sign. Of their wolfen guard there was no sign. There was just a collection of barns, one of them badly burnt. A number of wagons. And there had been no movement for an hour now.

Nevertheless when they'd first arrived, she'd seen wet glinting from the bucket used for the well. It had taken about a quarter of an hour for it to dry. All things being equal, that put the time of its last use a quarter of an hour before the Protektorate had arrived. And they hadn't passed any wolfen armies on their route. You don't miss a thing like that.

So – she'd come to the conclusion that they were still down there.

Around her the cardinals jabbered in Italian. She could

barely hear herself think so she hushed them. They gave her resentful looks as she went back to studying the farmyard.

Then made her decision. She indicated to Gaslini, the only member of the new Protektorate with any English, and in a mix of the two languages explained to him that she was going to lead a small squad on to the compound in order to establish the presence of the enemy. Just four of them. She held up fingers. They would use the hedgerow as cover to get down the hill then on to the farmyard in order to check the barns. The rest were to remain on the hill until given the signal.

Message received and the four of them set off, leaving seven behind, still bickering on the hill, pulling disgruntled faces and saying rude things about English women – especially the one in charge. A job hunting wolfen was probably the only job fit for a woman anyway, grumbled one of their number, Agazzi.

They were so busy grumbling that the men didn't see the wolfen until they were upon them.

Agazzi, in fact, who thought it below him to hunt wolfen, knew nothing until the first creature had stripped away most of his face with one swipe of its paw.

In a flash, the other wolfen descended. There was no battle or fight. The cardinals didn't even have time to moan about the fact that they had been taken unawares by the supposedly low-ranking Arcadians – and after such an abominable meal, too! Not one of them even got as far as drawing his sword. They were simply and quietly despatched in a welter of red blood and meat, a series of moans and grunts the only audible evidence they were even under attack.

When it was over, one of the wolfen was about to move off in the direction of the squad, but another stopped him. 'No,' he growled, 'Malchek wants to turn the leader himself.'

Meanwhile, Jane and the three other Protektors reached the bottom of the hill. Together they crept past the farmyard, then to a small coppice behind. They moved through, serenaded by the sound of the birds, of the woodland around them, until they came to the perimeter, which brought them on to the farmyard. There they lay in a shallow ditch, Jane beginning to worry now, because up close there was still no sign of life. No movement, no sound.

And yet. And yet . . .

She motioned for two of the men to remain in position then indicated to Gaslini to follow her. Now, keeping low, they moved out of the wood, quickly and noiselessly, past a large patch of something on the ground – something that looked like dried blood – until they reached the rear of the first barn.

Crouched against it, they faced the second barn, this one partly burnt. No sign of life there, either. She felt the wood at her back. Impossible to tell whether or not it was empty, but there was something – *something* about the way it felt that made her think they weren't alone. They were sitting targets if so. And as she took stock, casting a look around the farmyard, she felt sick at being so exposed, cursed the sunlight.

Then it occurred to her. How could she have missed it before? The sunlight. Of course! They rested during the day. She twisted in the dirt to try to peer through the boards of the barn with no success, then put her ear to it. Again she had that feeling. Were they asleep in there? Do wolfen snore?

She motioned to Gaslini and they began to move towards the front of the barn, crabbing awkwardly along its length, until Jane stopped.

A pair of feet were in her way.

Hairy feet – paws, really – with long curved talons that were attached to hairy ankles that disappeared into the legs of a pair of black breeches flanked by the hem of a robe.

Her gaze continued upwards, to the scarred snout of a wolfen, eyes fixed on hers.

Or *eye*, rather. For he wore an eyepatch.

By his side came a female wolfen, who regarded her with a smile.

'Come,' she said, reaching for Jane, 'join us.'

'Gaslini,' shouted Jane, and she rolled, snatching her sword from its sheath at the same time, landing between the two barns in a combat stance. In front of her were Malchek and the female, to her left the empty farmyard and the gate; while to her right she saw three more wolfen who stood over Gaslini, beyond them the woodland, where, as she watched, two more of the beasts appeared, dripping with blood, jogging towards the barns.

She'd been wrong about the daytime sleeping, then, she thought.

Gaslini, meanwhile, had been too slow, had not put enough space between him and the Arcadians that had come up on them from behind. One grabbed him, swung him back towards the others and they tore him apart. Literally, tore him apart. One on each arm, one with a leg. There was a sickening moment as Gaslini struggled, screaming. Then a sound of crunching, cracking and next a ripping sound as his leg came free, then his arms were torn from their sockets and his torso hit the ground with a wet thump, his scream cut off.

Jane was lost, she knew. It was a trap. They'd been forewarned. The second barn was at her back, wolfen in front and to her right. She heard the sound of bolts being thrown and saw the barn doors swing open. From behind her came a similar noise and she twisted around to see more doors flung open. The same was happening at the last barn.

Then, from the barns, came men, jogging out into the yard, almost silently despite their vast numbers. Hundreds of them. The wolfen army.

An army of men in nightshirts, it seemed to Jane, thinking that she had never before seen such an array of nightwear. Many of them still wore their hats. But if once they had been on the point of death, now they were alive, their faces expressionless as they filled up the yard around her. Still that space to her left, though. She glanced to where the gate stood unguarded and she supposed she could try running, but they probably expected her to do that; would catch her, kill her, or – *of course* – turn her. All she could do was fight, she realised, take as many of them with her as she could.

And make one of them Malchek. The leader was momentarily distracted by the appearance of his army, she saw, on his face an amused expression. And there was her chance. She leapt forward. At the same time thinking, *Horse*.

Hadn't she just seen a horse?

Malchek was fast, of course. He saw her coming and his smile widened but instead of meeting her with his claws he drew from beneath his robes a sword.

'Hold,' he commanded his lieutenants, showing his fangs. 'She's mine.'

Jane could have cheered. Arrogant: good. And he wanted to play. Great. He was playing her game.

Their swords met with a great clash that rang around the farmyard, and she darted to her left to come at him on his bad hand, but he grinned and tossed his sword from one hand to the other, easily parrying.

Great, she thought. He was playing her game. But maybe he was better at it than her. They fought on, Malchek driving her back. Behind him all she could see were blank faces and nightshirts, ahead of them the guards and Malchek's female. Jane almost laughed. It was her against thousands. Just her.

She wondered: if they turned her, would they give her a nightshirt?

But no. If she could take Malchek. If she could just take Malchek.

But he was strong and lithe and seemed hardly to be trying. He was good. She had to admit it, he was good. Maybe better than her. She bumped into something at her back and it was the well so she used the opportunity to turn and quickly run around it. Suddenly the gate looked even more tempting. Break into a sprint, perhaps? Try to make it. No, she wouldn't get as far as the gate before they were upon her.

Then she saw the horse again and it really *was* a horse. Not just a trick of the light or a product of some fervent wish. It was real and it was galloping down the lane, galloping down the lane towards them, hooves sending up a cloud of dust.

Riding it was the King. He wore a robe and brandished a sword. And as she watched, he transformed into a wolfen.

The Arcadians saw him at the same time, Malchek, too, his face darkening suddenly. Without taking his eyes from Jane he motioned to his men to move and they did, dropping to all fours and bounding past Jane to the gate. Briefly she saw Malchek's mate and saw the fear in her eyes.

And Jane started to believe. She saw the King jump the gate and swing his sword, meeting the neck of the first wolfen to attack and hacking into its neck with the sword so that it fell away screeching. A second beast leapt and pinned itself to the side of Henry's horse, which screeched and skidded, throwing Henry to the side so that he fell, chopping with his sword as he did so, thudding to the ground and rolling. Behind him horse and Arcadian hit the ground, the wounded wolfen pinned for a second and an easy target for Henry, who slashed its throat with the tip of his sword. His horse righted itself, whinnying in pain and bleeding, but otherwise, it seemed, all right. Then Henry was meeting the slashing claws of a third wolfen and was driven back temporarily.

And all the time his eyes darted over to the well where Jane crouched. Where Malchek stood with his sword drawn, stunned by the sudden turn of events, his army at his back.

And Henry, fighting, took all of this in. Then another was upon him, ripping with his claws so painfully that he dropped the sword and good riddance to it anyway. It had done its job. For a moment the two wolfen sized each other up, growling.

'Human,' mocked the Arcadian. '*Weak* human.'

'Arsehole,' said the King. 'Hairy arsehole.'

'You should look in the mirror,' growled the Arcadian and came at the King, the two of them going chest to chest, each holding the other's arms, wrestling, a test of strength that neither won as they came apart, breathing heavily.

Then they were both looking as, '*Attack*,' Malchek called, turning to command his troops and realising, perhaps too late, that his advantage was slipping.

And behind him the army of thousands of men became a force of wolfen. A mass transformation, a field of dirty nightshirts and pale flesh suddenly became a forest of hair and fangs and talons – and dirty nightshirts – only with a tighter fit than before.

At the same time, Henry saw Jane spring up from the well and run to Malchek. She'd seen her chance; the wolfen leader had turned away. And if she got to him before Henry – if she delivered the killing blow . . .

With a shout he thrust forward but was feinting, slashing with his claws and sending his surprised adversary spinning, spraying blood. Another was almost upon him, but Henry was running now, towards where Malchek was turning to meet Jane's attack, with a look almost of bemusement that things had, suddenly, gone very, very wrong.

And Henry went to all fours – just as Jane ran Malchek through.

The wolfen leader howled. With a roar Jane yanked her sword upwards to slice the beast open and at the same time Henry leapt, throwing himself at Malchek, jaws finding the Arcadian's neck, licking his jaws and chewing the life out of him, gulping down the dying leader's blood.

Was he in time? Was his the killing blow?

He didn't know and maybe it didn't matter, because now he rose from the body of Malchek expecting to see the wolfen army bearing down upon them, expecting to meet his death at their hands – or their paws . . .

Instead, the thousands of wolfen stood staring at him, silently, almost eerily.

In front of them stood the female. Henry tensed, still expecting the attack. By his side, Jane did the same.

But no attack came. Instead, as one, the wolfen army went to one knee before their King.

All of them, until left standing in the farmyard was just Henry, Jane and Aisha, who turned to regard her army then faced the King. She transformed back to human, her shirt now hanging loosely around her. She reached to gather her breeches at the waist.

Jane moved forward, about to strike her down, but Henry stopped her, and now he transformed, too, became Henry again.

Or was he? he wondered. Did he stand before them human or wolf?

'Go,' he told Aisha.

Jane went to protest but thought better of it, as Aisha bowed to thank the King, then transformed again, dropped to all fours, and bounded away.

They watched her go across the yard, to the hedgerow then up the meadow on the other side; she reached the top and stood for moment looking down upon them, then let out a howl and was gone.

The army had begun to stand as Henry collected his horse and helped Lady Jane to it; then they too became human once again.

'Thank you, good people,' he called. 'Please remain here, bury your dead and I will send food and supplies and physicians for any wounded.'

Some of them would leave, he knew, but most would stay, and he'd need to decide what to with them – how to deal with the men in a just and merciful manner. For that was him now: he was a good King, who ruled with the head and the heart, not the fist.

'Three cheers for Henry,' called one of the men as he and Jane turned and rode towards the gate.

'Hip hip hooray!'

LX

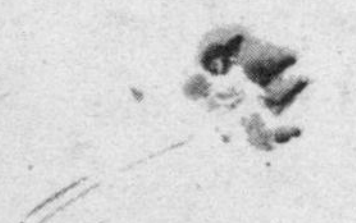

Sir Thomas More sipped a particularly fine French wine, stared out over the Seine and decided he was happy no longer to be involved at court. He preferred to experience it like this – at a distance – his news from England restricted to the letters he received from Agatha and Hob.

To say he had been pleased to see them on the afternoon of his beheading was something of an understatement.

It was they who were to be the executioners for the day, having bribed the official executioners with some of the money put aside for the chimney. The morning of the execution they had secreted the tied and hooded body of Strode beneath the scaffold. It was their thoroughness he had been admiring from his window in the Bell Tower. Later, it was the Hoblets who had entered his cell. Once the chief warder had withdrawn, they explained their plan, which was that Sir Thomas should jump from the scaffold as though trying to escape. Beneath the skirt was where the switch would take place, and indeed it had, the only hitch occurring when a yeoman had followed Hob beneath the scaffold.

More knew full well as they embarked on the plan that he had nothing to lose by trying it; they, everything.

After the rescue he had lived with them in the farmhouse

for a while, where they were occupied mainly in helping Master Brookes the builder adjust to his new life as a werewolf. While there had been teething problems, excuse the pun, Brookes seemed to have been adjusted to The Change, which pleased Mistress Hoblet a great deal. She missed witchfinding, she admitted, and on those mornings when the moon was full and Master Brookes sat down to breakfast with a satisfied and sated look about him, she would look wistfully at him. Perhaps in those moments she found herself missing the carnage. After all, she had enjoyed her life of bloodletting; she'd been good at it.

Still, she had a new interest now, and it was one that had made them rich. The Hoblets' cure for the sweating sickness was known far and wide, and sold by travelling apothecaries who came trundling down the path most days for extra supplies.

Hob had installed more hives to keep up with demand. Master Brookes was already hard at work on an outhouse to cope with the operation's expansion. Meanwhile, their miracle cure was a popular treatment at court, enabling the Hoblets to visit the palaces at Richmond, Greenwich and Hampton Court, Wolsey's old home. Thanks to their court visits More was able to keep up on all the gossip and from their letters he heard all about the birth of the Princess Elizabeth, but how the King yearned for a boy. He read that the King and Queen were known to argue. Then came the news that the King was courting one of Anne's ladies-in-waiting, Lady Jane Seymour. She would be a good influence on him, thought More, if only she could be his wife.

By the time of the next letter she was. Queen Anne had been executed for high treason and His Majesty had married

Jane Seymour. The next letter announced that she was pregnant.

And as he read the letters, More wondered if this meant his old friend and pupil, who had once been so determined to be a good and just King, had been cured of his lycanthropy? Or did Henry remain a wolfman?